TAKING LIBERTY

TAKING LIBERTY

KIM PRITEKEL

SAPPHIRE BOOKS

SALINAS, CALIFORNIA

Taking Liberty
Copyright © 2021 by Kim Pritekel. All rights reserved.

ISBN - 978-1-952270-24-6

This is a work of fiction - names, characters, places, and incidents are the product of the author's imagination or are used fictitiously. Any resemblance to actual persons living or dead, business, events or locales is entirely coincidental.

All rights reserved. No part of this publication may be reproduced, distributed, or transmitted in any form or by any means, including photocopying, recording, or other electronic or mechanical methods, without written permission of the publisher.

Editor - Heather Flournoy
Book Design - LJ Reynolds
Cover Design - Fineline Cover Design

Sapphire Books Publishing, LLC
P.O. Box 8142
Salinas, CA 93912
www.sapphirebooks.com

Printed in the United States of America
First Edition – March 2021

This and other Sapphire Books titles can be found at
www.sapphirebooks.com

Dedication

To Ryan, with all my heart.

Acknowledgment

A special thank you to Morgan, also known as T. Novan. Your knowledge was invaluable.

Chapter One

Liberty Faulkner sat there, not entirely sure what to say. She knew she was still in shock, the news not fully absorbing into her system. "But we just rearranged everything for better customer flow," she said, feeling stupid and helpless.

"I know, Libby, and I'm really sorry. The orders came down from corporate last week, and I had no choice but to carry them out."

She nodded, the rent check she'd just mailed out the day before floating through her mind. "Shit," she murmured, covering her face for a moment before nodding again. "Okay."

"Listen, Libby, you've been a wonderful employee, so if I can write any sort of letter of recommendation, anything…"

"Uh, yeah. Sure. Thanks, Mr. Tanner," she said absently, feeling like she was in a fog as she pushed up from the chair of her own office, taken over by the regional manager for this highly unexpected and devastating meeting. "Um, if you'll let me get in my desk there, I can get out of here."

The drive home was quiet, her music turned off when normally she'd be jamming to it. She glanced at her phone for the third time, thinking she should call her mom, but she knew she wasn't in the emotional space. Not yet. She didn't want to call and immediately dissolve into a pool of tears. No, she was an adult now, and had finally reached that stage where she *felt* like an adult. She had to handle this on her own.

Pulling into the parking lot of the apartment complex she'd called home for the last two years, she pulled into a space and cut her engine. Blowing out a heavy breath, she let her head fall back against the headrest and stared at nothing, her mind reeling.

The sound of a dog barking and kids laughing caught her attention, bringing her out of her reverie. She glanced over at the small playground the complex offered to its residents, smiling as a tail-wagging beagle chased around with boys who looked to be no older than seven or eight. Ah, to be a kid again, no responsibilities or bills to pay.

"If only." She gathered her keys, phone, and wallet and climbed out of her car, her first big purchase before leaving her hometown for good three years ago.

She slammed her car door shut and locked it, then headed up the cement pathway. Her kitten heels clicked a beat of progress as she reached the building and let herself in through the security door before heading through the lobby and up the stairs to the third floor.

Her apartment wasn't much, but it was hers—for the moment. She unlocked the door and stepped inside. She immediately kicked off her shoes. One thing she hated about being in management was dressing up. In fact, she didn't have to quite as much as she did, but she'd done it to try to impress the higher-ups. Truth was, she thought as she padded to her bedroom, she had impressed them. She was the youngest store manager in the district at twenty-five.

When she'd heard Elliot Turner was coming in to talk to her, she'd thought it was about her application for the District Manager Training Program, not to let her go as they were closing down her store. Downsizing company wide. Really? Thanks for the notice, asshole.

Desperate to get into a pair of shorts and tank top, she striped out of her blouse and skirt. She wanted to throw them out the window, but knowing that wasn't an entirely mature thing to do, she dropped them onto her bed instead.

Dressed, she padded to the bathroom and flicked on the light. Looking at her reflection in the mirror, she could see the emotion just under the surface waiting for the escape valve to be opened. She also saw the quirky, feisty young woman she saw every day whose short blond hair could be unruly at times. At the moment it was in a wavy bob to her jawline, one side tucked behind an ear as usual. Her eyes were dark brown, just like her dad's. She'd gotten his freckles, too, but she had her mother's proud jaw, straight nose, and athletic build. She hated sports and, honestly, was horrible at them, but all throughout school coaches pushed her to try out for whatever sport they were pimping because they thought she just "looked like she should be an athlete." Whatever that meant.

She did, however, enjoy hard work. Her father, Steve, was a builder in the small mountain town of Wynter, Colorado, population: Depends On The Day. Since their absolutely beloved mayor Faith Fitzgerald had taken the reins four years ago, the town had turned a corner nobody thought possible for the dying hamlet. Word had it even Walmart had been sniffing around to build a store in the area.

It was in fact because of Faith that Libby had planned to take the three-hour drive from her current home in Pueblo to Wynter, as Faith was finally marrying Wyatt Casey, a woman who had stolen Wynter's heart—and Faith's—the moment they met her. A transplant ten years before from Georgia, the Southern belle had melted them all. Their journey was an incredible one, but that was another story.

Grabbing a fabric headband, Libby slipped it on to hold her hair back as she washed her face. She hated makeup, absolutely loathed the stuff, but again, trying to look like the big girl the bigwigs would want to utilize, she wore the stuff. Her mother had been so happy. She'd announced when her only daughter turned twelve that she could finally wear makeup. Libby had stared at her, waiting to see if Lynne Faulkner would deliver the punchline. When none was forthcoming, she asked if she could go back out and help her father finish building the detached garage.

Feeling a bit refreshed and more like herself, Libby braced herself with her hands on either side of the sink and stared into her own eyes in the mirror. "What the hell am I going to do?" she murmured. "Damn it."

Head hanging, she felt the first real stings of hurt, fear, and disappointment prick the backs of her eyes. The first tear plopped on the vanity next to Libby's right thumb, the second landing in the sink.

Sniffling, Libby reached over and gathered a wad of toilet paper to wipe at her eyes, taking several deep breaths in the process. She walked back to her bedroom and stared at the duffel bag she'd left on the bed that morning before leaving for work. She'd already begun packing for her weekend back at home, but now she wasn't sure what to do. Should she stay in Pueblo and beat the pavement for a new job? Should she waste the gas and money for the drive, money she may need if she didn't find something right away?

Deciding it was time to call her mother, Libby blew her nose and went to the living room where she'd left her phone.

※※※※

The plan had been to take off for Wynter straight after work Friday night, but since work wasn't exactly a thing at the moment, Libby opted to load up her car Friday morning and hit the road right away. After a long, hot bath and a good cry the previous night, she'd decided to let it go for the weekend. Her bills were paid for the month and she had the little bit in the bank that she'd been saving for a down payment on a house. She just needed to allow herself to go home and have a good weekend.

She turned from her street onto Abriendo Avenue so she could hit the freeway. It was an admittedly beautiful late-mid-June day. Not one for the heat, it would admittedly be nice to head to the cooler temperatures of her hometown.

Pueblo was in the southeast region of Colorado, a small- to medium-sized town of a hundred thousand, give or take. One of the biggest steel-producing towns in the country, Pueblo was known as "Steel City." Being where it was located in the state, it hosted hot summers and far more mild winters compared to Denver about two hours away. Wynter added about an hour and a half to the drive.

She liked where she lived overall, and the cost of living was extremely affordable. Pueblo offered a family-friendly place with a small-town feel that was financially accessible to the average blue-collar worker.

She didn't feel like stale, manufactured air, so she rolled down her windows and let her blond locks fly as she blasted her radio. Sunglasses on and pedal to the metal, Libby sang along as best she could, faking it when she didn't know the lyrics or bobbing her head to the beat as though in agreement and a silent, hallelujah!

Since she was a kid, music and using her hands had been her escape hatch when life got a wee too much. When she'd graduated high school, her dad had been truly disappointed that she hadn't followed him into construction in some way, even building birdhouses, as he'd put it. Truth was, she hadn't really had a clue what she wanted to do.

Before Faith had come to Wynter as mayor, the town was dying and there was no industry left to speak of. Libby knew she'd have to leave, and as much as she loved and admired her parents, she didn't want a life of scrounging for any scrap of a job she could find. Her parents worked their butts off, doing anything and everything from cleaning houses to throwing paper routes to taking any shift possible at whatever store was still open in town. She remembered a particularly fun summer with her dad in Wyoming on a build site for a month when she was thirteen. She'd learned so much from him that summer, but at the time had no idea or way to understand what a hardship those years had put on her parents' marriage. Somehow they'd made it through, raising their only child in the process. The coming November would bring their twenty-seventh wedding anniversary.

A tale almost as old as her parents' marriage

was the fabled Wynter High School, which never materialized after the corrupt mayor who preceded Faith bankrupted the town years before. Libby, like all other Wynter teens, was forced to attend Tunston High nearly an hour away. After graduation, she was left feeling lost and unsure. She knew she'd have to leave the area, and a big part of her was fine with that. She'd miss and worry about her parents, but they had each other. She'd enrolled in online classes to get her core classes out of the way, but she still felt like she was floundering. She did well, carrying a 4.0 GPA, but her heart wasn't in it because she felt rudderless.

Two years into college classes, Faith had opened up Bessie's, an ice cream shop by day and local watering hole at night, and Libby had gotten a job there. She became really close with Faith and Wyatt and learned so much from them. Somewhere during that year she fell in love with the idea of running her own company. So, off to business school it was. She'd thrived and done well. Nobody had been as surprised as she was by her flair for numbers and her common-sense, no-nonsense approach.

She'd gotten the assistant store manager job right out of the gate and was promoted within nine months. Now, she was out of a job. She sighed, bringing up a hand and running it through the massive knot that was her hair, windblown to oblivion.

Before she knew it, she found herself close to home, the turnoff coming soon. She was excited, if she were honest with herself. She'd been so busy working sixty-hour weeks that she hadn't been back to see her parents and friends since just after Christmas when the retail season cooled for two minutes after the holiday rush, which really began in September with all the planning that was necessary.

The fields were filled with beans, squash, melons, and cucumbers. She smiled, thinking about taking some of those bad boys home to pickle, just like her mom taught her. She turned down her music as she got closer, the sparse farmhouses and fields ending with the old white church, which indicated she would soon be entering town proper.

She saw the bustling of cars and life. Kids ran across the street from Bessie's, ice cream cones in hand, to the park that was installed two years before when one of the old buildings was demolished, too damaged and neglected to repair. The new park was a huge hit with the kids and added more beautiful green space to the town.

She drove the streets, headed to the oldest part of town where her childhood home was. It was an original home, one that was once inhabited by the mining community that founded Wynter. Libby was pretty sure it was haunted. She remembered hearing a woman cry when she was a child, and saw a man pace a couple times. She'd never tell her parents that. Her mother would flip.

The little house stood by the creek, plopped down on three acres of wooded land. The treehouse she'd built with her father was still in the tree, though it looked a little worse for wear. She was always amused as an adult how truly low to the ground it was, maybe six feet high at most. As a child, she had thought it a skyscraper.

She pulled her little Sentra into the driveway, glad to see her father's work truck parked there too. She'd hoped to catch him home during lunch, but as busy as he said he'd been lately, she wasn't sure if the daily ritual of home for lunch with his wife would stand.

Cutting the engine, she climbed out of her car, grabbed the duffel bag and garment bag with her weekend attire from the back seat, and headed inside. The house was as it had been since her sophomore year of high school, when she and her mom had taken all of spring break to paint and update. It was definitely time to paint and update again, Libby mused as she walked through the living room straight down the hallway that led to her old bedroom, still appointed to her teenaged sensibilities of cool.

She tossed the duffel bag onto the twin bed, where it nearly bounced off to the other side were it not for her quick-reaching hand. She certainly wasn't used to that size bed anymore. But her childhood bedroom wasn't much bigger than a prison cell, so they'd done what they could to give her the things she'd wanted as a child, like a desk and chair in which to read to satisfy her endless appetite for books.

After a quick trip to the bathroom, she found herself alone in the kitchen, two unfinished lunch settings on the table. She glanced out the window to the backyard but saw nothing, so she went to the open basement door. She could hear two muffled tones talking, her father's deep resonating baritone and her mother's soft, almost little-girl-like voice.

Trotting down the wooden stairs, she found them huddled around the water heater, which her mom had mentioned they'd been having issues with. "Hey, you two."

Lynne Faulkner's head snapped up, a surprised look in her large blue eyes. "Libby!" She popped up, all five-feet-two-inches of her, arms opened wide to engulf her taller daughter. "You're home."

Libby grunted at the painful hug she received, glancing with pleading eyes at her father who also stood, a huge smile on his face. As the crushing hug continued, he began to make stupid faces, trying to make her laugh. She scowled at him even as she tried her best not to give in. Finally, the hug ended, punctuated with a loud kiss to her cheek before she was handed off to her father for his bear hug.

Letting her go, he said, "Want to help me with this? See what's going on—"

"Oh no you don't, Steven," Lynne said, grabbing their daughter by the hand and tugging her toward the stairs. "I'm going to steal my time with her now because I know damn well you'll have her building or sawing or sanding something every moment she isn't at the wedding."

Amused, Libby didn't argue as she knew her mother was right. Once they got to the kitchen, she was ordered to sit down and talk while her mother made her a sandwich.

"So, totally closed down, huh?" Lynne was saying, her back to the kitchen table as she made her turkey and cheddar to perfection like only she could. Her light brown hair was pulled back into a short ponytail, her dress casual as ever. It reflected both of her parents: very unfussy, easygoing people.

"Yeah. They closed down the entire region." She accepted the plate that held the sandwich, cut in two crosswise, and a handful of potato chips. She had to smile, feeling like she was eleven again. It felt nice, though, able to let go of responsibility for a minute and allow her mom to do what she did best—be a mom.

"I'm sorry, but that's just a crock of shit," Lynne said, reclaiming her seat and picking at her own half-eaten sandwich.

Libby nodded, licking some mustard off the tip of her thumb as she reached for a napkin from the ceramic holder at the center of the round table. "I agree."

"Thought Mr. Nike would be with you."

Libby glanced over to see her dad entering the kitchen from the utility room where the basement stairs were. He walked over to the sink and washed his hands. "Think I got it running for now, babe, but we'll have to replace it. It's what, thirteen years old?"

Lynne nodded with a sigh. "Damn, okay. I worried about that." She smiled when she received the kiss to the top of her head as he joined them at the table.

Libby watched her parents, their interaction. She hoped someday she'd have that. They'd had their ups and downs, and she even remembered a time during middle school when she worried they were going to divorce, just like the parents of the rest of her friends at school. She never really knew what was wrong, but one day the storm clouds seemed to clear up and the sun shone again, restoring her faith in them—and in love.

"I broke up with Tyson six months ago, Dad," she said, grabbing the cold glass of iced tea her mother placed before her. Lynne topped off her own glass and Steven's with the pitcher she'd gotten from the fridge.

"Never saw a guy so into shoes. I mean, I thought nobody could be as fixated on footwear like your mom, but that guy..." He whistled through his teeth as he shook his head.

She grinned. "Yeah, he was definitely different."

She was about to bring her sandwich up to her mouth but stopped, studying her father's face for a long moment. She'd gotten her unruly waves from him, though his hair was darker brown. "You shaved your beard," she said, finally realizing what was different.

Lynne grinned as she reached over and playfully rubbed his cleanshaven cheek. "Like a baby's butt."

"Yeah, let's just say a pilot light got away from me," he muttered.

※※※※

The acreage her parents had was all wooded land, except what had been cleared for the detached garage and her father's workshop, which were all part of the same outbuilding. She walked it with her dad, a long stick in her hand that she'd picked up from the ground. She absently peeled the bark off of it as they strolled, her dad pointing out random birds up in the trees. He'd always been a bird watcher, a lover of anything and everything nature, furry, or feathered.

"That eagle's nest I told you about," he was saying. "I thought I spotted one of the little eaglets the other day."

"That's really cool. Maybe they're here now that Buck isn't around to bark and scare the crap out of them," she said, a sad smile on her lips.

He snorted. "Isn't that the truth. That dog scared every bird and rabbit out of this county. I miss him, though. Your mom really wants to get a puppy, but I just don't know if I have the fortitude for that." He grinned down at her. "You know—"

"Okay, don't start on the grandbaby talk," she said, holding up a hand to stop him. "I can't even find a decent boyfriend, let alone a baby daddy." They walked on in comfortable silence for a moment before her heart became heavy. "Dad," she began softly. "Did I fail?"

"No, sweetheart," he said gently. "No, you didn't fail at all, pumpkin. Hell, you should be proud as hell of yourself, kid. I got friends out there my age who can't even get their kids out of the damn basement, playing video games all day and stinkin' up the place."

Libby smiled. Sadly, she knew some of those people.

"You're so young, yet you're so smart and so driven. Honestly, Lib, this was just a learning experience for you, something to cut your teeth on." He stopped their stroll to direct her attention to a rabbit thirty yards away.

Libby studied the adorable little animal pushed up on its haunches, little nose sniffing the air before it hopped away. "It's just frustrating, knowing you did everything right. You put your heart and soul into it, and for what?"

"For life to kick you in those teeth you just cut," Steven supplied. "Listen, I've got more work right now than I can handle. Ogden has us working all over the county and even up in Denver."

She glanced up at him. "Faith's dad?"

"The very same. He started that construction business here a few years ago, and now this place is booming. I'm his main contractor, and I'll tell you what," he said, whistling through his teeth again. "Your mom and I even made a little mini vacay out of it when he had us up in Evergreen for a couple weeks." He stopped and looked at her, a smirk turning up his lips. "What? Isn't that what you young people call a vacation?"

Libby chuckled, nodding. "That's great, Dad. But, no. I mean, I'm so happy for you, but I can't work for you. I need to..." She stopped her own words, not sure what she felt or even what she was trying to say.

"You wanna do it on your own, on your own steam," he said softly.

She nodded, grateful he understood. "Yeah. Guess so."

He wrapped his arm around her shoulders. "I get it, kid. You'll get there. Come on, I need to build some shelves for your mom's sewing room."

Chapter Two

Libby was not religious in any way, shape, or form, nor was she raised in any religion per se. She was raised to be a good person, that reward or consequence didn't come from a book but from the way you treated and were treated by others. She didn't attend the Presbyterian church in town, though did enjoy Father Brandon's sermons when she was there for a funeral, or for a wedding, as she was today.

The church nave seated roughly two hundred people, but for the day's ceremony, only about thirty of the seats were filled. It was meant to be a very small ceremony with only those closest to Wyatt and Faith. Libby counted herself lucky to be one of the invited. After the vows were made, the entire town would assemble for a massive block party, each guest mailed a ticket to receive a small snack at Pop's Café, a free alcoholic drink or coffee at Bessie's, as well as a free scoop of ice cream for the kids. Local bands would be performing the music in the dancing area set up in the park.

Father Brandon had kept the service light on religion and instead focused mainly on the two women, the love they shared, and their incredible journey together. As Libby sat next to Faith's father and his girlfriend, who for all intents and purposes had acted as a mother figure to both women, she studied the two brides who stood before all who watched.

Faith and Wyatt made an incredibly beautiful pair. Faith was the more quiet of the two, with her pixie-cut dark hair and dark eyes. She was adorable and wicked smart, an intellect. Then there was her wife-to-be-in-about-two-seconds. Wyatt was a redhead with all the feistiness that went with it. She was utterly stunning, with a natural sex appeal that radiated no matter what she was doing, yet had a kind, deeply compassionate nature with a heart of gold and a deep insight into people. Her Southern charm instantly put anyone at ease, while it took a bit longer with Faith as she studied you, trying to figure you out.

Libby, however, saw herself as somewhere in between, minus the sex appeal. She'd never been one to feel sexy and struggled in that area. She saw the two women as big sisters, as they'd pretty much instantly taken her under their wing.

Father Brandon announced that the two may "kiss the bride," and the room went wild with cheers and cat whistles as the newly married made it official with a surprisingly steamy kiss. Libby laughed, finding it amusing and totally their right as she brought two fingers to her lips and released a shrill whistle of appreciation. She wasn't a lesbian, but there was nothing wrong with a good smooch. Then again, she wouldn't exactly know. She'd yet to meet a guy who could kiss worth a damn, and she was always left disappointed. Actually, she could say that about all things in the physical romance department. It always looked way better in the movies and in her imagination.

Libby cheered the two on as they headed back down the aisle, no bridesmaids or any other such traditional cast members in attendance, simply the two of them and Father Brandon, who also applauded their achievement.

Faith looked striking in a lightweight women's summer suit in white, clearly tailored to fit her body to perfection, while Wyatt sported a white gown that looked much like a summer dress' higher-rent cousin, with a flowing skirt and fitted bust with halter top straps that showed off the allure of her décolletage and the delicate structure of her shoulders. Her long, auburn hair was pulled up in an intricate do with tiny white flowers weaved into the chignon.

"So glad y'all made it!" Wyatt gushed, pulling Libby into a quick one-armed hug before she was tugged along with Faith.

Smiling, so happy for her friends, Libby let out a heavy sigh as she watched them go straight out of the church. She could only wish and dream that someday she'd know love like that.

≈≈≈≈

After heading to her parents' house and changing out of the dress she'd worn for the ceremony and into casual summer wear, Libby grabbed her mother and they headed to the festivities that were well underway.

The streets of Wynter were filled with people, kids running around, chasing each other or playing games at the carnival-type booths that had been brought in: *Knock down three bottles with a single throw and win a stuffed unicorn!* Libby had gone to Pop's Café the night before to help inflate hundreds of silver and blue balloons festooned with *Congratulations!* in bold script. The helium-filled party favors now bobbed on ribbons tied to small wrists and added to the festive atmosphere. A few had managed to escape their handlers and were hanging out in trees or flew toward the heavens.

"I want ice cream," Lynne exclaimed, grinning like a little kid as she tugged her daughter toward Bessie's.

"Okay." Libby laughed. "While you do that, I'm gonna head upstairs and grab a mocha breve."

Lynne stared at her. "It's about eighty-five degrees out here."

"And?"

Lynne shook her head and joined the long line in the ice cream parlor on the first floor of the old two-story building. Daytime coffee and evening adult beverages were offered on the second floor, which was decorated in a saloon style to honor the original purpose of the oldest building in town.

Upstairs was busy, wall-to-wall customers either waiting to order or waiting for their order. Behind the original mahogany bar that had been used to sling whiskey in the 1890s, Libby saw two young women doing their best to keep up. She didn't recognize either of them, but the brunette was practically shackled to the register, unable to get away to help the overwhelmed girl who was trying to keep up with orders.

Libby could tell the poor thing was about ready to burst into tears. Not only was she overwhelmed by the volume of orders, she looked like she was probably new and sketchy on how to fill them.

"S'cuse me, pardon me, yeah you, move, please." Libby made her way to the bar and around to the other side She grabbed an apron from the extras hanging on a line of hooks and ducked her head slightly as she brought the strap over her head before securing the loose ties behind her back.

"Did Faith send you to help us?" the girl behind the register asked, hope in her dull hazel eyes.

"Something like that," Libby said, making her way over to the frazzled redhead whose frizzy hair was pulled back into a ponytail. "Okay, toots, move over."

The system was basically what it had been when she'd worked there three years before, and Libby was able to fall right back into the process like it was yesterday. It didn't hurt that it had been her favorite job of all time.

Picking up one of the paper cups that the order taker had marked up, Libby's eyebrows fell. "What's her name?" she asked the redhead, gesturing to the girl behind the register.

"Naomi," she said quietly as she turned to Libby. The nametag pinned to her apron read *Dana*.

"Hey, Naomi?" Libby said, holding up the cup when she got the cashier's attention. "Bold block letters with the Sharpie, not the pen and cursive. Won't fly over here. We have to be able to read this on the go, not translate Naomese."

Naomi gave her the stink eye for a moment before grabbing the Sharpie for her next order.

Libby caught the relief and amusement in her frazzled companion's eyes before they got to work together. She taught her how to make four and five drinks at a time, how to organize, and how to make it fun and not so stressful on herself. Soon enough, drinks were flying out, and the room was beginning to become more manageable as served customers left.

"Liberty Faulkner."

Libby glanced up from the half-and-half she was steaming with the wand at the sound of her full name.

She stared at the man dressed in a police uniform, blond hair shaved high and tight in a military style. It took a moment, but then she smiled. "Colby! I didn't know you were a cop."

"And I didn't know you worked here," he said, indicating the building around them.

She grinned, finishing the steamed milk before handing it to Dana for the next step in the assembly line they had going. "I don't. I used to, but these ladies needed some help." She accepted the newly made drink that Dana handed her, slipping a cardboard sleeve over the hot cup and reading the block writing as she snapped a plastic lid on top. "CJ, chai tea latte?" she called out.

Colby cleared his throat and hooked his thumbs into his utility belt, looking uncomfortable. "Yeah, uh, that's me."

Libby eyed him as she handed over the drink. "Chai tea, big boy? Mr. Tunston High All-American?"

He grinned, which brought back the boyish good looks that won him tons of female attention when he and Libby were in school together. "Hey, trying to impress my boss, okay?" he said, taking the cup from her. "She's a ball buster." With that, he lifted the cup in salute, then turned and disappeared into the crowd.

Two hours and three missed calls from her mother later, Libby felt Dana was okay on her own, especially since another employee had shown up to help. With a quick hug to her comrade-in-arms, she took off the apron and escaped the chaos with her mocha breve in hand.

The band in the park was blasting out music of just about every genre, and currently the male singer was doing a heck of a cover of "Hotel California" while the female vocalist sang backup. She walked over to a clear spot across the street and leaned against the streetlight to listen to the music and take in her surroundings. She found herself raising a hand or nodding in greeting as people she knew from her school days, her time at Bessie's, or parents of old friends walked by.

"My hero!"

Startled, Libby whipped around to see Wyatt and Faith standing behind her. "Hey!" The three women exchanged hugs, the two brides now changed into more summer-fun-appropriate attire. No matter how beautiful they both were naturally, Libby noted that today they absolutely glowed. She'd never seen them look so happy. "Congratulations, you two."

"Thank you, darlin'," Wyatt said, holding onto Libby's hand. "The girls told me what you did in there," she said, nodding back toward their business. "Thanks so much. Y'all saved their hides."

"You're most welcome." Libby grinned and turned to Faith. "You guys looked so gorgeous this morning. Seriously, I've been to my share of weddings, and dayum…"

Faith smirked. "And look at that. You're not even a lesbian and you noticed how hot we are."

Libby rolled her eyes good-naturedly. "Whatever."

Faith grinned and teasingly patted Libby's cheek. "So, listen," she said, her tone growing serious. "We'd like you to come over tomorrow morning for breakfast."

"Not too early, though," Wyatt added with a wink, then leaned in toward Libby conspiratorially. "Though we've already been practicin' our honeymoon," she said, and she and her wife shared a quick glance and a smile. "We're pregnant."

"Oh my god!" Libby nearly squealed in her excitement, tears instantly coming to her eyes.

"You have to keep it under wraps for now, though," Faith instructed.

Libby nodded, unable to speak as she tried to get her emotions under control. "That's so wonderful," she finally managed, hugging each woman again.

"Well, we'll talk more about it in the mornin'," Wyatt said, taking Faith by the hand as the song came to an end. "We're gonna have our dance."

Libby gave them a little salute and watched the crowd part for them as the opening piano notes of a very familiar song filled the air.

"Ladies and gentlemen," the female singer said into the microphone, her voice echoing over the town. "Our brides will now share their first dance."

Libby watched, her heart full. Yet she felt a bit of…what was it? Wistfulness? She couldn't quite put her finger on it, but she knew she was definitely happy for two of the finest people she knew.

"Okay, maybe I'm off base here, but isn't 'Crazy' by Patsy Cline a seriously unlucky song for the first dance at your wedding?"

Libby glanced over to see that Colby had stepped up where Faith and Wyatt had just been. He was nicknamed "Bull" in high school due to his broad shoulders and chest and huge hands, yet he had a surprisingly short stature. She chuckled, nodding as she sipped her hot drink. "Ordinarily, but it's a favorite song of Wyatt's, and I know it has some sort of personal meaning to the two of them, so…"

Colby was quiet for a moment, as if mulling the information over, then nodded. "Okay, I can respect that."

Libby watched the women who had the dance floor to themselves. They only had eyes for each other, and their connection was obvious as they moved together. It was as if one knew precisely what the other was going to do without needing to ask.

"You know, I'm surprised the town's so okay with this," Colby continued, indicating the couple. "Especially with Faith being the mayor and all."

Libby glanced at him, eyebrows drawn. "Why? Everyone here loves them."

He shrugged and met her gaze. "I've only been back here about nine months, and was just surmising, that's all. I haven't lived here since I left after graduation, so I don't really know either one of them."

Though she believed he hadn't meant anything by it, Libby was still a little offended by his words. "I used to work at the café with Wyatt senior year in high school, then worked for her and Faith at the coffee shop before I left a few years ago. Really good people."

Colby reached into the pockets of his uniform pants and withdrew a pack of cigarettes and a lighter. She was about to tell him to do that crap somewhere else when he suddenly shoved them back into his pockets and stood totally erect, looking like he was ready to salute. It was then that she noticed Grace Montez walking across the street toward them.

Grace was a detective with the Wynter Police Department, and had become a town hero a few Christmases ago when she saved Wyatt from her abusive ex-husband Lucas. Libby had only ever seen her dressed for work, always in a women's blazer, slacks, and pumps—all business—but today she was dressed casually in a pair of women's cargo shorts and a tank top.

Grace was in her thirties, but she exuded a quiet strength and confidence beyond her years. Even now, out of uniform, her muscular legs carried her easily with a long stride, her body feminine yet clearly capable. Montez was of Portuguese descent, and Grace had the complexion of a woman who looked like she was always sporting a tan, her dark brown hair wavy and just barely touching her shoulders. It was a bit shorter than when Libby had seen her last, and it flowed freely, looking shiny and healthy. But the most arresting thing about Grace Montez was her eyes. They were an olive green, the most unusual color of eyes Libby had ever seen. And, her gaze was so naturally intense, as though the detective were looking into your very soul, that Libby always found it a bit unsettling.

"At ease, Soldier," she said to Colby in a serious tone, though there was a touch of amusement in those eyes. "Things staying quiet?"

"Yes, Ma'am," he said, voice loud and clear as if he were addressing his drill sergeant. "Just people having a good time, no trouble to speak of."

Grace nodded, looking around before her gaze settled on Libby, who watched the interaction between the two with interest. "Hey, Libby. I haven't seen you around in a long time. Come for the wedding?"

Libby nodded. "Wouldn't miss it for the world. I don't remember seeing you at the church this morning."

"Yes, unfortunately I had to work," Grace said with a heavy sigh. "Just got off shift, actually. Was it nice?"

"Oh yeah, it was beautiful. They looked so happy." The three of them stood in silence for a moment before Colby excused himself, leaving the two women.

"Considering their crazy start, they so deserve this," Libby said softly.

Grace nodded. "I agree." She met Libby's gaze with a smile on her lovely face. "In my line of work things don't always have such a happy ending." She glanced back over to the two dancing women, the song nearing the end. "They usually don't," she added quietly. She turned back to Libby. "It's good to see you again."

"You too," Libby said, suddenly feeling very nervous in the intense woman's presence. "I have to say," she added, her nerves making her mouth shoot off, which was often a problem. "I've never seen you out of uniform before." She nodded at the summer outfit Grace sported. "I pretty much thought the blazers were permanently attached."

Grace stared at her, a delicately arched eyebrow raised. "Keep it up, Liberty, and I'll make sure Colby tickets your behind all the way back home."

Chapter Three

Libby glanced up when she heard the knock at the door. She set the box she'd been carrying down on the stack, all labeled KITCHEN. Wiping her hands on the thighs of her shorts, she pulled the door open to find three big, burly guys staring at her.

"Hey. You must be Ogden's boys?" she asked, meeting the gaze of all three before giving her attention to the one who stood in front.

"Libby?" he asked, though seemed to say that more to put her at ease that they weren't just some random muscle that had shown up at her door. "We've got the box truck and are ready to rock and roll."

"Great. Follow me." She led the way from the miniscule entryway to the living room where she'd staged all the packed and labeled boxes, her bookcase, and a standing lamp. "Um, this," she said, indicating everything that was there.

The main guy stood at the center of the room, hands on hips. "Did somebody already come get your furniture?" he asked, resting a large hand atop the emptied bookcase. He looked at her with quizzical gray eyes.

"Well, I gave my futon to the neighbor downstairs, so, uh..." She shrugged. "The bedroom. I got furniture in there."

While the would-be movers carried out the three sticks of furniture that she owned as well as the couple dozen boxes, she carried her closet items to her car, which were all the clothes she'd had for work. She was considering getting rid of a lot of it, but would wait to see if she'd need anything so dressy in her new position.

The Sunday after the wedding, Libby had gone to Faith and Wyatt's farmhouse on the hill at the appointed time, very excited for some of Wyatt's Southern cooking. After a tour of the house and all the cool stuff they'd done to it since she'd been there last, the journey had ended in the nursery, which wasn't finished but was well on its way.

After breakfast, they'd settled outside with coffee and the ladies had laid it on her.

"So, your mama told us what happened at work," Wyatt said, leaning against Faith on the porch swing as they gently swung to and fro. "Just not right."

Libby shook her head as she sipped her coffee from where she sat on an outside chair. "Not right at all."

"What's your plan?" Faith asked. "Knowing you, I'm sure you have one."

Libby nodded, resting her mug on her thigh as she smirked. "Yup. Get through this weekend without freaking out then start looking for a job tomorrow."

Faith grinned. "Good plan."

"Well," Wyatt drawled, an eyebrow raised as she raised her cup of decaf to her lips. "We got a plan."

Libby stared at her, leery. "Oh?" She took a deep breath, sliding a sweaty palm along her pantleg. "Why do I feel like I should be nervous/"

Wyatt gave her a saucy little grin. "'Cuz you should, darlin'."

Libby smiled at the memory as she was about to slam her trunk closed on her final load of clothes. A sound caught her attention: *squeak, squeak, squeak.* Glancing over her shoulder, she rolled her eyes and turned around, watching the man dressed in sagging basketball shorts, an oversized T-shirt, a backward baseball cap, and sparkling white Nike tennis shoes walk up to her.

"How on earth does parts of this country call those things sneakers when you couldn't sneak up on my grandfather in those, Josh—and he's nearly deaf."

He looked down at his footwear, then up at Libby with confusion in his eyes. "Huh?"

"Never mind," she muttered, eyes closing for a moment as irritation washed over her. "What do you want?"

"Well," he said, nodding up at the apartment complex. "I stopped by to tell you the good news that I'm moving into a place here." He raised his hand, which held rolled paperwork, and indicated the building. "Just signed the lease." He smirked as he added, "I mean, you always gave me such shit about moving out of my parents' house, so I figured you'd be all excited for me and wanna hook up or something."

She stared at him. *What the* hell *was I ever thinking? I need to evaluate my life choices better.* "I am happy for you, Josh. I knew you could do it if you just put a little effort into being an adult. And, no," she added, slamming her trunk lid closed. "I don't want to hook up. I'm moving out. Not that I'd want to hook up even if I weren't." She glared at him. "Just in case you forgot, we broke up almost three months ago."

"Yeah, but we were just, like, taking a break,

right? I mean, I got a job, got a place. What more do you want?" His heavy dark eyebrows fell, consternation on his face.

She looked him over, a fifteen-year-old boy hidden in the mirage of a twenty-seven-year-old man. "More than this," she muttered, walking past him. "I have work to do, Josh. Good luck with everything."

"Bitch!" he called out after her.

"Indeed." She sighed and let herself back into the building.

※※※※

It was cute. It was really, really cute. Libby was enchanted. It was a bungalow-style home, two bedrooms and one bath with a detached garage. It had a small front porch, just large enough for a couple of rockers if she wanted. But what she was most happy about was it had outdoor space: a small front yard and fairly okay-sized backyard. Definitely large enough for a dog.

She pulled up to the curb after the guys had backed the box truck up into the long driveway to the detached garage that was beside and just a tad behind the house. She hadn't been inside yet. In fact, it was the first time she'd seen the outside, painted light gray with white trim. She was really excited to see the chimney sticking up from the roof. Growing up in Wynter, she knew how much it could live up to its name.

"M'lady?"

One of Ogden's men's voices pulled Libby's attention, and she turned to look at him. He stood at the front door, ready to open it for her. Taking a deep, cleansing breath, she closed her car door and walked up the path that was straddled by two patches of lawn, no more than four lawnmower stripes wide on either side. There were three steps that led to the small porch, wrapped with white railing.

The front door was painted red, her favorite color, and had a beautiful beveled window. She was nearly bouncing with nervous excitement as she trotted up the stairs. The man stood aside to let her enter her new home.

"Bungalow, built in 1923," he was saying as he followed her in. "Two bed, one bath," he continued.

She knew he was one of the guys who had worked on the house, so was very interested in what he had to say as she took in all that she saw.

"Floors are original," he explained. "The wide plank, though we stained them dark, hope you don't mind. You can see it has the arched entries that were popular at the time. Crown molding, all original, except for the medallion there around the dining room light. Ogden had that specially made by a local plasterer, though it's to the exact specs as the original, which was just too damaged."

She nodded in acknowledgement. The house was a perfect starter home for a single person, or even a couple. The kitchen, living room, and dining room were all small, but the walls had been knocked down to make it all into one nice-sized room. Very functional, and beautifully restored. She loved the fireplace that set the space off, too.

"Now," he continued, walking them over to the kitchen area. "Your dad said you love DIY projects and are pretty handy, so Ogden had us replace the appliances, new fridge and stove, but that was it. So, it's pretty basic and you can do what you want in here."

Libby smiled, feeling a strong sense of pride that her father had conveyed his trust in her to take on such a project, something she'd always wanted to do. She'd worked on other people's houses for years, and now she'd finally get to work on her own.

He showed her the bedrooms and bathroom. All three were small, but more than perfect for her purposes. All painted the same neutral light gray, floors refinished, but a clean palate for her to do with as she wished.

"There is one problem, though," the main guy said, the other two finally joining the tour.

She glanced at them. "What's that?"

"All your belongings will fit in your kitchen."

༄༅༄༅

"Okay," Libby said, glancing up at her audience of two who sat on stools as she leaned over the lunch counter across from them. "I looked over the records you gave me—thank you very much, Madam Mayor," she said, pointing the pen she held in one hand at Faith as she scanned the pages laid out on the counter before her. "And, I also took home the books and printed out everything that I could for the last five years. I looked at food costs, profit margins, labor costs, supplies, all that jazz. Cross-referenced with the breakdown of age and gender here in Wynter, the population, blah, blah."

"A busy little bee," Wyatt said, sipping from her sweet tea.

"That's why, my sweet, we hired her to manage

the properties. She knows her stuff and has her finger on the pulse of what young people want," Faith said.

"Bet your buns," Libby agreed. "Okay, this place has made a profit every single year for the past five years. Now, I understand it's been open since God was a boy. But clearly Pops had it worked out, a good system. And Wyatt," she added, glancing at the redhead. "You worked here for quite a while. Even during the lean years here in town…okay, I'm being too nice. Like, when Wynter was about to implode, this café still managed to come out swinging. Sometimes barely, but still stayed afloat. I mean…" She tapped the pages on the counter. "I've got the numbers right here, but what do you think was the magic recipe? No pun intended," she muttered.

"Honestly?" Wyatt said, eyebrows raised as she glanced from Libby to her wife and back. "It was the only thing this town had left."

"As I thought," Libby said with a nod.

"Okay, so what are you thinking?" Faith asked, picking up one of the printouts and looking it over.

"Pop's has been open continuously since 1957," Libby said, planting her palms on the counter as she took in both women. "It's always been a breakfast and lunch café. I say we start offering dinner service."

Wyatt's smile and nod of approval made Libby feel better and that she hadn't gone too far, but Faith looked skeptical.

"But," the mayor said. "You just said it's always turned a profit. I mean, it's always been a Wynter staple."

"It still would be, baby," Wyatt argued.

"Exactly. Why would that change? Faith, right now the only place you can get a meal after two p.m.

is McDonald's, and that just came in what, a year ago?" She lowered herself to her forearms to be more on eye level with them. "Since you guys opened up the hot springs next to Bessie's and Ogden has redone the mining shacks for summer rentals and everything, your own town records show tourism has risen five hundred percent," she said passionately, tapping another page on the counter. "Let's give 'em a taste of Wynter when they're here."

Faith stroked her chin, eyebrows drawn thoughtfully. "I'm not sure. I don't know if it would fly, honestly."

"Why not?" Wyatt asked, turning her stool to face Faith. "We expand the menu, even." She glanced over at Libby. "I see y'all printed that out, too. Ain't much change, was there?"

Libby shook her head slowly and screwed her face up into an expression of boredom. "Nope. I was thinking the same thing, Wyatt. Why not add some of your Southern dishes? Or, why not something ethnic? The only thing 'ethnic,'" she said using air quotes, "has been the occasional spaghetti special."

Faith smirked as she rested her chin upon an upturned palm. "I'll admit, I miss a good Mexican food platter that I don't have to drive an hour and a half to get."

"See?" Libby grinned. "Now you're seeing the light."

"Okay, let's settle this the old-fashioned way," Faith said, glancing at the two women. "Both Wyatt and I are transplants. Baby, you've been here about ten years, me around four. Libby, you grew up here. Wyatt and I are on opposite sides of this. As a native, what do you think? Would the people here like it?"

Libby gave her a cocky little grin and shook her head. "No. They'll love the hell outta it."

❧❧❧❧

"Table thirteen!" Libby called out, glancing up at the ticket wheel. "Laci, you're up, girl," she said to the waitress who hurried back into the kitchen to grab her table. "Hey, did you see Jesse anywhere? His table's been up for almost five minutes now."

"I think he's having a smoke out back," Laci said, gathering the plates for her order and scurrying out of the kitchen.

"Damn him," she growled, gathering the dishes for Jesse's table. She delivered them with a smile and an apology, then marched right out back. Sure enough, leaning against the back of the building was her server, Jesse. He was taking a drag of his cigarette while scrolling through his phone.

"Excuse me," she said, satisfied when it startled him. He looked at her with wide eyes. "You just took a smoke break twenty minutes ago, Jesse." He opened his mouth to say something, but she forestalled anything he had to say with a raise of her hand. "It's not my fault you've made the life choice to be addicted to nicotine, but you're not going to make your tables suffer for it, either. Get it under control or find another job. Got me?"

He cleared his throat as he tucked his phone into the back pocket of his pants. "Yeah." He smashed what was left of his smoke against the brick building before tossing it into the sand-filled coffee can left out there for that purpose.

"And wash your damn hands. I don't want you

smelling like a damn ash tray as you serve those people their food."

"Yes, ma'am," he mumbled, quickly passing by her and into the building.

Inside, Libby walked through the kitchen and into the dining room to see how things were going there. She went behind the lunch counter to grab a package of napkins as she saw two of the napkin holders were out.

"Damn, you're just like Visa—'Everywhere you want to be.' You're at Bessie's, now you're here…"

She glanced up to see Colby grinning at her from the stool where he'd taken a seat. "Hey there."

"You helping out here, too?" he asked, readjusting his body to a more comfortable position as he snatched one of the laminated menus from where it was housed between the sugar shaker and ketchup bottle.

"Nope," she said, bringing the package of napkins to the counter and tearing into the brown paper band that held them together. "I legitimately work here now."

"As opposed to?"

Libby was surprised by the sudden female voice, and even more so that it belonged to Grace Montez, dressed in a matching beat cop uniform to Colby's. Not really a uniform girl herself, she had to admit that Grace wore it well. Her eyebrow raised in question. "Uh-oh. Demoted, Detective?"

Grace smirked as she slid onto the stool next to Colby. "As much as some would wish, no. With such a small department, we all take our turns on the beat."

"I see," Libby said, doubt in her tone. She grinned when she got the evil eye from the woman sitting just across the counter from her. "Filling holes, huh?"

Grace smirked. "Something like that." She accepted the menu Colby passed to her. "What about you? Last I heard, you were playing boss lady in Pueblo."

"Yes," Libby said with a nod, bracing herself with a hand on the counter. "I was, until in their infinite wisdom, Corporate decided to close my store and three others in the district so they could open up five more in Canada."

"Ouch. I'm sorry to hear that," Grace said softly.

"Sorry to hear that, too," Colby echoed, clearing his throat as if to remind the two women he was there. "So, you're a waitress here now?" he asked. "Dinner service and stuff?"

Libby shook her head, pushing away from the counter as she began to fill the empty napkin holder. "Nah, Wyatt will be easing her workload back quite a bit, especially—" Libby bit her tongue, as she wasn't sure what was common knowledge.

"Once the baby comes?" Grace offered.

"Yeah, that." Libby grinned. "So, before that happens, and this early on, she wants to get me trained and up to speed, and then I'll take over running all three businesses—Bessie's, the hot springs, and this place."

"Ah, I see. Overseer, huh?" Colby asked. "So, then what are you doing filling napkin holders if you're the big boss?"

"Filling holes," Grace muttered dryly. She met Libby's amused gaze.

"Well, I'll go grab Laci. She'll be your waitress this evening," Libby said, the napkin holder where it belonged before moving farther down the lunch counter.

"Oh! Hey, Libby? Wait," Colby said, hoping off his stool and moving with her, around a seated customer.

She paused and looked at him, a question in her eyes.

"Um," he said, glancing down at the patron he was standing next to and giving him a small smile before returning his attention to Libby. "I was wondering if you'd like to grab some lunch or something, coffee, whatever, and catch up?"

She studied him for a moment, noting the hope that lit up his eyes and feeling a bit obligated because of it. "Yeah, sure." She took one of the napkins from her pile and the pen from her back pocket. She scribbled down her number and handed it to him, then turned back to her task.

Chapter Four

"You were born to frame, kid," Steven said, hands on hips as he watched his daughter work.

Libby glanced over her shoulder at him, smiling with pride as she met his gaze. "Hey, taught by the best." She used her nail gun to secure the final nail then took a step back, standing next to him. "I think it's a good size, don't you?"

He studied her creation, a big hand coming up to stroke his chin. "I think so. I mean, you should have plenty of good pantry space, yet it doesn't suck up a ton of room from the kitchen area. Great idea you had putting your TV on the back side of the wall, too. Brings it all together." He put his hand on her shoulder and squeezed lightly. "Great job, Libs. Let's get that drywall measured and cut."

They headed to the backyard where wooden sawhorses were already set up along with fresh pieces of drywall. The drywall saw was plugged in via extension cord and ready to go. Libby just hoped she didn't alienate her neighbors too badly.

"Things going pretty good at the café?" her father asked, donning his safety goggles as he fished out the pencil he had tucked behind his ear. "Place is hopping seven days a week, it seems."

Libby watched as her father carefully and skillfully drew the lines on the drywall face from the measurements she'd made of her framing inside. "I'm thrilled with the response. The town has really gotten behind it. It's been satisfying to know that Faith's trust in me was well placed, not gonna lie," she said with a nervous sigh. "I knew my job depended on this all going well."

He nodded. "Speaking of job," he said, pausing, the blade of the saw placed on its first mark. "We got a smaller project here in town. Someone wants a detached garage completely transformed into a photography studio. Guess they do it old school, chemicals, the whole nine. So, we're gonna change the entire thing, add skylights, the whole bit. Want some extra money?" The smirk returned. "Maybe some furniture money?"

Libby raised an eyebrow as a hand went to her hip. "Will everyone lay off my furniture? Or lack thereof?"

☙❦❧

"Now, see, I totally would have taken you for a wine girl," Colby said, grinning as he sat back in his chair.

Libby eyed him as she took a swig of her beer. She swallowed and set the bottle down on the table, though kept her fingers casually around it. "I like wine," she said. "Though, mainly only while I'm eating something, like wine paired with something. I don't get into the hard stuff, though."

"No? Why?" he asked, reaching for one of the mozzarella sticks on the platter they were sharing.

"Learned the hard way," Libby said, watching him dunk the fried cheese liberally in his little cup of warmed marinara. "One of the few parties I went to in college, the girl throwing it had one of those huge plastic jugs with a spigot, you know like you'd take to a family picnic or something? She made margaritas in it, not bothering to measure just how much tequila she poured in there." Libby shivered at the memory.

Colby grinned. "I see where this is going."

"Yeah. One cup of that stuff was like four shots. The night did not end well for me." She grabbed her own mozzarella stick. Bessie's nighttime fare included adult beverages and appetizers but nothing more substantial than potato skins and nachos. Colby had offered to buy dinner across the street at Pop's, but Libby had been there all day and wanted a change of scenery. She also wanted to keep their meal far more casual.

"Yeah, I think I'd avoid that stuff like the plague, too." Colby shook his head and took another swig of his beer. "Unfortunately, being part of sports and all that in high school, the partying was part of it, almost expected." He set his beer down and glanced over at a couple playing darts for a moment before looking back to Libby. "Pretty sad, huh?"

She shrugged. "I never got into that stuff. But then, as my best friend so cleverly pointed out when we were, like, twelve, I was born forty, so…"

A burst of laughter erupted from his lips. "I remember you always sitting by yourself or with your little group of friends in school." Heavy, dark blond eyebrows fell. "Always alone. What did you do?"

Libby shrugged as she contemplated his question. "I guess just watched all of you act like idiots. Contemplated my world as I thought I understood it at the time." She shrugged again. "Built structures in my head. You know like, while you guys were fighting in the lunch line, I was rewiring my dream house."

His smile was affectionate. "I always admired how smart you were. I remember that treehouse you had."

"Still do," she quipped. "Well, at my parents' house, anyway." She studied him for a moment. It was the first time she'd seen him in street clothes since high school, no police uniform. He was a handsome guy with boyish good looks. Dressed in a simple T-shirt and cargo shorts, she could see he had a nice build, still the body of a wrestler. He met her gaze with a question in his eyes. "Why the police? I never would have thought that with you. Honestly figured you would have been a coach in a school or something."

"Funny you say that. I was approached by a scout senior year, but…" He shrugged. "It just didn't fit into the picture I saw of myself. I figured it would be military or law enforcement."

"No military?" Libby asked, dipping her mozzarella stick before biting it in half, the warm, gooey cheese inside nearly dangling to her chin from her lips before she tucked it inside her mouth.

"Honestly, I didn't want to get deployed," he admitted.

She nodded. "Understandable."

"I mean, I don't want to sound like a dick or anything, but I really would rather help the people of the US now, you know? Like, personally, not fighting bad guys off in a desert somewhere."

She nodded. "No, I get it, I really do. I think the military is a calling, and I really respect those who do it, but I couldn't either." She smirked. "Hell, I couldn't do what you do now. How do you stand the bad stuff?

Car accidents, violence, all that?"

"Howdy, y'all."

Libby looked up, surprised to see Wyatt walk up to their table, apron tied in place. "Well, hey there, boss lady. What are you doing working nights?"

"Well," Wyatt explained, placing a fresh beer in front of each. "We had a call off, and I decided not to ruin somebody else's evenin'."

"That's real nice of you, Mrs. Fitzgerald," Colby said, handing her his empty bottle before taking the fresh one in his hand.

"Well, I thank ya, Officer," she responded with a smile before turning to Libby. "Darlin', I'm gonna need you to take Mr. Billy his lunch tomorrow. I have to go see my doctor in Denver about the little one here," she explained, hand coming to rest on the just-barely showing baby bump.

"Sure, no problem," Libby said, accepting the piece of paper she was handed with both the lunch order and the address written on it. "I think I know where that's at."

"Just know that when you see a barn, ya found it," Wyatt said with a chuckle, which garnered her a confused look by both sitting at the table. "No house, just a barn."

"I haven't seen him much since I've been back," Libby said of the oldest man in town, who was the last living relative of the founder, Jeramiah Wynter. "Usually he's out and about in his sleigh or wagon."

"Yeah," Wyatt agreed, hand resting on their table. "Unfortunately, Stella died, so I think Mr. Billy is pretty under the weather."

"Who names a horse Stella?" Colby asked.

"Someone whose primary winter transportation

is a horse-drawn sleigh," Libby replied.

"The very kind," Wyatt said, nodding. "You'll be there for lunch shift, right, Libby?"

"Yes, ma'am," Libby said, folding the paper and tucking it into the pocket of her shorts. "I'm going in around seven, so no problem at all."

"Excellent." Wyatt placed a hand on both their shoulders. "Y'all enjoy the rest of your night," she said, then walked away.

Though Libby understood it was just Wyatt's affectionate way, something about her gesture that seemed to place them together, like a couple, irritated her. Ridiculous? Yes. Likely not at all what Wyatt was saying? Yes. Irritated all the same? Yes.

⁂

Wyatt wasn't kidding. A barn tucked in the woods with a dirt drive leading up to it was all that comprised Mr. Billy's residence. There were the two big barn doors with the expected white X on each one, then a smaller, human-sized door to the side. That was where she went. Her limited text message with Mr. Billy told her to enter that way, and that it would be unlocked.

Sure enough, Libby turned the knob easily with the hand that wasn't holding the plastic bag that contained Mr. Billy's lunch in its Styrofoam container. She pushed the door open and stepped inside. She could smell fresh hay, which was interesting because it was well known around town that Stella was gone. It actually made Libby a bit sad to see the sleigh and wagon sitting in their own little stalls, and the third stall where Stella had lived, empty.

"Mr. Billy?" she called out, looking around, noting a wooden ladder that had been built into the wall heading up to the hayloft. "You home?" She heard his voice drift down to her in welcome, so she began to climb the ladder, which was tricky considering she had a Styrofoam cup with lid of Wyatt's sweet tea to not dump.

Slowly, oh-so-slowly, she reached the top of the ladder to find herself removed from a barn and essentially climbing into a very small but totally functioning apartment. She set his food and drink aside so she could fully climb up and, once on her feet, regrouped and joined the old man next to where he sat in his recliner. She'd heard he was nearly a hundred years old or perhaps a bit older than that, and he was so frail, huddled in a cardigan with a crocheted blanket tossed over his legs. The blanket looked like one of Wyatt's.

"Good afternoon," he said with a warm smile, raising a hand in greeting.

"Good afternoon, Mr. Billy. Quite a setup you've got here. I could've used this for my treehouse as a kid," she said, noting the little kitchenette which was comprised of a small fridge, microwave, and a hotplate on top of a table that had an electric fireplace built into it. An old radio stood alone, and there was a small curtained-off area that she surmised might house a toilet situation. The loft was finished off by a small cot tucked into the corner, folded blankets atop it. What caught her eye the most, however, were the stacks of books all along the back wall, about waist high.

"Well," he said with a small chuckle. "I imagine your parents would never have gotten you to come down for dinner had you a setup like this in your treehouse."

She grinned, setting the plastic bag down on the wooden TV tray he indicated. Untying it, she fished out his packed lunch and set it down, opening it for him. She was pleased when fragrant steam wafted up to meet her face, and everything looked as scrumptious as it had when she'd lovingly loaded it into the container ten minutes before.

"Per your request, sir, we have our famous meatloaf, made specially for you, and all the fixins." She gave him a winning smile before returning to the bag for plastic flatware, a straw for his sweet tea should he want it, and the surprise. She withdrew a Tupperware container. "Wyatt asked me to stop by her place on the way here. She gave me a huge chunk of her iced lemon pound cake." Her smile grew wider when she saw how his eyes lit up.

"My goodness," he muttered, eyes wide as he took in the spread before him, including the sweet tea that she removed the plastic lid on. "I ain't been this spoiled since the 70s."

Libby grinned, thoroughly amused. "Well," she said, hands on hips as she looked down at everything, making sure she hadn't forgotten anything Wyatt had told her to add. "Anything else I can get for you, Mr. Billy? Real easy for me to head back to the café."

He looked up at her with tired, watery blue eyes. "Keep me company while I eat?" She noticed his voice was weaker than it used to be, more wispy.

She looked around. Seeing nothing to sit on, she pulled up some floor and sat cross-legged next to the table that held his hot plate. "This is a neat place you've got here, Mr. Billy." She noticed that on the walls he had framed pictures of people, most clearly taken long ago. He had a burial flag in a wooden frame, glass covering the flag inside, ceremoniously folded in the familiar rectangle shape. She spied a brass name plaque on the frame, but was too far away to read it. "Did you lose someone, Mr. Billy?" she asked, indicating the flag.

He glanced over his shoulder as he chewed a bite of food and nodded. "My son," he said around the bite.

Surprised, and saddened, she met his gaze. "I didn't know you lost a son, Mr. Billy. I'm so sorry. If you don't want to talk about it…"

He shook his head, raising a finger as he drank some sweet tea down. "My son, Justice. Lost him in Vietnam. He was twenty-two."

Libby felt her heart fall. "Oh no. I'm so sorry, Mr. Billy. I can't even imagine."

"Nearly killed his mother," he said, slowly reaching over to one of the stacks and lifting off the first two books in order to reach the third, which Libby realized was a rather thick photo album. He dismissed her offer to help with a wave, bringing the album to rest on his thigh. The leatherbound book creaked as he opened it and flipped through the heavy pages, all covered in pictures from just about every era, it seemed. Finally, he handed it over.

Libby took the heavy album and laid it across her crisscrossed legs. The page was filled with small pictures on one side, all of a younger boy, that looked to have been taken in the forties and fifties. The boy grew from baby to a handsome young man in uniform on the opposite page.

"Good looking boy," she said softly.

"He looked a lot like his mother. Always wanted to be a soldier. I didn't want him to do it, but he was determined, as most children are." He took another bite of his lunch.

Libby studied the picture, thinking it was such a waste. So many killed in that war, and for what? Something that the American government refused to even call a "war," yet that's exactly what it was. "Justice is an unusual name," she said, glancing up at the old man.

"He was named after a grandparent," Mr. Billy explained, pointing his fork toward the book in her lap. "See how they're marked there, at the top of the page by decade? Turn back to 1890."

"Holy cow," Libby muttered, flipping the pages and eyeing the handwritten dates at the top. "This thing goes back that far?" She glanced up to see his smile. Finding the page he requested, she was awed. She hadn't seen pictures that old that weren't in a book or a museum.

In the picture, which had the sepia tones of the age and the technology of its day, was a young couple on their wedding day. He stood while she was seated, which was a bit unusual for the time with pictures she'd seen. The woman was lovely, the smallest smile on her lips. Her dress was white and of the period with a veil that wasn't much more than filmy lace held onto her head by a ring of flowers. The man's bridegroom suit was dark in color, also of the period's fashion. His dark hair was cut neat and short, parted in the middle. He was handsome, face clean shaven.

"'Grandpa Justice and Grandma Theadora Kilkoyne's wedding day,'" she read. The caption was written in the same hand as the years that marked the pages. She glanced up at him. "So, Grandpa Justice was who your son was named after?"

Mr. Billy nodded as he chewed. He took a sip of his tea, then explained. "I always had so much respect for Justice Kilkoyne. Not an easy path, that one."

"Why? What do you mean?" Libby asked, intrigued.

"Do you see those flowers Grandma Theadora holds there?" He groaned as he leaned forward just enough to point to the item in question.

"Yes," she said, sparing a glance back to the picture.

"Those were placed ever-so-purposefully," he explained with a boyish grin. "You see, she had a secret."

Libby's eyebrows shot up. Oh, the scandal! "She was pregnant?" At the elderly man's nod, she let out a whistle between her teeth. "Bad girl. So, this like a shotgun wedding?" She delighted in interesting images of the father grabbing his shotgun off the wall from over the mantel. "'You will marry my daughter, you scoundrel!'" she said, imitating the voice of said angry dad.

Mr. Billy chuckled as he sat back up in his recliner. "Well, it was scientifically impossible for Justice to have fathered that child, see."

Initially, her mind went to the thought that he must be a nice guy to raise another man's child, but something in Mr. Billy's expression told her to take a closer look. She studied the couple again, her gaze settling on Justice. Again, she thought him handsome, but as she continued to study his features, she realized there was something delicate about them, something strikingly beautiful. Justice Kilkoyne had been an uncommonly pretty man.

She gasped. "Justice was a woman?" she whispered, staring wide-eyed up at her companion. At his nod, she blew out a long breath. "Wow." She studied the two again, mind blown. "Why is she dressed like a man? Lived as a man?" She glanced up again as a thought occurred to her. "Was Justice what would be considered trans today?"

He chuckled. "I don't know about all that. Honestly, I think she was a woman who knew her own heart in a world that wouldn't accept that. Like Wyatt and Faith."

"Wow," Libby said again.

"All I know is, Justice loved the little girl he raised with Theadora, who eventually went on to marry my daddy, Jeramiah Wynter's grandson, Henry."

"So, they were your direct grandparents? Do you remember them? What were they like?" Libby fired off her questions like a six shooter.

"I left as a young man to go to war, so my memories only go so far. Mama talked about them all the time. She loved her parents dearly."

"Did your mother know? Your father?" Libby looked back at the picture of Justice. She was trying to find any sort of hint in the way the clothing fit Justice's body, anything. She thought in today's lingo, Justice would have been called androgynous.

"Believe it or not, Liberty, lots of folks knew. Justice was just such a standup husband and father, as they saw it, it just didn't matter to those who mattered." He smiled.

"You know," Libby said thoughtfully. "That is something about this town I've noticed. I had a gay English teacher in seventh grade, and nobody seemed to care. For such a small little mountain town…" She shrugged, gingerly closing the photo album and hugging it to her chest. "Like Wyatt and Faith, as you brought up. Everyone just embraced them, especially after knowing Wyatt as a woman married to a man."

"Bah," he said, waving off Libby's words, a sour look on his heavily lined face. "Lucas Pennington was a waste of human space."

Libby nodded, pushing to her feet to return the album where Mr. Billy had gotten it. "That he was," she agreed, never liking Wyatt's ex-husband. "I need to get going, Mr. Billy," she said. "But, thank you so much. I'm utterly fascinated."

He reached up and took her hand in one of his, the skin dry and rough. "You come back and I'll tell you more anytime."

Chapter Five

"Don't fall. Be careful!"

Grace looked down through the branches and smiled, daring to raise a hand just long enough to wave at the small crowd gathered below. Returning her attention to the dangerous task at hand, she continued to inch her way farther out onto the limb that was as thick as her thigh.

"Good at climbing trees, I said," she muttered. "Yeah...when I was ten! No need to wait for the fire truck, I said. *Dumbass.*"

Gritting her teeth, she hissed as a nice big splinter made its way into the meaty part of her hand as she continued to play inchworm. She glanced up to mark her progress, noting that Whiskers was lounging and casually watching her.

"I'm coming, big guy," she said to him. He, of course, didn't answer and simply stared at her before he began to groom himself.

Focusing back on the branch and her surroundings, Grace continued her slow progress. She stopped when she heard gasps and chatter below. Glancing down, she saw the crowd, including Whiskers's owner, pointing upward. She followed their pointing to the large cat, who had pushed up to stand. He was staring right at her, and the look wasn't a friendly one.

"Hey, big boy," she said. "Easy, fella. I've got three just like you at home. I'm not going to hurt you, so you return the favor, huh?" She smiled at him. "We're way too high up for anything but nice, okay?"

A low growl began to emanate from the back of his throat. His pupils were large and he looked like he was getting ready for serious business. Her heart picked up a bit as Whiskers showed signs of growing anxiety and aggression.

"Whiskers," she said as soothingly as she could. "Hey, sweet boy. It's okay—"

With a yowl that would make any bobcat proud, Whiskers lunged at her. Grace wrapped her legs around the branch as best she could and ducked her head down into her arms to protect her face. She waited for the attack, but instead felt the weight of the cat for a brief moment as he landed on her back and scurried over her behind, then seemed to vanish.

Confused, the officer lifted her head when she heard cheering down below. Opening her eyes, she looked down just in time to see the giant cat run across the ground and up into the arms of his owner, who had called the police for help in the first place.

Relieved that the cat was out of danger and that he hadn't torn her face off as he made his escape, Grace found herself two stories up and out on a limb. Looking around for her options, she quietly cursed.

"Little bastard," she muttered, before working to reverse her progress and make her way back toward the thick trunk of the massive tree. She noticed the crowd dispersing, Whiskers being carried inside the house and followed by the majority of the crowd. Only a couple kids were left watching her.

Shoving them out of her mind, she concentrated on getting down while staying alive. She was doing fine, making good progress, and was about nine feet above the ground when the branch she was lowering herself to step onto snapped. With a gasp and a yelp, down she went.

※ ※ ※ ※

As it had been earlier in the day, progress was slow as Grace made her way from her personal car to her house. Her coworker had offered to drive her home from the police department after they'd left the medical clinic, but she'd opted to drive her own car since she'd be home for the next few days to heal.

Ankle severely sprained, it was tucked into a walking boot like a child tucked into bed, and her gait was slow with a limp. She was on some good pain meds at the moment and had a prescription as needed. She wasn't thrilled to be sent home for a long weekend and then confined to desk duty for a couple weeks, her mobility to be re-evaluated afterward.

Irritated with herself and the situation, Grace sorted through the keys on her ring until she picked out her house key and unlocked the front door to let herself in. Her house was a small two-story with three bedrooms and two baths. What she loved most about it, however, was the land that came with it. It sat back in the woods on four acres. It had come with a few sheds and an old garage, but she'd torn the sheds down and was having the garage repurposed into her home studio.

"Well, hello little miss," she said, greeting Mama Peeps, one of her three cats. She'd gotten her as a rescue, at just a little less than a year old. What she thought was her Mr. Peeps turned out to be not only female, but also pregnant. After a few chin scratches,

Mama Peeps followed her into the kitchen. Her two little one-year-old boys, Midnight and Shadow, fell in beside her. Grace looked like she was performing the reverse of the black cat curse, as three black cats followed in her path rather than crossing it.

"You're wondering what the crazy lady is doing home, aren't you?" she asked in the weird little baby voice reserved for her feline babies. She smiled as they gathered around her feet, all taking turns sniffing at her new footwear before six green eyes looked up at her, three tails lazily weaving through the air.

Squatting down, she gave them all equal loves. Shadow, so named not only because he was pure black but because he followed her around everywhere, rubbed his head all over her hand, purring like a little motor. His brother, more skittish like his mother, headbutted her twice before walking away. Mama stood by and watched.

"All right, babies, shall we do dinner a little early, or just a treat to celebrate the difference in today's schedule?" She laughed out loud as a chorus of meows met her use of the T-word. "Okay, okay," she said, attempting to take a step in the direction of the cabinet she kept their treats in. "Listen, fella," she said to Midnight, who stood his ground and looked up at her. "You gotta move or no treats."

That seemed to be all it took, as the cat scurried over by his brother and mother near the cabinet. After dropping a few bite-sized treats in front of each of them, Grace limped her way to the living room where she unlocked and opened the French doors that led out to the back patio. She'd converted the covered deck into essentially a screened-in porch, enclosing it with what amounted to mosquito netting stretched out over a frame so the cats could come out with her without running out into the woods or being attacked by anything *from* the woods.

Tired and hurting, Grace limped to her favorite chair and slowly lowered herself down, pulling the matching ottoman over to rest her foot on. Doctor's orders: elevate, elevate, elevate. Letting out a relieved sigh, she allowed herself to relax back into the comfortable seat and look out over her property. Most of it beyond the immediate backyard was heavily wooded, which she loved as she could watch the birds and small woodland creatures scurry about their lives. Once they'd all figured out her cats were nothing but meows and swishing tails, they'd apparently felt safe enough to get closer to the house.

Grace's house was one that was narrow but tall, with a steeply pitched roofline. This made for interesting room layouts upstairs, just one of the many facets that gave the hundred-year-old house its wonderful character. She often sat on her back patio and looked out over the grounds and wondered what those who'd sat in a similar spot had seen and thought over the history of her house. Were they happy thoughts? Sad ones? Were there worries and concerns that filled the thoughts?

Glancing toward the detached garage, she saw that it was quiet and dark, as she'd expected it to be. Steven Faulkner had let her know they'd poured the cement flooring two days before on Monday, so she didn't expect any movement on the project until next Monday, as he'd said he wanted to give it a full week to cure before continuing the construction, ensuring foot traffic and equipment being set on the floor wouldn't cause any issues. It would take nearly a month for the floor to be fully cured, but a week would be plenty for their purposes.

Though Steven and his workers had been respectful and extremely professional, she was glad they weren't around at the moment. She was in no mood to entertain or even visit with anyone. She was, however, always in the mood to take photographs. She had bird feeders and squirrel feeders and other such things placed around the yard to not only attract the animals, but also to give herself wonderful opportunities for a great shot.

Never taking her eyes off the two birds frolicking in a nearby branch, Grace reached absently to her left to the small table where she kept her older camera at the ready when the weather permitted. Her fancy new baby was reserved for hikes and outings.

Satisfied with the shots she got, Grace decided she should get out of her uniform and shower before she fell flat on her face. She could feel the beginning tinglings of the pain meds kicking in. She had very little tolerance to either drugs or alcohol, and it wouldn't take long for them to knock her out.

※ ※ ※ ※

Grace blinked her eyes a few times before they settled open. She lay in her bed on Sunday morning after a quiet weekend to give her severely sprained ankle a rest. She glanced to her left to see Shadow asleep on the unused pillow in the queen-sized bed, Midnight asleep on the dresser across the way—no matter how many times she shooed him off—and Mama Peeps at the end of the bed.

Staring up at the ceiling, Grace took a mental inventory of her body and all her moving parts. She was feeling okay. Her ankle hurt, but that was to be expected. Overall, she'd give herself a B+. Sitting up, she groaned and squeaked as she reached her arms high above her head before stretching out her neck and shoulders.

Bare feet hitting the floor, she gingerly pushed to her feet, using the bed, the wall, and other pieces of furniture to steady herself as she made her way to the bathroom to take care of morning business. As she expected, all three of her fur babies were still asleep, which meant of course she couldn't make the bed.

Shaking her head, she wobbled over to her boot and strapped in before heading downstairs. It was a beautiful August morning. Though the afternoons were still rather warm, the morning and evenings were beginning to cool a bit, just a hint of fall flirting with Wynter. She made her way to the kitchen, unlocking and opening the French doors in the process. Hands on the handles of each door, Grace closed her eyes and raised her face to the morning, inhaling the fresh mountain air. She loved that fall was on its way, and then her favorite, winter. There was nothing like seeing the forest floor transformed into a snow-covered wonderland.

School would be back in session soon, as well as the annual Wynter in August festival, which had begun four years before and consisted of a parade and all the businesses opening their doors for giveaways, samples, and good fun. The live band would be back and there would no doubt be dancing in the streets. The night would end with a huge fireworks show over the lake. It was great fun, and kicked off the fall season.

She was about to turn away and go make coffee when she noticed the door to the detached garage was open. Stepping out into the enclosed patio, she listened. She heard movement, something scraping across the cement, then a murmured curse. The voice sounded female.

Her training told her to grab the .38 she had hidden, strapped beneath the end table next to the couch in the living room. It was difficult to be as stealthy as she'd usually be with the awkward boot thudding everywhere, but finally she got herself outside, the gun still on safety as she held it up and close to her body.

Her senses sharp on high alert, she reached the opened doorway and, with a surge of adrenaline, snapped her arms out in front of her, pistol held between her hands. "Freeze!"

With a squeal of surprise, the woman in her garage whipped around, hands raised overhead.

Letting out a sigh of relief, Grace's state of readiness deflated like a balloon as her arms fell, gun pointed at the ground. "Liberty Faulkner, what the hell are you doing?" she demanded, her tone filled with both the relief she felt and the confused anger that replaced the concern. She ran a hand through her unruly dark hair as she looked around the small building, which had been completely transformed from the detached garage it had once been. If one didn't know what it had been in its previous life, they never would have guessed.

"Sorry," Libby said, hand to her chest as she took several deep breaths. "My dad had me come over to check out the floor," she explained, hands moving to her hips. She still seemed to be shaken. Finally, she studied Grace, her eyebrows falling. "What are you doing standing there in pajama pants with green pigs all over them, a seriously cute tank top, hair that makes you look like you just stuck your finger in an electrical outlet, and with a Saturday night special?"

Feeling a bit self-conscious, Grace ran her hand through her hair again, no doubt making it worse. She glanced down at her gun before meeting quizzical brown eyes. "I live here," she explained dryly.

"What?" Libby took a step forward before her gaze fell to the .38 at Grace's side, then seemed to think better of it as she stopped. "This is your property?" she asked, indicating the general area of the soon-to-be studio and land and house beyond.

Grace smirked, tucking the small pistol into the pocket of her pajama pants. "Yup." She looked around, noting a corner of the plastic tarp that had been spread out over the floor had been lifted, a layer of material beneath it. "So, what's up with all this?" she asked conversationally, realizing the presence of her gun and initial aggression had scared the younger woman.

Libby seemed to try to shake herself out of her unsettled condition as she looked around to see what Grace was talking about. "Oh, um, this is what's called a wet cure. Look," she said, squatting down next to the small section of upturned tarp. When Grace joined her, she explained. "We wet the crap out of this cloth and set it over the entire thing so it'll keep the cement from drying out as it hardens, or," she added with a smirk, "cures. So," she concluded, putting the material back down and the tarp on top of it. "We should be good tomorrow to continue."

The pain Grace felt as she pushed back to standing must have shown as Libby took her arm and helped her. "Thanks" she murmured.

"What happened?" Libby asked, looking down at the boot. "Chase some bank robber up a tree?"

Grace glanced at her, chuckling. "No, a fat cat named Whiskers *down* a tree. Gravity helped me."

"Oh my god." Libby looked at her with shock on her face. "Are you okay?"

Grace had to admit, the young general manager could be pretty adorable. She quickly pushed that thought straight out of her mind and focused instead on Libby's compassion. "Doctor says I'll live, so I guess that must be true." She saw that Libby kept glancing over at the pocket that bulged with Grace's gun, the thin cotton material of the pajama pants not structured enough to keep the weight tucked against her thigh. "Guns make you nervous, Libby?"

Libby nodded, meeting her gaze, eyes holding fear. "Don't like them."

"You know," Grace said, easing the gun out of her pocket, no quick movements to amp up Libby's anxiety. "Outside of my job, or a situation like this," she added, sending a cheeky smile Libby's way. "I'm not a fan, either. I don't hunt, don't go target shooting, outside of what's required for training purposes. But," she continued, popping out the cylinder of the .38 and dumping the bullets into her hand, quickly depositing them into her pocket before snapping the cylinder closed. She held the gun out to Libby, to take or not take at her option. "I found the easiest way for someone to get over gun anxiety is to handle one in a safe, controlled environment."

Libby stepped closer to her and swallowed, clearly nervous. "Gee," she said, an attempt at amusement in her tone. "You happy to see me, Officer, or is that a bunch of bullets in your pocket?"

Grace smiled. "Ecstatic." Libby gave her a genuine smile back, which made Grace's grow. The detective said nothing, but simply let Libby take the weapon at her own speed.

Libby was quiet as she placed the pistol in her palm initially. "It's heavier than I thought it would be."

Grace nodded. "It's got a little weight to it." She watched the younger woman, knowing Libby couldn't hurt herself or anything else but still wanting to make sure she didn't need to intervene if anxiety levels rose too much.

"I can't imagine carrying this around," Libby commented, no judgement in her voice, simply sharing her thoughts. "Can I pull the trigger?" she asked, glancing up at Grace, who was slightly taller.

"Normally the answer would be no, as you should never, ever pull the trigger of a gun unless your intention is to use it, but in this case, we both know the gun is secure, so go ahead." Grace was not sure why she was allowing protocol violations that had been beaten into her head for so many years in the military and law enforcement. Not only that, but dry firing wasn't good for the gun. For some reason, however, she was allowing it.

Libby simply wrapped her hand around the grip and, gun pointed naturally downward, pulled the trigger, which clicked harmlessly as the cylinder turned at the mechanical action as the gun was designed to do. Seeming more relaxed, Libby handed the gun back to Grace. "Thanks," she said softly.

"You're welcome," Grace responded, taking the gun back into her hand. "Now you can say you've fired a gun."

Libby smirked. "What a dubious honor."

Grace grinned.

Chapter Six

Hard gray eyes raised from the podium. "Problem with that, LaCroix?"

Colby readjusted his body in the hard, wooden chair in the roll call room. "No, sir," he muttered. "I just thought Biggs was taking that shift."

The sergeant, in his usual deadpan style, said, "Yes, and none of us expected Mrs. Biggs to pop out Baby Biggs last night. So, your, uh"—he cleared his throat—"budding love life will have to wait, Officer. I'm staggering all of you throughout the day so you'll be off in time for the fireworks." Though his words said he was being understanding and trying to compromise, his tone said he was amused.

Grace glanced over at Colby, who spared her a quick glance before he looked down at his hand that rested on the ankle crossed over his knee. "It's fine, sir," he said.

"All right then," the sergeant continued. "That's the lineup for the festival tomorrow, here's what we got tonight."

Grace took in the rundown of cases and calls that had happened earlier in the day. As this group was working swings, they began at four in the afternoon and got off at midnight. Tonight, Grace was on special duty. She was undercover, wearing street clothes. They'd been getting reports about a prowler who seemed to be stalking various businesses in town. He'd reportedly go in, wander around just long enough to make customers and employees uncomfortable, then leave, never saying a word, never buying or ordering anything.

Grace headed to the locker room after roll call, getting together her gear and radio before heading out. She looked up when she heard the door open and saw Colby walk in. He was in uniform but looked sullen and irritated. "You okay?" she asked.

He glanced over at her before opening his own locker, two down. "Yeah, just pissed."

"Why, because of tomorrow?" she asked. She was working the morning shift, and for just a split second she considered switching with him, but then decided against it. They'd been scheduled by seniority, and she wasn't about to let a whining young pup cut in line.

"Yeah," he groused, throwing the rag he used to polish his shoes into the locker, much like a ten-year-old throwing a tantrum.

Grace was not impressed. "You two getting serious?" she asked, trying to figure out why he was so angry. "I assume you're upset because you wanted to spend time with Libby, right?"

He sighed, plopping down on the long wooden bench that ran the full distance of the lockers. His shoulders sagging, he looked like a defeated kid. "I really like her. Tomorrow is my first festival being back here." He shrugged, glancing up at her. "I wanted to be able to show her a good time."

"She'll probably be working, don't you think?" she asked, attempting to toss some logic into his bonfire of self-pity. "Or, as the big boss, is she taking it off?"

"Yeah, she's working, but I promised her I'd

swing by to get her when she's done. She's not working the entire thing," he said, hands resting on his knees. "Do you know of a good place to get flowers around here? Or do I have to go all the way to Tunston?"

"No, there's a place on Eighth." Grace studied him as she reached up to put the chain over her neck that her detective's badge and credentials were attached to. The chain in place like a necklace, she put the business end into her T-shirt so it would only be seen if she needed to pull it. "Flowers, huh?"

He turned on the bench so he was straddling it. He pulled one of his legs up, the heel of his black work boot on the wooden surface as he unlaced and retied the boot. "What?" he asked, sounding a bit self-conscious. "You're a girl. Don't you like flowers?"

She gave herself a final look-see in the mirror attached to the metal door via magnet, then slammed the locker shut. "I'm a woman, not a girl. And flowers die."

As she tucked her service pistol into the holster at the back of the waistband of her jeans and walked toward the exit, she heard the soles of Colby's boots slap the tile as he ran after her.

"Yeah, okay, but wait," he said, catching her at the back of the building just before she was about to open the door. "They die, so, what do girls like?"

"No wonder you're single," she muttered before turning to face him, her hand resting on the push bar. "First of all, Colby, don't call a woman a girl. I can promise you every woman on this planet has lived through enough shit to have earned the respect to be called a woman. Second of all, yes, flowers do die, but yes, they are beautiful and smell great. You can go that route, but if you really want to impress Libby, find out what she likes. Honestly, I'd be far more impressed with somebody if they showed up with my favorite drink or my favorite candy bar than flowers."

Heavy, dark blond eyebrows drew. "Really? Why?"

"Because." Grace pushed the door open and trotted down the metal stairs that led to the parking lot beyond, Colby following. "That would tell me that person had paid attention, cared enough to notice."

Colby nodded, as though absorbing what she'd said. "Okay. So, how do I know that? Like, what she likes?"

Grace did a mental facepalm. "Do you talk to her, Colby? Have the two of you actually had a conversation?"

He glared at her. "Yes, of course. We just went to lunch the other day. I paid for it."

"And, what did she order?" Grace turned to face him as she reached her car. He stared at her blankly. "Come on, Colby. You're a police officer, trained to observe. What did you observe was on her plate?"

He let out a heavy sigh and ran a large hand over his close-cropped hair in a nervous gesture before dropping it back down to his side. "I don't know."

Grace shook her head and pulled her car door open. "Petals of Love," she said, climbing in behind the wheel.

"What?" He looked at her through the open door.

"The name of the flower shop," she said, pulling the door shut.

"That'll be four bucks," the vendor said, tying the clear plastic bag shut after filling it with fresh and incredibly fragrant kettle corn.

Grace pulled a five-dollar bill out of her wallet and handed it over, refusing the change as she accepted her treat. "Thanks." She gave the seller a smile before turning to make her way through the throngs of people that wandered the downtown streets of Wynter.

It was a nice evening, though the rains from the day before made the air feel a bit heavy and muggy, which wasn't common for usually low-humidity Colorado. Growing up in a tiny town in New Mexico, Grace had never lived very long anywhere humid, but when she did her hair frizzed out like a clown, all the natural curl springing to life like Shirley Temple. For now, her hair was pulled up in a ponytail and she was dressed in her uniform away from work—a tank top and women's cargo shorts.

"Whoa!" She cried out, startled, as a herd of nine-year-olds nearly ran her over. She lifted her hands above their heads so she didn't take out half the fourth grade class with her kettle corn or her phone and wallet. The stampede passing, she moved on.

The band had been up and playing for just over an hour now as evening fell. The sky was painted with the glorious colors of sunset. Many of the vendors had packed up their wares and booths as night fell, though some, like the kettle corn lady, were still up and selling. Employees from the surrounding businesses wandered around with either coupons for their wares or free samples.

"Look at you two, cuttin' a rug!"

Grace turned at the familiar voice, smiling when she saw Libby, a serving tray balanced on her palm, watching her parents dance on the impromptu dance floor in the middle of the street. She smiled as she watched the general manager do a little one-handed waltz with her father before scurrying out of the way. Somehow, even with all that movement, she managed to keep the little paper sample cups on her tray in place.

She noticed the relaxed grace of Libby's movements, her easy manner, as well as her tanned skin, which looked soft and supple in the shorts and Bessie's T-shirt she wore. Her wavy blond hair was pulled back from her face with a bandana, much in the same style as Wyatt. Truth was, Grace thought Libby was absolutely adorable. She was a beautiful woman, for sure, and her body was stellar, but there was something else so adorable about her that Grace couldn't quite put her finger on.

She'd have to contemplate that another time, as Libby was dancing her way over.

"Well, top of the evenin' to ya, Officer," Libby said with a welcoming smile.

Grace grinned and raised a hand to tip a nonexistent hat. "Evenin', ma'am."

Libby seemed to be delighted that Grace played along, her expression playful and joyous. She glanced down at the unopened bag of kettle corn Grace held. "I'll trade you one of these scrumptious, refreshing vanilla-blueberry smoothies for a handful of your kettle corn," she said sweetly.

Grace raised an eyebrow and glanced from the treat she held to the enticing sample on Libby's tray. She made a show of chewing on her bottom lip before shaking her head. "Go fish."

Libby threw her head back and laughed. "Oh,

good one. Come on…" She gave Grace a saucy little side-eye. "Please?"

Unable to resist her charm, Grace sighed. "Fine." She actually wanted one of the smoothies, but it was worth it to make Libby beg. The two made their swap. "This is seriously good," Grace said, raising the small paper cup. "May have to go get me a big-girl-sized one."

Libby grinned. "Glad you like it. This is pretty good, too," she said, tossing the last clump of sweet, chewy yet crunchy kettle corn into her mouth.

"Your folks have got some pretty impressive moves, I must say," Grace said, nodding in the direction of the still-dancing couple.

Libby followed Grace's gaze and nodded. "Yeah. Mom used to teach lessons when I was little. One of the million and one side jobs she had during my childhood."

"Oh yeah?" Grace asked, crinkling the paper cup in her hand before tossing it into a nearby trash can. "Did you learn, too?"

Libby nodded, grabbing another handful when Grace offered the open bag to her. "I did. Do you dance?"

"A bit," Grace hedged.

"Well," Libby said, grabbing one more handful and giving Grace's arched eyebrow a shit-eating grin in the process. "I have to get back to work. I'll see you," she said, walking away from Grace backward and pointing a finger at her. "Later."

Grace chuckled and sent the younger woman off with a salute. Shaking her head in amusement, Grace dipped her hand into the bag, finally enjoying the kettle corn herself. She munched as she stood back and watched. More people were beginning to join the dozen or so dancing couples as the volume of the band picked up. Now that the vendors and many of the businesses were closing up shop, the music was the main event.

A handful of songs later, Grace had found herself a place out of the way by sitting on the half wall that extended between two of the buildings along the main street. Her kettle corn was long gone, the bag thrown away. Her head bobbed to the music, heels of her tennis shoes tapping lightly against the brick structure she sat on.

"Hey, stranger."

She looked to see Libby walking up to her. "Hey, yourself."

"You're being antisocial," Libby accused, thumbs hooked into the back pockets of her shorts.

Grace grinned. "I'm observing."

"Ah, I see." Libby nodded out to the throngs of people who walked past them or were dancing. "Gonna make any arrests?"

"You do something wrong?"

"Me?" Libby asked, a hand splayed out on her own chest. "Never."

"Perfect little angel," Grace quipped, hopping down from the wall, careful to land on her non-booted foot. It had been more than a week since her fall and her ankle was better, but it still made itself known several times a day. "Did you get paroled, or out for another round of samples? If so, yes, please." She flashed her pearly whites at Libby, who burst into laughter.

"Outta luck, Chuck." Libby paused and glanced over at the crowd of dancers and the band on stage.

Her eyes lit up as she looked back at Grace. "Love this song!"

Grace recognized the opening fiddle of "The Devil Went Down to Georgia" by the Charlie Daniels Band. Instantly, her fingers began to tap her thigh.

"Can you move in that thing?" Libby nodded down at the walking boot.

Grace spared a glance down at it before meeting Libby's challenging gaze. "Guess we'll see."

Libby grabbed Grace by the hand and yanked her nearly out of her boot in her haste to join the crowd. It was a song she knew well. Growing up in New Mexico, she'd been in more country bars than she could count, not to mention those during the six years she'd been with her ex Maryann, who was from Houston.

Libby led them to a place with a bit of room, and that's when things got awkward. Libby looked utterly baffled. "I have no idea where to put these," she said, wiggling her hands. "I've never done this with a woman before."

Grace smirked. "I have." She took Libby's right hand firmly in her left, then placed Libby's other hand on her shoulder before resting her hand on Libby's waist.

Their moment of awkwardness disappeared as the music engulfed them. Grace looked into those deep brown eyes and felt the connection as they moved together in a country swing, all spins, twirls, a constant flow of movement. Libby was easy to move and lead, their bodies and movements fitting together like they'd been a dancing pair for years.

They moved around the street, everyone else disappearing. In that moment, for Grace, it was only the music and Libby's eyes, which never left her unless she was in the middle of a spin or a turn. As soon as she whipped back around, Libby found her eyes and together they moved on to the next sequence.

Finally, the song came to an end, Grace grabbing Libby and holding her close for a moment before she dipped her on the final beat. She wasn't surprised to hear applause, but she was startled to realize she and Libby were surrounded by onlookers and the applause was   for them.

Pulling Libby back up to a standing position, she grinned and quickly found herself in a tight hug, which she returned. She felt Libby look around, then her body tense as she noticed what Grace had.

"Oh crap!"

Grace laughed. "Guess we did okay, huh?" Movement caught her eye. She glanced over Libby's shoulder and saw a very angry-looking Colby starting back at her. He held a wrapped bouquet of flowers in his hand. Glaring at her, he turned and tossed the flowers into a trash can before pushing through the crowd and disappearing from sight.

Chapter Seven

Grace took in the building around her, nodding in acknowledgement to what Steven Faulkner was telling her. He explained what they'd done on the floor, and though it would take a few more weeks for it to be fully cured, it was perfectly safe for them to continue work. That day he had a crew coming in to start ripping the roof off, as Grace wanted skylights put in.

"So, with the pitch of the roof on this thing," he explained, pointing up. "I'm guessing it's going to take us about two days, three days, max."

Grace nodded. "Okay. That sounds great. Looks amazing already in here, with the walls put in for the bathroom. Really excited." Grace gave him a winning smile, excited for the dream of her studio to be taking shape. "Anything you guys need, just let me know."

"Will do," Steven said with a grin. "Glad you like it." He reached up and adjusted the brimmed hat he was wearing. "So, some fancy footwork you two engaged in the other night."

Grace gave him a sheepish green. "Yeah, well."

"How'd the foot handle it?" he asked, nodding down toward the walking boot.

She followed his gaze, tapping the rubber heel lightly against the new cement floor. "Limping a bit, won't lie, but it was fun."

"I haven't seen Liberty smile like that in a long,

long time," he said, sounding every bit the proud father.

"Yeah?" Grace asked, smiling at the memory of their impromptu dance. "I'm glad."

"What do you think of my little girl?" Steven asked, crossing his arms over his chest, well developed from years of hard, physical labor, though he had the burgeoning gut of a man hitting middle age.

Grace shrugged, feeling herself close off a bit, though she had no real idea why. She hugged herself and glanced away from him. "I think she's a great kid. Very bright. Seems to be doing an amazing job with Faith and Wyatt's businesses."

Steven nodded. "She is. We're real proud." He reached out and lightly patted Grace on the arm. "I'm gonna head out and gather all the stuff we'll need so we can get started."

"Sounds great. Thanks so much, Steven." She really liked him a lot. He reminded her a little bit of her oldest brother, who was only about five years younger than Steven. "I'm off to work, so be safe."

"Hey, you do the same, young lady," Steven said in a deep firm tone, slight amusement in his voice but seriousness in his eyes.

Grace left her studio building and pulled her car keys out of the pocket of her jeans. It was another undercover night. The man she was looking for had been seen again at a gas station the night before. He'd loitered around, seemingly waiting for customers to leave. A sharp-eyed customer caught on and hung around, and eventually the man left. Later that night, they'd gotten a call that he'd tried to abduct one of the high school girls who was walking home from her job at the McDonald's. She'd managed to get away. Grace's lieutenant had sent her a picture of the suspect.

She spent the morning studying the picture and doing some research to see if she could figure out who he was. Young guy, looked to be in his early twenties. His head was shaved in the picture, eyebrows dark brown or black with eyes black as a shark's. Hispanic-looking, with a slight build and scruffy facial hair. In other words, he looked like every other twenty-something she'd see ten of in a day.

One thing that people said about him, though, was that he had a tattoo on the left side of his neck that just barely stuck out from the neckline of his T-shirt. Nobody had been able to get a handle on what the design was. The picture she had of him had been quickly snapped with someone's phone, so the quality was lacking, but it was all they had. In a town of less than six thousand people, someone like this stuck out like a sore thumb. You may not know everyone's name, but chances are you knew someone who knew someone. Nobody knew this kid.

Since they had no name or any sort of identification on him, including a license plate on the old beat-up white truck the high school girl said he was driving, Grace had to do it the old-fashioned way: pound the pavement, even as her undercover persona.

She drove to Bessie's to get herself a coffee to start her shift. She smiled and waved to the crew working in the ice cream shop on the first floor before trotting up the long, narrow staircase to the second. Pushing through the mini saloon doors, she saw that the coffee shop was fairly slow at just after one thirty in the afternoon.

"Hey, Grace. Regular?" Dana asked.

"Yes, ma'am," Grace responded, going to the

register where the new girl waited to ring up her order. "Can I ask you a question?" she asked the short, African American woman who met her gaze in curiosity as she counted out Grace's change from the register drawer. "Have you ever seen him around town?" She brought up her phone and the suspect's picture. Grace noticed out of the corner of her eye that Dana joined her coworker and took a look as well.

"No," Dana said, returning to complete Grace's order.

"Yeah," the cashier said, her eyebrows falling as she seemed to be trying to recall. "Yeah. I saw this dude at the hot springs Saturday."

Grace's ears perked up. "What was he doing?"

The girl scrunched up her face as Grace took her phone back. "He was, like, watching us and stuff. Like, he was actually in the building, down below with us in the hot springs, but he wasn't in the water. He just sat back and watched us."

"Did he happen to tell anyone his name?"

"Nah. He didn't talk to nobody. Just stared. I really only remember because I thought it was creepy."

"Okay. Thanks so much," Grace responded with a smile. She reached into her pocket and retrieved a business card with her official title, work phone, and cell phone printed on it. "If either of you see him again, don't hesitate to call or text my cell," she said, handing the card to the cashier before turning to head to the end of the bar where Dana would hand over the coveted coffee.

"You want your change?" the cashier asked, holding up two dollars and some coins.

"Put it in the tip jar," Grace said. She leaned on the polished mahogany surface. Word was the bar was original to the building, which had begun life as a saloon and reported brothel. She wondered how many men had leaned on the very spot she was, hopes of striking it rich in the mining town in their hearts?

"Did you have fun?"

Grace turned to see Colby walk up to her, dressed in uniform. "Pardon?"

"Did you have fun?" he asked again, his tone curt, words clipped. He reached past her to grab a napkin out of the holder.

"Fun doing what?" she drawled, in no mood for his games. She could see in his eyes he was a man on a grudge mission. *Don't do it, boy*, she thought.

"Fun making me look like an ass," he said, shoulders squared and chest puffed.

Fool. A lazy little smile crossed her lips. "Colby, you made yourself look like a fool, stomping away like a ten-year-old who didn't bother to call 'shotgun' yet pissed that you got stuck sitting in the back seat."

"She's not even gay," he exclaimed.

Grace raised an eyebrow before she stepped a bit closer to him, her face no more than six inches from his. He held his ground. "Check yourself before you wreck yourself, Officer," she said, her voice low and dangerous.

He didn't move back from her but did lower his voice a bit. "What, you worried everyone here will hear what you are?"

She crossed her arms over her chest, weight shifting to one hip. "What's that?" she asked, chin raised slightly in challenge. Colby may have been a few inches taller, but she knew he was no match for her.

"I know how you girls work," he said. "It's all

fun and games to you, isn't it? You find out which one the guy is into, the *straight* one that you decide to wave your magic wand of seduction at. Turn her head, try and make her gay, too."

If Grace hadn't been so insulted, she would have actually felt a bit sorry for him as she could see the pain of a past experience in his eyes.

"Um," Dana said, clearing her throat. "Your coffee, Detective," she said, sliding the paper cup toward Grace, who smiled at the decidedly uncomfortable-looking young woman.

"Thanks, Dana." She smiled at the girl as she picked up her coffee and walked away, hearing Colby's footfalls behind her. She led them to a corner out of the way before turning back to him. "Listen, I have no idea what kind of girl you got hurt by, but don't you dare lump every one of us into the same mix. And, don't you dare treat Libby like she's your property or some piece of meat. She deserves better than that. Yes, she and I danced," Grace said with a dramatic shrug. "And yes, we did a good job at it together. But it was just fun, Colby. Libby and I are…" She thought about it and shook her head. "I don't even know if you could say we're friends. We're good acquaintances, I guess."

He snorted before taking a sip from his coffee that he'd carried with him to the bar. "Sure not what it looked like."

"I don't give two shits what it looked like to you, you insecure ass. Put your big boy pants on and knock off the possessive bullshit or she'll want nothing to do with you." She started to walk past him but stopped, looking him dead in the eye. "Take a lesson from me. If you can't even let yourself trust her before you're even really dating, perhaps you should take a look at what's missing inside you, because I know Libby has done nothing wrong to make you act like this."

※ ※ ※ ※

"Yeah, I remember this guy," one of the high school boys said. A group of them were hanging out outside the McDonald's, and she'd taken the opportunity to ask them about the suspect. "He showed up at the back-to-school bonfire we were having down by the lake," he continued, looking at the picture on Grace's phone.

"Did he say anything to anyone?" Grace asked, remembering what the cashier at the coffeeshop had said.

"Yeah," one of the other guys added. "He was talking to Callahan's girlfriend, trying to pick her up. He showed up and the dude was pissed, so he split."

"This guy split?" Grace clarified, indicating the image on her phone.

"Yeah. Totally wussed out and left," the first guy said, readjusting his backward-turned baseball cap.

"Did he tell anybody his name?" Grace met the gazes of all four boys gathered around her.

"I think it was, like, Salvador, something like that. He really wigged her out," the first boy offered.

Grace's cell phone rang. A glance down at the incoming number told her she had to take the call. "Thanks, guys," she said, stepping away from the group. "Hello?" she said into her phone.

"Hey there, Fred," came the voice on the other end.

Grace smiled, unable to help herself. "What's up, Ginger?"

"You got it!" Libby crowed. "You're so smart. So, listen, my cook said you were in here the other night asking around about some guy."

"Yes," Grace confirmed.

"According to Johnny, I'm staring at him."

Grace felt her stomach drop, both in excitement that she had a solid lead, but also in anxiety that he was in Libby's diner. "On my way. Do me a favor, take a surreptitious picture of him and text it to me, okay?"

"Surreptitious. Big words, Detective." Libby laughed. "No problem. I'll do it right now."

Grace smiled, despite the possible seriousness of the situation. "Is there anyone else in the diner?"

"Just a group of girls giggling in the corner booth."

Grace felt her heart drop. Young girls seemed to be the connection with every sighting of this kid. "Okay. Thanks, Libby. And, uh…" She shuffled her foot, grimacing when she accidentally kicked the side of the building with her toe. "Be careful." Grace didn't wait for a response before simply ending the call. She felt strange telling Libby to be careful, and more than that, she felt confused by the very strong sense of protection that suddenly engulfed her. It went beyond the normal concern she had for general public safety, and it made her feel very uncomfortable and unsettled to not know why she was reacting so forcefully.

A text dinged on her phone, and she was grateful for the distraction from contemplating her thoughts and feelings any further. It was the picture from Libby. From the direction and distance of the picture, it was clear Libby had been standing behind the lunch counter. The suspect was seated in a corner table for two by himself. He wore a red baseball cap, the bill pulled low over his face, though it could still be seen clearly enough for identification.

Grace glanced up from her phone and saw the four boys piling into an old beat-up Chevy. She ran over to them. "Hey guys, one more question," she said, leaning down to the passenger-side window. "This picture was just taken. Is this the same guy?"

The passenger took her phone and moved it so both he and the driver could see it. They made eye contact, both nodding.

"Yeah, that's him," the passenger said, handing her phone back to her.

Grace gave them a winning smile and pounded the roof of the car. "Thanks, guys."

She hurried to her car, almost throwing herself behind the wheel in her haste to get to Pop's. Her heart was racing, her palms becoming sweaty. She had to formulate a plan. Before backing out of her space, she made a quick call to the station and asked for a uniform to be sent to the young woman's house whom the suspected had allegedly tried to grab. She sent the newest picture along for the officer to show her, then sped off to the diner.

Chapter Eight

Libby was nervous. She hadn't been until she heard Grace's voice. Just before the detective hung up, there had been something that Libby hadn't been able to identify in her tone. Yes, there had been concern, and that worried Libby, but it was more than that. It was almost like a protectiveness, something that made Libby feel safe, like despite the fact she had no idea what was going on with the guy sitting in her diner at the moment, Grace would make it okay. It was…she tried to think of the word. Unsettling?

Clearing her throat and her mind, she glanced up when she heard a chair skid across the tile and saw that the young man in the red hat was heading to the bathroom. She gave him a polite smile as he passed, her stomach doing a little flip-flop in the process. If Grace was worried about this guy, clearly there was a reason.

Eyes on the closed bathroom door, Libby's phone vibrated in her pocket. She brought it out and saw it was a text message from Grace.

Grace: I'm in my car outside. I think I see what's been purported to be his truck. He still in there?

"I just love those big words, Detective," Libby murmured as she responded to the text in the affirmative, telling her he'd just gone into the restroom.

She'd no more than put her phone back into her pocket when the bells above the door opened and Grace came striding in. Libby was surprised to see her in regular clothes, considering this seemed to be a police matter. She also wondered why she wore a light jacket on a warm night.

Grace glanced toward the bathrooms before she hurried to the lunch counter. She braced herself with her hands on it and leaned over, murmuring into Libby's ear. "Just bring me a Coke and a side of fries or something, whatever, and we don't know each other." With that, she glanced to the bathroom again then hurried over to a table that was closest to the door. The girls who still sat and chatted at their table was between Grace and the guy, though a table closer to Grace.

Libby hurried back to the kitchen and asked Wayne, her cook, what he could have ready in just a few minutes. She had the distinct feeling that for Grace, it wasn't about craving a side of fries but rather looking like she belonged there.

"I got soup?" he suggested, glancing at her from the huge vat he was stirring.

"Perfect." Libby grabbed a clean glass and hurried to the drink station where she poured Grace a Coke with ice.

A few minutes later, Libby made her way out to the dining room with the bowl of soup with a side of crackers and the drink. "Here you go, ma'am," she said cheerfully, glancing over at the man's empty table. "He still hasn't returned?" she asked quietly.

"Nope," Grace murmured. "Thanks," she said at normal volume. "Looks good."

"Anything else I can get you?" Libby asked,

hands on hips. When Grace met her gaze, she could see the concern there, and it made her heart skip a bit.

"Not yet," was all Grace said, and all she needed to say. *Pay attention and stay alert.* She easily read between the lines.

Nodding, she gave Grace a smile. "Okay."

Libby walked over to the table with the girls to make sure they were okay before making her way back to the lunch counter where she'd been working on inventory for the next week's order. She got so lost in what she was doing—checking cabinets, making several trips to the walk-in, etc.—twenty minutes passed before she knew it. Back at the lunch counter, she was leaning over her checklist and notes when she glanced up to see Grace walking toward her.

"Hey," she said, straightening up.

"Hey. Listen, do you have a man working here right now?"

"Um, just my cook, why?"

Grace let out a heavy sigh. "I've got a bad feeling. Do me a favor and have him go to the bathroom door and knock, just ask if the guy is okay in there. You're positive that's where he went?"

"Yeah, I watched him go," Libby said, butterflies beginning to flap in her belly.

"And there's no back way out from there?"

Libby shook her head. "Nope. From the bathroom the only other option is the kitchen, so he has to still be in there." She looked past Grace and saw the man's table as it had been for the past half hour.

"Okay. See if your cook will do that, just see what he responds, and I'm going to ask these ladies if they wouldn't mind leaving." Grace hitched a thumb in the general direction of the girls.

Libby was surprised. "You think it's that serious?"

Grace shrugged. "I don't know. I'd rather be safe than sorry. Plus, this guy allegedly has a penchant for girls just that age, so I'd rather they not be around here for him to follow or anything in case he just decides to leave."

Libby studied Grace's features for a moment, once again noting just how beautiful she truly was. Not that it mattered, of course. Pushing those thoughts from her mind, Libby said, "You seem really troubled. What's going on?"

"I'm waiting to hear back from Colby. This guy has been seen skulking around here for the better part of two weeks. He's creeping people out, making them uncomfortable, and then a seventeen-year-old girl alleges he tried to take off with her."

Libby gasped, a hand going to her mouth. "Oh my god," she whispered. "Why don't you just arrest him?"

"He hasn't done anything provably wrong. I shared that picture you sent me a bit ago and Colby is supposed to be talking to the girl to see if she can make a positive ID. If she does, we have probable cause. Right now..." She shrugged.

"Just a creeper in a diner bathroom," Libby offered.

Grace nodded. "Pretty much." Grace turned away from the lunch counter, then stopped, looking deeply into Libby's eyes. "If something happens, if something goes sideways, either you try and get out or you stay close to me." Her gaze bored into Libby's. "Okay?"

Libby nodded, gripped by fear. She swallowed

and finally managed, "Okay."

Grace gave her a small smile and, to Libby's surprise, reached out and lightly squeezed Libby's hand before walking away. Libby took a long, shaky breath before heading into the kitchen to talk to Wayne.

Her cook agreed, and Libby decided to keep herself busy by washing tables down and disinfecting for the night. She also felt a bit more safe with the mobility, should she need it.

She watched as Wayne pushed out of the swinging door from the kitchen into the small hallway that housed the bathrooms. He wiped his hands on the apron tied around his waist before raising a hand and giving the wood door a solid knock.

"Hey man, you okay in there?" he asked.

Libby watched, frozen in mid-wipe over a four-top, nearly holding her breath. When there was no response, Wayne knocked again. She glanced over at Grace to see she'd pulled her police radio out of the pocket of the light jacket she wore and was quietly requesting backup. She also noticed that Grace's badge had appeared out of nowhere, hung from a chain around her neck.

Her attention shifted when she heard the bathroom door open. She saw the man inside for just a split second before she heard a scream as he raised his hand from his side, the knife he held glistening for just a second before he buried it in Wayne's stomach. She only realized the scream came from her when she felt the back of her shirt grabbed, and the next thing she knew, she was flying backward, sliding across the floor on her rear until her back crashed against the front door.

The breath knocked out of her and her head

pounding where it banged hard into the glass, she watched, horrified. Wayne stumbled backward, his hand covering where he'd been stabbed, and the man pulled the knife out, releasing a lot of blood that seeped between Wayne's fingers. He fell back against the kitchen door, which swung inward, sending him flying backward.

"Police! Stop!" Grace yelled, standing right in Libby's direct view of the man. She stood with her feet wide apart, Libby assumed her arms out in front of her.

It was then that she noticed the holster clipped to her belt at her back. The jacket had been covering it, but now the jacket was caught on the strap of the holster, revealing the empty leather pouch.

"Drop the knife!"

It hurt to move, but Libby did just enough to see around Grace's left leg. She shouldn't have. Looking at the man, it was clear he'd taken something in that bathroom. His eyes were wild, his teeth bared like a crazed lion. The blood-covered knife was held in his left hand, blood squirted across his knuckles. He was slowly advancing on her, knife raised Norman Bates style.

"Drop the knife!" Grace yelled again.

From this angle, Libby could now just barely make out the barrel of the gun aimed right at the man's chest. Libby's own chest heaved with her nearly hyperventilating breaths. Grace's yelled commands echoed in the room, but the man seemed totally oblivious.

"Drop the knife! Drop it, now!" Grace sounded more desperate as he slowly got closer.

Suddenly, with an almost animalistic cry, the

man charged. Libby screamed as three loud bangs pierced through the chaos. Her ears were ringing as she curled up as tightly as she could. The man didn't stop, even as scarlet flowers began to bloom on his light gray T-shirt.

BANG, BANG, BANG!

The acrid smell of burnt gunpowder filled the air. Libby screamed as the man cried out again, this time accompanied by the sound of the chair he'd thrown at Grace crashing into the table next to the detective.

Grace stumbled to the side as the table was shoved into her.

BANG, BANG, BANG!

Libby heard the wail of sirens go from distant to seeming on top of her. She felt trapped, nowhere to go.

Another chair went sailing through the air, this one catching Grace in the side of the head, causing her to nearly lose her footing. She did, however, lose her gun. The man lunged at her, just barely missing as Grace used a chair to push him away, growling like a raging bear as she did.

The guy stumbled backward, falling over a tipped chair. Like he had a spring inside, he was up and raging at her nearly instantly, knife raised.

Libby screamed again at the sound of an explosion above her, glass showering down. She covered her head and face as best she could. Then there was deafening silence, save for the sirens outside. Libby could feel her heart racing so fast she was worried she'd have a heart attack.

She cried out when she felt a hand on her shoulder. Looking up from glass-laden bangs, she saw Grace staring back at her, blood streaked across her face. Without thinking, she threw herself at her, whimpering as she clung to the detective, the tears coming hot and fast.

"It's okay," Grace whispered. "It's okay."

Libby allowed herself to be rocked, the tears slowing, though she still felt like she was in the middle of a bad dream. The only bright spot was the strong arms that held her.

"You guys okay?"

Libby sniffled, a hand coming up to wipe at her eyes, her entire face a mess of tears and snot. She used her shirt collar to restore some semblance of order to her face before she stood with Grace's help. Turning, she gasped when she saw that the entire top panel of glass in the door was gone. She was staring at Colby through the gap.

"We're alive," Grace said, her words clipped, curt, their feet crunching in the sea of glass on the floor as they stepped back so Libby could pull the door open.

She looked down, watching in awe as the metal frame of the door pushed the glass into a huge pile. She noticed little pricks and cuts on her bare arms, blood trickling in a few places at the small cuts. She stepped out into the night, barely noticing the crowd that had gathered, all standing in the street beyond the diner. They were little more than a revolving reflection of blue and red.

She saw an ambulance pull up, its lights swirling. She stopped and turned to look back into the diner, but Grace stopped her.

"No," she said softly. "Don't look." Grace cupped the side of Libby's neck until she looked up into Grace's face. Grace shook her head. "You don't want to see that."

Nodding, Libby turned around again and allowed herself to be led to the EMS people who were waiting to check her over.

❧❧❧❧

Given a clean bill of health, other than the cuts on her arms and face and a large bruise on her tailbone, Libby was taken into the police department, along with Grace, to give a statement. She'd sat with a kind and soft-spoken police officer who had asked her questions in a gentle tone, easing her through the process of describing what had happened.

Now, an hour later, she was tired. So, so tired. She'd spoken to Faith, who was more than understanding. She and Wyatt planned to visit her the following day at home to decide what to do regarding the diner. Faith told her that her father had offered to board up the destroyed door to get them through the night, so she had nothing to worry about.

The same officer who had interviewed her offered to give her a lift home, or at least to the diner to get her own car, but there was only one person she needed to see in that moment. So, she waited for her, sitting in a chair in the lobby. She'd been told that Grace, too, was being interviewed.

Finally, the exhausted-looking detective walked through the metal door that led from the innards of the police department to the lobby. She stopped when she saw Libby, and a small, soft smile spread across her lips, her bottom lip cut pretty badly. The paramedics had said she had no broken bones, but she was beat up and bruised pretty good.

"Hey," Grace said, walking again, headed to Libby.

Libby pushed up from the chair and returned the smile. "Hey."

Grace raised a hand, and her fingers went to Libby's hair. Libby was confused for a moment until Grace's hand came back holding a large sliver of glass in it. They shared a smile and Grace tossed the glass into a nearby trash can.

"Do you need a ride home?" Grace asked.

"To the diner. I need to pick up my car," Libby said quietly, feeling so small next to the woman standing before her. What she'd seen that night would stay with her for many reasons, but mostly because of the incredible bulldog warrior that was Grace Montez.

"Okay."

A handful of minutes later, Libby sat behind the wheel of her car, letting out a heavy sigh. She glanced over and saw that Grace was still there, not having driven off yet. She smiled and waved before starting the engine.

Driving the quiet streets, Libby realized that Grace was behind her, her car staying almost a respectful distance away as they turned onto one street after another before finally Libby pulled into her driveway. Grace pulled up to the curb in front of the dark house.

Turning the car off, Libby climbed out and looked back at Grace, who was watching her through the passenger window. On a lark, she walked the length of the driveway to Grace's car, the driver's side window buzzing down as she neared.

"You okay?" Grace asked.

Libby was ashamed to admit it, but she was

afraid. She knew the man was dead, the threat taken care of. But still, she was scared. "Um, would you mind waiting here for a minute, just until I can get in and turn the lights and stuff on?" she asked, feeling like a five-year-old.

Grace reached down and turned her keys in the ignition, the car falling silent. "Do you one better," she said, Libby stepping away as the door was pushed open.

Insanely relieved, Libby led the way to her front door, inserting the key and unlocking the doorknob and deadbolt. She took a deep breath, then pushed the door open. Grace followed her inside. Libby hit every light and lamp they came to, though she felt tremendously better having Grace with her. She knew that the detective would never let anything happen to her, and she found it as unsettling as she did comforting.

They toured the entire house, every light switched on before they returned to the living room. She smiled sheepishly at Grace. "Thanks. I know it's silly, but..."

Grace shook her head. "Not silly at all. You should probably look into talking to somebody about what happened tonight, Libby," she said softly. "It would be traumatizing for anyone."

Libby nodded. To her horror, the tears came back again. She tried to turn away, but Grace saw and grabbed her, taking her into the most gentle, warm hug Libby had ever experienced. She let the sobs really go then, her entire body shaking with them. Grace said nothing. There was no need to, from Libby's point of view, as her embrace said anything she would need to hear.

Chapter Nine

Libby glanced over her shoulder when she heard Grace open the bathroom door in the hallway. She was dressed in the mesh shorts and T-shirt she'd given her to sleep in. Grace's clothes from the night before were covered with blood, and Libby had her throw them away.

She smiled, noting the somewhat-tamed rat's nest that was the detective's hair. "Want some coffee?" she asked, removing a mug from the cabinet for her own brew.

"Please," Grace said. "I hope you don't mind, I borrowed your comb and some water to try and contain," she said, pointing at her head.

Libby's smile grew as she grabbed a second mug. "Yeah, I noticed. Clearly you have the same issue I do." She spared a glance at her unexpected guest. "Your hair has a mind all its own."

Grace chuckled. "Ohhhh yeah." She walked over to the couch and began to fold the bedding Libby had supplied her with the previous night. Libby hadn't wanted to be alone and, truth be told, Grace almost seemed as though she didn't want to be alone, either. They'd both grabbed a shower, Libby giving her guest first dibs and clothes to change into, then after a long hug had said their goodnights.

"What flavor do you want?" Libby asked, glancing across the open space to where Grace was folding the sheet, the light blanket still tossed haphazardly on the couch. "I have vanilla or chocolate coffee," she offered, holding up a K-Cup for the Keurig maker. "Or, if you're totally turned off by flavored coffee, I have some regular."

Grace glanced at her over her shoulder. "After making my coffee nearly every single day for over a year before you left for Pueblo, you have to ask?"

Libby stared at her and blinked a few times. "Good point." She went back to her task, searching through her cabinets until she found what she was looking for. "How'd you sleep?"

Grace responded with a heavy sigh. "As good as can be expected, I guess. Kept waking up from horrible dreams. How about you? Where do these go?"

"Hallway closet. You'll see where," Libby said. "About the same as you. Faith called this morning, which is what finally woke me up. Wayne's wife said he made it through surgery and it looks like he's gonna make it." When there was no response, she turned to look in the direction where Grace had been, surprised to see Grace standing next to the couch, the expertly folded bedding in her arms. She was looking down, almost looking as though she were in prayer. "Grace?" Libby said softly.

Finally, Grace's shoulders lifted and fell with the deep breath she took. She met Libby's eyes, relief in the olive-green depths of her own. "I'm so glad," she said so softly Libby almost missed it.

Libby held her gaze for a long moment, something passing between them that she couldn't quite discern. Perhaps the relief of two survivors? She looked away. "Are you hungry?" she asked. "I was going to keep it simple. I have some apple turnovers I got from the bakery." She spared a glance in Grace's direction to see that she'd walked to the hallway closet. "Can I interest you?"

Grace looked over at her as she heaved the folded blanket to lie upon its mate on the top shelf. "Yeah," she said. "You can."

Minutes later the two sat at the kitchen table, breakfast served. Libby sipped her coffee, glancing up at Grace when she began to speak.

"I'll be sure to get these washed and back to you by tonight or tomorrow," she said, indicating the shorts and Bugs Bunny T-shirt she wore.

"You really should just keep the shirt," Libby said. "It's big on me and actually fits you great."

Grace raised an eyebrow, coffee mug paused halfway to her lips. "Are you implying that I'm bigger than you?"

Libby's eyes widened as panic washed over her. "Oh god. No! No, just that you are taller and your shoulders are a little broader than mine, and of course you have bigger..." She shut her mouth with an audible click of her teeth.

Grace glanced down at her chest, which filled out the T-shirt much better than Libby's own more delicate, *smaller* size did. "I see."

She gave Grace the most adorable—she hoped—and disarming smile she could. "Sorry. Not sure that could've come out more wrong if I tried." She was relieved to see the amusement in Grace's eyes as she sipped from her coffee. Seeing it as a reprieve, she decided to move on to safer topics. "Do events like last night make you regret becoming a cop?"

Grace seemed to take a moment to consider the question before responding. Finally, she said, "No. It reinforces why I did, to be honest. Is it easy? Absolutely not. But, I think that guy was in town to do some serious harm. I think it ended the second-best way it could have."

"The first being his arrest?" Libby asked softly.

Grace nodded. "Life's about choices. He made his, but unfortunately for those types, their choices affect those around them in the most horrible ways. Look at Wayne. Look at Colby." She studied Libby for a moment. "Look at you," she said gently. "You should never have had to see something like that."

Libby sighed and looked down into the depths of her coffee mug. She nodded, so many thoughts going through her head.

"I'm serious about you talking to someone," Grace added. "No doubt you'll suffer some effects from PTSD."

Libby eyed her companion. "Can I talk to you?"

"Of course, any time you want." Grace gave her a warm smile. "But, just keep an open mind to talking to a professional if you need to. PTSD can be a real bear."

Libby nodded. "Duly noted. What made you become a cop?" she asked, suddenly her curiosity about the woman sitting across from her burning a question mark in her brain. She knew next to nothing about her. "Where are you from? I know you're not a Wynter native."

Grace shook her head, sitting back in her chair, coffee mug in hand. "That I am not. I grew up in a teeny tiny town in New Mexico that bordered Mexico. If you spit, you could pretty much reach the other side of town." She smiled, though it didn't reach her eyes. "I joined the army as soon as I could and did my four years. I became an MP while in and fell in love with it. Got out and joined the force in Rio Rancho and was there for a while, then decided it was time to move on." She knocked on the table as she took a drink of her coffee. "Ended up here," she said, setting her cup down.

    Libby studied her for a moment as she chewed a bite of pastry. She felt there was more to the story but wasn't sure if she should ask. Instead, she said, "Do you like it here? Whatever you were looking for, did you find it?"

    Grace glanced out to her right, the backyard beyond the window. At length, she nodded. "I think so, yes. Certainly professionally."

    Intrigued, Libby pressed. "Were you married back in New Mexico? Kids? I'd be surprised if you have kids, because I can't see you leaving them behind."

    Grace gave her a tight smile, almost looking pained for just a second, then it was gone. "No kids. Alaina wanted them, but I knew she wasn't the right person, and it wasn't the right situation to bring children into."

    Libby felt a rush of surprise wash through her. Looking at Grace, her natural beauty, gentle, somewhat nonchalant attitude, and longer hair, she never would have pegged her as someone who had been in a relationship with a woman. And then she realized just how ridiculous she was being, how much she was trying to stuff Grace into the same box as some of her lesbian friends from college. Wyatt popped before her mind's eye. That woman was the most naturally straight woman she'd ever known, yet she was as dedicated and committed to Faith as it got.

    She cleared her throat, deciding to file this information away and consider it another time.

"What are your plans for the day?" Grace asked, draining her coffee cup, her pastry long gone.

"I was going to head to the diner to help clean up, but Faith told me she didn't want me there just yet. As much as I feel it's my place to be there, I'm grateful. I'm not quite sure I can handle that today."

Grace nodded. "I agree. It's not a good place for you to be."

"Colby invited me to go hiking with him." She sighed, trying not to let her irritation show. "So, guess I'm going hiking."

Grace studied her for a long moment before saying. "Well, probably good for you to get out of town for a while."

※ ※ ※ ※

The forest was beautiful, the tree canopy creating wonderful pockets of shade on a hot summer day. Libby enjoyed her surroundings, taking in the colors, the warm patches of sun on her skin as they walked under a break in the trees. She could hear the birds singing out their warnings of the encroaching humans, unseen high up in the branches.

Her mind had begun to wander as Colby rambled on and on. She tried to listen, wanted to be a good listener, but she'd come to realize that her own thoughts or experiences weren't part of the discussion. She didn't think he was intentionally trying to monopolize the conversation but was simply enjoying telling her about himself and his life.

"So, it's not far up ahead now," he was saying.

This caught her attention, something perhaps

she should pay attention to. "Um, what is?"

He glanced back at her. "The deer stand I told you me and Dad use."

Libby stopped, shaking her head. "Wait, no. Colby, I don't want to see where you and your dad lay in wait to murder animals."

He, too, stopped and turned to look at her. He looked confused and a bit hurt. "Wait, I asked you if you hunt a while back, and you said yes."

Crap. "I'm sorry," she said, kicking herself for not fully paying attention, especially to something she had strong feelings about. "Sorry, not sure what happened there. No, I don't hunt. I hate guns, actually. They make me terribly uncomfortable."

Looking utterly crestfallen, Colby ran a hand over his hair, nodding. "Okay," he said, as though coming to some sort of decision in his own head. "All right. We can work around that."

Feeling her stomach do flip-flops—not the good kind—Libby suggested, "Hey, I know of a little stream just that way a bit," she said, pointing to the west. Nodding in agreement, Colby walked with her as they headed in the new direction, this time at a leisurely stroll rather than the march he'd had them on. "I used to come up here all the time when I was a kid," she said, trying to redirect the conversation from guns and hunting. "It's so beautiful, so peaceful."

Sure enough, after a few minutes walking, the trees broke and opened up to a small yet powerful little stream that gurgled over and around large rocks. A couple of the boulders were half-buried in the bank. Libby sat on one while Colby claimed the other for himself.

"This is nice," he said, looking out over the new

terrain. "I love the sound of running water."

"I do, too," Libby agreed. "I've been thinking of getting one of those garden fountain things for my backyard. You know, that always has the water running, like this," she said, indicating the flowing water before them.

"So," Colby began. "If you hate guns so much, it must have freaked you out last night when I made that killer shot through the door and blew that guy's brains out."

Libby looked at him, admittedly a bit disgusted by his framing of the events.

"I mean," Colby continued, oblivious. "I don't know what was up with Grace, but he was beating the crap out of her with chairs." He shook his head. "Figured she'd be able to handle herself better than that." He looked at her, curiosity in his eyes. "Was that the first time you've heard a gunshot?"

Libby stared at him, incredulous. "She shot him nine times before you showed up. He kept coming like some kind of horror movie monster, or something."

"Well, she probably missed," he said, his body language screaming he'd switched to defensive mode, and she had no idea why. "If she'd hit him center mass, like she *should* have—"

"His shirt was covered in blood, Colby." Libby was getting more and more angry at how he was diminishing Grace's unbelievably heroic actions the night before. "I'll bet you anything that tests come back saying he was on something. You could see it in his eyes. Meth, PCP, something. He wasn't acting like a normal person."

Colby looked like he wanted to argue but wisely kept his mouth shut. Instead, he gathered a handful of pebbles at his feet and began to toss them into the water, skipping a few across the water's surface.

"What's going on with you and Grace anyway?" Libby asked. "When I first saw you at the festival, you seemed to really respect her and look up to her. Now," she added with a shrug. "You act like there's some sort of bad blood there. Is she hard on you or something?"

He spared a glance at her before returning his gaze to his task with the rocks. "Grace is okay. Decent cop, I guess."

Libby was really surprised by those words. "She's an amazing cop. I've seen her in action before last night."

Colby's head whipped around to look at her. "What do you mean?"

"Well," Libby said. "Like the beating she took by that asshole last night. She kept going like a trooper, no matter what he literally threw at her. She's black and blue today," she said absently, picking up a smooth, flat rock nearby that she thought would make a great skipping stone.

"Wait, you saw her today?"

She sent the stone flying, eyebrows falling in disappointment as it sunk to the bottom of the stream with a splash. Her father had taught her to skip better than that. "Yeah," she said, glancing over at him before looking around for another stone, determined to redeem herself.

"Where? I'm guessing the diner wasn't open for breakfast," he said with a smirk in his tone.

She looked at him with hard eyes. "That's not even funny, Colby." She was utterly irritated now. "A man lost his life there last night, and Wayne nearly did. Grace followed me home, at my request, after we gave our statements."

"What for?" he pressed.

"Because I was afraid!" She looked at him, slowly shaking her head. "Why do you think? We got to my house and I didn't want to be alone. Honestly, I don't think Grace wanted to, either."

He cleared his throat and looked down at his feet. "So, she spent the night?" he asked quietly.

Libby heard something in his voice, a sadness, almost. "Yeah," she admitted, her tone lowering from rising irritation to that of understanding. "She slept on the couch, Colby. We had breakfast this morning and she left."

He nodded. "I get it."

She studied his profile for a long moment, trying to understand why he seemed upset. Again, the word *sad* came to her mind. "Colby, is there something that happened between you and Grace? Did she do something?"

He glanced at her before letting out a heavy sigh. He pulled a leg up so the heel of his hiking boot rested against the boulder he sat upon. "I just don't get why girls like Grace"—he stopped himself and smirked—"*Women* like Grace, seem to always win."

"What kind of woman is she, Colby? What exactly is she winning? Are you talking about last night? Because she saw the guy first, or…" When he said nothing, Libby gasped as something occurred to her. "Do you mean because she likes women? Because she's a lesbian?" She grinned as another thought, absurd as it was, popped into her head. "Did she, like, seduce your girlfriend or something?" The way his face fell made Libby's stomach plummet. "Wait, Grace?"

"Well," he said, meeting her shocked gaze. "No, not Grace."

"But someone did."

"Fucking stole her," he spat out. "I was going to marry Heather, but no, no, here comes that slut, took her from me."

"Wow." Libby was quiet for a moment, trying to imagine the heartbreak from something like that. "I'm really sorry, Colby. That's awful."

"I worked my ass off every day in the academy, you know, to build a future for us," he explained. "And that stupid carpet muncher was in one of Heather's classes. Who does that?" He met Libby's gaze. "Seriously, who steals someone from their longtime boyfriend like that? Dyke bitch," he growled. "That's who."

"Colby," Libby said softly. "Look, it's awful what Heather did. Cheating is never the answer—"

"She didn't cheat on me, Liberty. That bitch seduced her."

Libby raised her hand in supplication. "Be that as it may, she didn't abduct Heather and force her to live in a closet. Heather made her choices, right or wrong. She hurt you, anyone can see that." She studied Colby's profile again as he looked out over the water, looking to see if he was listening to her. He seemed to be. "But it's not fair to think that every lesbian out there is just like that one woman. I don't know Grace crazy well, but I can't even fathom her doing something like that. She's got too much integrity."

Colby looked down at his hands, clasped around his shin. "True."

"I just think your anger is really misplaced," she added gently.

He met her gaze and held it for a long moment before he smiled. "Yeah. You're right."

※ ※ ※ ※

After their talk at the stream, Colby's attitude and manner seemed to brighten significantly. The two continued their hike and had several amusing conversations about movies and TV shows they watched in common. Truth was, Libby found herself having a good time.

As evening descended, he tried to talk her into getting some dinner with him in Tunston, but she wanted to go home. Part of her had felt awkward about being out as it was, but after the events of the previous night, she thought she should be at home, resting and trying to unscramble her feelings about what she'd witnessed.

Colby pulled his truck up in front of her house and pulled the parking brake before turning to look at her from his seat behind the wheel. The familiar pangs of uneasiness batted at Libby's gut in the form of teeny tiny butterfly wings. It was never a pleasant feeling, and one that confused her. She knew that he was interested in her as more than a friend, and she couldn't necessarily blame him. If she were honest, she'd done nothing to give him any message that she wasn't interested right back. Instead, she found herself once again painted into the corner of an expectant man.

"Today was really fun," Colby said, his tone different from that of the lighthearted goof he'd become after their stream-side talk. Now, his voice was softer.

She nodded, not entirely sure how to respond.

"Yeah."

"Come 'ere," Colby murmured.

Libby swallowed, angry at herself for not making her friendship-only intentions clear. Now, obligation reared its ugly head. Again.

Not entirely sure where he wanted her to "come 'ere" to considering there was a giant console between their seats, she simply turned to face him. Libby's eyes closed as he got closer and she braced herself for what was coming next. She'd only let him go so far, which he managed to get to pretty quickly. The moment she felt his tongue trying to push inside her mouth, she backed away. He tried to follow, but she put her hand up as she slid toward the door.

"I need to go in," she said in explanation to the confused disappointment on his face.

"Oh, okay." He nodded as though trying to act the cool guy, like *he* was the one who ended the kiss. "I have stuff to do at home."

"Okay." Libby climbed out of the huge truck, falling the six inches or so before her feet hit the ground.

"Hey," Colby called out, leaning on the console as he looked down at her. "I'll see you again. Right?"

She nodded and smiled before closing the door.

Chapter Ten

She walked around, looking at everything. The meeting time was scheduled for nine in the morning, but Libby had come early. She wanted—no, she needed—some time by herself to absorb and process. The blood had been cleaned, the glass swept up, and the door replaced. The tables and chairs had been removed, and everything that had been on and behind the lunch counter was gone as well.

The place looked a lot bigger without the tables and chairs. She noticed just how worn the linoleum was, the green-and-white diamond pattern probably laid forty years ago. It was stained and creased. A few dents looked newer, and she wondered if they were from the events of a week before. She saw one thing that certainly was: the blood stain at the dead center of the room. It showed just how close that man had gotten to both Grace and herself.

She shivered at the thought of what could have happened. One wrong hit in the head and it could have been lights-out for Grace. The mere thought made her feel nauseous. She was grateful for the distraction of Faith's 4Runner pulling up next to her car, as it stopped her mind from even daring to walk down the avenue it was flirting with.

Libby watched as Faith and Wyatt climbed out of the large SUV, a smile curling her lips when she spotted the little baby bump that was Wyatt's tummy.

"Good morning, ladies."

"Hey, sweetheart," Wyatt said, her mama bear coming out as she walked over to Libby and took her into a tight hug. "How are y'all doin'?"

"I'm okay," Libby said into the hug. "Not sleeping well, but I guess it is what it is. Grace recommended I talk to somebody, so I might."

"You really should," Faith said, taking Libby into a hug once Wyatt released her and giving the younger woman a tight squeeze.

The three women were quiet for a moment as they looked around the space. Finally, Wyatt broke the silence.

"Faith and I were talkin' about maybe makin' some changes. Obviously, no matter what, we gotta take out this floor," she said, indicating the poor shape it was in and the new stain that had captured Libby's attention moments before.

Libby tried to look around from a new perspective, pushing away thoughts of the horrors of that night and focusing on what could be done.

"You know," she said, looking at the other two women. "This place has been a café for decades. The problem is, everything here has also been here for decades." She grinned. "We can still keep the café or diner vibe but bring it up to the twenty-first century." Getting inspired, she walked over to the far wall across from the lunch counter. "Right here," she said, expanding her arms out to indicate the entire wall. "A huge neon sign, *Pop's since 1703*, or whatever year this place opened." She turned back to them. "So, we get the original history of this place."

"I love that idea," Faith said, walking over to the tired and worn lunch counter. "We could beef this up, modernize it, and maybe run more neon along the edge, really make it pop." She grinned at them both, making her look like a schoolgirl. "Sorry for the pun."

Libby opened her mouth to say something when she noticed a Wynter Police Department squad car slowing as it reached the diner. A small smile began across her lips as the car pulled into the parking lot until she saw who was driving it. The smile fell away. She shoved her hands into her pockets and felt her body close off a bit.

The car parked and the driver's side door opened. The uniformed officer stepped out and raised a hand to wave before leaning back inside the car for a moment. Colby emerged with a cardboard drink carrier in his hands, three Bessie's cups tucked into the holders.

Libby felt eyes on her, and glanced over to see Wyatt studying her. At Libby's questioning expression, Wyatt simply smiled sweetly then walked over to the door to push it open for Colby.

"Well, good mornin', Officer," she said, standing out of his way. "Nice to see one of our local heroes."

"Aw, thanks, Mrs. Fitzgerald," he said, all smiles and charm. He turned to Libby, his smile growing. "Hey, babe," he said.

Libby bristled at that, taking a partial step back as he walked over to her. Seeming to sense his physical touch wasn't wanted, Colby stopped. His smile faltered for just a moment, but then it sprung back onto his lips.

"So," he said, looking down at the trio of cups in his tray. "I know you've said you like chai tea, so this is for you." He wiggled one of the cups free and handed it to her.

She took it and muttered a thank-you as he turned and headed to the other two.

"Ladies, I had no idea what you liked, so I asked the gal behind the counter." He pulled out the second cup and handed it to Wyatt. "Ma'am," he said. "A mocha breve."

Libby watched, eyebrows raised. She couldn't even imagine how much caffeine was in that cup, far too much for the little Wyatt inside.

"Ma'am," he said, handing Faith the final cup. "Vanilla latte."

"Thank you, Colby," Faith said with a smile, raising the cup in salute.

"Well, looks like you've got your work cut out for ya, huh?" he asked, tossing the drink carrier to the lunch counter and standing at the center of the room, hands on hips. He looked down at the gory reminder at his feet. Whistling between his teeth, he shook his head. "What a mess that must've been." He looked around the room at the three women. "Sorry 'bout that."

Libby just stared at him, not trusting herself to speak. She was bothered by how callous he was being about something so traumatic. She didn't think he meant to be, and was clearly proud of himself for ending a horrible situation, but she wished he'd understand it from her and Grace's point of view.

Like a welcome little gift from the Gods, Colby's radio went off, the dispatcher requesting his location. He leaned over to Libby, giving her a peck that felt like it had come from an angry rooster, then hurried out of the diner.

Left alone, the three of them just kind of stood there, staring down at their respective cups. As though preplanned and choreographed, Libby walked over to Wyatt and handed her the chai tea, took the mocha breve from her and handed it to Faith, who in turn gave her the vanilla latte.

"So…neon lighting, we were saying?" Faith said.

≈≈≈≈

"You are too cute. Yes, you. Okay, now you're just showing off." Libby grinned as she scooted from the chair to the floor as Charlie rolled over onto his back, legs in the air to expose his belly. The four-year-old chocolate Lab was a big goof with a wonderful personality. His right back leg scissored the air in pleasure as she rubbed his chest. "Silly boy."

"Okay, be kind."

Libby looked up from Charlie and got an up-close and personal view of a wineglass filled a third of the way with bright red liquid. She reached to grab it, but it was moved out of reach.

"You are of age to drink, right?" Faith asked, dramatic concern on her face.

Libby glared at her. "Funny."

Faith grinned and handed her the chilled glass.

"Are we becoming vampires tonight?" she asked, noting the unusually bright red color. She brought the glass down to sniff the contents. "Strawberry."

"Yes, it's more like a wine cooler than anything else. Not as strong, a bit more fruity and sweet," Faith said, lowering herself to the couch.

Libby gave the dog one final pat on his chest before pushing up to sit back on the easy chair. She got settled, careful not to spill her drink before taking an exploratory sip. Liking what she tasted, she took a bigger drink.

"Good?"

Libby nodded. "A little sweet, but yeah, that's really good."

"Your boy came into the ice cream shop today, asking around," Faith said, chuckling. "You need to school him. Clearly clueless, what, after the coffee debacle the other day?"

Libby stared down into the scarlet depths of her glass before letting out a long sigh. "He's not my boy," she said softly. "He's not my anything. A friend, I guess." She looked up when there was only silence. Faith was looking at her, confusion on her face. "What?"

"That's just not what he's telling people. And, you let him kiss you at the diner the other morning, so I just figured..."

Libby took another sip of her wine, mostly to keep herself from throwing the glass across the room. Finally, she shrugged. "I don't know what's wrong with me."

"Whatever do y'all mean?" Wyatt said, entering the room with a glass of water. She sat beside Faith.

Libby thought about what she wanted to say for a moment before she finally spoke the words she'd held inside for a long time. "Sometimes I think I'm nothing more than a cold bitch." She spared a glance to the two women, who sat silently, listening. "I consider myself a good person, a nice person," she amended. "I care about people, try not to judge, live and let live. I have friends of every color of the rainbow, female, male and everything in between." She smiled. "Gay," she added, indicating the couple sitting not far away. "Straight, whatever."

"You're one of the nicest people I know, Libby," Faith said softly. "What's going on?"

Libby smiled. "Thanks. My parents taught me to never judge someone by the color of their skin, sexual orientation, any of that stuff. But when it comes to a guy I'm dating or who's interested in me..." She shrugged, feeling frustration begin to seep in. "I instantly begin to pick them apart. I mean, there have been some genuine reasons with some," she conceded. "Won't get a job, won't move out of Mommy's house, whatever. But then...take Colby, for example. Known him for a long time, comes from a good family. He has a career, his own place, goals. I mean, he's basically a typical guy."

"Maybe that's the problem," Faith muttered.

"Hush." Wyatt lightly smacked her wife on the thigh.

Libby heard the comment, but it didn't fully register as she was deep in her own thoughts. "Why am I never satisfied when it comes to the guys that come into my life?" She felt near tears, confused and angry with herself. "Why can't I just be happy with what's offered? Again, like Colby. Everything I've complained about with the guys I've been involved with has nothing to do with him. But I just..." She sighed. "I just can't seem to make that connection."

"Darlin'," Wyatt said softly, leaning over Faith to place her hand on one of Libby's knees. When Libby looked at her, the Southerner smiled sweetly in that motherly way she always approached Libby. "Don't be so hard on yourself. Love is a finicky beast. Just because somebody looks good on a page doesn't mean they fit in your book."

Libby considered the wise words for a long moment before she nodded.

※ ※ ※ ※

"I still wish you guys would've let me help with dishes," Libby said, accepting a hug first from Faith then a tight squeeze from Wyatt.

"Nah," Faith said. "I did most of them while Wyatt cooked. Easy cleanup after."

Libby noticed Wyatt duck out of the foyer and into the home office. "So, are we still planning on meeting at ten tomorrow?"

Faith nodded. "Yup. Dad will be there to do his architect thing and we can start with some official plans for the diner. I really love the ideas we've come up with."

Wyatt returned, a thick trade paperback in her hands. "Here," she said, holding it out to Libby. "I think y'all will like this. I know you love to read."

Libby accepted the book. "*1049 Club*," she read. She glanced up at the redhead. "What, is it like *Fight Club*?" she smirked.

"Hardly," Wyatt grinned. "This book has a little bit of everything in it. I think y'all will appreciate it."

Libby's eyebrows drew. "How on earth do you say this author's last name?" she murmured.

Wyatt chuckled. "No idea, just love her work." She gave Libby another squeeze before Libby left with a promise to read and return the book.

※ ※ ※ ※

September had arrived, which meant temperatures would rapidly start to fall in the mountains, so

Libby decided to take advantage of the warm day and do some hiking. After a couple hours, she decided to take a break. Finding a nice, shady spot, she unbuckled her backpack and shrugged out of it, water bottles and snacks inside along with rain gear in case the heavens decided to dump on her.

Squatting next to a tree, she unzipped the backpack and was about to reach in for water when she was started by the discernable *click, click, click* of a camera shutter. She stood and looked around, seeing only trees and foliage until she glanced behind her. About fifteen yards away, Grace sat on a fallen log, a very nice camera in her hand with a huge lens. She was grinning.

Libby rolled her eyes and let out a breath. "You startled me."

"Sorry," Grace said, resting her camera on a thigh. "Couldn't resist."

"Well, I know I'm stunning and all," Libby said, brushing unruly blond hair out of her face. She returned the grin, knowing full well she looked like hell: sweaty, face probably smudged with dirt somewhere. Her tank top was plastered to her back.

Grace chuckled and pushed to her feet, holding her camera securely against her stomach as she grabbed her own backpack. "Mind if I join you?"

"Of course not," Libby said, lowering herself to sit down. She patted the forest floor. "Grab some moss."

Grace walked over and lowered herself to sit across from Libby, the younger woman's backpack between them. She set her own backpack to her side, setting her camera atop it. "I love coming out here and taking pictures," she said softly, looking up into the trees above them. "So peaceful and quiet."

Libby studied her companion for a moment, noting not for the first time just how beautiful Grace really was. Her skin was flawless, her heritage giving her the look of always having a slight tan. Her eyes, such an unusual color of green, were beautiful, yes, but also so deep, always seeming to look into the very soul of whomever she was looking at.

Softly clearing her throat, Libby looked away, turning her focus back to her backpack. "Water?" she asked, bringing out a water bottle slick with condensation. She'd put three bottles in her freezer overnight so that she'd have ice water on the hike when she was ready.

Grace looked at the reusable water bottle she had attached to the side of her backpack, then to the cold one in Libby's hands. She grinned. "As long as you're sure you won't need more later," she said, meeting Libby's gaze.

Libby waved her off. "I've got two more."

"Then, sold."

Libby watched as Grace twisted the cap off, breaking the seal before tipping the bottle back and taking long gulps. A bit of the water leaked out the corner of her mouth and made its way down her chin and an arched, graceful throat.

She looked away.

She pulled out a second bottle for herself as well as a protein bar, holding one up in offer.

Grace lowered her water bottle, nearly half the liquid gone. She wiped her mouth with the back of her hand. "You come prepared," she said.

"That I do. Learned from my mama."

Grace accepted the food and chuckled. "You'll

be the type that can literally pull out a playpen from your bag when you have kids, aren't you?"

Libby grinned. "Probably." She tore open her protein bar and bit off a bite. As she chewed, she studied Grace, head slightly cocked to the side. "Tell me more about you. You're such a mystery. From what you told me that one day, you were born, joined the army, then became a cop. The end."

Grace chuckled around the bite she was chewing. "Pretty much," she mumbled.

"Come on," Libby urged, lightly tapping the toe of her hiking shoe against Grace's bent knee.

Grace shrugged as she stared off into the trees as she finished chewing. She took a drink from her water, then cleared her throat. "Well, as I told you, I was born into a teeny tiny little border town in New Mexico. Youngest of seven. Five girls and two boys."

Libby's eyes widened in surprise. "Yikes. As an only child, I wouldn't know what to do with that." She met Grace's smile. "Are you close to your siblings? Your parents? What did they do for work to afford such a large family?"

Grace finished her protein bar then crumbled the wrapper, which she placed in Libby's outstretched hand, who tossed the trash into her backpack. She placed her hands back on the moss-covered ground and leaned on her arms.

"Well," Grace began. "My father, Guillermo Montez, worked as a janitor in the high school. He was of his generation, unfortunately. 'I am man and can do what I want. You are woman, so make me dinner, raise my babies, and shut up.'"

Libby grimaced. "I'd kill him."

Grace laughed. "I'm surprised Rosemary didn't,

to be honest. Anyway, he was married to Rosemary, a midwife. The funny thing about her was, she was an evil woman—cruel, lacking a conscience, I believe. But, when it came to 'her girls,'" she said with air quotes. "What she called the women she helped, a lot of women who'd cross the border to have their babies, but also women who lived in our town, she was amazing. *Angel de la vida*, they called her."

"Angel of life," Libby murmured. She smiled at Grace's nod and approving smile. "Did all you kids call your mother by her first name? Or is that just something you do now as an adult?"

"She's not my mother," Grace said simply. "My father had his flings, but he had a couple of mistresses through the years. One such mistress was a young woman named Diane Knox. She was a junior at the school where he worked. She got pregnant with me her senior year. As punishment, her parents made her carry to term, keep me for three months, then forced my father to take me or they'd expose him."

Libby stared at her, slack-jawed. "Oh my god."

"Yup. So, as my brother Edwardo told it, my father came home one night with a basket and a baby and told Rosemary to do something with it."

Libby sat there in silence for a long moment, not entirely sure what to say. Finally, all she could manage was, "Wow." She met Grace's gaze, those green eyes guarded. "Are you close to any of your siblings?"

"My oldest brother, Edwardo. Our other brother, who was two years older than me, was killed in a motorcycle accident several years ago. All my sisters are just like their mother. I was *not* sad to say goodbye to them, lemme tell you."

"Did you ever have to see any babies being

born?" Libby asked, taking a drink from her water, all the information she'd just been given whirling around in her head.

"Oh yeah, we had to help. Helped with my first baby when I was seven. Scared the living crap out of me," she said with a laugh. "That woman's scream was better than any horror movie."

Libby grimaced, feeling an irrational need to clasp her legs closed. "I can't even imagine. How terrifying."

Grace nodded in agreement. "Certainly had its moments. So, when I started high school, I decided I was going to get out. I worked my butt off and graduated a year early. At seventeen, I signed up for the army, then lived on friend's couches and worked until I was eighteen, then shipped out."

Though Grace's eyes were still guarded, Libby could see some pain seeping through. She gave as kind a smile as she could muster. She reached over and lightly squeezed one of Grace's hands. "Thanks for telling me."

Chapter Eleven

Grace tossed a baby carrot into her mouth as she continued to sort through the photographs she'd taken during her hike four days before. It was the first chance she'd gotten to upload all her shots. She'd used her digital camera that day as her studio wasn't finished yet, so she had nowhere to process film the old-fashioned way.

It always amazed her just how many shots she took: hundreds, when it seemed like only a few dozen. She was pretty impressed with some of the photos, while others made her wonder what she'd been smoking. What exactly made the nodule on that tree so interesting at the time?

She sent some of her more questionable shots to a separate folder to review at a later time and decide whether to keep or delete. Those she liked or loved were moved into a folder for keepers, those she often had printed and framed—even one she had blown up into a poster-sized picture for a friend's birthday.

A small smile instantly curled her lips when the quick series of shots she'd taken of Libby came across her screen. The first she deleted outright, as, unaware she was being photographed, Libby had jetted into frame and inadvertently turned herself into more of a blurred Bigfoot photo than the adorable little spitfire she was.

The second picture showed Libby caught in

mid-action of looking around. She was frozen in time looking up into the tree she stood next to. The third picture was similar to the first, though not as blurry. The fourth, however, was what stopped Grace.

Libby had just turned to look for the sound of the camera shutter and was looking straight into Grace's lens. Her face was relatively expressionless, so it was just the purity of her features. Her lips, full, just barely pink. Her eyebrows, slightly darker blond than her hair, slightly arched. Someone with a trained eye for symmetry like a photographer or an artist would notice that one was raised ever-so-slightly more than the other; the average person would simply get the message from their brain which got the message from their eyes that that barely perceptible raised eyebrow was a sign of cockiness from the feisty little manager. The impression was softened, however, with the dichotomy of the largish brown eyes that gave a sense of innocence, which was utterly destroyed by the impish grin so often on those full lips.

Grace smiled as she thought of it. She could only imagine what Liberty the child had been like. The only child of doting, loving parents. No doubt she got away with murder. *I want an ice cream. Okay. I want a puppy. Okay. I want a pony. Okay. I wanna go to Mars. Okay.* She laughed at her own machinations.

Her gaze drifted down to see tanned arms and shoulders, visible under the tank top she was wearing. She could see her upper chest with just the slightest start of cleavage, which she quickly tore her eyes away from. She noticed the glint of a tiny gold chain around Libby's neck where a choker would sit. There was something dangling from it.

Fingers gliding over the sensory pad of her laptop to access the enlarge tool, she enlarged the image, zooming in on the necklace. Dangling from the gold chain were tiny angel wings. She wondered how she hadn't noticed that day. Zooming back out, she looked at the whole picture that was Liberty Faulkner. Somehow the angel wings made sense for her, a small but mighty symbol of the divine.

Clearing her throat to clear her head, Grace saved the picture and sent it to the appropriate folder before moving on to the next shot.

※ ※ ※ ※

Grace read the report she was handed, shaking her head. She heard Colby whistle between his teeth.

"Dude was smoking pretty much everything but the wax on the floor," he muttered.

"That punk was on meth, PCP, and I'm sure whatever else he could get his hands on. I'm surprised his damn head hadn't exploded before he found his way into that diner," their captain said, sitting behind his desk across from Grace and Colby.

Colby smirked. "Well, I took care of him with my nine-mil."

Grace glanced over at him, disapproving. Before she could say anything, the captain added, "Yeah, well, as much lead as Montez pumped him with, he probably would've bled out in another thirty seconds."

Though she knew their supervisor was simply stating a fact, Grace saw how it hit Colby. She listened as the captain filled them in on a few more details before releasing them from his office.

Colby stormed down the hallway that led to the back door of the station and the parking lot beyond.

"Colby," Grace called, hurrying after him, his strides as long and powerful as he could make them. "Hey, wait up."

Colby burst through the door and continued on, ignoring her. Irritated but determined to talk to him, she followed, finally catching up to him at his assigned patrol car.

"Hey."

Finally, he turned to face her, his face the very mask of anger. "What?" he barked. "Coming to gloat?"

Grace, dangerously close to smacking him, took a deep breath to gather her thoughts and ground her emotions. "Colby," she said gently. "That night was a bad night with a really bad dude. Yes, the world is safer now that he's gone, and you definitely played a part in that. You did good."

"But?" Colby said, anger in his voice.

"But," Grace conceded. "Between the military and the civilian world, I've been in law enforcement for seventeen years. I've drawn my weapon plenty, but that was the first time I've fired it in the line of duty. A life was taken that night, Colby. There's nothing to *gloat* about." She looked deep into his eyes, needing him to hear her. "You and I took an oath to protect and serve, and that doesn't include being in competition for more notches on the utility belt."

He let out an irritated sigh and crossed his arms over his chest as he looked away.

"We did our jobs," Grace continued. "As your superior officer, I'm telling you, you need to watch your attitude." She met his gaze when he glared at her again. "Ego and temper have no place on the job for a cop. It's gonna get you in trouble or killed." With that, she turned away and walked over to her squad car.

She unlocked the newly washed car, the shiny black-and-white stark and true. She got settled inside and sorted through the few things she had to do at the beginning of her shift: divorce papers she had to deliver, a warrant to serve.

Starting the Crown Vic, Grace pulled out of the spot and onto the street. She thought she would deliver the divorce decree first since it was the farthest out of town, then work back inward. Twenty minutes later and that unpleasant task completed, she decided she wanted some coffee to try and forget about the poor woman's absolute fall-apart moments before. Though she headed to Bessie's, she found herself pulling up in front of the diner.

The restaurant had remained closed after the shooting, which was a bummer for those in town as it was the only nighttime eatery other than fast food and the bar snacks at Bessie's. But, the people seemed to understand, and had come together to help. Once the police department had done their investigation, the town had come together to help clean up the mess, sweep up glass, remove the furniture, all of it.

She recognized Libby's father's work truck in the parking lot and saw some of his guys hurrying back and forth from building to their own trucks for this or that. She'd heard a rumor that Faith and Wyatt had decided to go ahead and update the diner's interior décor earlier than planned since it had been so badly damaged and would need work anyway. She was curious what they'd do.

As she sat there in her cruiser, her words to Colby earlier came back to her. It was true: in all her years on the job, she'd never had to fire her weapon, and certainly had never shot anyone or been part of their death. Their captain had told her and Colby that it had been deemed a justifiable shooting, and both had been cleared of any wrongdoing. It was great that her record would be clear, but her conscience was not.

He wasn't a good guy, but somewhere out there, someone would be getting a call about their son, their brother, or their friend. Someone out there was hurting because of his death, and she was part of the cause of that death.

Movement out of the corner of her eye pulled Grace out of her somber thoughts. An instant smile came to her face when she saw that it was Libby, literally galloping to her car as though she were riding an invisible stick horse, replete with tongue clicks to mimic the hooves. Chuckling, Grace hit the button to send the window sliding downward with a quiet buzz.

"Well, hello, cowboy."

Libby grinned as she came to a dramatic stop with a hop at the driver's side window. "Howdy."

"What was that about?" Grace asked, bringing her hands up to pantomime holding the reins of a galloping horse.

"Frankly," Libby said, lowering her voice to an almost conspiratorial tone as she placed her hand on the roof of the car. "I'm so sick of working with stubborn, sweaty men and needed a little yeehaw to burn off annoyed energy."

A bark of laughter escaped Grace's lips. "I see."

"Hey, you gotta do what you gotta do." Libby grinned and knocked on the roof of the car. "What are you up to? Security for the diner?" Her grin said she wasn't being serious.

"Oh yes, I'll be here all night," Grace said,

playing along.

"Fabulous! We've got some of the old booths set out back if you need a comfy nap spot."

Grace nodded. "Thanks for the tip. I was actually just being nosy. I'm headed over to get a cup of coffee to start my shift."

"You know," Libby said, raising that naturally raised eyebrow just a bit more. "If you give me a lift that seventy-five feet, I'll personally make your coffee for you."

Grace glanced around to see who was watching them. Technically, it was a no-no and against department policy. Even so, she'd given people rides home before—those too drunk to drive home, or a woman once who got a flat tire on the side of the highway in Rio Rancho. Without a word, she nodded toward the passenger-side door, using the driver's side panel to unlock it.

With a whoop, Libby trotted around the front of the car and tucked herself inside next to Grace. She looked around, eyes wide as she took it all in. "I don't know why, but I'm surprised to see a laptop in here." She grinned, meeting Grace's gaze. "To look up people by their license plates and stuff?"

Grace put the idling car in gear and pulled away from Pop's. "Yes, as well as reports, things like that." She drove past the coffeehouse, Libby so involved in taking in all the fun buttons and switches that she didn't even notice. "Press that," Grace said, reaching down to lightly tap one of the buttons on the small black box on the dash below where the laptop was mounted onto a moveable platform.

"Here?" Libby asked, her finger poised above the indicated button.

"Yep."

Whoop! Whoop!

Libby snatched her hand away as though she'd been burned. She looked over at Grace with the huge eyes and expression of a child in uh-oh mode. Grace burst into laughter as she steered them toward the less-populated area for a moment so she wouldn't garner any unwanted attention.

"Can I do it again? Libby whispered.

"Sure. Go for it. Then hit the one to the right of it," Grace said.

Whoop! Whoop!

"Most excellent!" Libby crowed. As told, she hit the other button and the siren began to wail the song of somebody's really bad day. Libby cackled before hitting the button again, the siren cutting off mid-wail. "I would get myself in way too much trouble."

Grace grinned, pulling a U-turn in the middle of the empty road to head back to town.

"Where have you been?" Libby asked. "Haven't seen you since our hike."

Grace nodded. "I know." She took a deep breath and let it out slowly as she pulled up to Bessie's. "Been working a lot, but honestly," she added with a shrug, glancing over at her passenger. "Just been keeping to myself." She wondered what Libby saw in her eyes, because suddenly her own softened and the sweetest, kindest smile crossed her lips.

"What time do you get off tonight?" Libby asked softly.

"As long as there's no drama that erupts, ten. Why?"

"Do you have a bathing suit? Or something you don't mind getting wet? You know, shorts and a

T-shirt, whatever?"

Baffled, Grace's eyebrows fell but she nodded. "I do."

"Good." Libby wrapped her fingers around the door pull. She met Grace's curious gaze. "When you get off tonight, grab 'em and meet me back here."

Grace stared at her, definitely confused. "Okay."

"Come on, Montez. Let's go get you that coffee," Libby said, pushing the door open.

Grace turned off the car and secured it before following the younger woman inside. As the days of summer were coming to an end, the ice cream parlor was jumping, especially since they'd added ice cream cakes to their roster.

Grace turned her attention away from the counter where an employee seemed to be taking just such a cake order from a customer and found herself right at face level with an incredibly shapely behind lovingly wrapped in denim. Like a punch to the lower gut, Grace looked away as she mounted the stairs behind Libby, following her to the second floor.

The coffee shop wasn't as busy, a few patrons scattered about in the seating area, one young woman wearing headphones and typing on her computer at a corner table. A few people glanced up at Grace, something she was used to when in uniform. Some gave her a nod or smile of respect while others looked a bit nervous.

Grace headed to the cashier but was waved over to the barista area by Libby, who smiled at the guy behind the counter and said something to him, sending him off to begin wiping down tables.

"I'll be right back, Libby," Grace said, nodding toward the cashier. "I need to go—"

"Nope," Libby said, grabbing the largest cup they offered. "You do a lot for us, keeping us safe." She gave Grace a sweet smile. "It's on me."

"That's very sweet," Grace said softly. "I don't want to get you in trouble with the boss."

Libby gave her a crooked grin. "I *am* the boss. No worries."

"Well, all right, fine. I guess I'll just have my usual, then."

"Actually," Libby said, eyeing her. "Do you like mint cookies?"

Grace considered for a moment, then nodded. "I do. I will tackle a Girl Scout for a Thin Mint any day."

Libby raised an eyebrow as she began to do her mixing magic. "Oh my, Detective."

Grace smiled. "So, what are you guys doing over there at the diner? I hear some updates are being made." She rested a palm on the bar top and leaned her weight against it in a casual stance.

Libby nodded. "That is correct." Like a seasoned bartender, she grabbed this bottle, that bottle, then another one, pouring what seemed the perfect amount of this, that, and the other thing into the cup. "Faith, Wyatt, and I decided to give it a facelift. You know?" she asked, glancing over her shoulder at Grace as the steam wand buzzed, frothing the milk in Grace's drink. "I'm actually really excited about it. We're giving Pop's a new century look."

"I think that's wonderful. Updated the food already, so why not the space?" Grace reached over and grabbed a cardboard sleeve for her cup as she saw that Libby was nearly finished. She was loading up the stainless-steel bottle with ingredients for fresh whipped cream that she'd shake to nitrous-oxide-assisted perfection to become the creamy white swirl atop her drink.

"Here you are, madam," Libby said a few moments later as she set the cup in front of Grace, carefully pushing a plastic white lid down on her creation. "What do you think?" she asked, sounding a bit leery.

Grace blew into the drinking hole, trying to cool the liquid down enough to take an experimental sip. She focused on the tastes as they finally hit her tongue. Immediately, her eyes closed at the warm, minty heaven that aroused her senses. "Absolute minty bliss," she murmured.

Libby grinned big, bouncing on the balls of her feet. "Yes!"

Grace took another sip, tempted to ask her to make a second drink so she'd have more for her shift. "This is amazing, but," she said with regret. "I have to get going." She raised her cup. "Are you sure I can't pay you for this, Libby?"

Libby waved off her offer. "Nope. On the house. See you tonight, Detective."

Chapter Twelve

"I'm pretty positive you're taking me down into the depths of Hell," Grace muttered, the stone staircase they were heading down seeming to never end.

Finally, they reached the ground floor of the basement and she saw an opened doorway to the left that, from what little she could see in the dimly lit hallway, looked like an office, probably for the managers. They continued on, the hallway narrow and a bit claustrophobic. They passed another door labeled with a sign that read: *PRIVATE* before they turned down another hallway, even more narrow and noticeably warmer.

"You know I was joking about the Hell reference, right?" Grace said, wondering where on Earth Libby was leading her.

"A line from one of my mom's favorite movies," Libby said. "'You whine like a mule.'"

Grace chuckled. "Love that movie, too. *Robin Hood: Prince of Thieves.*"

Libby slowed her pace and partially turned to look back at Grace. "Very good, Detective," she said. "Big words and nineties movie trivia."

Grace grinned. "I have many skills."

Libby snorted as they headed down the final hallway, which ended in a downright medieval-looking door. Libby produced a huge, brass key.

"Your mom's favorite movie, huh?" Grace asked, waiting patiently for the manager to disengage the locks.

"She says she likes the strong character of Maid Marion created by Mary Elizabeth Mastrantonio," Libby said, turning her wrist to disengage the lock with a loud *click*. She glanced at Grace over her shoulder. "I think it has more to do with Kevin Costner's butt, myself."

Grace was still laughing at that as Libby pulled the heavy, thick wood door open with a grunt of exertion. Grace reached over her to help, surprised at the heft. The wave of humidity and heat that met them nearly took Grace's breath away.

"You really are taking me to Hell." She laughed.

"Hell, yeah, baby!" Libby said, laughing as well. "Watch your step."

They walked through the oversized doorway and down another flight of stairs, each step lit like those in a movie theater. As they descended, a light fixture along the wall sprang to life, illuminating their way down into the dark depths.

Finally, they reached the bottom to step onto smooth, naturally cool stone. It was such a strange dichotomy: the huge, cavernous space of naturally carved rock which sent a random cool breeze over the skin; then, the natural hot spring, nearly the size of a large inground swimming pool, sending off plumes of warm, humid air. Like a public pool, the deeper areas were marked and roped off from the shallower ones. Off to the side was another breach in the stone floor, a smaller pool of water with lots of steam rising from it.

Suddenly, light began to shine from the depths of the smaller pool and around the edges of the large one. Turning, Grace saw Libby standing at a metal box affixed to the wall. The door was open, revealing a jumble of switches and knobs. Libby glanced out at the space, watching as lights grew bright above then slowly dimmed down to a more relaxing level. The colors began to slowly change from red to green to blue and on and on, giving the cave an ethereal feel.

Grace shrugged the backpack from her shoulder and walked over to Libby, who had shed her own backpack, which hit the stone floor with a plop. Dressed in swishy track pants and a lightweight hoodie, she could feel the tight confines of her suit beneath it. That thought had no more entered her brain when Libby whipped off the T-shirt she was wearing. Revealed was a bikini top, black with neon orange goldfish printed all over it, though from afar they looked more like orange polka dots.

The cute bikini top was not, however, what had Grace's attention. Despite the nice tan of her arms, face, and legs, Libby's torso was pale, as were the swells of her breasts. They were full, and looked to be a perfectly sized handful. She could just barely see the rigid outline of small nipples.

Always a breast woman, Grace was drawn to them like a child to candy. These particular breasts, as beautiful and enticing as they were, absolutely were not an option. The delicate structure of Libby's throat and collar bones leading down into that creamy cleavage called to her like a siren's song, so Grace forced herself to turn away.

She grabbed the hem of her hoodie and tugged it up over her head. As she heard Libby continue to disrobe, she wondered just how bad an idea this actually was. She knew she would keep her hands to herself but could make no such promise about her eyes. After all, she reasoned, it had been a very long time since she'd been this close to a half-naked woman.

She used the toe of one slip-on shoe to help remove the other, then returned the favor with her bare foot. Pushing her track pants down her legs, she stepped out of them and wadded them and her hoodie into her backpack after removing the bath towel she'd brought. She took her time getting settled, trying to get her racing heart to settle down. It wasn't until she heard the splash of Libby diving into the water that she felt she could let out the breath she hadn't even realized she was holding.

Turning to face the water, she saw Libby's head break the surface, the wavy blond locks smoothed back from her face with her hands. She turned in the water until she spotted Grace walking over to the water's edge. She smiled.

"Look at you!"

Grace looked down at herself. She was dressed in a ruby red bikini top with matching boy shorts rather than traditional bottoms. "What?" she asked, feeling self-conscious.

"I can now see why you make a pair of jeans look so good," Libby said, swimming toward the side. "Not fair."

Grace felt shy at the compliment, her hand coming up to rub the back of her neck. "Thanks." She eased herself down to sit on the edge of what was marked the four-foot depth.

"How do you stay in such great shape? Your abs are just gorgeous." Libby stood up once she reached the shallower end, the very breasts that had garnered

Grace's attention so completely earlier back in view, though this time wet and with tantalizingly hard nipples.

Again, Grace forced herself to look away, angry with herself for her lack of self-control. She slid down into the water, which felt like her body was being engulfed in warm satin. It felt amazing, and as much as she hoped it would take her mind off the gorgeous young woman just a couple feet away from her, it made her need greater.

She fully thought now that it had been a very, very bad idea to accept Libby's cryptic invitation. As she'd come to understand just a bit ago, it had clearly been too long since she'd gotten laid. She thought perhaps a trip to Denver on her next weekend off was in order.

When she felt Libby's gaze on her, she remembered there was a question still on the table. "I kept my routine even after I got out of the army," she explained. "Running and an exercise regime I've managed to pare down to civilian life." She lowered herself into the water until she could raise her face to the cave ceiling to get her hair completely wet, smoothing it back into a rope down her upper back. "I'm a believer in healthy body, healthy mind."

Libby gave her a crooked grin. "Yeah? Do all those lattes count for a healthy body?"

Grace gave her a wicked smirk right back. "Nope. That's for the healthy body of others." She grinned as she heard a burst of laughter erupt from her companion right before Grace pushed off the wall and darted across the water just beneath the surface. It felt good to let her body go, the blood pumping and muscles working as she swayed her way across the length of the natural pool before turning back the way she'd come. It was a bit eerie—and very cool—how the changing lights changed her underwater world, too.

When Grace broke the surface again, Libby had moved to the shallowest part, which was just a couple feet deep. She was lounging, watching. Grace made her way over to her, feeling relaxed and almost like she could hum in contentment as endorphins ran through her brain.

Reaching Libby, she got comfortable next to her. The water looked unnatural and almost alien with the underwater lighting. She smiled. "This is cool."

"You've never been here before?"

Grace shook her head. "Nope. Heard about it, of course. Just never got around to coming."

"You know, I didn't even know this place was here," Libby said, meeting Grace's gaze.

Confused, Grace's eyebrows fell. "What do you mean?"

"Yeah, people just kind of forgot this place was here. Faith stumbled upon it when she was renovating the building," Libby explained.

Grace was fascinated. "I had no idea. What's the history of this place, do you know?"

"Well," Libby said, bringing her hands up to push some spring-like hair out of her face that had begun to dry. "According to Mr. Billy, this was used back when Bessie's was a saloon and brothel."

Grace's eyes widened. "You're serious? That's what this building was?"

Libby grinned. "Yup. So, the guys who paid the big bucks got to come down here and entertain their lady friends, or impress their guy friends."

With this new knowledge in mind, Grace

looked around, enjoying the gentle lapping of the water against her. "Lotta deals made down here," she imagined out loud.

"I think a whole lotta everything happened down here." Libby chuckled. "Anyway, so yeah, even as a kid, I had no idea this was here. I think Wynter just fell into such disrepair as a town." She shrugged. "And people forgot."

Grace glanced over at Libby, happy to see the look of contentment that softened her beautiful features. "Are you sure you won't get in trouble for bringing me down here after hours?" she asked softly.

"Nah," Libby said, her gaze drifting down. "You're twisted," she murmured, reaching a hand over to untwist one of Grace's bathing suit straps.

Grace gasped softly when Libby's finger just barely grazed her upper chest. "I thought I just wasn't straight," she managed, though her words were a bit more breathy than she wanted them to be. Her skin burned where she'd been touched. Looking down, she was surprised she didn't see a fiery fingerprint glowing just above her left breast.

Libby smiled, her hand falling away after her task was finished. Surprising Grace, she moved away toward the center of the pool, which put several feet between them. "I let Faith and Wyatt know so nobody would call the cops because cars were parked outside the building this late." She smirked. "The cops are already here."

Grace chuckled. "I seem to be lacking my badge and my gun at the moment, however."

"Oh, I don't know," Libby murmured. "You seem pretty dangerous just the way you are."

Stunned, Grace opened her mouth to reply but

Libby dove off into deeper water, vanishing beneath the surface. "What was that about?" Grace muttered.

Libby popped up halfway across the length of the hot spring, putting even more distance between them. "Do you like to read?" she called out.

Feeling silly yelling her response, Grace moved closer to the four-foot section where she'd entered the water to begin with. "I do." She stopped before the water got too deep for her to stand, as she wasn't as strong at treading water as Libby was. "Why?" She was confused by the total non sequitur.

"Have you read *1049 Club*?" Libby asked, seeming to ignore Grace's question.

"No. Is it good?"

Without responding, Libby again disappeared beneath the surface of the water. Grace was confused and a bit concerned by Libby's strange and somewhat out-of-character behavior. She waited patiently for the young woman to resurface and, hopefully, explain this new direction of topic.

Libby broke the plane of the surface, spitting a bit of water out of her mouth as she headed for the side. She held on with one hand as she used the other to push her hair out of her face. "Wyatt leant it to me," she said finally. "I'm not sure why."

"What do you mean?" Grace asked. She was feeling a bit overheated, so she braced her hands on the side of the spring and used her arms to lift herself out, sitting on the side with her legs dangling over the side.

Libby was quiet for a moment again, so long, in fact, that Grace wasn't sure if she was going to respond. "It's a really good book so far, about plane crash survivors with about a billion characters. But two of them, well, kind of, are lesbians."

Grace, unsure what the issue was, simply said, "Okay," to let Libby know she was listening.

"Do you think that's weird?" Libby glancing at her, her face suddenly very guarded.

"To have lesbian characters?" Grace asked.

Libby smiled and shook her head. "No. That Wyatt would give it to me to read." With a grunt, she also pulled herself out of the water but kept her distance where she sat on the edge. "I mean, obviously I don't have any issue with lesbians," she said, indicating Grace with a wave of her hand. "But…" She shrugged, looking down at her thighs, which her hand plopped down upon. "Just not sure why she thought I'd want to read it."

Grace considered for a moment, not entirely sure what was bothering Libby or what to say. Clearly, she was troubled by something, and it almost seemed as though Libby weren't entirely sure herself what it was. "You said there are a lot of characters in it?" she finally said.

Libby nodded. "Yeah. I mean, there's like ten main characters alone," she responded with a chuckle.

"Are they all gay?" Grace asked.

"No. Gay guys, lesbians, straight people, old, young, all over the map." Libby glanced over at Grace again. "A little bit of everything, I guess."

Grace smiled at her. "There you go. Maybe it wasn't about the lesbians at all. Maybe Wyatt just thought you'd enjoy something new."

≈≈≈≈

Grace's mind was an absolute tempest of thought, emotion, confusion, and concern as she went about her nightly tasks. She'd fed the cats when she'd stopped in at home after her shift to change into her bathing suit, but that didn't mean they didn't need a treat before bed—according to them.

The furry ones taken care of, she made sure everything was closed up and locked for the night before heading upstairs to take a shower. The swim had been wonderful, the company even more so. But something had been bothering Libby, Grace figured, and even when they parted with a quick hug, something had been wrong. Libby's eyes were clouded, a wrinkle formed between them as though she were in deep contemplation of something.

Flicking on her bedroom light, she tugged off her hoodie, tossing it toward her laundry basket as she'd put it on over her damp swimming suit top. Her track pants followed next, then her bathing suit itself.

Naked, Grace made her way to the bathroom, wanting a shower before bed. She was exhausted, however her body was letting her know that it wasn't so tired. Arousal the concept seemed like a vague memory, but the feeling was still familiar. She ignored it. Reaching the bathroom, she winced time and time again as she brushed out the snarls from her hair. Again, her body made its presence known, and again, she ignored it.

She tried to force her mind to what was on the agenda for tomorrow. She had to work, but she didn't go in until later, so she planned to do some yardwork. Yes, yardwork would be great. Her body and its need trickled back into her brain.

"Damn it, no!"

She wasn't in the mood. She didn't want to.

She turned on the shower and adjusted the

temperature to her liking, then stepped beneath the spray. A loud gasp escaped her lips as the warm water pounded against rock-hard nipples that were incredibly sensitive.

She was annoyed, she was frustrated, and she wanted to cry.

Eyes closed, Grace rested her forehead against the coolness of the tile, the water raining down over her neck and upper back. Her breathing was shallow, her body pulsing with sensations and growing arousal. She could feel the heaviness between her legs, and before she could command it to stop, her hand trailed down over her tummy to the soft, trimmed thatch between her legs.

Grace gasped at the copious wetness she found there. As her fingers trailed over the slick skin, she was surprised to feel how swollen she was, how ready. It had been so long, her body neglected and ignored, much like her heart.

A long, shaky breath escaped as her fingers found where they were needed most, so hard, so ready for release. A gasp and a whimper tore from her mouth as her body finally gave in, volcanic wetness flowing over her fingers. Grace's entire body shuddered as her orgasm swept through her, leaving her feeling weak and ashamed.

"I can't do this," she whispered.

Chapter Thirteen

Lying on her left side, Libby smiled, her arm folded beneath her head. She looked into the face of the woman lying next to her, her position mirroring Libby's. So beautiful. They lay no more than a foot apart, no less than six inches. She noticed the dark hair against the white of the pillowcase, a stark contrast. The red of her bathing suit top was stunning against her skin, her Portuguese heritage making her skin tone slightly darker than Libby's, even the parts that were pale from lack of sun.

Her gaze fell to those parts, mainly the breasts cupped in red. With her lying on her side, the swells of her breasts became enticing cleavage, which made her fingers itch with curiosity. Would the skin be soft? Would the breasts be heavy? They were larger than her own, so what would they be like to touch? To hold in her hands?

As though reading her mind, Libby's hand was taken and gently rested upon one of the breasts. The material of the bathing suit felt slick on her palm, even as her fingertips rested on the warm softness of the skin around it.

She gasped slightly, eyes riveted to where her hand lay. She squeezed a bit, amazed at the combination of firmness and softness. She trailed her fingernails over the red cup and was rewarded with a hardened nipple.

Libby's eyes fell closed when a hand came to cup

the side of her face just before soft lips touched her own. She was pushed to her back, the weight of a soft, warm body following. She buried her fingers in long, dark hair which fell around them, the soft tendrils tickling her cheeks. Her tongue felt like velvet against Libby's, as did the bare skin of her back as Libby's hands found the soft warmth. She could feel the tie of the bathing suit against her finger, and though she wanted to tug it loose, she just couldn't quite make herself.

A sigh left Libby's lips as the hot mouth and tongue moved to explore her jaw and her neck. The tongue licked a fiery trail down her throat before teasing the hollow. Libby's felt her heart quicken as her breasts felt heavy and needy, nipples straining against the material of her own bathing suit top.

Libby felt cool air brush her nipple as the black material of her bathing suit top was tugged down, revealing her naked breast. Her eyes fell closed and her head fell back into the pillow as it was engulfed in wet warmth.

With a loud gasp, Libby's eyes opened wide and unblinking. Her heart was racing and her chest heaving with every heavy breath. Her hand came up to her chest, only to find it resting on bare skin. She looked down and saw her breasts bared, nipples hard and extremely sensitive, almost painfully so.

Taking several deep breaths, she looked around, shocked to find herself alone in her bed. How could that be, when just seconds before… Libby's eyes closed and her hands moved up to cover her face, the dream in its entirety coming back to her.

Opening her eyes again, her hands dropped back to the bed. She stared up at the ceiling, unable to shake the images and sensations that her mind had conjured in the realm of make-believe and fantasy. Fantasy. Essentially, imagining or creating images of something that was unlikely or impossible. Yes, impossible, Libby concluded.

She sat up and looked down at herself, noting she was only wearing a pair of panties and naked from the waist up. Looking around, she saw the clean tank top she'd intended to wear still folded on her dresser, precisely where she'd left it prior to her shower the night before. Further investigation showed the crumpled bath towel on her bedroom floor and Wyatt's book, *1049 Club,* lying facedown and open on the bed.

She remembered the events of the night now that had left her in this confused position. She'd come home from her time at the hot springs with Grace exhausted and, frankly, feeling a bit out of sorts. She hadn't been able to put a finger on what she was feeling, and that had put her in a dark mood.

She'd gotten home, set out the clothes she intended to sleep in, then got in the shower. Feeling overheated, she'd decided to hold off getting dressed until she went to sleep, so, just in her panties and wet hair, she'd reclined on the bed and decided to read a bit. The contents of her dream made it clear that it had been a mistake. It was the book, she reasoned, that was to blame for her strange dreams. There had been tension building up between two of the female characters for a few chapters, a sexual yearning and longing.

Padding to the bathroom, Libby looked at her reflection in the mirror. "That's what it was," she muttered. "It was Rachel and Denny's fault." She looked at the mop that was her hair, the downside of falling asleep with wet, wavy hair. "Who the hell's fault is this mess?"

She felt just as irritable as she had the night before, and decided yet another long, hot shower was in order.

※※※※

Irritated. She was irritated, damn it! Why weren't these kids cleaning the machine out properly at night, damn it? Why wasn't the cleaning checklist she'd created and trained them all on being followed, damn it? Why was she in such a bad mood, damn it?

Libby had taken the secondary ice cream maker apart as she'd gotten a text that morning saying it wasn't working again. Faith had advised she call someone in to take a look at it, but Libby knew she could handle it. It was a simple machine and easy to take apart. So, when Wyatt showed up, she found Libby sitting on the floor of the ice cream shop's kitchen, machine parts scattered around her as she got to the problem.

"Oh my," Wyatt said, stopping just inside the room and looking over the mess.

Libby nodded. "Yup. These damn kids aren't following the cleaning schedule," she growled. "I'm going to work closing shifts until I can train everyone all over again on how to properly take care of these damn machines." She looked back down at the component she was taking apart by removing the eight Phillips head screws. When she heard nothing but silence, she looked up again to see her boss staring down at her. "What?"

Wyatt squatted down and looked Libby in the

eye. "How'd it go with Colby in the springs last night?" she asked softly, concern in her eyes.

Taken aback, Libby blinked. "Colby?"

"Well, when you mentioned you were bringing a friend, I figured he would be the one." Wyatt picked up one of the disassembled parts of the machine and looked it over before shaking her head and setting it back down.

"Oh, hell no." Libby smirked. "I don't want to see Colby in a bathing suit."

Wyatt smiled and nodded. "So, who'd you invite, then?"

"Grace," Libby said, as though it was so utterly obvious who she'd bring. "What?" she asked again when Wyatt studied her for a long moment.

"Did you gals have a good time?"

Before Libby could respond, her openers arrived, and clearly they'd heard the last part of her discussion with Wyatt.

"Oh, wow, you took Officer Montez down into the hot springs?" Julia, their fresh-out-of-high-school employee, asked as she walked into the kitchen, followed closely by Micah, another of their employees. "Dude, isn't that the chick you're always scoping?"

Strutting into the room with his usual swagger, the African American college student nodded. "Ohh-hhh, wee! Hell, yeah. That chick comes in all the time to get her coffee. She's hot." He grinned as he walked over to the computer to clock in. "She look hot in a bathing suit, Libs? Great set of—"

"Can you please watch where you step?" Libby erupted as Micah accidentally kicked one of the pieces of the machine. "If you guys would actually do your goddamn jobs and clean this stuff properly, I wouldn't have to come in early and fix it!"

The silence in the room was nearly deafening after Libby's outburst. Feeling like an absolute asshole, Libby pushed to her feet and stepped over the mess she'd created, past the shocked-looking trio.

"I need to grab a part," she muttered, leaving the kitchen and hurrying to the door that led down to the manager's office, the very door she'd taken Grace through the night before.

Blowing out a breath, she trotted down the stairs and pushed open the door to the office. It was nothing special, containing just a long desk with a computer, a floor-mounted safe, and open shelves of supplies such as receipt tape, tools, and the like. Since she had the skills to fix many of the things that went bump in the night, she'd also started making sure she had basic supplies that she may need to fix any of the machines or furniture.

Now, standing in the center of the office, she looked around, hands on hips as she tried to remember what she had gone in there for. Shame filled her and her head fell when she heard footsteps coming down the stairs. Not surprisingly, Wyatt appeared in the office doorway. She glanced over at the silent woman whom she respected greatly. Wyatt and Faith had taken Libby under their wing, not only as business owners and her bosses, but also as friends and mentors.

Wyatt entered the office and closed the door behind her with a soft click of the latch. She walked over to the desk and sat down in one of the two desk chairs, her hand automatically going to the little belly she was getting, an unconscious action that always made Libby smile.

"Y'all wanna talk about it?"

Libby wasn't even sure where to begin as she wasn't entirely sure what was wrong. She was just... bothered. She was trapped, cornered, and felt the need to lash out. "Why did you think I'd like a book about lesbians?" she blurted, no clue those words were going to come out of her mouth until they were floating in midair between her and Wyatt, hanging like a floating white elephant in the parlor.

Wyatt, seemingly unfazed by the verbal outburst, crossed one leg elegantly over the other before responding. "The book isn't about lesbians, darlin'."

Anger bubbling out of irritation, Libby began to pace, a hand coming up and running through her hair. She knew the move made it stand up in strange ways, and that only added to her anger. "I had this dream this morning," she began, again surprising herself by her own words. "I've never had a dream like that and it left me feeling..." She was afraid of the words that popped up in her mind to say, so she left the sentence hanging.

"I thought you'd like that book 'cause it's about finding yourself and startin' over, Liberty," Wyatt said softly. "Vicky, the woman who's all but married to Faith's daddy, has it listed as one of her most favorite books. There's a little somethin' in there for everyone." Wyatt pushed to her feet and walked over to Libby. She gave her a loving smile. "I'm thinkin' maybe you need ta do a little thinkin' on why the lesbians got you so upset." She leaned over and left a motherly kiss on the side of Libby's head, then quietly left the office.

Left alone, Libby took the seat Wyatt had just vacated. She wanted to cry, and the truth was she had no idea why. Elbows resting on her thighs, she buried her face in her hands for a moment before blowing out a loud breath and deciding to try to get on with her day. She had a machine that needed to be cleaned and put back together, and some employees to apologize to.

"No, nothing, yet," Libby said into the phone as she stared up at the double skylights. She continued to watch. "Nope."

She heard *Damn it* on the other end of the line, then quiet before she saw her father pass by one of the skylights before he disappeared. Knowing he was heading back down, Libby took a moment to look around. The studio was essentially finished, just a few little tweaks like the skylights to get done.

Hands shoved into her pockets, she strolled through the space, which was parsed out into three rooms as ordered by Grace: bathroom, darkroom, and the larger room, where she currently stood, that could be set up for photoshoots or displays or whatever her little heart desired. Obviously, none of Grace's belongings had been moved in yet, though they'd installed the equipment, tubs, and shelving she'd ordered, giving them a detailed outline where everything needed to go.

All in all, it was a pretty cool space. Libby wondered what it would look like once it was all finished and Grace had it the way she wanted it. She hadn't been inside a photographer's studio since she was about thirteen and her parents went to the mall in Denver to get a family portrait done. It certainly wasn't as nice as this one.

"Okay," Steven said, rushing inside and over to

the metal box mounted to the wall just inside the door. He pulled out a small handful of loose keys, trying to insert one into the box. "Ah hell, here, Lib," he said, holding it out to her. "Keep this for me, would ya? It's to the front door," he said, nodding to the door in question. "I'll get it from you later when I gather all the keys for the reveal."

Libby took it, noting it was a typical-looking house key made of brass. She flipped it over and over in her fingers before tucking it into her pocket. She watched as her father found the right key to the control box and pulled open the door.

Libby wandered away as he tinkered, muttering what she fondly called "Smurf curses." They were when he was annoyed and muttering but not angry enough for the four-letter big boys. She walked back over to the skylights and, again, looked up. She'd been quite proud of herself for finding a really cool set that could be electronically manipulated into opening and closing. There was also a feature that blacked them out completely to make the entire building pitch-black, along with the new windows that had the same capability.

"Okay, think I got it," her father said, hurrying out the door again. She pulled out her phone from where she'd stowed it when he'd come back inside. As she waited for him to climb the ladder back onto the roof, she remembered the text she'd received earlier that day. She glanced at it as she waited:

Colby: Hey Libs. How about some shopping tomorrow? I need to get a gift for mom's bday. Want to go? U can help me pick something out.

She let out an irritated breath as she glanced up again, waiting for directions from her father. She needed to do something about Colby—she knew that. Though she wasn't meaning to, she was leading him on. She'd heard from far too many people that he saw them together, a burgeoning couple. Not so much, in her mind. She had no real reason why she was being a chicken and not just telling him flat out. She'd never had a problem with that before.

Her father calling her phone gave her reprieve for a moment as together they worked to get the skylights to work properly. Finally, the Smurf curses ended, and the two stepped out of the building and into the cool evening. October was coming, and rains had been prevalent, as they always were in the fall before the snows came.

"You comin' over for dinner Sunday night, kid?" Steven asked, opening one side of the toolbox custom made for the bed of his F250 as he stowed some of his tools away.

"Not sure," Libby said, leaning against the side of the truck, toe of her shoe kicking at the ground. "I'm not sure if I'll have to close for Micah or not."

Steven nodded before he gave her a side-glance. "You okay?"

She met his gaze and nodded, even as she tucked in her bottom lip. She looked out over Grace's house. The detective wasn't there, likely at work, She hadn't seen her in almost two weeks. Yes, she'd been working a lot of hours retraining everyone on cleaning, but she was also busy with the work happening at the diner. She'd done a lot of it herself. Putting in seventy-hour weeks was a wonderful way to keep herself not only busy, but out of pocket for just about anyone who may wish to see her or talk to her. Like Colby. Like Grace. She was such a coward.

As though God or whoever was pulling the puppet strings were punishing her for just that, she heard the crunch of gravel underneath tires as a car slowly pulled into the driveway. It was Grace in her personal vehicle. She felt her stomach begin to flip-flop in all sorts of unladylike ways. She felt downright nauseous.

"Hey, guys," Grace said, climbing out of her car dressed in a women's pantsuit. Libby thought she looked stunning.

"All dressed up, huh?" she asked. Her voice sounded weak, and she knew it.

Grace smiled. "Yeah. Had to do the detective thing today. Damn people just can't stay out of trouble."

Libby met her gaze, the two holding for a moment before she finally looked away. The intensity of those eyes was just too much for her in that moment. She cleared her throat before finding the courage to look up again. She was pleased with herself when she managed to keep the image of Grace in her bathing suit out of her mind. "I hope it went well."

Grace nodded. "It did, thanks for asking."

Libby replied with a nod of her own. She hated how uncomfortable it clearly was between them. She knew a lot of it was from her own standoffish behavior, but the truth was, she didn't know what to do. She was confused and had absolutely no understanding of the person she'd been over the past couple weeks. Ever since that damn dream. Oh, who was she kidding? Ever since she'd seen Grace in that damn bathing suit.

Chapter Fourteen

Owls. Owls as far as the eye could see: owl clocks, owl salt and pepper shakers, owl figurines, owls on pillows, owls on a comforter set. It was a downright owl-palooza. Libby picked up a collector's plate with a little family of owls painted on it.

"What exactly does she like, Colby?" she asked, setting the plate carefully back on the little wooden display, which was also for sale. When she heard nothing forthcoming, she glanced over at him. He had picked up a little pewter...something. She assumed it was an owl, but to her—and clearly to Colby, judging by his expression—it looked more like a blob of metal. "Colby?"

"Huh?" He met her gaze. "What?"

"What does your mom like? Like, is she into baby owls, family of owls," she asked, indicating the plate. "Stuffed animal owls, *real* owls?" She shrugged. "What?"

With a heavy sigh, he shrugged, putting the pewter item down. He looked around the little boutique. "I don't know. I'm not even sure she will like the owl stuff, to be honest."

Libby took one breath, she took three, then four. Not wanting to lose her cool, she managed to keep her tone even. "Then why are we in here?"

Looking defeated, he shrugged again. "Thought maybe something in here might catch my eye."

Libby was truly getting irritated. She looked down at her phone to see the time. "Look, we've been at this for two hours already." She glanced up at him. "Beginning to doubt your mom even *has* a birthday at this point."

Colby looked at her, a wounded expression on his face. "Jeez, Libby. I thought you'd enjoy spending some time with me."

"I have to be to work in just over two hours, and I still have to drive back to Wynter," she explained, not doing a stellar job of keeping her growing irritation out of her voice.

"I told you I'd drive you back," he argued. "There was no reason for you to take a separate car."

She'd taken her own car to make it clear she was not under his control nor in a relationship with him. She sighed internally. Fine, it was time. "Look, why don't we grab some lunch and come up with a game plan for your mom's birthday, okay?"

He nodded, dutifully following her out of the shop and out to the sidewalk on the 16th Street Mall, an outdoor shopping promenade spread out over several blocks in downtown Denver.

They settled on a burger joint and got seated and their drink order taken. Libby looked across the table at her companion who was all but hiding behind his menu. She knew he was mad, or perhaps disappointed was a better descriptor for his energy. She felt bad, as she was responsible for this. She should have been honest with him before now, as she'd known full well he was interested from the beginning. Perhaps, she thought, she'd waited to make sure he wasn't actually an option. Over the past weeks, she'd come to the conclusion that he decidedly was not. She wasn't entirely sure why but knew in her gut that Colby was not on the path of her future, except perhaps as a friend.

"So, what exactly is your mom into?" she began, deciding not to jump into the "It's-not-you-it's-me" speech right out of the gate.

Colby tossed his menu to the edge of the table atop Libby's. "She likes to eat," he said.

Libby nodded, remembering his mother's struggle with weight issues went way back. She'd been on every diet known to man and had finally resorted to surgery their junior year of high school. Her battle was the main reason she pushed him so hard in sports. He'd shared with her that his mother had always told him she never wanted him to struggle as she had.

That in mind, she said, "How about you get her some yoga classes? Or, I know they're starting up a weekly program for the elderly at the hot springs for water aerobics."

He nodded as he tapped his fingertips against the table, seeming to be considering what she said. "Not a bad idea. Not sure if she could get down those stairs, though. Have you ever been down those?"

Suddenly, a flash of Grace in her bathing suit, particularly the magnetism of her breasts, swept before Libby's mind's eye. She looked down at the table where her hands played with her napkin-rolled silverware. "Yeah," she murmured. "I have."

"So, then you know what a challenge that would be." He smirked.

Their drinks arrived and their lunch orders were taken before Libby spoke again. "Why don't you make a really nice dinner for her? Maybe see if you and your dad can work on that together or something."

Colby's face screwed up in an expression of non-interest. "I can't cook to save my life. Can you cook?" he asked, face brightening. "You know, maybe you can join us. I'd like for them to meet you."

"I've met your parents before, Colby," she said. "And, this isn't about me. It's about your mom and—"

"Yeah, but…" He shrugged and grinned a grin most women would likely consider adorable in that moment. Libby, however, just wanted to slap it off his face. "Last time they met you it was as my classmate, or the chick who made their coffee."

Libby cleared her throat and sat up a little straighter in her seat. "Colby, yes, you and I were classmates, and yes, I've made your dad coffee before. Only person I've ever met who likes an Americano with a shot of peppermint syrup in it." She looked him in the eye, making sure he was paying attention. "But we can never be more than that. More than friends."

He stared at her for a long moment, as though her words needed that time to fully penetrate. Finally, he said, "But, you kissed me."

She nodded. "I did return your kiss, yes. And, other than hurting you or upsetting you, I don't regret that I did. I've been trying to figure out what I want for my life right now, Colby, and after everything since I've been back home, I just really don't want to be in a relationship. I honestly just want to be alone and focus on getting the diner back up and running, and growing Faith and Wyatt's businesses for them." She met his hurt gaze with a pleading one. "I need to focus on me."

Colby sat back in his seat, his jaw tightening, muscle bulging before relaxing. He nodded as his arms crossed over his chest. "I see."

"And, no, this has nothing to do with anyone else. This is about me, Colby. It's about me figuring out what's next for me. What my next phase in life is. So, I don't want you making assumptions or getting angry at anyone. If you want to be mad, be mad at me."

Colby cleared his throat and brought a hand up to rub the back of his neck. Without a word, he shoved his chair back and pushed to his feet, grabbed his phone from where it sat on the table, and left the restaurant.

Libby sat there, blowing out a heavy breath, filled both with relief and guilt. She should have said something so much earlier.

"Okay, who had the buffalo burger?" their server asked, walking up to the table, all smiles, their lunch dishes held in both hands.

Libby glanced at the food, then gave him an apologetic smile. "Can I please get those to go, and the check?"

※※※※

Libby stopped at a gas station and bought one of those quickie Styrofoam containers that she filled with a bag of ice and the two packaged dinners. She wasn't entirely sure what to do with Colby's once she got back to town. Take it to him? Just put it in her own fridge for dinner tomorrow?

Driving along the long, lonely stretch of highway that led back home, she tapped her fingers on the steering wheel to the almost native-like beat of the Within Temptation song "Firelight." She thought about her discussion with Colby, and though she felt bad that he'd gotten upset enough to leave her there, she was relieved that it was over. And relieved she'd had the foresight to drive her own car.

She considered her time spent with him, thinking back even to the early days. Had there ever really been a chance for him? For her? She didn't want to be so quick or jaded to say no, but she just couldn't see it, yet another disappointment in an attempt to find love. She'd had so many. Hell, she felt she'd never even been kissed properly. Her girlfriends always talked about how great sex was or how much they enjoyed the bodies of their boyfriends or, for the few that were married, husbands.

Libby was as human as anyone. She could enjoy beauty in all its forms, like a beautifully sculpted body of a man, say, a gymnast. Truly Michelangelo's *David* come to life. She could also admire and enjoy a woman's lines, her décolletage, the delicate beauty that spoke to a woman's femininity. There had always been something about the grace of a woman's neck, the softness of her skin, the fullness of her lips.

Yet again, Grace's breasts cupped in the red material of her bathing suit top came back to haunt Libby's mind. Frustrated, she tried to push it away. The image went away, but it was replaced by her eyes, their color unusual, their intensity paralyzing.

Eyebrows furrowed, she blew out an aggravated breath. Running her hand through her hair, Libby reached out and turned up the music, attempting to lose herself in it. It was then that she noticed the skies above. She was getting closer to Wynter, and the clouds were gathering. Storms were definitely on their way.

By time she reached her house, the rain had

begun to spit, but nothing too terrible. Weather reports gave it a forty percent chance of rain, so she felt things would be fine. She quickly stowed the two food containers then changed for work and headed out, going in early so she could get out early. It was actually her day off, but she'd decided to go in and do the scheduling and inventory for all three businesses so she could focus on other things during her actual shifts.

The office in the Wynter Splash, the building next door to Bessie's that housed the public entrance to the hot springs as well as showers and locker rooms for those who were going to soak and swim, was much more conducive for Libby to do her work. The hot springs were currently closed so she didn't have to worry about the noise or constant interruptions from her employees with questions or issues. She was in no mood for issues.

A few hours later, the music on her phone turned on, she was finishing up the third schedule, the one for Pop's. It was due to reopen in two weeks, so she made out the schedule for that first week, which no doubt would be insanely busy. She was so glad she'd been able to talk Wyatt and Faith into setting up a computer network so she could log in to all three businesses from any of their locations. It certainly made her job much easier.

She was inputting a couple of notes for her servers on reopening night when she yelled out in surprise, a massive boom rocking the town. "What the hell was that?" she muttered, pushing her rolling desk chair back and getting to her feet.

Walking over to the window, she looked out into the night. As she watched, the darkness was split in two by a dazzling bolt of lightning.

"Wow," she whispered as another clap cracked and the sky opened as rain began to pour down, pounding aggressively against the window.

She hurried back to the computer, saved her changes, and backed out of the system and logged out of the computer. The last thing she needed was for the building to get hit by lightning and the computer to get fried.

As she was gathering her belongings, her phone rang. Glancing at it, she saw it was her father.

"Hey, Dad...I'm at the hot springs right now, why?" She turned off lights as she went, trotting down the stairs past the women's locker room. "Okay, yeah, I can stop by there on my way home. You have the lockbox on the door with the key?" she asked. "Okay. Text me the address and the code for that lockbox and yeah, I'll absolutely check the windows." She started as the entire building was rocked by more thunder as she reached the front door. "Damn," she murmured. "Do you want me to check that house on Mango, too?" She listened to him as he gave instructions before she pulled open the front door and hurried out, crouching her body as close to the building as she could as it was pelted with cold rain.

Hair and clothing plastered to her body, she finally got the door locked and ran to her car, throwing herself inside. She closed and locked the door, watching as the storm raged outside her windshield.

She watched, leaning forward to look up into the sky, which was alive with Zeus's power and fury. "Okay, Dad. Yeah, no worries. Just text me that stuff and I'll get on it. In my car, now...Yeah, you be careful, too. Love you, bye."

She sat behind the wheel as the car was rocked by the storm, waiting for his incoming text. They were going to split up the project check, something she'd done with him even before she was old enough to legally drive. When storms hit, which happened often in the mountains, he'd toss her the keys to the minivan and send her out to check on half the properties he was working on while he went to check the others.

As soon as the text came in, she turned her car on and headed the way of the first address. The house was one of the tiny shacks the miners lived in during the heyday of the town. Faith's father had bought them and had been renovating them one by one to use as rentals for Wynter's whitewater rafting, fishing, and hot springs industry. It had done wonders for local tourism.

Libby pulled up to the one in question. She reached around to the pocket attached to the back of the seat and tugged out the rain slicker she kept there. Feeling like Paddington Bear as she climbed out of her car, she hurried through the punishing storm, trying to hold the yellow hood in place until she reached the door. She punched in the code—her mother's birthdate—and yanked down the lockbox to reveal a house key.

It took several attempts to get the key into the door, as the lightning wasn't cooperating and flashing when she needed it to, and she wasn't about to bring her phone out for light. Finally, she got it and the lock disengaged.

The house was small, not much more than a main room with space for bedroom furniture and kitchenette, which had been installed the previous weekend. A small, three-piece bathroom was the only other space, two separate rooms all told.

She tried one of the light switches, but nothing happened. Pulling out her phone, she activated the flashlight function. She went around to every newly installed window, making sure there was no leaking as the storm pounded down on the small building.

Shining the flashlight beam into every nook and cranny and running her fingers along windowsills, she was satisfied that everything was tight and dry. Time to move on to the next property in the text.

She was pleased by the windows and the seals at each address, nothing getting wet or leaking. The lightning and thunder were beginning to slow down, the brunt of the storm moving away. The rain was still coming down pretty good, though no longer in dangerous torrents like it had been. Even still, she was very careful as she drove along the streets, headed back home. Puddles were deep, and if a driver wasn't paying attention, they'd find their car ass end up out of a ditch full of water.

As she slowly made her way down along a deeply rutted dirt road, she splashed through the mud as slowly as she could so as not to lose control of her car. Her phone rang. Not feeling safe enough to answer while driving, she stopped right where she was, as hers was the only vehicle on the road anyway.

"Hey, Dad. Yeah, everything looks great. I think there will be some roof damage on the house on Mango, because a tree branch was knocked down and took some shingles with it. Other than that..." She listened as he asked her a question. Eyebrows falling, she turned to look at the center console and opened it. "Shit, I hope so. Hang on, let me look."

She turned on her overhead dome light and

searched, finding an empty mint container, which she tossed in her in-car trash bag—no clue why it was in the console empty. She shoved aside random things, such as a small hand sanitizer bottle, some loose change, a tire pressure gauge…

"Aha," she crowed in triumph, the brass key in her hand. "Yep, I still have it," she said into the phone. "Okay, yeah, I'll head over there…Yup, okay, yeah. I'll text you and let you know I got home okay. Rain's slowing down here, now…Okay, bye."

Ending the call, Libby set her phone on the console and stared at the key that she held, the brass glinting off the light above. She looked up in the general direction of her destination and let out a resigned breath.

Chapter Fifteen

Somewhere in the back of her mind, Grace could hear the rumbles of thunder building outside. She kept her focus where it most needed to be, however. The young woman sitting before her on the couch was still crying. Grace noticed a box of facial tissue lying on its side on the floor, next to all the other things that had been on the coffee table that now lay in pieces.

Grace reached down and gently tugged a tissue free before handing it to the woman. "Mrs. Hammond, are you sure you don't want me to call medical?" she asked softly, squatting in front of the woman again. "Get you checked out?"

The woman accepted the tissue with whispered gratitude before gingerly dabbing at her eye and wiping her nose. "A few days, it'll be gone," she said bitterly, indicating her deeply bruised eye.

Clearly someone who was familiar with the healing process. Grace felt her heart ache. She kept her expression sympathetic yet tried to remain professional. "As you know, your husband was taken to the Wynter Police Department to sleep it off for the night," she explained, then jumped, startled by the crack of thunder that split the night. Hand on heart, she looked from the living room window to the woman who also looked rattled. "Oh my," she said with a small, nervous laugh. "Guess the Gods are talking tonight, huh?" She smiled, then grew serious once more. "So, what I need to know is, do you want to press charges?"

The woman let out a heavy sigh as she hugged herself. She glanced over at the broken table before looking down at her lap, knees pressed together as she seemed to be trying to make herself as physically small as possible.

"I don't know," she finally said.

Grace had seen this situation so many times in her career. It was more than obvious that the violence was not new to this couple or this household. Anita Hammond was a beaten down woman, not just physically, but her very spirit. She wasn't sure what she wanted to do because Leonard Hammond wasn't there to tell her what to do, what to think, or how to respond. Now, for Anita, decision-making was a terrifying prospect, as the consequences could be deadly no matter what she chose.

"Listen," Grace said softly, dropping her professional veneer. She stood and removed the small, thin wallet she used for work—just thick enough to keep a few credit cards, her ID, and a few folded bills—from her back pocket and retrieved a business card. Printed on it was a name and phone number: *Ally D'Giovanni—advocate*.

"This lady is a good friend of mine out of Pueblo." Grace handed the card to Anita. "She came from a life of abuse and trauma and managed to not only get her life back," she explained, lowering herself back to squatting in front of the battered woman, purposefully lowering herself below Anita to take a nonthreatening position. "She married a detective in Pueblo named Nia. The two of them have begun what's basically an Underground Railroad to help women like you get to safety and get help." She smiled encouragingly. "Okay?"

The woman looked down at the card before meeting Grace's gaze with tortured eyes. "What about my boys?" she whispered as though they may be overheard by someone.

"Your boys are part of you, Anita," Grace responded gently. "Where you go, they go. You call Ally anytime, day or night, and she'll know exactly what to do."

Anita Hammond nodded. "Okay. Thank you, Officer."

Grace smiled as she pushed to her feet. "Let us know what you decide to do, okay?"

※ ※ ※ ※

By time Grace was back in her squad car, the rain was coming down in torrents. The only good thing about a night like this was that with such bad weather, things were pretty much quiet, unless a natural disaster came out of the storm. Her plan was to head to a parking lot to catch up on paperwork and ride out the storm.

She made her way back up the dark road that connected the small trailer park where the Hammond situation happened to the outskirts of town. She tried to keep focus on the raging storm around her and the muddy roads she traversed, her tires threatening to slip out from underneath her. Most times after a call was complete, she'd have one hand on the wheel and the other on her mounted computer to see what the next call was. Tonight, however, both hands were planted so firmly on the wheel her knuckles were white.

The night sky lit up as lightning zigzagged across the sky, Grace yelping when the loudest crash she'd ever heard rent the air. Another blinding flash was followed by a waterfall of sparks that fell down around the squad car as Grace slammed on the brakes, the black-and-white sloshing through the mud for a moment before it came to a stop just off the side of the road. It was then that a massive crash sounded behind the car.

Heart palpitating, Grace gripped the steering wheel, trying to get herself grounded and her heart rate under control. She radioed in that she was stopping to deal with a large branch that seemed to be blocking the road due to a lightning strike on the tree, and would let Dispatch know if she needed assistance.

Unbuckling her seat belt, she climbed out of the car and, with a grimace, stepped out into the thick mud and rocks that had become the road as the rain continued to come down. Standing next to the car, Grace reached down to pull her Mag light from her utility belt and switched the powerful flashlight on, the beam revealing that, yep, indeed a massive branch had fallen from the sky, completely blocking the road.

"Shit," she muttered, eyeing the situation to see if she could handle it on her own. She thought she probably could, at least to clear the road enough for workers to come and fully clear it in the morning.

She opened the trunk of the car and unzipped her personal bag to fish out leather work gloves she kept for situations just like this. Wiggling them on, she put her still-lit flashlight back into its holster on her utility belt, offering at least some semblance of light, and made her way to the branch. With a little help from her flashlight, a little help from another bolt of lightning farther away, and a lot of touchy-feely, Grace found a place to grab that was sturdy enough to move the branch but small enough for her to get a good grip.

With a mighty grunt, Grace dug her heels into the mud and used the strength in her thighs to move the heavy branch. She was getting some good movement with it, taking steps backward as she used every bit of muscle she had. Her teeth gritted and eyes squeezed closed, she growled like a wild animal as she tugged.

Everything was going smoothly until it wasn't, and inertia worked against her. She let out a part yell, a part *shit!* as she landed flat on her back in a mattress of mud, her body slowly sinking in. She lay there, stunned for a moment, until she couldn't breathe as the rain poured down on her, filling her mouth.

Turning her head, she spit it out and peeled herself out of her insta-mud bath. She managed to get to her feet, slipping two more times and once doing a face-plant, before she finally made it to her feet. Covered in mud, wet and more determined than ever, Grace put even more effort and vigor in moving the tree branch. She yelled into the storm as she pulled the branch the rest of the way off the road.

"Ha!" she howled in triumph.

She could feel her feet squishing in her boots and cringed. She radioed to her partner that she was headed home for a quick shower and change of clothes then would be back out on the street.

She dreaded the cleaning her car would need on her day off, but for now she had no choice but to climb in and head home, which wasn't far. She wiped her hands on the thighs of her uniform pants, trying to at least clean them off enough to be able to turn the steering wheel.

Finally, she reached her street. Everything was quiet and dark, except for the occasional lightning. The storm seemed to have gotten the majority of its fury out, now mostly rumbles of disquiet with rain that wasn't exactly puddle-stomping pleasant but certainly wasn't the deluge that it had been.

Grace glanced over into the trees that were her property, and her heart lurched. Through the thick foliage she saw a quick glimpse of a flashlight beam shining across the side of her studio.

"Damn it," she murmured.

She reached down and switched on the flashers atop her car, letting out a single, *WHOOP!* of the siren before pulling off the side of the road. She'd go on foot to investigate. Before she got out of the car, she turned on her spotlight and aimed it in the direction of the studio, but the denseness of the trees and such didn't allow for much light penetration.

Climbing out of the car, never taking her eyes off the location, she hurried around the squad car and into the trees. As she went, she saw another glimpse of the flashlight, this time behind the small building, the beam bouncing off a nearby tree trunk.

Grace reached down to grab her Mag light and cursed when she felt nothing there. She felt all around her utility belt. Nothing. *Crap.* She'd have to return to the road with the tree branch, guessing she lost it when she took a fall.

Definitely at a disadvantage, she tried to be as stealthy as she could as she made her way through the copse of trees to the small building. She saw the beam of light snaking its way around from the side to the front, where she was ready for the person holding the light.

"Freeze! Drop the flashlight, now!"

Instantly, the flashlight fell to the ground where immediately half the beam was covered by the mud it had been dropped into. Now, they were plunged into darkness. Grace knew she had to act quickly, taking advantage of her surprise.

"Turn around, now! Hands on the building!" As her eyes began to adjust, she saw the silhouette of the person follow her instructions, arms raised and hands high above their head on the side of her studio. Taking her hand away from her holstered gun—the last thing she wanted to have to draw again—Grace placed her hands on the person's shoulders, ready to pat them down. "Do you have any weapons on you?" she asked. "Anything I need to know, tell me now," she warned, hands moving from the slender shoulders down to a small waist. A small person. A woman.

"Of course not. Grace, it's me."

Grace froze, her hands resting on the hips of the woman standing less than a foot away from her. "Liberty?"

"Yes," the smaller woman affirmed.

Grace's racing heart slowed only to pick up in a new way as their close proximity seeped into her consciousness. "What are you doing here?" she asked softly, her fingers flexing a bit on Libby's hips. Her eyes closed when she got a whiff of the younger woman's shampoo.

Libby began to turn around, and something inside Grace, almost something primitive, reacted as though the younger woman were about to bolt. Her hands shot up and grabbed Libby's wrists, holding them together above the blond head. Now, they were face-to-face, nearly breast to breast. She heard the soft gasp of surprise and could just barely make out Libby's features. Her eyes were wide as they looked at her.

"We've got to stop meeting like this at your studio," Libby said, her voice breathy.

Grace couldn't tell what she was hearing in Libby's voice, but worried it was fear. Not meaning to scare her, she loosened her grip, making it obvious Libby could slip her hands away at any time. Curiously, she didn't.

"What are you doing here?" Grace asked again.

"Dad asked me to go check some of the properties," Libby explained. "The ones that aren't finished, make sure they weren't leaking. All the new windows and everything put in recently."

Grace considered the explanation, and it made sense, for sure. "Okay," she said, making it clear she bought what she'd been told.

"So," Libby continued. "Dad wanted me to make sure your skylights weren't leaking. This was the first rain since they were installed, and we had trouble with them, so…"

Grace felt one of Libby's fingers graze her hand. Somehow—how, she'd never know—their hands ended up coming together with magnetic force, fingers entwining up against the wall of her studio.

"You could have gotten hurt," Grace murmured, her body moving in a bit. She could feel the rain coming down, dripping off her brows into her eyes, but in that moment, all she saw was Libby, all she felt was Libby, all she *knew* was Libby.

"I'm sorry," Libby whispered, the words barely audible above the rain. "Your car wasn't here, so I figured you were at work and would never know I was here."

Grace smiled. "A little thief in the night, huh?"

Libby's smile could just barely be made out in the dimness. "Something like that."

Grace's gaze became fixated on that mouth. Though she couldn't see the details at the moment, she didn't have to. She knew the lips were full, the bottom a bit more so than the top. She knew the tiny little smirk that always seemed to pull the left corner up, giving Libby a look like she knew something you didn't. It always kept Grace on her toes. She loved that about her.

An alarm beginning to scream in her head, Grace pushed away from Libby, nearly falling into the mud as she stumbled backward. "I can't do this," she muttered, hand going to her chest as her heart felt as though it were going to beat right out of her skin.

She felt disoriented, intoxicated by all that made Liberty who she was. She gasped for air, taking in cold raindrops instead. She remembered why she'd come home and turned toward the house.

"Grace!"

She didn't stop when she heard Libby yell her name, loud above the rain. Instead, she reached into her pocket for her house keys, anger beginning to build and replace the euphoria of moments before.

"I'm not just some damn kid!"

Grace stopped, able to hear the hurt and anger in Libby's voice. She stood there for a moment, not entirely sure why, her hair hanging in her face, her body cold and shivering. She turned around and saw that Libby had stepped away from the studio, now standing halfway between it and the house, fifteen feet away from her.

She could see that Libby was just as wet as she was, her T-shirt glued to her body, her hair stringy and hanging in her face. That beautiful, beautiful face. Before she could scold her feet, they were moving, and they were moving fast.

Grace brought her hands up and grabbed Libby's face. Those soft lips that she'd thought of so many times were stiff and cold at first, but it didn't take long before they responded. The kiss quickly heated, becoming desperate, sloppy, and intense. Libby's hands came up, her fingers clawing at Grace's uniform shirt, pulling her closer.

As she moved her hand from the wet and chilled flesh of Libby's face and into her hair, Grace slowed the kiss down, needing to truly taste her, to truly say with her lips and tongue what she'd never be able to say, to ask, or to give. It all had to be in that moment, that one perfect moment in time. She had to know; had to know what it was like to indulge, to understand what lay beneath the surface; had to give, something she didn't really know how to do. In that moment, with Libby leaning against her and their lips caressing and tongues exploring, she knew how.

Their little world was interrupted and intruded upon when Grace's work radio came to life as Dispatch called for her location. As if in a daze, Grace lifted her mouth from Libby's, their eyes meeting and holding for the briefest of moments before she moved away from her, reaching for her radio to respond as she turned and walked to her house.

Chapter Sixteen

In the area set aside behind the department for just such a task, Grace sprayed down the squad car she'd been driving the night before. It was filthy inside and out. She felt like she was cleaning out a car belonging to the cartoon strip character Pig Pen.

"Heard you had quite the, shall we say, *interesting* night last night."

Grace felt her heart leap and stomach roll. *Shit.* It was exactly the person she did not want to see. Releasing the handle on the spray at the end of the hose, she turned, forcing herself to meet Colby's gaze.

"Yeah?" she said noncommittally.

She noted that he was dressed in uniform and was walking over to her from the parking lot, the door on one of the squad cars behind him standing open. He walked tall, thumbs hooked in his utility belt. She felt horrible, filled with guilt. Every single thing he'd been suspicious of, worried about, and feared had been realized the night before, and she was at fault. His face was basically expressionless, his eyes hidden behind the aviator sunglasses he wore.

"Couldn't resist, could ya?" he said, head slightly cocked to the side as he studied her. He looked down as the toe of his black work boot kicked at one of the soapy tires of her black-and-white.

"How'd you find out?" she asked quietly, her heart racing and rolling stomach turning into high tide.

He smirked and glanced at her, muscled arms crossed over his chest. "The whole department knows, Montez."

"Nice goin', Sarg."

Really wanting to throw up, Grace looked over toward the building to see another of their beat cops heading their way. He was a twenty-year veteran, chubby guy with a constant smile. He held something in his hand, and that something began to make her feel a mixture of confusion and hope.

"Left this behind in your big adventure," he said, tossing what he held.

Grace followed it with her eyes, which was a good thing. It looked to be heavy, and if she missed it, either she or the car could end up with a nasty dent. She looked down as the Mag light landed in her hands. It was still covered in dried mud.

"Did you really have to make the rest of us look like assholes?" he asked, walking over to her and Colby, nudging Colby playfully with an elbow.

"I could have moved that," Colby muttered, looking away as though he'd lost interest in the conversation.

"Yeah," the older officer said. "Well, I'm man enough to say I woulda walked away with a hernia. Nice job, Montez." He clapped her on the shoulder, which was covered in the department-issued navy blue fitted T-shirt with the department logo on it. His hand moved down from her shoulder, which he squeezed experimentally before it slid down her arm, again squeezing. "Okay, yeah," he said, hand falling away. "I give." He met her gaze. "Semper Fi, right?"

She shook her head. "Army Strong."

"No kidding?" the officer said, surprise in his voice. "I always took you for a Marine."

She chuckled. "These days I'm having a hard enough time just being a Grace."

He leaned in a bit. "Yeah, well, try being a Doug," he said, indicating himself.

She burst into laughter. "Get the hell out," she said, playfully shoving him away. "Go stop some bad guys, you two." The relief washed through her as if she'd just stuck the mouth of that hose down her throat.

Turning back to her task, she felt goose bumps erupt all over her skin, her physical reaction to the relief that Colby didn't seem to know. Also, she admitted, it was her own guilt. What the hell had she been thinking? That was the question that had gone through her mind all evening, all night while she tossed and turned, and all morning. Now, heading into early afternoon, she was still pondering.

She could no longer deny it to herself; she was attracted to Liberty Faulkner. That was a fact. What wasn't attractive? Beautiful. Intelligent. Feisty and funny. Fun. Responsible and reliable. So, what was the problem?

"She's straight for one," she muttered in response to her own thoughts. She shook her head. "But she sure as hell didn't kiss like any straight girl."

No, Libby was an incredible kisser. That had been such an unexpected, harried situation. She couldn't help but speculate how Libby would be in a more relaxed—and dry—situation. She smiled at that thought, considering that, regardless of the outside climate, there hadn't been a single thing dry about her panties after that kiss.

She felt like a high school girl with a crush, something she hadn't felt in a very long time. Too long, she thought as she began to spray her car again. Her first relationship of any real consequence had been in the army. They'd been more like friends than lovers, and it had ultimately ended for simple mutual lack of interest from busy careers that took them in different directions. That breakup had happened over beers and a shared bowl of peanuts at the E-club on base. She still had Maryann's number in her phone as the two had maintained a friendship, where it always should have remained.

Then there was Alaina. Grace had been on the force in Rio Rancho for a couple years when they met. Alaina was a teacher at a local middle school and Grace worked a couple days a week as the School Resource Officer on school grounds. Pretty much from day one, theirs had been a deeply passionate relationship, something Grace had never had before.

On any day off, they would fight and argue all day, then fuck like crazy all night in makeup sex. What had at first been exciting and exhilarating soon grew exhausting and, at times, deeply unsettling. After a while, Grace began to do some research and ask questions of some peers in the social work and counseling areas. Upon her description of Alaina's wildly erratic behavior, they suspected mental illness was a factor.

Mental illness wasn't something that exactly scared Grace, as she'd dealt with it before in her family and knew it was something that could be handled if controlled. Alaina, however, simply proved to be out of control. What had begun with passionate fire had ended in flames of infidelity and a restraining order. The one time Grace had given her heart, her patience, and her understanding, she'd gotten severely burned.

After the breakup she was stuck in a nowhere job and strongly felt that physical distance from Alaina and her new girlfriend—the final one she cheated on Grace with—was needed. Deciding there was nothing worth staying for in New Mexico, she'd scoured the internet looking for new opportunities in law enforcement. Finding the re-establishment of the Wynter Police Department, Grace felt she could be of service not only to the people of the town, but to help rebuild the defunct department.

Now, in an incredibly fulfilling job, a homeowner for the first time, and with a trusted and loved circle of friends, Grace was satisfied. Right?

※※※※

A week later found Grace in the woods, camera around her neck, backpack firmly attached to her back with more equipment like lenses, extra film, and myriad other toys. One of the things she loved most about living in Wynter was the fact that the mountains were virtually her backyard.

They were pushing a good distance into September, and the aspens were already turning gold. It would be a bit still before the other trees began to follow. The nights were becoming downright cold, and the days of shorts were coming to an end. At the moment she was dressed in a pair of comfortable track pants and fitted T-shirt, her daywear when not at work. Soon enough, though, the track pants, T-shirts, and tennis shoes would be replaced by jeans, layers, and boots.

She took a deep breath, breathing in the fresh

air which filled her lungs and made her feel instantly happy. Grabbing her water bottle from where it dangled from its clip on her backpack, she brought it to her mouth and took a healthy swig, enjoying the chilled liquid as it cooled her off from the inside the entire way down into her system. Clipping it back, she continued on.

She could tell by the shadows where the sun was and just how much time she had left to get the main thing she'd come for. Hitching her backpack up a bit higher on her back, she continued on. It took about forty-five minutes to finally reach the summit.

"Wow," she whispered.

From where she stood, she had a clear view of the entire town and all the surrounding areas. She could just barely make out the steeple of the Episcopalian church, one of the tallest structures in the entire town. She smiled as she could see the golden arches of McDonald's. In such a historic town, with most businesses housed in historic and original buildings, the fast food joint stood out like a sore thumb. Even so, it had been a hit with the younger folks, and certainly good for jobs.

She turned to look in the direction of her house, completely unable to see it due to the tree coverage. Instantly, she found herself looking farther to the west, the quiet area where Libby's small but adorable house was. She wondered if she was there this evening. Grace hadn't spoken to nor seen the younger woman since that night in the rain more than a week ago. She'd avoided any of Wyatt and Faith's businesses, but in a town so small it was impossible not to pass them. She hadn't seen Libby's car there, but that didn't mean it couldn't have been parked around back or she'd simply driven by at the wrong time of day.

Where was she in that moment? What was she thinking? Was she angry at Grace? Disgusted with her? Perhaps she'd be going in to talk to the detective's supervisor. After all, Grace thought, she'd taken that night, she'd taken from Liberty, and she had no idea how it had been perceived, digested, or absorbed.

She let out a heavy sigh as she turned back to the reason she'd come, watching as the sun began to fall, sending out its fingers of colors across the sky. She felt her energy calm and a peace wash over her as the pinks, oranges, and golds spread like molasses, painting the undersides of the clouds as they went. The contrast with the beautiful little mountain town was stunning.

Reaching down, Grace grabbed her camera and checked the settings before raising it, the viewfinder eyepiece at her eye. She clicked away, her finger working like it was on a trigger, unloading nature's most beautiful moments onto the film cradled inside the body of the Nokia in a staccato of clicks.

"Gorgeous," she whispered, lifting her face away for a moment to get the full view before returning behind the camera.

※ ※ ※ ※

Humming to herself, Grace looked down at her phone and followed the instructions as she synced it with the sound system Steven and his crew had put in for her. Finished, Sarah Brightman's *Eden* began and Grace headed to her developing room.

Three days before, she'd come home from work to find what amounted to be a dress box—squat, though large and square—tied with a maroon satin ribbon sitting on her front porch. Inside had been all of her studio keys bundled together on a keyring, granting her access to the front door, installed cabinets, her developing room, and the like. There had been a framed copy of the blueprints for the studio, all remotes with instructions on what they controlled, and any manuals she needed.

There was a small photo album with pictures from the first to the final day, showing all the progress from an old, rundown detached garage to the state-of-the-art photography studio it had become. There was also a bound itemized report on every single dollar and dime that had been spent, where and on what, compiled by *L. Faulkner*. That had made Grace smile, as well as the detail that had gone into the report, down to, literally, the nuts and bolts of the project. To top it off had been a Welcome Home card signed by Steven, Libby, and their entire team, and a homemade loaf of banana bread baked by Libby's mother.

Grace nibbled on a slice of said bread as she went. She personally felt the woman should sell it at the diner or at Bessie's. It was amazing. Now, with her studio done, in a strange sort of way, Grace felt sad. It was hard for her to admit to herself, but when Steven or his crew was there, no matter how sick she got of the hammering or drilling or generator, it was a connection to…

She shook her head, popping the last bite of bread into her mouth. She wasn't going to let herself finish the thought. She'd gone to develop pictures, not wax philosophical on matters that had nothing to do with her.

Getting into the music that played through the

embedded speakers throughout the building, Grace enjoyed the sultry song. Sarah's voice always calmed her, no matter her mood. She was going to develop the three rolls of film she'd used on her hike to catch the sunset, as well as some others she'd taken once she knew her studio would be completed soon.

She walked over to the tall cabinet and pulled open the doors. Inside, the shelves were filled with equipment and supplies which she'd stocked the previous night. She grabbed her puffer brush, loupe, protective eyewear, focus finder, and multigrade filters. She carried it all to the table next to the anchored area where her farmhouse sink and developing trays were.

The cabinet above the sink was where she kept her chemicals. Opening one side, she reached up and took down the large bottle of developer, which of course made the image from the negative appear on paper. She grabbed the stop bath, which would bring the development process to an end, and the fixer, which would make the development permanent on the paper, thus the picture. She also collected all the containers and stirrers she'd need for the chemicals before they were poured into their respective trays.

Walking over to her light table, she flipped the toggle switch so the surface lit up. She'd use that to select from her negatives what was going to be developed. Her goal was to decorate the sadly bare walls of her house with pictures she'd taken—nature, animals, and she'd even snagged a few of friends.

Her mind went to the one she'd taken of Libby that day they'd run into each other hiking. That seemed so long ago now, she thought, especially considering their last interaction. She'd printed out a copy of that picture, toying with the idea of framing it and giving it to Libby as a gift. After all, it was of *her*. But, she wondered if that was creepy. "Hey, Liberty. Remember those pictures I took of you that you gave me no permission to take? Yeah, well here's one framed. I think it'll go great on your mantel."

She chuckled at the thought. Perhaps a better idea would be to give it to Libby's mom as a thank-you for the banana bread.

※※※※

Dressed in uniform, Grace took a quick glance around the ice cream parlor as she removed her sunglasses. Yet again, she hadn't seen Libby's little Sentra, and didn't see her on the main floor, either. Shoving her sunglasses to the top of her head, she jogged up the stairs to get coffee for the first time that week before her shift began. Admittedly, she'd missed her caramel macchiato.

Upstairs, it was fairly quiet, as she'd missed the morning rush by not having to be at work until eleven. She walked up to the counter, her smile growing. "Mayor!"

"Hello there, Detective," Faith said with a bright smile as she hurried around the bar, the two meeting in a tight hug. "Good to see you."

"I haven't seen you here in forever," Grace said, walking to her place in front of the cash register as Faith walked back behind the bar and met her there. "Yes, well I'm doing double duty. With Wyatt now in her third trimester, we want to keep her home and relaxed, and with Libby home sick, it leaves me holding the bag."

Grace's smile instantly fell away, even as she

tried to keep her voice sounding normal. "Yeah? What's going on with Libby?"

"She's sick as a dog, from what her mom said," Faith explained. "Your normal?" At Grace's nod, she tapped the buttons on the register as she continued talking. "Has the flu. She's been out for about four days now."

Grace felt a combination of concern and guilt. Had she not kept her out in the rain... "Have you spoken to her?" she asked quietly, handing Faith the money for her drink.

"No, but Wyatt did," Faith said, punching in the amount and giving Grace her change, which went promptly into the tip jar. "She's the one who talked her into staying home that first day. Since then, her mom has been calling in for her." She shook her head as the two moved down the length of the bar for Faith to make the latte. "Poor kid." She spared a glance at Grace. "You should go see her. Probably cheer her up since you guys are friends."

Grace nodded as she blew out a long, slow breath. "Yeah."

Chapter Seventeen

With the unshakable feeling that she wasn't alone, Libby finally fought through the medicine-induced haze to the surface. Her eyes opened, though not much more than a drowsy slit. She was in her bedroom, as she expected to be, and it was daytime, though it was hard to tell exactly what time. She was covered in layers of covers, as her fever had her freezing even though she sweat beneath the down-filled warmth.

A glance toward her window shot her eyes open a bit more in surprise. Grace sat in the folding camping chair with attached footrest her mother had brought in to sit with Libby over the past week. She wore loose-fitting track pants and a fitted navy blue T-shirt with the emblem of the police department on it.

A month ago, Libby's gaze wouldn't have dropped to how beautifully that shirt hugged full breasts, or strong biceps, or well-developed shoulders. Now, well...Now was not a month ago. She noted that Grace's hair was pulled back into a ponytail and tucked through the back of a simple black baseball cap with *Be Nice* scrawled across the front. She had one tennis-shoe-covered foot up on the footrest while the other was flat on the floor, *1049 Club* open and in her hands as she read quietly.

Libby hadn't seen Grace since that night in the

rain, though she'd thought about her nonstop. She'd thought about that kiss nonstop. Finally, she'd found out what it was like to be *really* kissed. It was different than anything she'd received or shared from any guy she'd kissed or been kissed by. It was light-years better: more passionate, yet gentle and deeply erotic.

She let her gaze fall to those lips, as clearly Grace wasn't aware that Libby was awake. She had to admit she was enjoying the unabashed study of the enigma that sat in her room reading Wyatt's book. She was deeply intrigued by Grace yet had no real understanding of what the nature of that intrigue was. Yes, Grace was beautiful, and she was very sexy. Libby didn't feel strange thinking that, as she'd always been one to freely admit if she saw someone—woman or man—she found attractive. Finding someone attractive didn't mean "attracted to," she reasoned.

As she studied Grace, she again felt the softness of her lips, the gentle firmness of her hands on her face holding her as the kiss began. She could easily remember how Grace's tongue felt against her own, the velvety softness of it, stroking, coaxing, not shoved down her throat like every other kiss she'd ever had. Frankly, the aggressive way she'd been kissed prior to a week ago had literally made her want to shy away from kissing altogether. It grossed her out far more than turned her on. Until a week ago.

Libby watched as Grace's eyes lifted from the page to meet her gaze. Libby smiled, feigning innocence. "I think my doctor must have given me some strong meds," she muttered. "I think I'm hallucinating."

Grace closed the book and gently tossed it to the end of the bed. "Oh?" she said, a welcoming smile on her lips. "You weren't expecting a random detective

sitting in your room reading your books?"
 Libby grinned and shook her head. "Yeah, no." She felt so weak; she hadn't eaten much in the last few days, and used what little energy she had to bring her arms up out from beneath the covers to push them down a little so she could use her legs and feet to move up a bit in the bed.
 Grace instantly was on her feet and moved over to her, helping. She plumped Libby's pillow and grabbed a second one to create a better, more comfortable place for Libby to recline against.
 "Is that okay?" Grace asked softly, her face no more than a foot from Libby's. "Comfortable?"
 Libby nodded, unable to speak as a wave of emotion and sensation washed through her, leaving her temporarily speechless. It wasn't until Grace sat back down that she felt the spell break. She blinked a few times before adjusting her position slightly and swallowing nervously. Her throat was Sahara-dry.
 She glanced over at the bedside table to see a sea of medications and the signs of illness: pills tucked into foil and plastic, bottles of syrup for this-that-and-the-other, a box with facial tissue sticking out like the white flag of surrender, as well as wadded up tissues that had been sneezed into, coughed into, and who-knew-what-else-into. What she didn't see, to her groan of unhappiness, was the bottle of water that had been there.
 She sat up, intent on heading to the kitchen to get one, but Grace stopped her with a hand to her leg atop the covers.
 "What do you need?"
 "Water," Libby said, grunting with exertion as she began to push the covers off herself.

"No, no, I can get it." Grace pushed to her feet. "Cold? Out of the tap?"

"There's bottled water in the fridge," Libby said, relieved as she fell back into the little pillow nest Grace had made for her. She was exhausted now.

"Be right back."

Left alone, Libby closed her eyes for a moment, hating herself for feeling so weak and crappy. She was tired of being tired and tired of being sick. She was grateful when Grace came back in, cold bottle in hand. She twisted off the cap before handing it to Libby, laying the white cap on the bed within easy reach.

"Anything else I can do?" Grace asked, standing next to the bed. "Food? Wyatt sent me over with homemade chicken noodle soup for you," she said with a smirk.

Libby chuckled after taking a long drink, relishing in the cool, refreshing water as it coated her throat. "Yes, Wyatt does make some amazing soup." She recapped the bottle and set it aside on the bedside table. "But, no. Not yet." She studied Grace for a moment, her eyebrows falling. "Why are you here, anyway?"

"Your mom asked me to sit with you while she went to get some groceries for you. She said the place was pretty empty," Grace explained, reclaiming her seat.

"Oh lord. She made you babysit, huh?"

Grace smiled, adjusting a bit in the seat as she got comfortable. "No, I think she just realizes how sick you are and doesn't want you left alone. She's a great lady. Chatted with her for a bit before she left."

"She's one of my best friends," Libby said. "I'm really sorry you got stuck here, Grace. Honestly, I'm okay. You can go."

Grace studied her for a moment, head slightly cocked to the side and expression guarded. "I don't see it as being stuck here," she said gently. "I came for two reasons, and if me making sure you're okay becomes a third, so be it." She smiled.

Libby returned the smile, though she knew she, too, was guarded. Grace's energy had changed, her walls up, which made her own walls creep up. "You look like a cast member of *Police Academy*," she blurted, feeling the need to bring down the energy level with a bit of levity.

Grace's eyebrows fell as she shook her head. "I don't get it."

"You never saw those cheesy eighties movies with Steve Guttenberg?" she asked. "The first one came out in like, 1984. You're older than me…"

Grace grinned. "In 1984 I wasn't even born yet."

Libby gave her a sheepish grin. "Oh. True."

"How on earth did you see that?" Grace asked, amusement in her voice.

"Mom," Libby said with a winning smile.

"Ah yes, Kevin Costner's butt. Your mom and her movies." Grace's foot slid down off the footrest as she leaned forward, her demeanor becoming very serious. She cleared her throat and looked at her hands, which were clasped between her knees before she met Libby's gaze again. "I came here to check on you, make sure you were okay when I found out you were sick. But also, I came to apologize."

Libby cleared her throat again, sitting up a bit more, bracing for whatever Grace had to say. "Okay. For what?"

"For the last time we saw each other," Grace said

softly. "If I were a man, you would have had every right to slap me or even press charges. The fact that I'm a woman doesn't change anything. I still touched you in an inappropri—"

"You kissed me, Grace," Libby interjected firmly. Her voice softening a bit, she said again, "You kissed me."

Grace met her gaze, silent for a moment as though Libby's interruption had derailed what she'd planned to say and do. Finally, she nodded. "Yes, I did. I had no right to."

"And," Libby continued as if Grace hadn't spoken. "I kissed you back. Not because I was forced to," she added, shaking her head with her words, "Not because I felt compelled to."

Grace took a deep breath, and Libby wondered if it was relief. "Why did you, then?" she asked.

"Because I wanted to," Libby said simply. What she didn't say, however, was that she'd wanted Grace to do something more that night, though she hadn't fully known what it was. She'd called her back for reasons she'd yet to fully analyze.

Grace nodded but said nothing more. A moment of uncomfortable silence passed between them, so Libby spoke.

"What do you think?" she asked, nodding toward the novel lying on the bed.

Grace followed Libby's gaze then nodded with a smile. "It's pretty good. When you're finished with it, I'll ask Wyatt if I can borrow it. I have to say, though," she added, grabbing the book and fingering the bookmark sticking out. "I figured you'd be a lot further in than seventy-two pages after having it so long."

Libby grinned a little sheepishly. "It's my third time through it."

A bark of laughter burst from Grace's lips. "Clearly you got over your issues with it."

"Maybe," Libby hedged. She eyed Grace, trying to get a feel for where she was now, her energy, her emotions. Were those walls still up? "Would you read to me?"

Grace's eyes widened. "Read to you?"

"When I was in high school," Libby began softly. "I was in an advanced placement English class my junior year. Our teacher, Mrs. Gray, was so cool. She was probably like forty-one or forty-two at that time, but she would wear broom skirts and these crazy cheesecloth blouses. Lots of bracelets and dangly earrings. She looked like a relic of the sixties. Such a cool lady. Wicked smart. Anyway," she continued. "Since we were an advanced class, it was small, so she'd sit on top of one of the empty desks up front, her feet on the seat of the attached chair, and she'd read to us."

"She'd read to you?" Grace asked, looking amused. "The smart kids, she's reading to you?"

Libby nodded. "Yup. All of us sixteen, seventeen years old, eating it up like kindergartners on story day." She chuckled at the memory of how much she'd loved it. "You see, Mrs. Gray had this amazing voice, soft, and it would absolutely put you at ease immediately. So when she read to us, it wasn't hard for her to lull us into whatever place the story was guiding us to."

Grace's head tilted slightly to the side. "That's really sweet. She sounds like a neat lady. And, after that glowing endorsement, you expect me to follow?" she asked, holding up the thick volume.

Libby grinned and nodded.

"Okay," Grace said, sounding less than confident.

She began to open the book to Libby's bookmark, but Libby stopped her. "No, start reading where you left off before I woke up," she suggested. "So you won't miss anything."

Grace nodded. "I can do that."

Libby watched as Grace searched through earlier pages, reading quietly for a second before turning a few pages ahead and repeating the process until she found what she was looking for.

"Okay, here we go." She cleared her throat, looking nervously up from the page to Libby. "Ready?" At Libby's enthusiastic nod, she began. "'Pull it out, come on!' Pam ordered with a groan, using her full body weight to try and tug the raft onto shore, flanked by Mia and Rachel."

"You're just as good as she was," Libby whispered.

Grace glanced up at her again, a quirk of a smile on her lips. "Well, I'm no English teacher, and I don't even own a broom skirt."

Libby smiled at that. Then, out of the blue, something she had to know. "Do you regret it?"

Grace met her gaze again. "What?"

"Kissing me?" She shrugged a shoulder. "I know it's a childish question, but I need to know."

Grace looked down for a long moment before clearing her throat. "I saw Colby the next morning," she began softly, sparing Libby a glance. "I felt terrible. Horribly guilty."

"You don't need to, Grace," Libby murmured. She was feeling tired again, her interaction with Grace draining what little energy she'd had when she woke up. "Ironically, earlier that day I told him there wasn't a chance for us."

Grace held her gaze for a long moment before asking, "Why not?"

"I'm not interested in Colby," Libby stated.

Grace looked down at the book in her lap. "How did he take it?"

"He was pissed. So pissed, in fact, he left me in a restaurant in Denver."

Grace's head flew up. "What? He left you stranded?"

Libby smiled, touched by the fire she saw in those green eyes. She shook her head. "No, I had my own car. But, yes, he left."

After a moment, Grace nodded, as though coming to some sort of decision or understanding in her own mind. She held up the book, a question in her raised eyebrow.

Libby noticed that Grace hadn't answered the question, but she wasn't going to push. She'd wanted the older woman to know about Colby, though she wasn't entirely sure why. Now Grace knew.

※ ※ ※ ※

Libby slowly woke, vaguely aware that it seemed her fever had finally broken. She shoved off the heavy covers atop her, desperately needing to cool down. Sitting up in bed, she found herself alone in her bedroom, her mom's chair folded and leaning against the wall. She thought about earlier in the day, as now night had fallen.

She wondered how long she'd been asleep. Grace. The last thing she remembered was Grace reading from the book, then—a dream, no doubt—a hand had brushed fever-dampened hair from her face just before soft lips touched down on her forehead.

She noticed something on her dresser next to the book. Pushing the covers the rest of the way off her legs, Libby swung them over the side of the bed and, after giving herself a moment to gather her strength, pushed to her feet and padded over to it. She smiled when she saw a new bookmark slipped between the pages, clearly where they'd left off, though at the moment Libby couldn't remember the last thing she'd heard.

Next to the book was a silver picture frame, a sticky note stuck to the glass that read: *Feel better soon.* She smiled and peeled the sticky off, carefully lying it atop the book before returning her attention back to the picture frame. The eight-by-ten photo inside was of her.

For a moment, she was confused wondering when on earth Grace would have been able to take the picture. It was of Libby in the woods, looking straight on at the camera. She looked at what she was wearing and remembered it was the day they'd run into each other while hiking. Grace had gotten her attention with the clicks of her camera shutter. Libby smiled as she realized the picture she was looking at had been one of those shots.

Her attention was grabbed by her phone ringing. She looked around the bedroom until she saw it on the bedside table. She walked over to it and answered, seeing it was her mom.

"Hey, Mom...Yeah, fever finally broke. Feeling better, considering...Yeah, I agree," she said into the phone, looking down at the framed picture in her hand. "I think it was really sweet she came, too, and no, it's fine you sent her on. I doubt sitting here watching me snore was how she intended to spend her day off."

Libby walked into the living room, looking around as she decided where to put the picture, the phone tucked next to her ear. Finally, she opted for the mantel.

"She mentioned the soup. I do have an appetite, so that's good...No, Mom. No, really. I'm okay tonight. I'm sure Dad has really missed you. I plan to take a shower to attempt to feel human again, get some soup warmed up, and maybe watch a movie or something. You stay home with him." She smiled, able to hear the love her mother still had for her father all these years and decades later. She wanted that kind of love, that kind of friendship. Everlasting. "I love you, too, Mom. Bye."

Ending the call, she set the phone aside and moved a few things around on the mantel so everything would be balanced. Stepping back, she cocked her head to the side contemplating her choice of placement. Part of her felt a bit strange having a large picture of herself displayed in her own house, but Grace had taken it. Clearly, in her framing it and doing whatever else she had to do to it, Grace saw value in it. Therefore, Libby did, too.

She picked up her phone again and got to the camera app, taking a picture of the picture on the mantel. She was amused by the situation. Finding Grace's previous text messages, she attached the picture and sent it off, no message added. Feeling good about it, she smiled and padded off to take a shower.

Chapter Eighteen

Though cooler, it was a beautiful day, and it was made even more beautiful by the fact that Libby felt the best she had in more than a week. She had lost some weight while sick from lack of appetite for a few days, but she was certain to get it back by the weekend at the rate she was going.

She wanted to get outside, so on her third full day out of bed, she was out in her front yard pulling some weeds, doing end of the summer yardwork. She was up near her porch, where she'd planted flowers when she'd moved in. She heard a child's laughter at the house to her right, where the moving truck had been parked all morning. And, like the other times, it was almost like a ghost, as she saw no child connected to the laughter.

She smiled as she turned back to her flowers. She loved the sound of children's laughter, and was so excited for Wyatt and Faith to have their baby in late December. Libby was in talks with some of the other girls at Bessie's and Pop's to throw them a shower.

Bracing on one arm, she reached her body out like a cat to grab a particularly difficult to reach weed sprouting from next to the foundation of the house. Wrapping her fingers around it, she yanked, only to come back with a handful of leaves.

"Little bastard," she muttered, noting the stalk of the week still very much intact, taunting her.

Irritated, she sat back on her haunches as she shook her hand out, leaves falling to her little pile of pulled weeds. She was about to lean back over to go into full attack mode when she felt a soft tap to her shoulder, startling her. She glanced over her shoulder and came face-to-face with the most handsome little boy she'd ever seen.

His complexion was darker, though he didn't look like he was black, so she assumed he may be biracial. His head was shaved into what amounted to a buzz cut and was dark brown. His eyes, however, were what caught her. They were a gray/blue that seemed to look directly into her soul. He looked to be about four, and he didn't look happy to see her.

Libby was immediately concerned when his little face screwed up, looking like an upset was on its way. She turned to fully face him but didn't stand, not wanting to scare him any more than he already seemed to be.

"Hey, sweetheart," she said cheerfully. "Are you lost?"

His eyes got big and tears welled up in them as a finger went to his mouth.

Not entirely sure what to do, she smiled at him. "What's your name? Where's your mommy?"

"Noah? Noah, where'd you go?"

Libby glanced up and over the little guy's head toward the disembodied woman's voice that seemed to be coming from the house next door with the moving truck. Considering the little boy turned and looked that way, too, Libby concluded he must be Noah.

"Over here," she called to the woman. "Front yard next door."

A young black woman came running out of the

garage, her eyes wild with fear. When she saw the little boy, who ran over to her, she seemed to melt into a puddle of relief. When Noah reached her, he pointed back at Libby, speaking quietly to the woman Libby presumed was his mother.

Libby stood but stayed put, not wanting to interfere with mother and son. The woman picked up the boy, her arming coming to rest underneath his bottom as his legs straddled her side. The two chatted for a moment, the woman glancing over at Libby before looking back at the boy and saying something to him before giving him a broad smile. He tucked his head on her shoulder, that finger still in his mouth.

Feeling the moment was over, Libby walked over to the two, both women standing just inside their property line. "Hey. Not sure how, but I think I startled the little guy."

The woman rubbed the little boy's back through the cartoon dog T-shirt he wore. "Sorry about that. He thought you were his aunt," the woman said with a smile. "His dad's white," the woman continued, clearly something she explained a lot by how easily it fell off her tongue. "She has hair a lot like yours, about your build, so…"

Libby grinned. "Sorry, little guy," she said to the boy, who spared her a glance from his mother's shoulder. "He's really a handsome little boy," she complimented. "I'm Liberty, by the way. Obviously, this is my house." She nodded toward her little bungalow.

"Frankie," the young mom said, extending her hand, which Libby took. "This sleepy little one is Noah." She ran her hand over his head to his back. "It's been a long day for him."

"Moving is hard enough on us, let alone them," Libby said, smiling at the clear bond between mother and child. "Well, welcome. If you need anything, feel free to pop on over. I work a lot, but if I can, glad to help."

"Thanks so much," Frankie said with a kind smile on her lovely face. "It's not easy to start over somewhere new, but I wanted to get landed before this one started school." She gave Libby a final smile before turning and heading back into her garage.

Libby watched them go then returned to her weeding.

※※※※

Hoping for a second reading session, Libby had been disappointed when all she heard from Grace since she'd shown up at her house three days before was a simple *Hope you're doing well* text. It had been sweet and thoughtful, but Libby had felt a certain coldness or detachment behind it. She wasn't sure why, but tried to keep her own emotional distance in order to not get hurt. Hurt, why? That was the problem. There was no real reason to be hurt, but she couldn't help but have a heavy heart.

Grace had really seemed to enjoy the book she was reading out loud the other day, and Libby felt guilty that she hadn't been able to take it with her or finish it. Libby had finished her latest read of it and had gotten permission from Wyatt to loan it to Grace. So, with the book sitting on her passenger seat, Libby drove through the quiet Wynter streets, headed to her house.

The strange thing was, they hadn't spent a ton of

time together, but the time they had spent had been of incredible quality, substance, and meaning. She'd not known that type of connection with anyone outside of her parents. She had friends, had certainly had boyfriends over the years, but with them she'd never felt a connection, such an easy flow as she did with Grace. It was confusing, and she had no idea what it meant, if anything. But one thing she absolutely was aware of was that she craved it. When they weren't together she felt the absence, could literally feel it when Grace wasn't with her.

It was unsettling and greatly confusing. She and Grace were friends—yes, friends with an interesting set of circumstances a week ago, but friends. She didn't feel this type of connection with her closest girlfriends or guy friends. Didn't feel this type of connection with anyone she'd ever been in a relationship with. She didn't even feel this type of connection with her parents, and she was very close to them.

What did it mean?

Libby's little Sentra pulled up in front of Grace's house, which was quiet. Grace's car wasn't there, so she assumed she was working. She felt her stomach do a little flip-flop as she climbed out of the car. Her mind went back, as it had thousands of times, to that night in the rain.

She'd changed it in her mind before. What if it had been a guy who had been that forceful and aggressive initially? Even with her against the wall, holding her there? They would have ended up with a nasty red mark across their face or a knee to the nuts. Yet with Grace, all she could do was sink into it.

She looked over at the side of the house, where she'd walk to go to the studio. No way was she going to do that. Next thing she knew, Grace would show up again, gun drawn. She smiled at the thought. Or, maybe that wouldn't be such a bad thing.

Book in hand, she walked up the path to the front door and pulled open the glass-and-metal screen door. She'd taken a sticky note from the same block she kept in her kitchen that Grace had used to leave a note on Libby's picture. She kept a pen on the counter at all times and would jot down things she found that she needed to grab at the grocery store as she saw she was out of them.

On the sticky note attached to the cover of the book was written: *I think three times is enough, so your turn with Wyatt's blessing. Enjoy.* She positioned the book so that it would sit flush between the glass door and the solid front door, allowing the glass door to close. Satisfied, she closed the door and trotted down the few stairs of the front porch. She turned to look at the house as she walked backward down the path, just observing. Blowing out a breath, she turned around and walked to her car.

Climbing behind the wheel, she got settled in and seat belt buckled. She took another moment to look at the house, a strange sadness washing over her before she started the car up and pulled away.

꽃꽃꽃꽃

Libby was excited to go inside. She'd missed her people, missed her customers, and missed her job. She'd never had missed so much work before, save the times she'd taken the week off during finals in high school and college. She still felt a little tired, but beyond that, knew she was over the crud and was ready to get back to life.

"There she is!"

Libby smiled as she found herself engulfed by hugs from the two employees who were scheduled to work the ice cream shop that morning. She returned their hugs before taking a quick glance around. She was pleased with the state of things, though she'd do a more thorough look-see later when she toured all three locations, as she did most days she worked.

After answering a few questions about her health and her week, she left the two to get back to work while she headed upstairs. She was happy to see several people sitting at the tables taking advantage of the free Wi-Fi offered to their guests. Music played softly overhead, a change she'd made when she'd taken over. She liked music in the space but didn't want it blasting so loud that it made for an unpleasant atmosphere. She was happy to leave that experience to the commercial coffee guys.

Waving and greeting a couple of their regulars, she made her way back behind the bar. She accepted hugs from her girls upstairs before heading back into the kitchen area to see how things looked. She'd gotten a few texts while sick about the fryer giving them issues. When the "adult" portion of the shop opened up in the evenings—the only place that served liquor in the entire town save for the actual liquor store—they also served a small menu of appetizers to go with the drinks.

Humming softly to herself along with the music playing, she began to take the fryer apart. She'd see if it was something as simple as grease getting somewhere it shouldn't have, or if it was a problem with the actual brain of the fryer, which would require a professional service. She hoped she could save Wyatt and Faith that money and fix it herself.

She'd been back there working for about forty-five minutes when one of her girls poked her head into the kitchen and called her name. She looked up at her from where she sat on the floor amongst a sea of parts.

"Someone needs to speak to the manager, Libby."

Libby looked around at the mess she'd made and nodded. "Okay. Give me a sec."

Left alone, she put out the bright yellow *Wet Floor* sign to garner attention to her mess so somebody wouldn't accidentally kick the parts on the floor or trip over them should they come into the kitchen.

Washing her hands, she tossed the paper towel she'd dried them on into the trash bin as she left the kitchen. To her surprise, standing off to the side at the bar was her new neighbor. Her hair was pulled into tight braids on her head and she was dressed in green scrubs. Considering she was the only person at the bar, Libby assumed that was who she'd been called to help.

"Hey, Frankie," she said in a friendly tone as she walked over to her on the business side of the bar.

Her attractive neighbor met Libby's gaze, smiling. "Well, hello there. Are you the manager here?" She turned to face her, Libby now noticing the papers she held in her hands.

"I am. How's the house? How's Noah?" Libby asked, leaning casually on her forearms on the bar top.

Instantly Frankie's smile grew brighter. "He's great. Just dropped him off at daycare so I can head on to my job at the hospital in Tunston. It's been a trip unpacking and organizing with a curious, rambunctious four-year-old." She laughed.

"Oh, no doubt." Libby grinned. "He's a doll."

"He's a handful, is what he is."

Libby pushed up to stand at her full height, cognizant that her neighbor still had a drive ahead of her. "What can I help you with? Can I get you a coffee for the road?"

Frankie glanced over at all the fixings, clearly contemplating the offer as she chewed on her bottom lip.

"It's super yummy," Libby said in a singsong voice, then grinned.

"Okay, you talked me into it." She laughed, walking over to the register where Libby met her. She ordered her drink and Libby punched the keys and waved away her credit card when Frankie offered. "Thanks," Frankie said, taking it back. "So, the reason I'm here is, I wanted to know if you minded if I hung one of these up in here?" She held up one of the pages she held, which Libby realized was a flyer. "Single mom, and though I love my job in the X-ray lab, things can get tight, so I clean houses or businesses or whatever, on the weekends when Noah will be with his dad in Tunston."

"I can imagine," Libby said, taking one of the flyers and looking at it. Immediately she thought of Wyatt and Faith. Wyatt was the ultimate housewife, as it were, but she wondered if she may want extra help once the baby came, or during the last trimester. "We have a community bulletin board right over there," she said, pointing, business cards and such already pinned on its surface. "If you let me keep a couple, I'll make sure one gets pinned up downstairs as well as at the diner when we reopen this weekend."

"Oh yeah? Great, thanks!" Frankie handed Libby a few sheets. "I really appreciate this, Liberty. I'm good at what I do, I'm fast, and I'm reasonable."

"All excellent qualities," Libby said, setting the flyers down on the bar top. She walked over to the area where drinks were made and began to fill Frankie's order. "So, where you from?" she asked conversationally. "I know you said you work in Tunston."

"Yep," Frankie acknowledged, watching Libby work. "I'm from Colorado Springs, which is where I met my ex-husband and Noah's father. We moved to Tunston, where his parents live, five years ago, when I was pregnant with Noah."

Libby nodded. "I was born here but lived in Pueblo for a couple years. I actually just came back here myself." She indicated the building they stood in. "Took over as general manager here and some other businesses in town." Libby lifted the hot cup in her hand. "Whipped cream?"

Frankie studied the cup for a moment before finally she nodded. "Yeah. Hit me."

Libby smiled and did as asked before smooshing the yummy cloud down with a plastic lid. She slid the cup into the cardboard sleeve and handed it over. "Here you go, ma'am. Enjoy."

Frankie took the cup and looked down at it. "I so look forward to this," she said, laughing. "Tasty caffeine is my friend."

Libby grinned as the woman began to turn to leave. "Have a safe drive, Frankie. See you 'round the neighborhood."

Frankie lifted her cup in salute then hurried toward the stairs and out of sight. Libby liked Frankie's energy, and she was certainly glad to have a good neighbor. The house had been empty the entire time she'd lived in her house, so she had been worried what would come in. After experiences of bad neighbors in such close quarters as an apartment building, she'd learned to be mindful.

She headed back to the kitchen and her previous task with the fryer. She had just reached her work spot of parts when she heard the little desk bell they left on the counter for when a customer needed service.

Rolling her eyes, Libby turned back around and headed out to the bar, wondering where her girl had disappeared to. Her steps slowed when she saw Colby standing at the bar, dressed in casual civilian clothes. The last time she'd seen him, he'd been storming out of a burger joint in Denver.

Libby's jaw tightened and her energy cooled as she made her way to the cash register. She met his gaze when he looked at her. "What can I get you?" she asked. *Just an average customer.*

Colby cleared his throat, a hand coming up to rub the back of his neck. At least he had the decency to look sheepish, she thought. "Um, I'd like the Mocha Smoothie, please," he said quietly.

"Size?" she asked, eyeing him. She knew full well what he'd say, but she liked seeing him uncomfortable.

"Large."

She nodded and punched his order into the register before giving him his total. She watched as he dug his wallet out of the back pocket of his pants and sorted through the various bills before selecting the appropriate one. Libby took it and was counting out his change when he grabbed the flyer that she'd left there, intending to post them at the other locations.

"I've never understood people who hire help like this," he said, waving the page to emphasize his point before setting it back down. "Just seems lazy to me."

She glared at him, hand suspended in air with his forty-four cents in change. "Not everyone is good at it, Colby," she explained, her voice hard.

He looked at her, eyebrows falling as he accepted the coins, dropping them into his pants hip pocket. "It's not that hard, Liberty," he retorted.

She said nothing, simply shook her head and moved on to the area to make his drink. She began the process, her back to him. "Not everyone is as talented as you are, Colby," she muttered, loud enough for him to hear.

"Why are you so pissy with me?" he asked at length.

Libby shook her head, bemused. "Is that a serious question?" she tossed over her shoulder with a glance. She felt like he was looking to pick an argument, and she wondered if he thought doing so would somehow justify his behavior last time they'd seen each other. She hadn't given him what he wanted before, and she sure as hell wasn't about to start.

He was silent for a moment, though she could hear him messing with something. From the sound of it, she figured he'd grabbed one of the sleeves and was tapping it on the counter. "How's Grace?" he asked, though the tone lacked any curiosity.

Libby didn't respond as she poured everything into the blender and held her hand down on the lid as she turned it on, the shrill chewing sound a nice reprieve from his voice. Finished, she removed the lid and poured the thick mixture into a clear plastic cup used for cold coffee drinks and smoothies. She put the clear plastic dome lid on with a large hole at the top, big enough for the nozzle of the whipped cream canister. Filling it, she dipped in a straw and turned to set it on the counter, sliding it his way.

"She's amazing," she said sweetly, then turned and walked away.

Chapter Nineteen

The sky was a vivid blue, like the depths of the Caribbean Sea. The air was warm, but not as warm as her hand, which rested on the side of her neck as they kissed. She could feel her back being gently pressed into the rough bark of the tree behind her as the warm body before her leaned in closer against her.

Hands buried in dark hair, she drew her in closer, desperate for her touch. Lips so soft and pliant against her own, tongue easing inside to deepen the kiss. She sighed in pleasure when one of the hands on her hips moved up and cupped one of her breasts through her shirt. She could feel her flesh respond and moaned into the kiss, encouraging more.

She wanted more...

Libby reveled in the coolness of the tile against her forehead as the tepid water beat down on her back. Her body felt like it was in a constant state of fever. After just suffering from the flu, this was not welcome. The dreams wouldn't stop. The one she'd just woken up from was pretty tame and mild compared to some of the romps her mind had conjured up in slumber.

Her body beginning to shiver, she pushed off the wall and turned more of the hot water on until the temperature was what she wanted. She was off that day, and had made plans to spend the day with her mom. She knew there was a new recipe her mom wanted to try, and had offered to pick up a few of the ingredients the older woman didn't have on her way to the house.

An hour later, Libby was showered and dressed, the few things her mother needed picked up, and was pulling into her childhood home driveway. She turned the car off and gathered the grocery bag from her front seat before climbing out of the car and heading inside.

The thing Libby loved about her parents' house was that it was always very clean, things put away in their place, yet the house didn't feel like a hospital or a showplace. She felt free to move around, use things, sit on the furniture without being yelled at. But then, she'd also been taught to clean up after herself. As much as it had sucked as a kid to have to come home from school and immediately do chores, she was grateful for the lessons of respect for her surroundings and self-pride it had taught her, lessons she'd taken into every aspect of her life.

"Mom?" she called out, setting her keys and wallet on the small table by the door, ready to grab on her way out. "Where you at?"

"In here," Lynne called out from somewhere in the house.

Libby rolled her eyes at the non-helpful hint and went searching after she left the grocery bag on the counter in the empty kitchen. She found her mother in the master bedroom making the bed. Obviously she'd just changed the sheets, the dirty ones in a pile on the floor. Libby gathered them up and carried them to the hamper.

"Thanks, sweetie," Lynne said, walking around the freshly made bed and giving her daughter a tight one-armed hug and a kiss to the cheek. "I was hoping to get this done before you got here, but not quite, Almost, though."

Libby grinned and followed her mother back to the kitchen. "So, why are you attempting this cake today?" she asked, grabbing her grocery bag as she passed it and carrying it to the kitchen table.

She removed the few things she picked up, crushing the bag and placing it in the larger bag her mother had hanging in the pantry. The bags were taken out as needed for some of her father's messier projects and were great for greasy clothing or implements. It was the compromise her parents had come to years ago: you don't get my house dirty or greasy and I don't kill you.

"Well," Lynne responded, pulling one of her many cookbooks from the shelf that held her collection. She opened it up to a marked page and placed it on the cookbook stand that Libby had made for her out of wood years ago. "Your dad wanted me to make him an eggnog cake last year, but I just ran out of time during the holidays, and he's been working so hard," she explained, sparing a glance to her daughter. "I wanted to surprise him."

Libby stared at her. "Mom, eggnog isn't even sold in the stores yet."

"Of course not," Lynne said, walking over to the fridge. She removed a glass pitcher, which she used to make Libby's Kool-Aid in when she was a kid. "I made some," she said proudly, holding up the pitcher.

"Of course you did," Libby muttered. "You and Wyatt..." She brought over the things she'd bought and set them on the counter one by one next to the cookbook stand. "Here is your rum extract, though I had no idea such a thing existed, your confectioner's sugar, and two thingies of eggs."

"Thingies?" Lynne asked, eyeing her daughter over the top of her reading glasses. "Is that the technical term?"

Libby grinned and nodded.

Lynne chuckled, turning back to her cookbook. "You are your father's daughter." Taking the reading glasses off, Lynne placed them on the counter and began to open cabinets. "Libby, go into the pantry and grab me my mixing bowls."

Nodding, Libby went off to fulfil her mother's request.

The two settled into the task of mixing things in the separate bowls, only to combine them in stages. Lynne chattered on and on like a monkey in a tree about this and that. Libby tried to keep up, but eventually her mind began to wander. Nothing at all against her mother; she actually enjoyed her mom's little tales about her friends and random things she and Libby's father had done.

"Honey?"

It took a moment, but finally Libby realized her mother's rambling had stopped. She looked over to see Lynne looking back at her. "Hmm?"

"Help me with this?" Lynne said softly, indicating the large mixing bowl she held and the three round baking pans they needed to fill.

"Yeah, sorry." Libby cleared her throat and took the heavy glass bowl from her mother.

Lynne eased the gooey batter with a rubber spatula as Libby gently tilted the bowl for a slow flow. "What's wrong with my girl?" Lynne asked conversationally, never looking up from her task, which could easily turn very messy if she took her eye off the ball.

Libby chewed on her bottom lip, considering her options. Should she say something? Would her mother understand? Would she be disappointed in her only child? She knew it wasn't something she could talk to her dad about, no matter how close they were. This was different.

"What if I told you I kissed...a girl," she hedged, gently pulling up on the mixing bowl to stop the flow as her mother quickly swapped the filled pan for an empty one. They began the dance anew.

"Did you like it?" Lynne asked, her gaze never leaving her task.

Libby spared a quick glance. "Huh?"

"Were you wearing cherry ChapStick?"

Annoyed, Lilly pulled the mixing bowl away and set it down hard on the table and walked away. "Forget it." She felt stupid and wished she hadn't said anything.

"Honey!" Lynne hurried after her, catching up to Libby as she gathered her keys and wallet by the front door. "Oh, honey, I'm sorry." Lynne brought her hands up and cupped Libby's face, her own looking contrite and concerned at the same time. "You looked so scared, Libby, utterly terrified, and I just wanted to try and ease the moment. Clearly I chose to do that in the very wrong way." She took the keys and wallet from Libby's hands and placed them back on the table before gathering her daughter in a warm hug. "I'm sorry," she murmured again.

Libby squeezed her eyes shut as finally she returned the hug. She was confused and she needed her mom. Eventually, Lynne got Libby to return to the kitchen. They reclaimed their positions and filled the other two pans in silence. Libby sensed her mother wanted to get the cakes done and in the oven so they could fully focus on what she had to say.

Finally, they finished and cleaned up the kitchen from round one. They'd be starting round two in just a little less than a half an hour. Setting the timer on her phone and with a fresh cup of coffee for them both, Libby and her mom headed to the back porch.

They got situated on the glider, both bundled as it was a chilly early autumn day. The sky was overcast and heavy. Libby wondered if perhaps they'd get an early snow. She took a careful sip of her coffee, wincing when it touched her lip, too hot still.

"So," Lynne said, slapping her daughter's knee with a hand. "Tell me about this young woman. What happened?"

Libby chewed her bottom lip for a moment, not sure if she should be *that* honest or if she should just keep it vague. Looking into her mother's eyes, she knew she had to tell her. Needed her to know the entire story, including identity, to get her opinion, thoughts, and hopefully reassurance that she hadn't lost her damn mind.

"It's Grace Montez." She couldn't bring herself to look at her mother after saying that, and instead feigned interest in blowing on her coffee's surface to cool it down.

"The detective?" Lynne asked softly. At Libby's nod, she asked, "She's a little bit older than you are, isn't she?" There was no judgement in her voice, simply gathering information.

Libby finally met her mother's gaze as she nodded. "About nine years." She took a small sip and cleared her throat, remembering there had been another question in there earlier. "It just happened. Literally, although I can't exactly say out of nowhere." She looked down at her hands, which were wrapped around the coffee mug that rested in her lap.

"What do you mean?" Lynne asked gently, reaching up and brushing a few wavy strands that had escaped from behind Libby's ear to fly around her cheek.

"Well," Libby said, shrugging a shoulder as she looked out over the wooded property. "It wasn't planned, to my knowledge, but spontaneous isn't exactly correct, either."

"Building?" Lynne suggested.

Libby nodded, meeting her gaze. "Yeah. I think that's fair."

"Was that the day she stayed with you while I went to get our groceries when you were sick?" Lynne asked, voice soft and kind.

Libby shook her head and smiled. "No. That was the first time we'd seen each other after, actually."

"Has it happened again?"

"No," Libby said, angry at herself for the frustration that managed to enter her tone in that one tiny word.

"I see," her mother said softly, her hand returning to Libby's leg, patting it lovingly before squeezing her thigh just a bit before her hand slid away again. "So, what do you think?"

"I don't know," Libby said. "I really don't know." She met her mother's gaze, feeling so relieved to have this out in the open, to talk about it with another person.

"Well, honey, is it about Grace specifically?"

Libby looked at her, not sure what exactly the

question was. "What do you mean?"

"Well, are you simply curious about this one woman? Grace is sweet and a very beautiful woman. Or, is this bigger than that? Are you bisexual? A lesbian?"

A shard of white-hot panic lanced right through Libby at those two words. She suddenly felt very uncomfortable and very nauseous. "Wait, whoa, whoa, whoa," she said, pushing up from the glider and hugging herself, nearly dumping her coffee in the process. "That," she said, shaking her head. "That's a little much."

Lynne's head tilted slightly to the side, a trait her daughter had picked up from her. "Sweetheart," she said gently. "How can you contemplate it if you can't even say it?"

≈≈≈≈

Libby lay in bed, reading one of the books she'd ordered online. She'd considered borrowing more from Wyatt but decided she didn't want to answer any questions at the moment. Nothing against Wyatt or Faith, two of her closest and most trusted friends, but she needed to do some exploring on her own.

She'd gotten some books by the same author as well as a couple from another author Wyatt had mentioned at one time. The one thing all the books had in common was that the main characters were all lesbians. She was finishing up the first one she'd ordered and, as the angst-filled storyline was coming to an end, she'd be lying if she said her body wasn't burning with the desire the characters felt in the situation the author had created.

She set the book down on the bed beside her, fanning herself and laughing at the predicament she was in. A glance at the clock showed that it was only nine twenty-three. She decided to get up and walk it off for a moment.

Pushing the covers off her legs, she padded to the kitchen and got a drink of water. It had been two days since she'd been at her parents' house and spoken to her mom about the situation with Grace. They'd gone back in and had finished the cake, not mentioning it again, especially since her dad had come home. The three of them had fallen easily into banter and family discussion.

Even so, she'd taken to heart what her mother had said, and she'd ordered the books before she'd even pulled away from her parents' house. Leaning back against the counter in her kitchen with a bottle of cold water, she thought about something that she'd been considering for a few days. Deciding to try, she pushed away from the counter and walked back to her bedroom to grab her phone. Sitting on the edge of her bed, she pulled up her contacts list and the one she was looking for.

Libby: Hey stranger.

It was simple, nonthreatening. Just saying hi to a friend. So why did she feel so nervous?

Grace: Hi. How are you?
Libby: I'm okay. Hey, we're going to be shutting down the hot springs for a few weeks to get them ready for the winter rush, so I was going to go swimming soon, like in the next few nights. Want to join me?

Libby's heart was racing as she waited. It seemed like forever. She chewed on her bottom lip, her leg bobbing with nervous energy. Finally, her phone dinged with a response.

Grace: Sure. I'm free Thursday night.
Libby: Thursday night it is. Same bat cave, same bat channel?
Grace: 10 p.m.?
Libby: Yes, after closing and everything.
Grace: See you Thursday at 10.

Libby blew out a relieved breath as she set her phone aside. From the short, somewhat clipped responses, she figured Grace must be at work. So, she left her alone. She had no plans for the hot springs, wasn't going to set up some sort of rematch, but she did want to spend time with Grace. She wanted to get her away from the grind of both their jobs and lives to see.

"See what?" Libby muttered, taking another sip from her water. She stared down at her phone. "I guess just to see."

❧❧❧❧

Libby waited upstairs until 10:20. When Grace still hadn't shown, she decided to go on down and get things ready, turn lights on and such. Backpack hitched on one shoulder, Libby carefully made her way down the steep staircase, able to feel the extra weight in the bag that wasn't there last time. She'd decided to buy a bottle of wine and an insulated bag that was specifically made to keep wine or any other type of alcohol chilled while on the go.

Reaching the bottom of the stairs at the hot springs, she turned on the lights they would need and set her backpack down around where she had the first time. She opted to leave the wine in her backpack, not wanting to be presumptive. But, if Grace said she wanted some, if the situation seemed right to offer it, she'd have it.

She unzipped her jacket and let it slide down her arms and into a pile on the ground next to her backpack. Whipping her long-sleeved T-shirt off over her head, she set it on top of the jacket. In her bikini top, she squatted down next to the bag and unzipped it to retrieve her phone. It was pushing 10:30. She looked to see if she had any missed messages, text, or calls, and she had none. She sent a quick text off to Grace, understanding if she was running late and told her to just come down, the doors were open. She was waiting.

Setting the phone back on her backpack, she removed her shoes and socks then shoved her track pants down and off, leaving her in bikini bottoms. Standing there in her bathing suit alone, she admittedly felt extremely vulnerable. She was slightly regretting leaving the door open, and wondered if maybe she should go lock it. Deciding she was probably fine, she opted to take a dip while she waited.

The water was amazing, so warm and soothing as she dove in, allowing her body to shoot through the depths, her fingertips coming into contact with the smooth stone of the bottom before she arched and soared back up to the surface. She broke through, gasping for air as she pushed her hair back from her face and wiped at her eyes.

Glancing to the side of the spring, she saw she was still alone, though she thought she heard a text come in. Excited, Libby swam over to the side and pulled herself out, ignoring the ladder bolted into the stone wall. She made wet footprints over to her bag and dried her hands before picking up her phone.

Grace: I'm not coming. I'm sorry.

Chapter Twenty

She stared at him. More accurately, she stared him down.

"I'm tellin' you the truth," he exclaimed, eyes wide, eyebrows nearly in his hairline as he leaned into the table that separated them in Interrogation Room 1.

"Though I appreciate your passion, Kendal, I know you're lying," she said evenly.

"How can you say that?" the teenager demanded. "You don't know me, lady."

"You're right, I don't. I do, however, recognize you on the security video," she explained, lacing her fingers where her hands rested on the table before her. She studied him, noting the redhead's light blue eyes flashed to the side before quickly returning to her.

"Wasn't me. That camera's video is so shitty, you can't see nothin'." He sat back in the hard plastic chair, crossing wiry arms over a narrow chest. He looked smug, which made her that much more eager to bat around her mouse for a bit.

"So," she said, making a show of turning back a page or two in her notes. "You said that you've not been back to the McDonald's here in town since you quit…" She ran her finger over her handwritten notes until she found what she was looking for, though she didn't need it. This was all theater for his benefit. She wanted him to feel at ease. "…back in March, correct?"

She glanced up at him.

"Correcto, amigo."

"Okay. So, your contention is it's not you on the security camera?" she said, shoving her notepad away and sitting back in her chair. "Right?

"Yes," he said, sounding exasperated.

"Hmm, interesting."

"Look, lady," he said, a bit of desperation in his voice. She figured it was desperation for her to believe him at his word and let him go, although, she mused, he could leave at any time. "Why are you wasting your time with me instead of going out there to find the real person who did this?"

Grace eyed him for a long moment, just long enough to make him squirm before she cleared her throat and said, "I'm going to need your shoes, Kendal."

He looked down, eyes widening. "What? Why? I just bought these, paid a shitload for them."

"Well." She smirked. "We all make our life choices, don't we? Give me the shoes."

"No."

Grace laced her fingers again and leaned forward a bit on her forearms. She knew the light overhead would shine down on her features to blur them into a creepy mass of shadow. "We can do this the hard way or the easy way, Kendal," she said softly.

"I'm not giving you my shoes," he said, defiant, though a bit of fear edged his voice.

Grace said nothing, simply reached over to her notepad and pulled out two sheets of paper, both folded separately into thirds.

The young man watched her movements and locked his gaze on the documents for a moment, even though she knew he had no idea what they were.

"So, about those shoes," she said, pinning him to the spot with her gaze.

He cleared his throat, visibly uncomfortable now. "What are those?" he asked, nodding toward the two folded documents.

Grace didn't move a muscle. "Warrants."

"For my arrest?" he asked, the tough guy long gone now.

"Search warrants," she hedged, wanting him to continue to sweat. Truth was, she wanted the kid to just confess to what he did, get it out and over with. If she could subtly push him in that direction, she would. If he wouldn't go there, she had backup. "Should you be arrested, Kendal?"

He cleared his throat again and readjusted in the chair. "What's the other warrant for? My socks?" He smirked, though she'd done the job long enough to know he was trying to get some of his bravado back to make himself feel better.

"No, for your DNA."

"What?" He gasped. "Nobody was raped!"

She cocked her head slightly to the side. "How would you know? I thought you weren't there." Grace grabbed her phone and sent off a quick message to the person waiting on the other end. "You see, Kendal, a little birdy told me you have that disgusting habit of spitting on the ground, you know, hocking a loogie?" She wrinkled her nose as she set her phone aside, message sent. "Really primitive stuff."

"Hey, when a man has to clear his sinuses—"

"He gets a tissue. You see, Kendal," she said, again staring him down. "Our guy, who we have on camera, somehow knew that the back door of the restaurant was pretty temperamental and if it was jiggled just the right way, the lock would give. Now, who could have known that?" She pretended to ponder before waving the thought away with a hand. "Anyway, our guy, who we have on camera," she added again, "also had a really unique tread pattern on his shoes. Pretty rude, really. Tracked mud all the way from the back door to the manager's office."

He fell back against the chair, his shoulders sagging and his entire tough-guy façade crumbling.

"But here's the coup de grace, Kendal," she added, voice softening just a bit so he really had to listen to hear her. "Our guy, who we caught on tape, decided it was a fantastic idea to hock a loogie on the floor by the fry station. Do you know what's in spit and mucus, Kendal?"

"DNA?" he whispered, face beginning to flush as it looked as though he were about to cry.

The door to the interrogation room opened and the crime scene tech came in, snapping on a pair of latex gloves as he did, DNA swab test and paper evidence bag with him.

❧❧❧❧

Kendal Sparks's confession in the can and mug shot in the books, Grace felt satisfied about a job well done. Before they'd taken him away to booking, she'd had a heart-to-heart with him. She'd told him he was a nineteen-year-old kid who did not want his life starting off this way. She suggested he use his time behind bars to finish high school, which he'd dropped out of, and find a purpose and some self-respect. Make his mother cry tears of pride instead of the tears of shame and fear she'd cried when she'd shown up at the police station after he'd been officially arrested and had called her.

That was the worst part of her job. People always thought of the family and friends of the victim, as they should. But what was never taken into account were the family and friends of the accused and convicted. Families were utterly destroyed by the poisonous and selfish decisions of a loved one.

She'd seen elderly parents forced onto the street after they'd put their house up to bail their kid out who ran, leaving his family to pay his debts. She'd seen children torn from their parents only to get lost in the foster care system. Couples divorced or horrible life choices, such as one more drink at the work party that left someone dead from a DUI. Grace loved righting wrongs, but sometimes it was hard to watch the fallout.

Now, she sat in her personal car in the parking lot of the police station. Head back against the headrest, she blew out a long breath. It had been a very long thirty-six hours since the break-in and robbery, but she was really proud of her team. They'd gotten it done. Unfortunately, that meant work was over and she had nothing to focus on. Which also meant, she realized with a heavy sigh, she had to focus on real life.

"Shit," she whispered.

Lifting her head, she looked around, smiling at a couple colleagues who were walking past her car to clock in for their shift. A glance at her phone told her it was pushing five. She was tired and needed a hot shower and a good meal. Reaching up, she gripped the steering wheel as she considered her options.

Ultimately, she decided first and foremost she wanted a shower and change of clothes. Getting the car started, Grace headed home. Her mind raced back over the last few days, various images flashing before her mind's eye: the extensive damage done to the restaurant by a rebellious and stupid strung-out teen. She saw the look of shock on Kendal's face when she and another officer arrived at his house to arrest him. And again, she saw his mother's tears.

Blowing out a breath, Grace ran a hand through her hair as she pulled into her driveway. The property was quiet and beautiful, trees really beginning to show their colors. Slowing the car to a stop, she cut the engine and gathered her things before climbing out and heading to the house. It was good to be home.

Though very happy to see her fur babies—it felt like it had been forever—trying cases like this one truly made her wish there was a hug waiting for her when she walked through the front door.

Taking care of the cats, she noticed the copy of *1049 Club* that had been left between her doors with a little note several days before. She'd been surprised, and found it very sweet. She hadn't had a lot of time but had been reading the novel steadily when she could. She had less than a hundred pages to go in the thick tome.

Walking past the book, she headed upstairs, removing articles of clothing as she went. Wisps of her perfume had long ago been replaced with the smell of sweat and clothing long hours worn. The hot water that rained down on her felt like heaven. Her body was sore, her head hurt from both being hungry and tired.

As she washed her hair, her thoughts went back

to what she'd been avoiding—or trying to—for three days. Libby. She found the younger woman to be intelligent, incredibly curious and kind, fun, and amusing. Her loyalty and dedication to those she cared about was such a rare thing, in Grace's experience. She was beautiful and quite sexy.

These were all things that made Libby dangerous. There seemed to be a vulnerability about Libby lately that would be so easy for Grace to take advantage of, but she couldn't do that. She'd grown to care about the spunky blonde, far more than she cared to admit, and knew that a good fuck and handful of orgasms wasn't worth damaging Libby's trust in her, or causing damage and confusion to Libby's psyche.

Libby's invitation to the hot springs had kicked Grace squarely in the gut. No, squarely in the crotch. Her knee-jerk reaction had been, *Hell yeah, see you there!* Then, once she'd reminded herself she was a thirty-five-year-old woman and not a fourteen-year-old boy, she'd recalibrated and talked herself out of the gutter and back into the burgeoning friendship she knew she was capable of and had agreed to.

Then, the night had arrived.

Grace stepped out of the shower and, naked body wrapped in a towel so as not to drip on the floor, walked to the mirror and used a washcloth to wipe away the steam. She studied her reflection. Her focus went to her eyes, which looked tired, the skin a bit puffy beneath and the whites of the eye a bit red. As she looked into her own eyes, something seemed to be missing.

She looked away, not wanting to explore that. Instead, she grabbed a brush and began the careful and sometimes painful process of brushing out the tangled curls. She needed to talk to Libby, she knew. She needed to offer her an explanation. What could she say?

"Gee, sorry I stood you up. I was afraid I'd give in and fuck you three ways to Sunday right there on the ground next to the hot springs," she muttered, her clit jumping at the very thought of it.

She could tell her she'd gotten called in to work. Technically, that wasn't a lie, she reasoned. Grace met her own reflected gaze again. "Bullshit, you coward." She'd gotten the call about the robbery after eleven, an hour after she was supposed to meet Libby.

She couldn't lie. She couldn't tell the truth.

Brush set back down, she used the towel to dry her body then squeeze-dry her hair, careful not to re-tangle it. It seemed no matter how good her conditioner was, her hair was never on her side.

Hanging the towel to dry on a hook mounted on the bathroom door, Grace padded into the bedroom, thinking about what to put on. She stood in front of her dresser, staring at it as though it would give her inspiration. Undecided but wanting to at least feel somewhat productive, she grabbed a clean pair of panties.

She balanced on one foot as she slid the silky material up over one leg before reversing her position. She glanced back toward the bathroom when she heard the alarm for an incoming text message. Tugging the panties over her behind and adjusting them comfortably into place, she walked back into the steamy, soap-scented room. She reached for her phone which rested on the counter within grabbing distance of the shower, an always-on-duty-cop habit. Her heart sank when she saw the text was from Faith offering a dinner invite.

It wasn't that Grace was disappointed with the invitation, but the person offering it. Ludicrous, she knew. Unfair, she knew. She stared at the message and tapped the edge of the phone with her pointer finger as she considered what she wanted to do. Finally, she responded in the affirmative, then left the phone on the counter after seeing Faith's very excited reply confirming the time, and sighed as she again went to look for something to wear.

~~~~

Deciding to see if perhaps she could kill two birds with one stone, find a way to apologize to Libby and then spend a little time with her as a friend with Wyatt and Faith all in one trip, Grace headed in the direction of Libby's house. She hadn't seen her Sentra at any of the three businesses downtown, so figured she must be home.

Sure enough, Libby's car was parked in her driveway, the house quiet. Grace pulled up to the curb across the street, taking a minute to decide how to handle this. She turned off her car, her hands flopping down into her lap as she glanced over at the house again. Her heart was beginning to race a bit just being there, knowing that Libby was just beyond those walls.

"What the hell am I going to say?" she muttered, angry at herself.

Why couldn't she just have been an adult? Why couldn't she just give Libby what the younger woman seemed to be asking for: friendship. That was easy enough, that was innocent enough. Grace was capable of that, could give that much. Right?

Grace's head fell back against the headrest as, yet again, her thoughts went back to that kiss. That goddamn kiss! Why she had to open that Pandora's box, she'd never know. Now, she couldn't think of Libby without that damn kiss flooding back. The taste of Libby's mouth, how soft her lips were. She couldn't help but think of the desperate hold Libby had on Grace's uniform shirt. Even now, she couldn't wear that particular shirt without taking Libby with her on her shift, no matter how many times she'd washed it.

She'd been a coward. For a good reason. Right?

"Fuck!"

Grace slammed her fist into her denim-clad thigh. She looked over again at Libby's house, movement catching her eye. The house next door. A very cute black woman was walking across in front of the closed garage door, headed toward Libby's house. She looked to be around Libby's age, perhaps just a bit older. She was dressed in medical scrubs, but what caught Grace's attention was that she was carrying a bottle of wine.

Grace sat up a bit in her seat, following the woman's progress across Libby's lawn. The woman made her way up to the front door and, before she could knock, the inner door opened and Libby appeared behind the still-closed glass screen door. Her smile was instant when she saw her visitor. She pushed the glass door open and took the woman in a tight hug. When they parted, the woman held up the bottle of wine, seemingly for inspection. Libby took it and nodded her approval with another welcoming smile.

Grace felt a coldness spread through her like molasses made of ice, all heading into her gut and wrapping itself into a hard ball. Anger sprouted from that hard ball, and the ugly pangs of jealousy.

Libby's head fell back as she seemed to be laughing heartily at something the woman said. Mid-laugh, she glanced out of the glass door and seemed to notice Grace sitting in her car.

Grace met her gaze, the jealousy burning bright and completely irrationally, but she couldn't help it. The woman had moved on deeper into the house, leaving Libby standing at the door by herself. She faced the door now, her full body in view as she stared Grace down.

For just a moment, Grace considered getting out of her car and walking across the street. To do what, exactly? She had no answer. Instead, she reached up and gripped the steering wheel, fingers like talons around it.

Libby lifted her chin slightly, as though in defiance, before stepping back and closing the solid wood door. She was gone.

Chapter Twenty-one

Grace checked the last two boxes and added a few more notes to the report before saving it and sending it off. She glanced at the clock on her desk computer's screen, then pushed back from the desk and stood.

"Okay, Colby, I should only be gone for an hour or less," she said, whipping her department-issued jacket around and her arms into the sleeves as she shrugged into the quilted warmth. "If you need me, just call," she offered, patting her radio mic tacked up near her unformed shoulder.

"You're seriously leaving me here alone?" Colby asked from his desk, which was placed in the main room with a smattering of other desks Tetrised to fit in the limited space.

Grace stared at him before glancing at his computer screen. "You're playing solitaire, Colby. Honestly, I think you'll be okay while I drop by Wyatt and Faith's baby shower on my lunch break." She decided to take a black-and-white just in case she was needed quickly while there, no matter how unlikely that was. "Want me to pick you something up on my way back?" she asked, headed toward the back door.

He looked at her thoughtfully for a moment before rattling off his order.

"Okay, see you in a bit with food," she said, pushing on the push bar to open the door.

She was met with a bone-chilling blast of wind with tiny snowflakes stinging as they were blown into her face as she headed outside. She made her way down the stairs and to the parking lot where her squad car awaited her.

She and Colby had been out earlier in the day and had made some stops, nothing major: speeding, a minor accident on the ice, and a fight between two brothers who'd had a bit too much to drink at a family reunion. She'd tried to get the day off for the baby shower, but due to being shorthanded at the station as they'd lost an officer to retirement, she went ahead and worked.

The streets were relatively clear after the previous storm a few days ago, but Grace figured it wouldn't be long before accumulation started. She guessed that by the end of shift today, the streets would have a nice frosting layer on the streets and rooftops.

As she drove through town headed to the old farmhouse on the hill where Wyatt and Faith lived, Grace thought back to her childhood and the rare times they had snow, or when she'd see it on TV. She would look at the thick layer of white stuff and immediately think of her favorite cookie, Oreos. The snow to her was the cream in the middle. Imagine her disappointment at six years old when she took a bite of that "cream" and didn't get quite the same effect as her before-bed snack.

"So," she mused, looking out the windshield up into the sky. "Will it be a regular day or a Double Stuf?"

She chuckled at her own joke as she turned onto the long winding road that led up to the farmhouse, the gate left open for guests. She loved the old farmhouse, once upon a time no doubt grand for its day but now just a lovely piece of history lovingly renovated back to life by its current owners.

There were a handful of cars already there, considering the celebration had been going on for an hour already. From what she'd been told, the day was meant to be a pre-birthday party for baby Abbigail, though no gifts. Just fun, friendship, and food, or so the invitation had read.

Grace parked the squad car where she could easily get out and not get blocked in by any other incoming cars. She turned off the car and reached over to the passenger seat for the wrapped gift she'd brought. Though the moms-to-be had said no gifts, there was something special she wanted the baby to have.

She locked the car and walked toward the house, her boots crunching on the snow-covered gravel and ice. She noticed Libby's Sentra buried in the pack. Likely she'd been one of the first ones there to help set up. Her stomach did a little flip. They hadn't spoken on any real personal level at all since Grace had read to her while Libby was sick, other than the couple of text messages regarding the hot springs invitation. That day in front of Libby's house had been more than a week ago, and other than once when Libby had waited on her at Bessie's, there'd been no interaction. In that meeting, Libby had been polite to the extent that her profession required.

It had hurt. She hated to admit it, but damn it, it did.

She made her way up the stairs to the large wraparound porch and to the front double doors of the beautiful old home. She could hear women's voices within talking and laughing, and muffled music. Hugging the wrapped box to her chest with an arm, she used her other hand to ring the bell.

Grace blew out a breath as she waited for her call to be answered, her nervousness coming out in a white puff of steam. A moment later, the door was pulled open, Libby standing on the other side. She'd clearly been in the middle of laughing on her way to the door, but the moment she spotted Grace, the mirth seemed to die on her lips.

Libby cleared her throat and gave Grace a polite smile as she stepped aside to allow her entry. "Hello."

"Hi, Liberty. How are you?" Grace said softly.

Libby nodded, hugging herself, her body language and energy completely shutting Grace out. "Good." She glanced down at the gift Grace held. "They'll be pissed at you. Didn't want any gifts or anyone to spend money."

Grace looked down at the gift then met Libby's guarded gaze. She smirked. "Well, technically I didn't spend any money except on some wrapping paper and a bow. But, it's something I want Abbigail to have."

Libby nodded. Her jaw worked for a moment as she glanced down, looking as though she had something to say, but instead she simply pushed the front door closed behind Grace and turned to rejoin the festivities, leaving Grace to stand there or follow.

Blowing out a breath and bringing up a nervous hand to run over her hair that was smoothed back into a tight bun, she followed in Libby's wake. The guests were spread out over the large space that was the kitchen, dining room, and living room, one narrow wall separating the kitchen and living room that held the fireplace, a fire popping inside and warming the space.

She had to laugh as Ogden, Faith's father, was over in the corner where the dining table had been moved and a music unit brought in. All he was missing was a pair of sunglasses and headphones as he dished out the tunes. There were a couple women she didn't know but thought she'd seen around. Wyatt and Libby's mom Lynne were talking away like two long-lost best friends at the banquet of food laid out on the long kitchen island. Grace was amused, as Wyatt's plate was loaded with a little bit of everything. From the expanse of her belly, she was definitely eating for two.

A glance over to the sink sent a jolt of surprise through her. It was the same woman who had joined Libby with the bottle of wine. She stood with Faith talking about something amusing, both bursting into laughter as they rinsed and cut vegetables to refill the veggie tray. Their comfort level with each other indicated that the woman had been around Faith much longer than just this baby shower.

Grace was startled as suddenly she was hugged from behind, a bulbous belly pressing into her back.

"Don't y'all think ya can sneak in here without sayin' hi, Grace Montez."

Grace grinned and reached down to grip and squeeze the hands clasped at her belly. "I wouldn't dream of it," she assured. She was released and turned to give the lovely redhead a proper hug, receiving a kiss to the cheek in the process. "How are you, Mama?" she asked, looking down at a very pregnant Wyatt.

Wyatt lit up like a Christmas tree, her hands going to her belly. "Happier than a tick on a Retriever's butt."

Grace chuckled. "That happy, huh?"

"What is this, missy?" Wyatt asked, nodding toward the gift Grace held. "I told you, now," she added, wagging her finger.

Grace thought she had that disciplinary move down. "I know. It's just a little something I wanted you guys to have for Abbigail."

Wyatt's entire face softened as she accepted the package, the box about ten inches all around. She turned to her wife. "Faith, darlin'?"

Faith turned from her task, an instant smile coming to her lips when she saw Grace. "Hey!"

"Hi there, lady." Grace accepted a tight hug and an apology, as Faith's hands weren't fully dry.

"So glad you could come," Faith said, moving to stand next to her wife. "I think you know pretty much everyone here," she said, looking around. "Oh! Frankie, have you met her, yet?" The black woman who was still at the sink glanced over to look at the group.

"Uh, no. I've seen her, but don't know her," Grace said.

"Frankie, come meet our good friend," Faith said. "She's a real sweetheart," the mayor explained to Grace. "She's an X-ray tech but also cleans houses and businesses part time. Been one hell of a help to us here."

Drying her hands on a kitchen towel, the attractive young woman walked over and joined them. "Hi," she said with a beautiful smile. "I'm Frankie."

"Hi." Grace accepted the hand that was outstretched in greeting. "Nice to meet you. I'm Grace."

"I've been wanting to meet you," Frankie said, her smile and hand warm. "These two talk about you all the time," she added, indicating Wyatt and Faith with a nod of her head.

Grace felt a presence move up just behind her and to her left. She knew it was Libby without even looking at her. She kept her attention on Frankie but felt Libby's presence like a flame licking at her back.

"Well," she said, a smirk on her face. "I'm so sorry they've bored you like that. They're far more interesting than that usually."

"No," Frankie said, laughing. "You've played such an important role in their history." She looked from Grace to the couple and back. "Really inspirational."

Grace smiled. She liked this young woman, and she didn't want to. "Thank you."

"She brought us a gift," Wyatt told Faith. "Shall we?"

Grace felt panic for a moment, as she'd wanted a more private setting. Now, they were surrounded by everyone at the event, including Ogden and his longtime girlfriend, Vickie. Again, she felt Libby and glanced over to see her moving to the couch where she sat by herself. Grace ignored the urge to go to her and stayed put. As she stood there, Frankie left their little group and joined Libby, sitting next to her.

Grace fought the extremely unpleasant jealousy that had been her companion for more than a week. It sucked.

Wyatt handed the present to Faith, who set it on the island. "Heavy," she commented.

Grace watched as the paper was carefully removed, revealing the plain white cardboard box she'd found that was the right size. Again, she could feel that heat, and a surreptitious glance showed her that

Libby's eyes were on her, quickly darting to Faith and the gift.

Faith opened the top flap on the box to reveal the small silver elephant tucked inside. From the coiled trunk to the tip of its tail was about eight inches, large feet to the top of its head about six inches. Fat elephant belly and big elephant ears. The expression on the animal's face was joy. On the underside of the large belly was a rubber stopper, which could release the coins slipped into the slot atop the elephant's head.

The "piggy" bank was obviously not new, the silver aged. Grace looked on, slightly mixed emotions as the two moms looked it over. They looked at her for explanation.

Grace felt the weight of the room as every pair of eyes was on her, including Libby, the house silent in expectation. "When I was three months old," she began, "my mother left me with this and a note. She explained that the dollar's worth of dimes inside was to get me started on my future." She cleared her throat as she continued, surprised that she nearly choked up over those words. "I used this to save every penny I could until I was able to buy my bus ticket to head to the army and start my life." She spared a glance at Wyatt and Faith before looking back to the elephant. She reached into the hip pockets of her uniform pants and withdrew the five silver dollars she'd gotten from the bank the previous day. "So," she said, holding them up for the moms to see before slipping them, one by one, into the elephant's body where they landed with a metallic *clang*. "Here's to Abbigail's future."

Grace found herself engulfed in hugs from Wyatt and Faith, which she returned. A quick glance showed her Libby was blotting her eyes with a tissue. She knew that Libby was the only person there who knew her story. She looked away for fear she'd tear up as well. Her eyes did well up, however, as the gathered group began to dig through pockets and purses, bringing out coins and slipping them into the piggy bank one by one.

She stepped out of the way, snagging a baby carrot off the veggie tray and popping it into her mouth. Suddenly, her radio squawked to life.

"*Grace, what's your 10-20?*"

Grace grabbed her hand radio and clicked the button. "I'm at the mayor's house," she responded, knowing Dispatch knew where that was.

"*Officer LaCroix has an 11-99,*" came the staticky voice from Dispatch.

"What's his location?" Grace said, waving to the room at large as she darted out of the house, everyone able to hear the radio and waving goodbye in return. She hurried back out into the cold afternoon, the snow easing a bit, though it seemed colder than it had thirty minutes ago.

"Hey!"

Grace turned to see Libby hurrying down the porch stairs and over to her, Grace's hand on the door handle of the car. She waited patiently for the younger woman to reach her.

"That was a really decent thing you did," Libby said, out of breath. "Diane gave that to you?"

Grace nodded. "Yes."

Libby, only dressed in jeans and a sweater, hugged herself as a cold breeze whipped past them. "Didn't think you were gonna come," she said, meeting Grace's gaze.

"I couldn't get the day off," Grace said, though Libby's remark rubbed her wrong. "I see you brought your friend, though." She couldn't keep the bitterness out of her voice.

Libby stared at her. "Seriously? I come out here to tell you that I was really touched by what you did for Wyatt and Faith and *that* is what you have to say?" Her arms dropped only for her hands to rest on her hips. "Yeah, I did bring Frankie. She works for them, Grace. She does the things around here that Wyatt can't at the end of her pregnancy." She glared at Grace. "At least she's dependable."

That one hit Grace right in the gut, the flames shooting out of those brown eyes nearly burning her alive. Her guilt morphed into anger. "Oh, I'm sure," she bit out.

Libby literally took a small step back, looking as though she'd been punched. "You're jealous?" She gasped. "Are you fucking kidding me?"

Grace looked away, unable to meet that gaze any longer. Her jaw worked as her anger built.

"How dare you," Libby continued. "Something was happening between us, Grace. I may not fully understand it, but it was there. *You* are the one who made it clear you're not interested."

Grace glared at her, lips not much more than a thin line, her emotions all over the place—anger, guilt, regret.

"You seem to have an issue with the fact that I'm nine years younger," Libby nearly growled. "But you seem to be the one who can't handle it. So, before you start your jealousy shit, *Colby*, remember your own choices."

With that, Libby spun on her heel and stormed

back to the house, leaving Grace standing out there in the cold, literally and figuratively.

Grace grabbed the door handle and yanked the door open. She dropped into the seat behind the wheel, her anger alive and well. She slammed the door shut and started the car, blaring her lights and siren as she tore off the property.

Chapter Twenty-two

Compartmentalizing her confrontation with Libby to examine and deal with another time, Grace focused solely on her job as she pulled up behind Colby's squad car. He'd pulled over a man speeding in a pickup truck. As Grace made her way to the scene, Dispatch had let her know that the man had an outstanding warrant. Colby wasn't going to act on making an arrest until he had backup as there was a passenger in the truck as well.

Colby was standing at the driver's side window talking to the driver, so Grace sat back and watched for a moment, trying to get a feel for the situation and see if perhaps she should call for backup from the sheriff's department.

Something in her gut told her to call Dispatch and give them a reading on the situation and prepare them they may need to act. That done, Grace stepped out of her car and walked in front of it to the passenger side of the situation.

"I don't care what you are. I ain't gonna get outta my truck," the driver was saying as Grace neared the passenger window.

She removed her baton from her utility belt and used it to lightly rap on the passenger-side window. The man sitting there, who looked like the teen-something version of the thirty-something man sitting behind the wheel, glanced over at her. She smiled at him and indicated he should roll down his window.

Once the window was rolled down a bit, she smiled at both occupants. "Good afternoon, gentlemen. I'm Sergeant Montez. How's it goin'?" She met Colby's gaze through the cab of the truck and could see the irritation and strain in his face.

"This blowhard is tryin' to get me outta my truck," the driver explained. "If I was speedin', fine, gimmie a ticket and let me and my boy go. I ain't got all day to waste talkin' to this asshole," he added, hitching a thumb at Colby.

"Well, Mr. Sears," Grace said, her tone kind yet firm. "Tell you what. It's cold out here and none of us want to be standing out here in the snow, so…" She pulled open the passenger door of the truck, smiling at the teen who stared at her. "Let's all just have a chat and then we can all get on our way. Okay?"

Grace stepped aside as the teen stepped out of the truck. He looked no older than probably thirteen or fourteen from the fear that was on his face and willingness to comply with her. She gave him a comforting smile. Not his fault his dad was an ass.

"Hey, get away from my kid!"

Following her lead, Colby opened the driver's door. "Sir, please step out of the truck."

"Fuck you! Get away from my son, bitch," the driver yelled toward Grace. "Patrick, get back in here!"

"Let's go over here out of the way, huh?" Grace directed the boy to well off the side of the road. They were already basically out of any real traffic, but moving the son away from the vehicle also gave Dad an incentive to cooperate. He no longer had his kid to use as a shield.

Assured that the boy was secured and safe, Grace

turned back to the situation, making her way over to the truck where Colby was still trying to coax the man out. She stood at the open passenger door to let him know he had no way out. She'd put her baton away and now held her hand casually near her holstered pistol.

Suddenly the man took a swing, coldcocking Colby, who stumbled backward and landed on his behind in the middle of the street. As Grace went to unholster her gun, she saw the driver reach down to the bench seat next to him and retrieve a pistol from beneath a jacket that was lying there.

Before she could get her gun released, his 9mm was pointed at her and firing. Grace felt a sting of fire at her temple before she dove to ground, wincing as she landed on her shoulder. The sound of the firing stopped, replaced by the squealing of the truck's tires as the man put his foot on the gas and took off, passenger door flopping around helplessly with the motion before it slammed shut with his hard turn left.

"Dad!" the kid yelled, running out into the street.

Dazed, Grace rolled to her back before sitting up. She brought a hand up to her head and saw blood. She figured it was just a grazing wound, but it was bleeding pretty good.

"You okay?" Colby gasped, hurrying over to her. "I'll call an ambulance—"

"No," Grace said, taking his offered hand to get to her feet. "No, just a flesh wound. Call someone to pick up the boy and let's go."

Sirens screaming and lights flashing, Grace flew down the street, on the radio back and forth with Dispatch and Colby, also in pursuit. They'd caught up to the truck, which had sped up once he realized he was being followed. An all-out car chase was underway.

The sheriff's department was on the case as well and were setting up down the highway in the direction he was headed, with spike strips laid in the middle of the road. When the truck's tires ran over them, it would shred the rubber, forcing the truck to a safe stop.

The warrant he was wanted for wasn't that big of a deal, so Grace had to wonder what they *didn't* know about that was making him run like this. Colby's car was at the truck's left flank, so she sped up and moved to the right. Seeing this, the driver hit the gas even harder.

"Gonna pit," Colby called out over the radio, referring to the pit maneuver, which was where he'd edge the front right side of his squad car up to the back left of the truck and, using inertia against the truck, spin the truck around, forcing a stop. "Move back!"

"You sure about this?" she asked. The move was incredibly dangerous, and to her knowledge Colby had little to no experience doing it. "I can—"

"Move back!"

Concerned but knowing she had to trust her partner, she eased back to give him the space he and the truck would need. Grace watched as he eased over to the truck before moving away. Clearly Colby didn't feel it was a good moment. He eased back over.

Grace's heart was pounding. She knew they had to stop the truck before he hit the more populated portion of town, and didn't have long to do it. "Come on, Colby," she whispered. "You can do this."

Colby eased the car back into position before

yanking the wheel hard left and then hard right into the truck. Metal screeched and tires squealed in protest as the truck spun around, the driver behind the wheel desperately gripping at the wheel trying to gain control.

Grace was impressed and relieved, but then the truck hit a patch of ice, sending it flying into Colby's car like a missile. The squad car, already unstable due to the contact, careened off toward the other side of the street where it plowed through a split rail fence, sending the car airborne, flipping several times as it landed in the field beyond, pieces of the car flying off with every spin and hit to the frozen ground.

"Jesus!" Grace exclaimed, though she had little time to worry about Colby as the truck was headed straight for her.

She gripped the wheel and yanked it to the left to get out of the way, but it was too late. She braced herself for impact as the truck hit her right front quarter head-on. As if in slow motion, she watched as the driver was pulled from behind the wheel, as though sucked by an unseen force, crashing headfirst through the already-cracked windshield of the truck and straight into hers with the most horrible sound. Her windshield instantly shattered, scarlet painting the spiderwebs all the way across.

After what seemed like an unending roller coaster, the car came to a stop. Shaken, bumped, bruised, and her head still bleeding, Grace sat there trying to catch her breath. Getting her bearings, she struggled with her seat belt, her hands shaking. Finally free, she pushed open her door and nearly fell out of the car as her legs gave out from under her. She braced herself on her door before fully rising to her height. A glance at the driver of the truck, whose body was pinned within the mangled front right end of her car, made it quite clear he hadn't survived the crash.

"Colby." She turned to look at the field to her left. "Colby?" she yelled out, forcing her legs to work as she did a part run, part gallop over to the hole the car had made in the fence and the torn ground that marked the path to where the car rested on its top, all four wheels still spinning up in the air. "Oh my god."

Grace finally reached the car, grabbing her radio as she did, breathlessly relaying events to Dispatch and requesting medical. She was absolutely terrified of what she was going to find. He'd yet to respond to her calls, nor did she hear anything else—moans, cries, or calls for help.

Reaching the car, she fell to her knees and instantly cried out in pain. Now she understood why her legs had failed her, as she'd banged the hell out of them in the accident. It didn't matter as she ducked to look inside the cruiser.

Colby was still strapped inside, upside down. His face and head were covered in blood. She looked around, trying to see if it would be possible for her to get him out. The car was in terrible shape, the driver's door crushed in. She moved around to the passenger side, which wasn't as badly damaged.

"Colby?" she said, tugging on the door handle. It pulled up but the door didn't release. "Colby, can you hear me?" she called louder. No response. She stopped when she realized she smelled gasoline. "Fuck."

The side window had been broken out in the crash, so she crawled in through it, wincing as a shard of glass sliced into her leg in the process, cutting through the material of her uniform pants.

She ignored the pain and kept going. Once inside, effectively curled up on the roof of the inside of the car, she contorted herself so that she was sideways, her boots pressed against the passenger door. She pushed using the significant strength in her thighs, trying to budge the door open. Nothing.

The smell of gasoline was getting stronger, along with the stench of Colby's blood. Panic kicked in and she brought her knees up as much as she could and slammed her boots into the door over and over and over again until finally the door popped open with a distressed whine.

With more room to maneuver, she turned around and began to work on Colby's seat belt release. "Buddy?" she said, looking into his face, hoping against hope he was alive. She reached up and used two fingers to find his pulse in his neck. She nearly burst into tears when she found one, as weak as it was. "Gonna get you out of here, Colby," she promised, looking around to figure out exactly how she was going to do that.

She worked again on his seat belt, the mechanism crushed from the accident and unable to release. From her cramped, contorted position, she managed to shimmy her hand down to a cargo pocket in her uniform pants and grab the knife she always kept there.

"All right, dude," she said, voice breathy from pain and fear. "We got this, Colby. Hold on, buddy."

Teeth bared in effort, she sawed at the nylon of the belt that kept him hostage. She was getting tired with the exertion and loss of her own blood. She kept at it, her hand aching and getting shaky.

"Come on, you fucker!" she growled, desperation

bringing out aggression in her movements and her vocabulary.

Finally, the nylon began to fray enough from the sharp blade that she was able to get it to give and slice through the last stubborn strands. She knew it had been mere moments, but it felt like an hour.

Exhausted and hurting, she knew her mission wasn't done. Now she had to get Colby, a large, muscular, heavy man out. She looked at his legs tucked beneath the steering wheel and was relieved to see that they didn't seem to be crushed or pinned.

"Okay." She pushed the tattered ends of the seat belt away. "Come on, Colby," she said, taking hold of his arm closest to her. "Let's get you out of here."

She pushed aside the arm that normally held the tray his department laptop was mounted to, the tray and laptop no doubt in pieces flung into the field. As she backed out of the car and tugged on his arm, gravity began to do its thing and Colby's heavy body began to slide out of the seat. She did her best to keep his head stabilized, not knowing what his injuries were.

It took all of her strength to get him pulled halfway out of the seat, simply because of the confined space and angle. If she'd been able to use her legs properly, she'd have had him out in a heartbeat. But, as it was, she had to use nothing but her upper body strength, which was substantial in its own right but challenged against two hundred pounds of dead weight.

Colby's upper body was now on the roof below the passenger seat, only his legs still on the driver's side of the car. Now outside the car herself, Grace scrambled to get her feet under her, squatting down in a crouch. She dug her heels in as she tugged, her growl loud as she pulled with all her might.

Colby's body hit a snag, which caused her to fall back on her butt. She was sweating profusely. She moved to get back to her squatting position and stopped, her senses on high alert.

"Oh Jesus." She gasped when she recognized the smell.

Smoke.

"Come on!" She pulled with every ounce of her strength. This time, she didn't stop. She used her thighs to propel her backward, Colby's body sliding out of the damaged doorway like a baby from the womb.

Panting, she stopped for a moment when she saw the flicker of flames at the rear of the car. Her heart nearly leapt out of her chest. Now at least she had both of his hands, which she grabbed, holding on as best she could. His left hand was bloody, which made it a bit slippery. She grabbed his wrist, getting a better grip on it. She heard the popping of flames and saw the fire getting bigger.

"Oh god, oh god, oh god," she growled through bared teeth as she backpedaled away from the crash, kicking aside debris as she went so Colby wouldn't get caught on it and stop their progress, or be further hurt.

She saw the fire spreading, moving from the rear up to the front of the car, the seat catching fire. Still pulling Colby away as quickly as she could, she looked behind her to see a ditch. It seemed so far away, but she knew she had to get them to it. She could hear sirens wailing in the distance, and as wonderful as that was, it would do nothing for them now.

Whoosh!

The entire car went up in flames, Grace able to feel the heat on her face as she sent prayers up to anyone willing to listen that she needed all the strength they could give her. She finally reached the ditch and had no sooner gotten Colby rolled into it than the car exploded, sending her flying into the bank of the ditch on the other side, knocking the wind out of her.

She fell to the bottom of the three-foot-deep ditch next to Colby. She glanced over at him, then all went dark.

Chapter Twenty-three

"Okay, ma'am, this is the last one," Libby said, placing the filled grocery bag on the butcher block countertop next to the sea of other bags.

Frankie, who stood at the open fridge unloading a bag, glanced at her over her shoulder. "Thanks so much, Libby. I really appreciate your help. My little man is coming home in just a bit from his dad's, and I want to make sure I make his absolute favorite dinner ever." Her smile was nearly blinding, making Libby smile in return.

"How are you doing with that?" she asked. She wasn't sure what else to do, so she began to empty the bags, unloading the cans, bottles, bags, and canisters she'd watched Frankie put in her buggy as they wandered around the grocery store after they'd left the baby shower. "You seem in much better spirits this weekend than you were that first, brutal one."

Frankie shrugged, sparing a glance at her friend as she grabbed the produce bag of tomatoes from the counter near the sink. "It sucks," she said simply. "But, he's his dad. Noah needs him."

Libby wadded up all the empty plastic grocery bags together in one bag and set it on the counter, not sure what Frankie did with them. "I'm so grateful my parents managed to figure things out along the way. It can't be easy on Noah, either."

Frankie shook her head. "It's not. The thing

is," she added, closing the fridge door. "I really loved Tucker. I never would have left him. He was just so goddamn weak when it came to his mother." She shook her head, grabbing more items to stow in the cabinets near the fridge. "That woman would literally come into the house, *my* house," she clarified with a raised eyebrow, "and rearrange the cabinets, go through the fridge, and," she added, hands on hips as she faced Libby. "That bitch had the nerve to strip Noah down when we'd drop him off for her to spend some time with her grandson, wash all his clothes, *iron* them, then bathe my child like I, as his mother, had no idea what I was doing."

Libby stared at her. "My god. What did Tucker do?"

"Not a damn thing," Frankie said with a sigh. "I'd talk to him and tell him he really needed to talk to her, and he wouldn't. His dad died when Tucker was a teenager, so it was just the two of them, and I get that, but good lord. Grow some balls!"

Libby smiled. "Agreed. I'm so sorry it broke up your marriage, but I can see how. Is he a good dad, at least?" Libby leaned back against the wall by the stove, trying to stay out of the way.

"I suppose, for the most part. I mean, I've certainly heard horror stories of far worse. I think if he'd get away from her he'd be a better man, overall." Frankie moved to the sink to wash the apples she'd bought. Libby moved the fruit bowl from the small cooking island over to the sink for her to put them in.

"So," Frankie said, glancing over at Libby. "Let's get back to what we were talking about in the car. You and Grace?"

Libby blew out a breath as she ran a hand

through her hair. She couldn't believe she'd said anything. She'd been so angry when she'd gone back into the house after Grace had left. Frankie had asked what was wrong, and she'd promised to tell her after they left, not wanting to spoil Wyatt and Faith's day.

"Yeah."

"So, are you guys like a couple?" Frankie asked. She grabbed herself a coffee mug and tapped a second with a questioning expression.

"Please." Libby walked over to the island and pulled out one of the two stools and sat down. "Is there something I can do, lady? I feel like a lazy ass sitting here while you buzz around here like a fly on crack."

Frankie threw her head back and laughed as she prepared her Keurig coffee maker. "You're fine. Just talk to me. Did you guys break up?"

Libby shook her head, her stomach flopping at such a notion. If they'd broken up, that meant they were together at one point, and that made her heart flutter for reasons she couldn't quite grasp. "No. We…" She wasn't entirely sure what to say. She decided to just start at the beginning. "Technically I've known Grace since she moved here when she joined the department four plus years ago. I was still living in town and going to college. I basically only knew her from waiting on her at the coffee shop, but…" She shrugged. "I don't know. In retrospect, there was always something about her, something that really caught my attention."

"Well, she's absolutely beautiful," Frankie said, removing a bottle of flavored creamer from the fridge. "Sugar? Splenda?"

"No, the creamer is fine." She watched as Frankie set the bottle and two spoons on the island before returning to the single-cup coffee maker that was sputtering to a finish with the first brew, which was placed before her. "Yes, she's very beautiful," she admitted. "She's incredibly kind, smart as hell." Despite her earlier anger, a soft smile crossed her lips as she thought about the time they'd spent together. "There's a calm about her," she said softly. "A gentleness to her energy." She looked down into the black depths of the coffee as she absently reached for the creamer, a chocolate-caramel flavor. "Like, there's nothing I couldn't tell her, nothing she'd judge me for." She looked up to see Frankie studying her. "Does that make sense?"

Her new friend nodded. "It does. She sounds like a really good, solid person. Clearly you have a lot of respect for her, and you like her. What went wrong?"

Libby let out a heavy sigh. "That part I don't know. When I came back here in August, we met up again and started to become friends. Hung out together, usually by accident," she said with a smile, thinking of their day hiking. "Things began to…" She shrugged again as she poured creamer into the coffee, using a spoon to stir it in until it reached the color she preferred. "I don't know. Something was happening. Definitely an attraction."

"Did it get physical?" Frankie asked, joining Libby at the island with her own cup of coffee.

Libby could feel Grace's mouth, so aggressive, demanding initially, then softening to introduce her to a sensuality she had no idea existed, all with just a kiss. She cleared her throat to try to push away the memory and nodded. "We kissed."

Frankie was silent for a moment as she prepared her own coffee. Finally, she said, "You know, something just occurred to me." She met Libby's gaze.

"Maybe Grace got freaked out. I mean, she may not be gay, Libby. Like, maybe she got in over her head with you, thought she could, but..." She waved her hands absently like she was searching for words. "Freaked out," she said again. "I mean, my cousin, TaRhonda, we're really close, and she's this out-and-proud lesbian, and some women are really intimidated by that, even though they're drawn to her like a moth to a flame." She shrugged. "Maybe that's what happened with Grace. Attracted to you, drawn to your confidence as a lesbian woman, but maybe it scared her." She smirked. "Maybe she liked it a little too much."

Libby stared at her, dumbfounded. "You think I'm a lesbian?" she asked, indicating herself with her fingers.

The smile that had been on Frankie's lips seemed frozen in place as she stared at Libby. The smile fell and so did her jaw, her hand snapping up to cover it. "Oh my god!" she exclaimed from behind it. "Please don't tell me I've misread this and you're not gay."

Libby ran a hand through her hair and gave a bit of a nervous chuckle. "I don't know what I am, Frankie."

"So, Grace—"

"Is a lesbian, yes."

Frankie burst into laughter, her hand slapping the island with her mirth. Libby couldn't help but smile at the situation, as ridiculous as it was. "Oh my god, okay. Sorry," Frankie said, blowing out a loud breath as she calmed herself down. "This is a new one. So," she said, eyeing Libby. "You date guys?"

Libby smirked. "Well, I did up until about three months ago."

"What changed? Grace?" Frankie asked simply

before taking a sip of her coffee.

Libby considered that for a moment before shaking her head. "No. I don't know." Her eyebrows drew as she considered, a bit frustrated with herself that she had no real answers, for Frankie or for herself.

"Look, from what TaRhonda has told me over the years, women like you are dangerous for lesbian women. Maybe interested, maybe even want to have sex, but then what? At the end of the day, you're straight and are going to absolutely break their heart. Hell, maybe she's afraid of you, Libby. Maybe she really, *really* likes you, but is scared."

Libby studied her friend. "Scared? Scared of getting hurt? By me?"

"Yeah," Frankie said. "Absolutely. And, she's a bit older than you, so I imagine there's probably some sort of history there for her. What exactly has she done? To you. To make you so angry."

Libby played with the spoon in her coffee as she felt the pain again, the rejection, the growing chasm between them. "She's pushing me away," she said softly. "I never thought that could be so painful." She sighed, then took the spoon out and rested it on the small plate Frankie had provided. She met an understanding, dark gaze. "It definitely hurts." She took a small sip before adding, "You know what's crazy, though, why I was so upset when I came back into Faith and Wyatt's house today, is that she's jealous."

"Of what?"

"You," Libby said with a smirk.

"What? Of me? Why?"

"Remember that weekend, the first one Noah went with Tucker and you were crying on your porch after they left?" Libby asked gently.

Frankie looked down at the mug of coffee she held in her hands. "All too well. You were so wonderful. And that lasagna you had made was spectacular."

Libby smiled. "Yes, well the bottle of sweet red you insisted on contributing totally topped it off. Well, anyway, she'd come by, not sure why, and saw you come to my place with the wine."

"Ah hell. She thought—"

"She did," Libby said, nodding.

"Shit." Frankie set her mug down. "Should I say something to her?"

"Absolutely not," Libby said, shaking her head. "She's a grown ass woman. If she wants to know, she can ask me." She took another sip. "Frankie, Grace has no claim on me. Believe me, she's made that very clear. You and I are friends, and you were having a really horrible night dealing with your son being gone with his dad for the first time over an entire weekend. We have nothing to apologize for or explain."

"Which, I can't tell you how much I appreciated you being there for me that day, Libby," Frankie said earnestly. "I mean it. Doing the single mom thing is hard enough and sure as hell lonely, but watching my baby boy leave my house for two whole days…not cool." She cleared her throat as the last couple words were tripped up by threatening emotion in her voice.

"Aww," Libby said, touched. She reached over and covered one of Frankie's hands in friendly affection. "I'm so glad I was home that night." Libby glanced over at the coffee table in the other room where she'd left her keys and phone when she heard it ring. "Be right back."

Libby slid off the stool and hurried to the other

room and picked up her phone. Noting that it was Faith calling, she answered.

"Hey, lady. Did I forget something?" She listened, immediately alarmed by her tone. "What?" Her heart jumped into her throat. "Where?"

⁂

She kept hearing Faith's words over the phone in her head over and over again: *horrible accident... one fatality...Grace and Colby involved...* Faith knew nothing more than that those involved had been taken to Tunston.

She was halfway there, the tears refusing to stop. Frankie had stayed behind, as Tucker was due back at her house with Noah within the hour. So, she drove alone, pushing the speed limit, determined to get there as quickly as possible. She reached up, yet again, and wiped away more silent tears that continuously slid down her cheeks.

Her mind replayed her conversation with Frankie just moments before. It raced to all the feelings that it had brought up, feelings she didn't fully understand. What she *did* understand in that moment was that she didn't know what she'd do if Grace had been killed. What if she never got to talk to her again? Touch her again? Tell her that she meant something to her? What if...what if their final interaction on this earth had been words of anger?

Libby sniffled as she absently reached around inside the console between the front seats for the small package of tissue she kept there, not taking her eyes off the road. Finding what she was looking for, she used her wrist to slam the console lid down and fingers to tug a tissue out of the plastic package. She wiped her cheeks and blew her nose, sending silent prayers to the heavens as she drove.

Making the forty-some minute drive in just over thirty, Libby found a place to park and climbed out of her car, locking it before she ran toward the red brick building that served as the trauma hospital for Wynter when their little medical facility was not sufficient.

She found the information desk, nearly out of breath from her parking lot sprint. She braced her weight on her hands. "Hi." She gasped, swallowing as she tried to catch her breath, the man sitting behind the desk looking up at her like she'd lost her mind. "Sorry. I need to know where Sergeant Grace Montez and Officer Colby LeCroix of the Wynter Police Department have been taken."

The man turned to his computer and began to type on the keyboard using slow, chicken-peck strokes. Libby wanted to shove him out of the way and look for herself. Somehow, she managed to keep her composure together even as her heart raced in her chest.

"It was John LeCroix, you said?" he asked, glancing up at her over the top of his glasses.

"No, Colby," she corrected.

"Colby," he murmured. "With a 'C?'"

"Yup," she nearly bit out, her anxiety growing by the second.

"Okay, Colby LeCroix is just now being moved from recovery into ICU from surgery," he explained.

Libby felt a stab of fear in her gut. "Okay. Is he okay? What happened?"

"You'll have to speak to his doctors, ICU is on the fourth floor," he said.

She nodded. "And, Grace Montez?" This time she spelled out both first and last names.

Bushy gray eyebrows drew. "With a 'Z', not an 'S,' correct?"

"Yes."

He typed in a few more things then shook his head. "I have nothing here for a Grace Montez."

Libby felt her stomach drop. "Wait, you have to. They were brought in together. Grace Montez," she said, her voice growing a bit shrill with her desperation. "Please look again."

The man struck a handful of keys with fat-tipped fingers before again shaking his head. "I have no record of Grace Montez, ma'am."

"What, what does that mean?" Libby asked, terrified of what he'd say.

"Well, it means either she was never admitted into this facility or she passed on. I don't have death records, only those who were admitted."

Libby's hand flew to her mouth as she felt like she was about to throw up. "Oh god," she whispered, eyes closed as she tried to calm her stomach. "Okay," she breathed, hand falling away. "Where did you say ICU is again?"

Libby headed in the direction she was pointed to. She stood with two other people on the elevator, which seemed to take three hours to reach the fourth floor. Finally, they arrived with a cheery *ding* before the doors slid open.

She hurried down the corridor, no clue where the main desk was. Her heart was racing and she was near tears. She had no idea what to do. Should she continue to look for Colby, or start calling around to find out where Grace was? She decided to find the desk for ICU to see what she could find out about Colby, but also ask what she needed to do to find out about Grace.

The corridor she was walking down was about to come to an end at a perpendicular hallway. Stopping at the juncture of the T, she looked to her right and saw nobody, only closed hospital room doors. Turning to the left, she saw a doctor standing at the center of the corridor, white jacket over green scrubs. He was talking to someone. The person was a woman, and Libby's heart nearly bounced out of her chest.

The doctor said a few more things, then with a smile turned and walked away, leaving the woman standing alone. Libby took a couple steps closer, unable to breathe. Her eyes bore into the back of the woman's head, but she could see the woman was dressed in BDU pants and a dark quilted jacket. She desperately wanted to believe it was—

"Grace," she whispered as the woman turned around to face her, standing thirty feet away.

Grace's hair was down, no longer in the bun it had been earlier that day. She had a white bandage at her left temple and there was dried blood on the right side of her face. The front of her uniform shirt was badly stained with blood.

Recognition entered Grace's eyes and she took a step forward, which seemed to knock Libby out of the daze she was in. She took off toward Grace, who caught her up in her arms, holding her almost painfully tight.

Sobs burst from Libby's throat as she held on, her face buried in a warm neck. She could smell a strange menagerie of scents: sweat, blood, and smoke. "Oh my god," she breathed out. "Oh my god."

Grace held her, one of her hands cupping the

back of Libby's head. "It's okay," she whispered, Libby's entire body trembling with her sobs. "It's okay. I'm okay."

Slowly, Libby's sobs began to ease into tears and finally into sniffles. She lifted her head and looked into Grace's face. She looked battered and bruised, and her eyes were hollow. Libby's hand came up and lightly cupped her cheek. "Are you okay?"

Grace nodded. "Overall. Gonna be sore as hell in the morning, but nothing's broken." She gave Libby a weak smile.

"What happened?" Libby asked, the two of them moving over toward the wall as a couple of nurses headed their way and needed to pass.

"Guy ran from us, wanted on a warrant. Caused a horrible accident." She let out a heavy breath, running her hand through her hair, which was badly matted with knots and blood. "He didn't make it, and Colby…" She nodded toward a door a few doors down from them. "He may never walk again. They don't know yet."

Libby's eyes grew wide and her hands raised to her mouth. "Oh no."

"Yeah, the doctor said they just won't know until some of the swelling goes down how bad the damage is. Nobody can see him tonight." Grace looked so tired.

Libby's hand cupped Grace's face again, olive-green eyes sliding closed as Grace leaned into the touch. "Let me take you home."

Grace said nothing, simply nodded.

Chapter Twenty-four

"I think your mama fibbed," Libby said softly, enjoying the feel of the soft fur underneath her fingers. "She said you didn't like anybody, sometimes not even her. Yet, here you are, all rumbly." She smiled, charmed as the cat lying on her lap rolled from her side partially to her back. "I see a tummy."

"I never thought I'd ever see such a thing."

Libby glanced up to see Grace standing in the entryway of the living room. She was freshly showered, her face cleaned of the blood and grime, hair slicked back from her face. Her bandage had been replaced at her temple. She was dressed in a simple pair of cotton pajama pants and T-shirt. Cleaned up, Libby could see how bruised and cut up Grace's beautiful face was. She wondered about the rest of her—how bad of shape was she in?

Libby smiled at her before looking back down at the cat in her lap. "Yeah, after I finished making the pot of coffee you asked me to make, this little one jumped up on the couch." She glanced up at Grace, who was walking over to the couch. "Hope she's allowed, sniffed me for about two minutes then plopped down next to me. Slowly she made her way onto my lap."

"Traitor," Grace muttered as she sat down just over from Libby and Mama Peeps.

"Me or the cat?" Libby asked with a smile.

Grace raised an eyebrow. "Yes!" They shared

a smile for a moment before Grace looked away, her shoulders slumped and hands tucked into her lap. "Ready for a cup of coffee?" she asked, hands placed on the cushion on either side of her and looking like she was about to stand again.

"Let me," Libby said, reaching over and placing a resting hand to Grace's thigh. Realizing what she was touching, her fingers slid off and onto the cushion. "After all," she added with a rueful grin. "I know how you like it." As though sensing she was about to be moved, Mama Peeps jumped up on all fours, digging her claws into Libby's lap before jetting off to the floor. Libby sat there, stunned. "What did I do?"

Grace chuckled. "You breathed. Cats don't like when you do that."

Libby met her gaze then shook her head. "Ay yai yai."

She stood and moved around the coffee table toward the kitchen. She'd found where the coffee mugs were when she'd gotten the pot started. There had been one in the sink strainer placed upside down. She figured it was probably from that morning and Grace's favorite cup, or certainly one she liked if she'd used it, so she grabbed it for Grace and another from herself out of the cabinet.

A handful of minutes later, she returned to the living room. She half expected Grace to be asleep, but she sat there, elbow resting against the back cushion and her uninjured temple resting against her hand. She looked so tired, so weary. Libby set Grace's mug down on the coffee table just long enough to retrieve a coaster from the set at the center of the table, placing one on the table in front of Grace and the mug atop it, then one for herself.

"You look so tired, Grace," she said softly. "Are you sure you don't want me to leave? Let you get to bed?"

Head still braced against her hand, Grace's eyes met Libby's and held for a long moment. Libby thought she saw in Grace's eyes the same thing that had been in Libby's heart the night of the attack at the diner, which seemed so long ago. That need for Grace to stay, for her comfort.

Libby decided to go out on a limb. "Do you want me to stay?"

Grace said nothing for a long moment before softly saying, "I do."

❦❦❦❦

Her eyes slowly opened, blinking a few times before they stayed open. She tried to make anything out in the darkness of the room around her, but wasn't able to. A moment later, she realized what it was that had woken her. The bed began to shake again. She glanced to her left, where Grace lay. Just barely, she heard the tiniest sound of a sob.

Libby's heart broke. There was no reason for Grace to literally suffer in silence. That was why she was there. "Grace?" she whispered.

The shaking immediately stopped, followed by a sniffle clearly trying to be stifled. "Yeah?" came the small, thick voice.

"Can I, can I hold you?" Libby asked. She had no clue how to do such a thing but felt utterly compelled to ask.

There was silence for a moment before sounds of Grace moving and covers being shifted. Libby, who lay on her back, simply stayed put, not sure what to do. She felt her left arm lifted and Grace's body move until it was snuggled against Libby's side, her arm coming down over Grace's shoulders as Grace's head adjusted to lie upon Libby's shoulder.

Libby was angry at herself as she felt a wave of arousal shoot through her when she felt Grace's breast press up against her side. She pushed the thought, sensation, and image out of her mind as she focused on why she was there.

"Is this okay?" Libby asked, feeling Grace adjust her body a bit more. "Are you comfortable?"

"Mm-hmm," Grace murmured. "I've never been held before."

Libby smiled. "I've never held anyone before, so guess we're doing good."

As they both got settled, they lay in silence for a long moment. Libby could feel the softness of Grace's cotton T-shirt beneath her fingertips, could smell the freshness of her shampoo as dark hair was so close to her nose. She could feel Grace's soft, warm breathing brush against her upper chest, the bit that was revealed as the neckline of her T-shirt scooped a bit. She could feel Grace's hand resting against Libby's right side, fingers just lightly curved around beneath her back.

It felt wonderful.

"What's the bandage for?" she asked softly.

"The guy shot at me," Grace said evenly.

"What?" Libby gasped. "Oh my god. What kind of monster was he?"

"The kind who left his fourteen-year-old son on the side of the road while he went scurrying off like a scared little rabbit. He only grazed me. Took a few stitches."

"I'm so sorry. So unnecessary." Libby rested her cheek against Grace's forehead. "Am I hurting you?" she whispered, concerned about the injury to the older woman's left temple.

"No," Grace said, snuggling in a little more. "Not at all. You see," she added. "That's what gets me about crime and criminals—it's *all* unnecessary. It's all about choices, and these people make some really bizarre, stupid, and selfish choices. It really makes me sad."

"Does it frustrate you?" Libby asked, her fingers finding themselves playing lightly in the strands of dark hair, careful to stay away from the bandaged area.

"Oh, absolutely. Sometimes I just want to smack them around and be like, 'What are you doing? You're destroying your life, fool!'"

Libby smiled. "I can imagine."

They remained silent for a moment until Grace said, "Libby, I'm sorry I didn't show up at the hot springs that night. I'm really sorry."

Though surprised by the words, Libby was glad to hear them. "Why didn't you?" she asked gently.

"I…" Grace pulled away just a bit, resting on her side next to Libby as she braced her head on an upturned palm. Libby looked up at her, just barely able to make out her features now as her eyes adjusted to the dimness. "Can I be honest with you?" Grace asked, her voice soft. "Like, really honest?"

"Of course." Libby's eyebrows fell as something occurred to her. "Are you seeing someone?"

Grace grinned and shook her head slowly. "No. Definitely no."

"Okay. Yes, Grace. I need you to be honest with me," Libby assured. "No matter what it is," she added, a bit nervous what Grace would say.

"Okay. The truth is, I'm really, really attracted to you, Liberty," Grace began softly. "And I don't know what's going on with you, if it's just a random thing with me or if you're beginning to discover some things about yourself, but if I allowed myself to be near you in that cute little bathing suit of yours, I knew I wouldn't have been able to keep my hands to myself."

Grace's words sliced right through Libby's clit, nearly making her gasp. A little voice in her head surprised her by saying, *What would be so wrong with that?* She cleared her throat, and her mind remained quiet, as it was clear Grace had more to say.

"I really like you, Libby. I respect you and I think you're a really amazing woman," Grace said, a soft smile gracing her lips. She shook her head. "I can't do that to you. I can't use you like that, and that's what it would be, because I'm not capable of anything more." She smirked. "Not saying you'd want anything more, mind you. But, I just can't..." She seemed to be searching for what she was trying to say. "I can't just do casual like that, one time deal or friends with bennies. It's not in me. Not for someone I genuinely like."

For reasons that she couldn't quite put a voice to, Libby was disappointed with Grace's admission. However, she chose to focus on her honesty. "Thank you for telling me that. I don't really know what's going on with me, either, but I know that I'm very drawn to you, and I know that I really want us to be friends. Can we do that?"

Grace's smile was radiant. "I'd like that. Very much." She looked down and away before looking back at Libby, a bit shy. "I've really missed you."

"I've missed you, too," Libby whispered.

Her eyes fell closed as Grace lowered herself and pulled Libby into a hug, a warm, wonderful hug that lasted for several minutes. It was almost like a reset, she felt. Like, everything that had happened over the past couple months, the negative, the confusing, just disappeared, replaced with a silent acceptance.

Grace raised her head and, as if it were the most natural thing in the world for her to do, she brushed her lips against Libby's, who responded, their lips moving together in a beautiful dance of lips. Though sensual, Libby understood it was meant as an understanding of a connection and bond they had that could never be more than it already was.

The kiss came to a natural end and Grace urged Libby to turn over on her right side. When she did, Grace moved up behind her and wrapped her in her arms. Libby fell into a deep, dreamless sleep.

※ ※ ※ ※

She stood there looking down at him. The entire left side of his face was a mass of bruises, a long laceration running down along his left cheek to his neck. She figured that would likely be a scar. His eyes were closed, face relaxed. He was intubated, the tube coming from his mouth taped to his face and leading to an intricate system of machines that beeped and gasped along with his vitals.

Libby glanced behind her and saw the chair so she reached for it, pulling it up to the bed. She sat down and reached through the bars of the bedrails to take his hand. She was careful, as an IV had been inserted into and taped to the back of his hand, the line connected to an IV that sent lifesaving fluids into his body.

"I'm so sorry, Colby," she said softly, her thumb rubbing gently across the backs of his fingers. She'd seen the condition of the accident scene on the news that morning, and it had been horrific. If she hadn't spent the night in Grace's embrace, it would have been so much worse. Just knowing she'd literally walked away from that, somehow, had made it palatable. Or, perhaps, emotionally survivable for her.

Now, looking at this young man, only twenty-six, her heart went out to him. Colby certainly went about things the wrong way at times, but he wasn't a bad person. She felt for the right woman, one who could hold his feet to the fire and knock him down a peg when he needed it, he could be a really good partner. He deserved that chance.

Doctors wouldn't tell her anything since she wasn't family, so she was going to talk to his parents. She was just grateful they allowed her in for a few minutes to see him. She intended to do all she could to help as his friend.

❦❦❦❦

The reopening of Pop's had been a huge hit with everyone except for Pops himself. The townsfolk said they liked the changes, it was bringing in a younger crowd, and tourists seemed to love it, too. Pops was not a fan of the new look.

Libby wandered through the dining room, stopping at the tables to make sure everybody had everything they needed and to find out how their dining experience had been going. So far, so good.

"How are you, Mr. Banks?" she asked, walking over to a table where a man, probably in his seventies, sat eating alone. "I haven't seen you in forever."

"Been at my grandson's place in Tucson," he said, looking up at her and smiling, a pug's worth of wrinkles smiling along with him.

"Oh, yeah? I think you got yourself a tan, too," she said with a little grin. She lightly squeezed his shoulder before moving on.

As she headed toward the lunch counter, she noticed a familiar figure that had just sat down, back to her. She smiled as she snuck up behind her.

"Freeze," she murmured in her ear. She grinned when Grace jumped, her head whipping around to see who was behind her. Libby waved with her fingers.

"Brat," Grace muttered.

"You know it," Libby said as she made her way around the counter to stand in front of her favorite cop. "How are you, stranger?" she asked. It had been a week since they'd parted the morning after the accident, though they'd stayed in contact nearly daily through text and a couple phone calls.

"I am exhausted," Grace said, resting her cheek against her hand. Libby thought she certainly looked it. "I've been working doubles this week, filling in for Colby."

Libby's eyebrows drew. "Why were you working at all this week?"

"We'd be entirely too shorthanded if neither Colby nor I were there, Libby. It could be dangerous."

Libby nodded, understanding even as she was concerned. "You look like you're about to drop, Grace. You have no idea how much I admire your grit." She eyed the bruises and cuts on the beautiful face, which had begun to fade. "You got your stitches out," she noted. "Coke or coffee?"

"Coke. Yup. Yesterday," Grace said, taking one of the laminated menus from the chrome holder.

"Oh yeah?" Libby said conversationally, filling a glass with ice before filling it with the carbonated drink from the machine. "Did you have to go back to Tunston for that?"

"Nope. I did it at Casa de Grace."

Libby glanced at her over her shoulder in confusion.

Grace grinned, bringing a hand up to her left temple and imitating the motion of scissors with her fingers. "Snip snip."

"Ouch! Grace!"

"Liberty!"

"Rebel," Libby muttered, setting the filled glass with straw in front of the detective.

"Hey, the doctor said they'd need to be taken out in five to seven days. I took them out on day six."

Libby braced her hands against the counter and stared into Grace's unrepentant gaze. "I bet you were a difficult child."

A smirk crossed her lips. "Still am."

"Oh, I'm sure," Libby retorted, her voice nearly a purr. She cleared her throat and stepped away from the counter when she realized where her mind was going. *Bad girl.* "So," she said, changing the subject. "I heard Colby is doing well." She leaned down on her forearms on the counter. "I've been twice, but he was asleep both times."

Grace nodded. "He's doing okay, I guess. He's supposed to go home next week sometime." She let out a heavy sigh as she tore off the paper from her straw and slid the neon orange drinking implement into the liquid. "With a broken back, he's got a long road ahead of him."

"Will he walk?" Libby asked, concerned.

"Not sure. His doctors seem to be optimistic, but I guess we'll see how he heals, how well he takes care of himself, how responsive he is to physical therapy." Grace shrugged. "Up to him, honestly."

Libby studied Grace for a long moment, cocking her head slightly to the side. "Why do you look like you want to ask me something?"

"'Cuz I do," Grace murmured, a lopsided grin appearing that Libby hadn't seen before. She found it adorable. "Your…Frankie. She cleans houses and stuff. Right?"

Libby made it so she was directly in Grace's line of sight and looked her in the eye. "Grace?" she said softly.

"Yes?"

"Frankie and I are just friends," she said. "Got it? She's a single mom who moved in next door with her adorable little boy, Noah, who I'm pretty sure I'm in love with, and we became fast friends. And Grace?"

"Yes, Liberty?"

"She's straight. Very familiar with Kevin Costner's butt, just like my mom."

Grace smirked. "Is being familiar with Kevin Costner's butt a measure of a straight woman, or something?"

Libby mirrored the smirk. "If so, then I'm in trouble. I've never been particularly drawn to Kevin Costner's butt."

Chapter Twenty-five

"You ready back there, Libby?" Grace asked, gritting her teeth under the weight.

"Yup. Come on back." The response came from down the extremely narrow, wood-paneled hallway.

"Ready?" Grace asked Gus LeCroix.

"Yup," he muttered, face red from his load.

"Okay, Colby, here we go."

An arm wrapped around Grace's shoulders and one around his father's, the trio made very slow progress down the hallway, having to sidestep as there was no way for the three to walk normally. Colby was supposed to be in his wheelchair, but that thing barely fit in the living room, let alone down a hallway so narrow that a walking Colby's shoulders brushed either wall.

Colby groaned and grunted along the way, doing his best to help them even though it was clear he was in a lot of pain.

"Almost there, buddy," Gus said with effort.

Covered in sweat, Grace glanced up to see the back bedroom had been prepared for him. Libby had moved the room around so there were no obstacles such as his weight bench in the way, and the linens had been changed with hospital-corners care.

"Libby, can you hold on to the end of the bed to make sure it doesn't move or rock too bad?" Grace managed.

Without comment or question, Libby jumped to

action, using her body weight through her hands to do as asked.

Grace and Gus were able to get Colby turned around so his back was to the bed, facing a Gold's Gym poster taped to the wall above the dresser. Grace was slightly amused, but only for a second as they slowly got the very heavy man lowered onto the mattress. He grunted in pain again, eyes closed as he seemed to be trying to breathe his way through it.

She glanced over at Gus, who was getting to his feet from the bed. "You okay, Mr. LeCroix?" she asked.

He nodded, running a hand over his buzz-cut hair, turning to look down at his son and Grace. "Thanks for helping me. He's just too damn big to do it myself."

Grace stood. "Absolutely no problem." She turned to see that Libby was already on the opposite side of the bed helping Colby to move into the right position with his head lying on the freshly fluffed pillow.

"I gotta get to work, got an overnight run, but I'll be by tomorrow, son," Gus assured Colby.

Colby, lying there with his eyes closed, face somewhat contorted in pain, simply nodded a bit in acknowledgement.

Grace chatted a bit with Colby's father, but she kept her peripheral eye on Libby. She watched how she spoke to Colby, how she was with him as she gently removed his tennis shoes and then his socks at Colby's nod. He was already dressed in sweatpants and a T-shirt. She made sure he was comfortable, lightly joking with him, bringing a ghost of a smile to Colby's chapped lips.

She watched the way Colby responded to her as she essentially tucked him in. The way that her gentle touch, deep compassion, and almost ethereal understanding of what he needed seemed to bring him out of himself for just a moment. She hadn't seen that since he'd woken from the three-day medically induced coma they'd had him under to get the swelling to go down in his brain.

Libby glanced up from her task for a moment, her gaze meeting Grace's and holding it before her attention was brought back to Colby, who said something to her so quietly Grace couldn't hear.

A small smile touching Grace's lips, she turned her focus back to Gus. Their conversation finished, she walked with him back down the narrow hallway to the cluttered living room.

"I'm gonna bring a truck over here tomorrow," he said, looking around. "Get some of this stuff out of here for the time being." He met Grace's eyes. "Doctor said he needed to be up and walking and without anything to trip on." He indicated the small living room around them. "This place is one giant tripping hazard."

Grace heard what he said and, as she looked around, she agreed. It wasn't that the place was messy, it was just a small trailer, so cluttered was basically the rule of the day. "I think we can get this chair out of here," she said, resting a hand on the back of an aged plaid armchair. "It's big and bulky, and I think the couch would be better for him right now. Even three of the four kitchen chairs can be taken out for now."

Gus nodded, stroking his chin. "I can make that happen." He turned to Grace and extended his hand, which Grace took. "Listen, Sergeant," he said. "Me and Colby's mom owe you more than we can ever repay for saving our boy. Thank you."

"Of course. He's done the same for me, sir."

After a firm shake of the hands, Gus nodded and left the premises. A few moments later, Libby joined Grace in the small kitchen. The place was a mess, but the mess of a bachelor who had run out of the house to get to work on time, fully expecting to return home after his shift and wash the dishes in the sink and fold the laundry tossed out on the couch. He certainly hadn't thought he'd be returning home only after nearly two weeks in the hospital, one week of that spent in ICU.

"Do you want the laundry, or do you want the dishes?" Libby asked, hands on hips as she looked around.

Grace quirked her lips into a rueful grin. "I'll flip ya for it."

A handful of minutes later, Grace was up to her elbows in soapy water, scraping food that seemed to be glued on. Clearly, Colby didn't believe in rinsing his dishes after they were used, especially if they had to sit for a minute before handwashing, as there was no dishwasher.

"What all does Frankie do for her clients?" Grace asked, looking over to where Libby was folding yet another T-shirt. She had to wonder just how many her colleague had. There were already two piles of them.

Libby met her gaze, tucking the collar of the current shirt under her chin as she folded the sleeves and garment into a perfect department store square. "What do you mean?"

"For extra money, her side hustle, she's cleaning Wyatt and Faith's house, right? Does she do any organizing or anything like that?"

Libby stared at her and a slow smile spread across her lips as she finished with the T-shirt and tossed it down onto the coffee table to start a third pile. "That's friggin' brilliant." She indicated the trailer around them. "You mean here, right?"

Grace nodded. "Yeah. I mean, I don't have the time." She smirked. "Or the patience, and not sure that's exactly what you want to do with your free time. His mom is wheelchair bound and can't even get into this place, and Gus is busy driving his big rig, so..."

Libby looked around. "I think that is such a good idea, Grace. This place isn't that big, so it honestly wouldn't take much." She chewed on her bottom lip for a moment before giving Grace a side-glance. "Want me to ask her? I know that you're not a huge fan—"

"Hey," Grace said softly, walking over to the breakfast bar, just big enough for two stools, that separated the kitchen from the tiny dining nook and living room. She rested her hands on the Formica bar top, stained and scarred from decades of use and abuse. "I have nothing against Frankie, Libby. I truly don't. I acted like an ass, and I'm sorry for that. I needed to use my big girl words, and didn't. That's on me. Frankie did nothing wrong, nor did you."

Libby walked over to the breakfast bar, opposite side of Grace. She looked down at her hands for a moment, which rested on the back of one of the high-backed stools, then reached over and wrapped her fingers around those of Grace's right hand. Without thinking, Grace returned the gesture. It was such a natural thing to do.

Grace had never allowed herself to be a very

touchy-feely person, but for whatever reason, when she was around Libby physical affection just seemed like what was supposed to happen—both for her to initiate it and, most importantly, to accept it.

"Thank you for that, Grace," Libby said, her voice soft and earnest. "She's a good person. I think you'd really like her." She squeezed Grace's fingers and, to Grace's surprised disappointment, slid her hand back to her side of the bar. "Want me to ask her about this?" Libby asked, indicating the trailer around them.

Grace considered the offer for a moment then shook her head. "No. If it's okay, I'd like to talk to her about it. Hire her, if she's game."

Libby studied her for a long moment, head slightly cocked to the side. "You know, tomorrow night Frankie and Noah are coming over for dinner. Four-year-old's choice, which of course, means little worms in goo with doggie bites."

Grace stared at her. "What on earth is that?"

Libby chuckled. "Basically, mac and cheese and cut up hotdogs. Why don't you join us? And," she added. "Noah is obsessed with fire trucks and police cars."

Grace: Are they there?
Libby They are.
Grace: Okay, I'm just down the street. Call for him?
Libby: Yes! So excited!!!!

Grace smiled. She texted her friend and

colleague and then set her phone on her thigh as she pulled her car up to the curb in front of Libby's house. Something in her rearview mirror caught her eye and her smile returned when she saw the flashing police lights followed by the *whoop, whoop!* of the siren.

She watched as the squad car pulled up to the curb in front of Libby's driveway, lights continuing to flash. The front door to Libby's house opened and she stood there, a *very* wide-eyed four-year-old standing with her. He was a handsome little boy, hands braced against the glass of the glass-and-metal door.

Grace had initially considered bringing a squad car herself, but with the department being down two cars now, she wasn't comfortable borrowing one. At least Officer Tate was on duty, ready to go at any time he may be needed, whereas she was off duty.

Grace chuckled when she saw Frankie come up behind the little guy, wrestling with him to put his winter coat on as he struggled to get out of the house. Finally, he was appropriately dressed for the cold October night. He pushed open the door and jetted across the snow-covered grass to the squad car that her colleague had exited and was standing next to. Grace noticed that Frankie and Libby were also stepping out of the house, Frankie following literally in her son's footsteps and Libby walking over toward Grace.

The two women stood side by side, shoulders touching, as they leaned against the passenger side of Grace's car, watching. The officer gave Noah a complete tour of the car, let him turn on the siren and the lights. He even got to "arrest" his mother.

"Isn't he adorable?" Libby whispered. "He's utterly enthralled."

"Yeah," Grace agreed softly. "Cute kid."

"I can't believe you did this for him," Libby said, shaking her head, a look of wonder on her face. "Probably the sweetest thing I've ever seen someone do."

Grace looked away, feeling a bit overwhelmed by the radiance of Libby's gratitude, like a warm summer day if the sun's spotlight could be directed at one person alone. "Glad I could do it," she finally said, feeling a bit short for words under the weight of Libby's direct attention. And presence. Under what amounted to their truce of intentions, Libby felt so close was yet so far; so near to hug, even for an unexpected kiss between friends, yet so utterly untouchable.

"So, I was thinking," Libby said softly, too quiet to interrupt what was happening with Noah and his special moment. "Halloween is just around the corner, which means the holidays are next."

Grace nodded. "Yes."

"Soooo, how about coming to my parents' house for Thanksgiving?" Libby asked.

Grace watched Noah try on the policeman's uniform hat and smiled as it fell over the boy's eyes, far too large for his head. She felt nervous at the invitation, though she wasn't sure why. "I'm working on Thanksgiving this year."

"How do you know this far out?" Libby asked, meeting Grace's gaze.

Grace grinned. "Because I volunteered. Every year I usually alternate Thanksgiving and Christmas, let the people with families or significant others have that time."

"Well, that's sweet of you to do that, but what about you? You're off Christmas, then?"

Grace was surprised to hear the tone in

the younger woman's voice, almost a mixture of sadness and desperation. "Yes, for Christmas, unless something happens. But, what do you mean, 'What about me?'" She shrugged, shoving her hands into the pockets of her heavy jacket as the cold was beginning to settle into her bones from lack of movement and leaning against an ice-cold car. "What about me? I don't really have any family to see, certainly don't have a significant other." She shrugged again. "The gals and guys I work with do. It matters to them."

"But you have people here who care," Libby insisted. "Who want to be with you, share that with you."

Grace stared deeply into Libby's eyes, seeing so much open honesty there that she had to look away. It was simply too much. It was an honesty that she didn't know how to respond to. "I've never had a holiday that didn't turn into an absolute shit show," she said softly. "Drama, fighting, far more trouble than it was worth."

"It doesn't have to be like that, Grace," Libby said. "It just doesn't. I'm so sorry that's been your experience, but not every family is like that. Not every person needs that sort of bullshit to function." She turned to Grace, a soft, affectionate smile on her beautiful lips. "Look, I'll leave you alone about Thanksgiving. If you have to work, you have to work. But please consider spending Christmas with me and my family, okay?" She gave Grace a smile that warmed Grace right up. "I'm having it at my house this year. First time I've ever been able to do that, ever had the room." She laughed. "I mean, my house isn't as big as my folks', but it's sure as hell bigger than a one-bedroom apartment."

Grace smiled, remembering all too well those cramped days of her past. "Won't your mom be disappointed not having it at her house?" she asked, hating the need to take the topic of conversation off herself with a distraction.

"Are you kidding? She's thrilled not to have to deal with the mess or the possibility of my dad blowing up the house with his crazy fantasies of deep-frying the turkey."

Grace smiled at that. "I can imagine."

"Please?" Libby said, stepping a bit closer to Grace, her hand reaching out to wrap around Grace's arm. "Please tell me you'll think about it at least?"

Grace studied Libby's face for a long moment, not wanting to commit to anything, but finally nodded. "Yes, I'll think about it."

As seemed to happen every time they were together in recent days, Grace felt an unmistakable and unspoken connection between them, a silent communication, though she wasn't entirely certain what the conversation was about. And, true to form, as yet another link formed in her chain of need for Libby, so did another brick fall into place in the wall around her heart.

Forcing herself to look away from those seemingly bottomless brown eyes, it was only then that Grace realized they had company. Frankie stood on the sidewalk holding a newly "deputized" Noah in her arms, the boy proudly displaying the plastic gold badge Officer Tate had pinned to his jacket before leaving. Each squad car had a clear plastic bag of the child-sized badges in the glove compartment for community relations.

She noted Frankie had an interesting expression

on her face, a small smile that seemed to be part amusement and part concern. She cleared her throat and turned her attention to the excited little boy.

"How'd it go, Noah?" she asked.

"Can you tell the sergeant thank you?" Frankie asked her son.

To Grace's surprise, he held out his arms to her. She accepted the bundle of adorableness as well as the tight hug he gave her with his arms around her neck. Unable to hold back her smile, she hugged him in return.

"Thank you for making the officer come here," he said into the hug.

She chuckled. "Any time, kiddo." She looked past the handsome little boy just in time to see a look pass between Frankie and Libby. For some reason, she felt like she was the answer to a riddle that she hadn't known they were trying to solve.

Chapter Twenty-six

Grace pulled onto the LeCroix property. A glance in her rearview mirror showed her that Frankie's little SUV was following behind. The property was hard to find unless a person knew where they were going. The ten-acre property had a small two-story house on it, which was where Gus and Misty LeCroix lived, their son in the trailer mounted on a cement foundation at the rear of the property off by itself.

She pulled to a stop in front of Colby's trailer, noting his truck parked there. Somebody must have gotten it from the police department parking lot for him since she'd been there the week before. She raised her hand in greeting as Frankie pulled in beside her. The trailer didn't have much of a defined yard nor driveway, and at the moment was nothing but snow-packed ground.

"Hey there," she said.

"You were so right." Frankie laughed as she climbed out of her SUV. "This place would've been a bear to find, especially only living here for such a short time."

"Hey," Grace grinned. "I've lived here for nearly five years now and I almost pass up that road back there every time." She clapped her gloved hands together. "Ready?"

"Wait," Frankie said, reaching out to touch

Grace's arm to halt her.

Grace turned and looked back at her. "Have you changed your mind? If you don't want to do this, I totally—"

"No, that's not it." Frankie gave her a reassuring smile. "I just wanted to talk to you for a second."

"Okay, sure." Grace turned to face her. "What's up? Are you okay? Noah?"

Frankie grinned. "Oh yeah, he's just fine now that he likes Officer Tate more than his own mother, thank you very much."

Grace returned the grin. "Yes, well."

"Yes, well nuthin'." The two shared a short laugh. "Anyway, no we're fine. I just wanted to thank you again for what you did for my son. This has been a tough year for him, with the divorce and the move and everything. We're both still adjusting, and Libby has truly been a godsend for me. I've never connected with someone on a friend level as quickly as I did with her. I'm grateful for her, you know?"

Grace nodded, definitely able to understand that. "Sure."

"She does so much for so many people in this town. I'd really like to see her happy. She deserves that." She smiled. "I don't know you all that well, but I'd like to see you happy, too, Grace."

Not sure what to say, and feeling a bit cornered, Grace nodded. "Thank you," she said. She didn't know if Libby had spoken to her about their situation, or if Frankie had picked up on something on her own, but Grace felt very uncomfortable. She wasn't one to share her personal situations or feelings with friends, and she pushed down a small spark of irritation that perhaps Libby had.

"So," Frankie continued, fidgeting a bit. "Um, ready?"

Grace forced a smile. "Let's do it."

Grace led the way up the somewhat rickety steps to the small wooden stoop at Colby's front door. She brought up a hand and rapped firmly on it in the way only law enforcement could, even if they weren't there for a raid or an arrest. She heard nothing, so knocked again. A moment later, she received a text. Looking down at it, she saw it was from Colby, telling her to come in, the door was unlocked. She'd spoken to him the night before to make sure he was still on board with the plan for Frankie to help him out.

"He must be lying down," she said, glancing down the stairs at Frankie, who waited with her gloved hand on the wooden railing. "He said go on in."

Turning the doorknob, Grace pushed open the front door of the trailer to see that the work she and Libby and Gus had done was all for naught. The place looked like a tornado had torn through it, leaving behind a trail of clothing, food wrappers, and dishes in its wake.

"Uh boy," she muttered, looking around.

"I can certainly see why he needs my services," Frankie said, stepping in behind Grace, shutting the door behind them.

Grace gave her a rueful grin. "So, you're sure?"

Frankie laughed. "Believe it or not, I've dealt with a lot worse."

"You are a better woman than I. Hey, Colby, where you at?" she called out.

"Bedroom," she heard in response.

"You decent?"

"So I'm told."

Grace rolled her eyes and headed that way, Frankie following. In the bedroom, Colby sat up in his bed, braced by a nest of pillows. He looked like he hadn't shaved in a couple days, his facial hair growth uneven and grizzled. He looked tired, but Grace was grateful to see him sitting up, watching TV.

"Hey," she greeted, looking around the bedroom. It wasn't as bad as the living room and kitchen, but definitely needed some attention. "Colby, this is Frankie. Frankie, Colby."

Colby glanced over at the woman who stood next to Grace and raised a hand in greeting. "Hey."

"Hi there," Frankie said cheerily. "Nice to meet you. So," she asked, hands on hips. "What exactly do you need from me?"

He shrugged. "I dunno. She hired you," he muttered, nodding at Grace.

"And, your gratitude is earth shattering," Grace quipped. "How about you try being grateful instead of an asshole?"

Colby stared at her, eyes wide with what seemed to be surprise. He brought up a hand and ran it over his hair, which was longer than she'd ever seen it. Gone was the high and tight and in its place was a messy short mop. It made her sad, as Colby was always a very well-put-together man, on the job or off. Now, he was the poster boy for depression and lack of give-a-shit.

He took a deep breath, then turned back to the women standing next to his bed. "I can't really bend over all that easy," he said. "So, it's really tough for me to pick stuff up. Can't really stand in one place for long."

Frankie patted the edge of the bed. "Mind?"

He indicated with his hand she was free to sit. She did and brought her phone out of her pocket. Grace figured she must be using a notepad app or something. "Okay, let's go over what you need done, okay?" she said sweetly, meeting Colby's gaze before returning her attention to her phone.

"Are you guys good here?" Grace asked, noting the time. She needed to get home and get ready for work.

"Oh yeah, all good," Frankie said, her focus never leaving her phone.

Grace reached over and squeezed Colby's shoulder before turning and leaving.

༄༄༄༄༄

With a sheepish grin, Grace opened the door. "Thanks for coming." She stepped aside, allowing Libby to enter, toolbox in tow. "I'm the worst lesbian ever. Can't even use power tools," she said with a chuckle, closing the door before leading the way to the kitchen. "Think they'll revoke my lesbian card."

A cackle escaped Libby's throat as she followed behind. "Does that mean you'd have to switch teams?"

Grace glanced at her over her shoulder, and raised her eyebrow. "I'd slit my wrists first."

"Oh my," Libby responded. "Got it. I shan't push the pee-pee on you, then."

"Have you been hiding something from me?" Grace asked, playing along.

Libby eyed her, a sexy little grin on her lips as she stood in front of Grace's dishwasher, which had stopped working. "Wouldn't you like to know," she said, her tone nearly a purr.

Grace felt a flush wash through her, Libby's gorgeous body once again flashing before her mind's eye. "Not if you have a pee-pee," she managed.

Libby grinned and shook her head. "I do not. I've heard, however, that they make detachable ones." She burst into laughter again as Grace felt that earlier warmth consume her. "I had no idea you could turn that shade of red."

Grace brought up a hand to rub the back of her neck, the flesh warm to the touch. "Fix my damn dishwasher," she growled good-naturedly, though her body was about to spasm from the images that comment evoked.

Grace hopped up on a counter on the other side of the kitchen to get out of Libby's way, but also to be near in case she needed her to grab something or had questions about the dishwasher. She also wanted to spend time with her. They'd both been busy with their respective jobs, and as the holidays were coming, all the businesses that Libby managed were incredibly busy. She never knew what it was about this time of year, but people seemed to eat out more, be out more. Perhaps it was the magic of the season and the snowy weather.

"I hear it's going well at Colby's place," Libby said conversationally as she pulled out the appliance and began to look it over before taking it apart.

"Yeah? She hasn't killed him, yet?" Grace asked, lightly tapping her heels on the cabinet below.

"No, she said they've had a few really great conversations, actually." Libby looked up from where she sat on the floor. "Do you have a bucket of soapy water I can get from you?"

"Yeah, absolutely." Grace hopped down from

the counter and went about fulfilling the request Libby gave her.

"I think I found your problem," Libby said, grabbing yet another tool from her toolbox.

"Do you need a scalpel, Doctor?" Grace asked, setting the bucket of warm soapy water on the floor next to the toolbox. "Do you want a rag or a sponge?"

Libby grinned at the joke. "Sponge, please. One that you're okay with being tossed."

Grace took one from a new package under the sink with the rest of her cleaning supplies. "No worries," she said, dropping it into the bucket. "Anything else?"

"No, ma'am," Libby said, holding up a bent and crud-encrusted fork. "This was your culprit," she said, handing it up to Grace, who took it. "Yours?"

Grace looked at the pattern of the flatware and shook her head, amused. "No. God only knows how long it's been stuck in that thing."

Libby grinned as she used the soaked sponge to wipe down the innards of the dishwasher components. "These get gross over time," she explained, indicating the grease layer that coated parts of the appliance. "It's a good idea to take your stuff apart every six months or so and give it a good wipe down."

Grace threw the fork into the trash. "And what if I'm not as good as you are at taking it apart, cleaning it, and putting it back together? Well, the cleaning part I rock at, the rest, not so much."

Libby eyed her from where she was on the floor. "Then call me, silly goose and I'll do it for you." She stopped scrubbing for a second. "I'm almost done, so chop chop on that dinner you promised me."

Dinner eaten and dishes loaded into the newly working dishwasher, the two sat in the living room, a fire going on the bitterly cold late October night. The snow had stopped and it was supposed to clear up over the next few days, but November was due to come in with a bang.

Libby was curled up on the oversized chair while Grace stretched out on the couch. They'd ordered pizza and had eaten it with easy conversation. Now, they sat drinking coffee in silence. Grace stared into the flames, so loving a fire on a cold night.

"Can I ask you something?" Libby asked.

There was something in her voice that caught Grace's attention. "Of course," she said, taking a sip from her coffee.

"How'd you know you were gay? How old were you?" Libby asked softly.

"I think I knew something was different about me when I was eight or nine. When I was around fourteen, I finally came out to myself and to a couple friends at school. Honestly, it was one reason I knew I needed to get out of that house."

"The one you grew up in?" Libby clarified. When Grace nodded, she asked, "Why? How did you know that you were a lesbian?"

"Yeah. My father's wife was very religious, Catholic. Crucifies affixed to anything that would stand still. We'd always have to pray over the women who came to give birth at the house." She shook her head as she remembered it. "Just crazy. And, I knew because I was in love, as much as an eight-year-old can be, with the teenage girl who lived across the street."

She grinned, thinking about her. "Never even knew her name. But she was my standard for a long time."

"What did she look like?"

Grace grabbed her phone off the coffee table and sat up. She got on her social media account then went through the pictures of her friends until she found what she was looking for. She patted the couch. "Here."

Libby moved off the chair and to the couch. She took the phone. "She's really pretty. Is this the neighbor girl?"

"No, that's Maryann, my ex. We're still good friends. I honestly just realized that I ended up with her because she reminded me of the neighbor," Grace explained with a chuckle.

Libby glanced over at her. "Kinda creepy, there, Detective." She handed the phone back.

Grace nodded, still amused. "I know."

"Why did you come out?" Libby asked. "Like, what did it?"

"I kissed my first girl," Grace said simply.

"Really?" Libby asked. She didn't move back to the chair, but instead reached over and grabbed her coffee from where it sat on its coaster and scooted it over to where she now curled up, partially facing Grace on the couch.

"Yup. Friend from school on a dare. I knew right then and there. I had never been interested in boys, and now I knew why," Grace explained. Despite the subject matter they were discussing, she was glad Libby had moved closer. It was nice to have her near, even as she held her at arm's length.

"Oh yeah?" Libby said, interest in her voice. "So, was it like our first kiss or our second kiss?"

Grace looked down into the depths of the coffee in her mug that she held in both hands in her lap. She smiled at the memory of both kisses. Clearing her throat, she said, "Neither. It wasn't quite our second kiss."

Libby sipped from her coffee, giving Grace a side-glance before she set the mug down on the coaster and turned to her. Scooting a bit closer, she said, "So, was it like this?"

Grace's eyes fell closed as the softest touch pressed against her lips, then was gone. She slowly opened her eyes to see Libby looking back at her, six inches away. "Um," she managed. "It was a little bit more than that." She was trying to be honest about the kiss twenty years ago, but what she wanted to say was, *No, we actually got buck naked and made out. Why don't you try that?*

"Like this?" Libby murmured, again moving in.

The kiss was more than the lingering peck of the first attempt, Libby's soft, full bottom lip brushing against Grace's top lip, asking for entrance, retreating before it was granted only to return for another pass of lips moving against lips until finally, those lips disappeared for good.

Grace's heart raced. She wondered how on earth such a sweet and simple kiss could get her entire body humming, so ready to be touched. For a moment she couldn't speak, deeply affected. She brought her coffee mug to her lips and took a drink. Though the coffee had cooled, it was still warm enough to give the comfort from the inside that a hoodie or a hug gives on the outside. She felt so lost.

"Are you okay?" Libby asked quietly, moving a bit away so that her back rested in the corner made by the arm of the couch and the back cushion.

Grace nodded, grateful for a bit of physical distance. The energy between them, the connection so intense, it almost made her nauseous. She had no idea how to handle it or what to do with it. "Yes," she said finally. "And, um, yes. That was very much like it," she added with a smirk, trying to add a bit of levity to distract from how deeply she'd been affected by what amounted to a simple kiss.

Libby ran her hand over her hair before letting it drop into her lap. "I can see how that would make you come out," she murmured.

Chapter Twenty-seven

"Happy Thanksgiving!" Libby was excited to see the couple standing before her. "Woman, you're about to burst," she said, placing her hands on the bulging belly before her.

"You're tellin' me." Wyatt laughed, hands resting on her lower back. "I'm about tired of bein' a walkin', talkin' bassinet. This little one needs to get her own place, already. Happy Thanksigivin', darlin."

Libby smiled, accepting an awkward hug from the very pregnant woman. "Almost time."

"Just around a month to go," Faith added, offering a tight, one-armed hug, a large pie balanced on the palm of her other hand. "Happy Thanksgiving."

"Let me take your coats," Libby said, taking the pie from Faith and setting it on the sofa table near the door in her parents' house.

"Smells amazin' in here," Wyatt said, tugging the scarf she had loosely wrapped around her neck off then shrugging out of her winter jacket. "Thanks, darlin," she said, as Libby took the items from her.

"Is Grace here yet?" Faith asked, removing her own jacket and handing it to Libby.

"Not yet. She's working today." Libby closed the front door enough to be able to open the coat closet to hang up their items. "But she promised she'd try to come by for a piece of Mom's prized pumpkin cheesecake, so…" Libby saw another car pulling onto the property as she closed the closet door and opened the big door. "You guys go on in. Mom and Dad will be thrilled to see you."

The small SUV pulled up to the house and Libby smiled. She was glad Frankie had taken her up on the invitation to spend the holiday with her and her folks. Her neighbor and friend hadn't been sure what she was going to do, as Tucker was giving her fits. Clearly, she'd gotten it straightened out.

Her happiness was eclipsed by surprise when she saw that Frankie had a passenger in addition to her son, who was strapped into his car seat in the back. Pushing open the front door, Libby stepped out onto the porch, not sure if Colby would need help or not.

"Happy Thanksgiving," Frankie exclaimed, climbing out from behind the wheel. "I hope you don't mind, but I picked up a hitchhiker on the way."

Libby grinned, trotting down the stairs then walking over to the car as Colby pushed open the passenger door.

"More like I was hijacked," he muttered, swinging his cane out so the business end rested on the snow-covered ground.

"Hey, mister," Frankie said, opening the back door where Noah waited. "You haven't left that trailer since you got home from the hospital. There was no way in hell I was going to let you stay hidden away in there and miss such a wonderful holiday."

"Hey, I was just fine watching football in my jammies, thank you," he said good-naturedly. "I had a turkey lunchmeat dinner planned."

"Dream on, big boy," Frankie, retorted, glancing at him through the space of the SUV as she unbuckled Noah.

Libby watched the two, bemused. They sounded like an old married couple. *What the hell?* "Well, I for one am very glad you're here," she said, reaching the vehicle and holding the door open and still as Colby pulled himself out of the passenger seat. Truth was, she was thrilled to see him, and it nearly brought tears to her eyes to see him standing tall. To show that, she took him in a tight, meaningful hug once he was steady on his feet and the cane. "Happy Thanksgiving, Colby," she whispered into the hug.

"Libby!"

Libby pulled out of the hug and looked down to see a wild Noah running around the car to her. "Hey, you!" She squatted down just in time to nearly be bowled over back into the snow by the little bruiser who threw his arms around her. She returned the hug, squeezing him tight and making obnoxious noises as she pretended to bite his neck, making him giggle. She looked into his handsome face. "Are you hungry?" She grinned at his overdramatic nod.

Standing, she took the boy by the hand and accepted a hug from his mother before the four of them walked into the house.

Colby received a true hero's welcome from everyone inside, and it warmed Libby's heart to see it. As much as he tried to play it cool, she could tell he was eating it up. Maybe, just a little bit, he was getting some of his self-esteem back. He'd become a shell of the confident, cocky man she'd come to know again over the past many months. It had been hard to see that change in him. Though it was good for everyone to be knocked down a peg or two to keep perspective, she thought, he'd been knocked off the whole damn ladder.

Libby was sent to the basement to grab an extra chair for Colby. To her surprise, Faith followed her down. She turned to the older woman and smiled. "Come to help?"

"I did," Faith said with a smile. "Also to ask you for a favor."

"Sure. What's up?" Libby asked, indicating that she needed Faith to grab the other end of a folded table that was placed against the stack of folding chairs she needed to get to.

"Well, on the fourteenth, I need to fly out to California for a couple days." Faith grabbed the end of the table and helped to move it. "This has been planned for quite a while now, and I can't get out of it. It's about a company that's considering moving one of their factories into the area," she explained. "Would bring a lot of really good jobs to Wynter."

"Okay," Libby said. "Totally understandable." She grabbed two of the folding chairs just in case another surprise guest showed up.

"Wyatt isn't due for another couple weeks after that, but I'd really appreciate it if you could keep an eye on her while I'm gone," Faith said, helping to move the table back into place and accepting one of the folding chairs. "It would make me feel better and, though I don't think she'll admit it, Wyatt too."

Libby looked at the older woman, honored. "Of course," she said. "I'll move the schedule around to make sure I'm either off or have coverage if I had to leave."

"Thanks so much," Faith said, giving her a quick but tight hug. "I appreciate it more than you know."

"I can't blame you, Faith. Truly. I mean, your first baby." She shrugged as Faith stepped away from her after the hug. "I imagine I'd do the same thing." She returned Faith's smile before the mayor turned to head toward the stairs and rejoin everyone. "Faith?"

Faith stopped and turned back to her. "Yeah?"

Libby chewed on her bottom lip, wishing she'd kept her mouth shut, especially as Faith seemed to see something in her face as she leaned the chair against the wall by the stairs and walked back over to Libby.

"What's up, hon?" Faith asked softly.

And then profound humiliation. The tears came in a rush, unexpected and hard. Libby found herself in a warm embrace, soft words of comfort murmured into her hair. It took several moments, but finally her emotions became manageable. She took several deep breaths, using the sleeve of her shirt to wipe at her eyes and cheeks. She looked at Faith, afraid of seeing annoyance or irritation. All she saw was understanding and affection. That almost made her burst into fresh tears. She managed to hold it together.

"What's going on, sweetheart?" Faith asked gently, a hand on Libby's shoulder.

Libby considered the question and rolled it around in her own mind. What, indeed? She took another deep breath to center herself, then met Faith's troubled gaze. "Had you been in love before you met Wyatt?"

"I thought I was," Faith said simply. "But it took meeting Wyatt for me to truly understand what love meant, where I belonged." She shrugged with a sheepish grin. "If that makes sense."

Libby nodded. "It makes perfect sense."

Faith studied her for a moment. "Is this about Grace?"

Libby was startled by the question. "Why would

you ask that?"

Faith's expression was soft and gentle. "It's not hard to see when you guys are together, Libby. We don't know what's going on, but it's clear something is. Why the tears? Are you struggling with it?"

Libby burst into laughter, amused at the question but also a bit relieved to finally be able to talk about it. "No, ironically."

"Oh boy."

"Yup. I'm figuring things out with me, understanding more and more who I truly am, but one thing I don't question is my feelings," Libby admitted.

"And, what about Grace? Or," she added, "have you guys gotten that far?"

"No, we've talked about it." Libby hugged herself, she suddenly feeling very small, very alone. "We both admit there's an attraction, but Grace was honest and said she can't offer any more than that, and she doesn't want to use me. So, we agreed to just keep it friends."

"But you don't want to be just friends?"

Libby considered those words for a moment, then shrugged. "I don't know, Faith. I mean, I *think* I'm a lesbian. The jury is still out, but I'm pretty sure the verdict will come back guilty." She gave her friend a weak smile. "But I do know that today, looking at you and Wyatt so beautiful together, so happy, so loving toward each other, and even Frankie and her newfound friendship with Colby…"

"You crave that closeness," Faith finished softly.

Libby looked at her. "How did you know?"

"Because that's exactly how I felt when I left New York and came back here to Colorado even though I swore I was done. A garden-variety touch-me-not."

Libby grinned. "And then you meet the Southern octopus."

Faith let out a loud cackle. "Isn't that the truth. Listen," she said, sobering. "I see a lot of myself in Grace, so afraid to put herself out there after being beaten down so badly. Honestly, I think that's why she puts her all in her work. She can give of herself without losing her heart, because she is a natural giver."

"But I can't force her, Faith," Libby said, feeling deeply sad.

Faith shook her head. "No, you can't. That's up to her. All you can do is decide if perhaps she came into your life to help you find your truth and nothing more. Maybe Grace isn't your path, Libby."

Those words tore into her very soul, taking her breath away. She took a moment before asking, "How will I know that?"

Faith brought a hand up and lightly touched her cheek in a motherly gesture. "I don't know, sweetheart. I think you just need to really search yourself. How much are you willing to do without in order to have Grace in your life? Is it more painful with her there and what she's willing to give you, or without her? Only you can decide."

※ ※ ※ ※

Libby tapped her chin with her forefinger, staring at the screen before her. She stared at the different names, hoping that would give her some sort of inspiration. She had a handful or so of people that were trained for all three businesses that she could move around to fill in holes. Right now, she had a big hole. She had been the putty to fill in holes for most of the month of December, but since Faith needed her for those few days, that left brand-new holes.

"Okay, Jerry," she muttered, reaching out and pacing her hand on the mouse to highlight his name. "Let's move you to an opening shift, 'kay?"

"What if he doesn't want to open?"

Libby gasped, startled by the unexpected voice behind her. Grace stood in the open doorway, though the smile that was on her lips fell quickly away, which made Libby wonder what exactly she'd seen on her face.

"Um, they told me to come on down," she explained, hitching a thumb to the hallway and stairs beyond. "Is that okay?"

Libby hated the doubt she'd put in Grace's voice, but she also couldn't push aside how she'd been feeling the past few days since Grace had been a no-show at Thanksgiving. She indicated the other chair at the long desk that ran along the wall.

Grace entered, closing the office door behind her. Hands tucked into the back pockets of her jeans, she looked around. "Strange to see behind the curtain, as it were." She took in the wall that was dedicated to Libby's tools and "extra pieces" parts, as she called it. She smiled, glancing over at Libby, who still sat, though no longer working on the schedule. "Handy here too, huh?"

"I try and save them money where I can," Libby said, turning the office chair to face the general direction that Grace was, the older woman leaning in to look at a picture Faith had hung on the wall from opening day of the business.

"I heard about this day," she said, tapping the picture with a fingertip. "I hadn't been hired yet as the police department hadn't been brought back from the dead quite yet." She turned her full body to Libby. "Were you there that day?" she asked, taking the other seat.

"I was. I was one of the first people they hired," Libby responded. She hated how uncomfortable it was between them. It made her feel sick to her stomach. She knew why from her end, but had to wonder from Grace's. It reminded her of when somebody knew they'd screwed up and were trying to make casual chitchat to either avoid the situation or buy time.

"How was your Thanksgiving?" Grace asked, crossing an ankle over her opposite knee.

"It was nice. Colby came with Frankie." She was doing her damndest to sound conversational, though she wasn't entirely sure how successful she was.

Grace smiled with a nod. "That's what he said. Do you think there's something going on there? Between those two?"

Libby ran a hand through her hair, eyebrows drawing as she felt her emotions rising. "I don't know," she said, trying to keep her voice even and her emotional turmoil out of it. "I know they get along pretty well." She smiled, looking down at her hands in her lap. "She kicks his ass quite often to keep him in line."

"The kind of woman he'd need, for sure," Grace said, her voice trailing off. She cleared her throat. "I'm sorry."

Anger rushing to the surface, Libby's eyes flashed at her. "For which thing?" she barked. "For not showing up? For not bothering to call or text? For making me look like a fucking idiot by holding aside the last piece of pumpkin cheesecake, even when my dad wanted it, for you?"

"I ended up in Tunston until nearly ten Thanksgiving night," Grace said softly, meeting Libby's angry gaze. "Helping them with a nasty pileup accident. I didn't call you or text you because you said you had to be at work early for Black Friday the next morning."

"And the next day?" Libby demanded. "And the day after that? And the day after that?"

Grace looked down at her hand, which rested on her ankle. Her shoulders slumped and she looked like an admonished child. She simply nodded before she said, "I hope you ate that or finally let him have it."

"I fucking threw it away," Libby bit out. "Look, I don't own you and you don't owe me anything, Grace. You don't. You made it very clear to me that you don't want me for anything more than either a fuck or a friend. You're not getting the fuck, so I'm guessing I'm not worth much to you as a friend." She was angry at herself when she felt tears sting the backs of her eyes. She aggressively snatched a tissue from a nearby box, cursing under her breath when the single tissue didn't release but rather threw the box halfway across the small office.

Grace said nothing as she leaned over and grabbed it off the floor, tugging free the tissue and handing it to Libby before she placed the box gently back on the desk. "You have every right to be angry," she said. "I have been working, but you're right. There's no excuse, Libby. I'm not going to insult you further by giving you one."

"I deserve better, Grace. It shouldn't hurt me more to have you in my life than to simply walk away from you completely."

Grace's head whipped up from where she'd been once again looking down at her lap. "What?"

Libby studied her for a long moment, looking

at the beauty that was Grace, those eyes which had haunted her dreams countless times. Those lips that had tormented her, aroused her, helped her find her way home to who she truly was. She looked away as she used the tissue to wipe at her eyes, trying to catch the tears before they showed themselves.

"I just can't do this anymore, Grace," Libby said. "I can't. The shitty way you treat me sometimes aside, though that certainly plays into it, my heart hurts. I'm obviously not going to force you to be something you don't want to be, but in so doing, I can't force myself to be something I don't want to be."

"Which is what?" Grace asked, meeting Libby's gaze, hers filled with such sadness.

"Your friend. I don't want to be friends. Well, just friends. Hell, you won't even give me that." She threw her hands up. "Looking around my parents' house on Thanksgiving, the happy couples, even the growing friendship, or whatever it is, between Frankie and Colby, everyone had someone. Even Noah bonded with the dog." Her lips curled in a rueful grin. "Even with you legitimately working, and I believe you that you were, there was no special person waiting for me at home. No special message coming in just for me. Nobody out there who couldn't wait to see me again. Be with me." The tears were pushing forward again. "I want that. I need that, and I can't find my person if you're still haunting me like a ghost. Popping in when it's convenient for you, getting what you want and giving nothing in return." She sniffled, wiping her eyes.

Grace's head fell a little lower, but she nodded. "If that's what you need," she whispered.

Libby nodded, eyes closing as her heart broke. "It's what I need."

Chapter Twenty-eight

Libby went over in her mind what she'd packed into the duffel bag, ticking items off on her fingers to make sure she wasn't forgetting anything. She'd only be gone for a few days but didn't want to have to come back to the house. It was supposed to snow while she was up at the farmhouse, though thus far the weatherman wasn't calling for anything crazy.

Initially, she was just going to pencil herself in to bop around to the three locations as what she called a ghost employee—not scheduled so not expected—who could pop in and cover lunch breaks, call-outs, etc. But after talking to Wyatt she decided to just go ahead and take the three days off. There were some things Wyatt needed done that she could no longer do in her last days of pregnancy and Faith just hadn't had the time to do, so Libby offered to be Wyatt's surrogate honey-doer while Faith was out of town.

She'd told her people she was on call at all times, and that if there was an emergency she'd run in, but otherwise she was officially "out of the office." Confident she had everything, she zipped her duffel bag and slung it over her shoulder to carry out to her sedan. She had been saving money over the past months to trade it in for an SUV that would do better in the snow. Living in Pueblo, where four inches of snow was considered a good storm, the Sentra had been fine. Back in Wynter, four inches was just the appetizer.

Not that she was terribly worried, but she'd filled Frankie in about her absence, and her friend had agreed to keep an eye on her house. House locked up and herself loaded into the car, Libby was excited to head out for a few days with Wyatt.

When Libby reached the gate on their property, she stopped her car and got out. Faith had walked her through how to deactivate the automatic close feature so the gate would stay locked open. They did this before any expected measurable snow to avoid the gate being snowed shut. Gate taken care of, she got back into her Sentra and continued the rest of the way to the house.

Libby had always been one to notice the energy of a house or even a building. Yes, the people inside certainly added, both good and bad, to the energy, but she truly felt a house had its own soul, its own beating heart. She loved that of this farmhouse. The immense love and dedication of those inside of it added to the calm and peace. She hoped for that very same thing someday.

Grabbing her duffel bag and slinging the thick vinyl strap over her shoulder, Libby made her way up the stairs to the large front porch, letting herself into the house as Wyatt had texted her to do. She had been told by her doctor to stay off her feet as much as possible in the final days, so she was reclining in the living room on the couch when Libby entered the house. She also noticed the plastic tubs full of Christmas decorations Faith had brought down from the attic, asking if Libby would mind getting the decorating started. Wyatt was so miserable and ready for the baby to be born, Faith explained that the decorations and lights would help brighten Wyatt's spirits. Faith herself simply hadn't had time, trying to get everything with her work done before the baby's arrival so she'd be able to spend all her family leave focused on Wyatt and the baby.

"Hello, sweet girl!" Wyatt exclaimed from the couch, her arms already outstretched for a hug, as awkward as it was in her current position.

"Hey, lady," Libby said, squeezing as hard as she was squeezed. "It's so good to see you. I miss having you around downtown."

"Oh, believe me, darlin'." Wyatt chuckled. "I can't wait for the day me an' this little one stroll in as two separate individuals."

Libby grinned. "I'm going to go run this upstairs. Did you eat breakfast, missy?"

"I was waitin' on y'all," Wyatt called out as Libby headed for the stairs.

"Okay. I'll whip us up something when I come back down."

The one guest bedroom that was set up for guests—the other bedroom transformed into a whimsical nursery—was small, the size of the original room in the more than one-hundred-year-old farmhouse, unlike the master bedroom which had been expanded into a true master with en suite bathroom. The bed was a queen with an authentic antique brass headboard that looked to be nearly as old as the house. She dropped her duffel to the bed then headed back downstairs.

"Okay, lady," she said, standing beside the couch where Wyatt still lay. "What is Abbigail craving this morning?"

"Oh lord, don't even ask her that. If she could, she'd have y'all makin' tacos with extra hot sauce."

Wyatt grunted as she began to sit up. Libby helped her get to her feet. "Thank ya, darlin'." Once steady, she rolled her eyes. "I have to pee…again. How about waffles?"

"Waffles it is," Libby said. "Your maker still in the corner cabinet?"

"Yes, ma'am," Wyatt said, hands on her back as she waddled toward the downstairs restroom.

Thirty minutes and roughly four trips to the bathroom for Wyatt later, the two sat at the kitchen table. Libby's plate was empty, her jelly-slathered waffle and sausage links long gone while Wyatt still worked on her third helping.

"Feel like a damn beached whale," Wyatt muttered, stuffing the last of her sixth sausage link into her mouth. She chewed for a moment before eyeing an amused Libby. "Don't you say nothin' neither," she said, pointing her fork in Libby's direction.

Libby raised her hands in supplication. "Nothing to say. You're beautiful."

"You're sweet," Wyatt said, sitting back in her chair, which creaked under her as she chewed what Libby assumed was her last bite. "Have y'all talked to Grace?"

Libby shook her head. "No." She grabbed her glass of orange juice and finished what was left in it. "Like I told you that night on the phone a week or so ago," she said, placing the glass back on the table. "I need to move on. It was because of her that I found my truth and that I can say, mostly with confidence, that I'm a lesbian. I'm honestly not sure how much longer it would have taken me if I hadn't met Grace again by moving back here."

"Can I ask you somethin'?" Wyatt said softly,

finally pushing her plate away.

A bit nervous about what that "somethin'" might be, considering the quiet, thoughtful tone it was asked, Libby nodded. "Sure."

"Do you love her?"

The simple question stole Libby's breath. "Holy cow, that's a big word."

Wyatt grinned. "Just four itty bitty letters."

"Yeah, with ginormous meaning and consequence."

"Love is the most amazing and scariest thing in the world, all at once."

Libby listened to the words coming out of Wyatt's mouth, but she also focused on her eyes, noting so much brewing behind them. "Can I ask you a question that may be difficult?" she asked at length.

"Of course," Wyatt said. "But can I go pee real quick?"

Libby burst out laughing. "Tell you what, you go pee and I'll get this cleaned up, then I'll meet you in the living room."

As she cleaned up the kitchen, Libby thought about what she planned to ask the older woman. She looked up to Wyatt and Faith for so many reasons. But, as she was easing her way out of a dark, lonely closet, she was really paying attention to their relationship, how they treated each other, their dynamics. She knew they'd been through a lot in the early days of their relationship, and she'd had a front-row seat to a lot of it, but wondered how they'd found such balance between them.

She knew Wyatt and Faith were flesh and blood, human and loaded with flaws and faults like everyone was. She wondered how they'd managed to turn their differences into something that enhanced their relationship like her own parents had.

Kitchen done, she made her way to the living room and restoked the fire, noting it was beginning to burn down and it was getting cold in the house. She heard the toilet flush and a groan, which made her smile. She felt bad for Wyatt, who looked absolutely miserable. She made a note to herself that if she ever decided she wanted kids, she should do what they did and get pregnant in the spring or the summer so she wasn't huge and miserable in July.

Fire perked up, Libby went to the first storage tub and popped the lid off. She was sorting through the decorative contents when Wyatt waddled her way back to the couch.

"Oh, thank ya, darlin' for gettin' the fire rip roarin' again." She let out a heavy, tired sigh as she lowered herself back to the couch. "Now, I don't mean this as any sort of judgement," she starts. "But for those women out there who have a dozen kids on purpose…why?"

Libby grinned and shook her head. "No idea. Want this in its usual place again this year?" She held up one of the two beautiful wreaths that usually hung on the double front doors.

"Yes, ma'am," Wyatt said. "What was your question?"

Libby held the large wreath, looking down at the silver and white ornaments that were wired into the greenery and gold bells. "I know you were married before…Lucas, and obviously that ended terribly, but I have to imagine you loved him at some point. In the beginning, maybe? I say that because…can you compare how you felt about him to how you felt about

Faith when you realized you had feelings for her? Was it different? Well, other than the fact that one was a guy and one was a woman."

"Hand me that, will you, darlin'?" Wyatt said, pointing at a smaller tub that was stacked upon the other large one. Libby placed it on the couch beside Wyatt, who began to unpack it. "I was very young when I met Lucas, and looking back on it now, over time I did grow to care about him, but I know I never loved him." She spared a glance over at Libby, who was untangling lights. "Certainly not in the way that a wife should. But I also knew, in some part of me, that I liked women."

Libby stared at her. "Really?"

Wyatt grinned. "Why do y'all think I have that lovely collection of lesbian literature in there?" she asked, nodding toward the home office.

Libby grinned. "Well, shut my mouth."

Wyatt chuckled. "But, as for Faith." She stared down at the stained-glass angel she'd just unwrapped from layers of newspaper to keep it from breaking. "The first day I met her, when she came into the café to use the restroom, there was something about her. It wasn't because she was beautiful or sweet or anythin' else like that. It was deeper. Somehow inside I just knew this precious woman was gonna play a huge role in my life."

"Did you think it would be love?" Libby asked, hanging on every word the redhead said.

Wyatt shook her head. "No. Certainly not." She smiled. "But I knew I didn't wanna lose touch with her. When she walked outta that door, I felt so sad. I was so worried I'd never see her again."

Libby considered what she'd just heard, and

she recognized those same thoughts and worries. She conjured up Grace's face in her mind's eye. She'd met Grace for the first time as a college student working at the coffee shop. Their communication was relegated to how Grace liked her coffee, but there had always been something there. She'd always been drawn to the detective, though she hadn't understood why in those days. She simply took it as admiration for the older woman who wore a gun and a badge and always seemed so calm and collected, so with it. She was even nice to everybody she met, including a college student with a crush.

"Over time," Wyatt continued, "Faith became the center of my world. I couldn't hold a thought in my head that didn't start without my seein' her face in my mind."

Libby looked away, feeling like she'd been busted even though she knew Wyatt had no idea what she'd just been thinking about.

"Liberty?" Wyatt said softly.

She looked up from her spot sitting on the floor on the other side of the coffee table.

"Honey, it's obvious you care. We all see it. But you have to live your life based on what's right for you, what you're ready for." She shrugged. "If Grace isn't where you are, isn't strong enough, you can't wait around for her to figure it out."

Libby felt her heart breaking—again. She stared down at the Christmas lights in her hand, only a small portion detangled. Finally, she looked up at Wyatt. "So, you think I did the right thing, walking away?"

"I think you did the only thing you could do, darlin'." Wyatt set the angel aside and grabbed another wrapped decoration. "We both know Grace is a fine,

fine person, a heart of gold. But love is a scary thing, and it's just not for the faint of heart. Love—real honest and true love—takes a whole lotta work, Libby. Don't settle for anyone who isn't up to the challenge."

The last sentence hit Libby hard, in a good way. Wyatt was right. She'd seen what her parents had gone through together, what Wyatt and Faith had gone through together. Never had any of them run from the situation or disappear because it got too hard. She nodded, steeling her resolve.

"You're right. I need to be with someone who deserves me. Who is willing to take what I have to give and give it back."

Wyatt's smile was big and bright. "I'm so proud of you, darlin'. Come 'ere so I can give ya a hug."

༄༅༄༅

The rest of the day had passed with a new Libby at the helm. Wyatt's words and strength had given *her* the strength to focus on herself and the woman she was becoming. Though she knew they'd support her, she still needed to sit down with her parents and tell them directly, but she decided to give herself a little more time first. She wanted to make sure that she truly was a lesbian and not just a Grace lesbian.

Now, night had fallen and Wyatt had thrown in the towel a couple hours before. Libby was in the guest bedroom, enjoying the quiet as the snow fell peacefully outside. It was a nice, easy snow that would leave Wynter blanketing in winter beauty in the morning.

Reclining against pillows in bed with covers pulled up to her waist, Libby scrolled through the pictures posted on the social media account of a young woman named Kristy that Wyatt had told her about. Kristy was a cute little blonde—though from the more recent pictures, she was currently more of a purple-head—who lived in Colorado Springs. She was the lesbian daughter of a woman Faith worked with in the mayor's office. Recent college grad and recently single after a five-year relationship with her high school sweetheart.

Apparently Faith had mentioned Libby to Kristy's mom, who had then mentioned her to her daughter. Curious, Libby was checking her out. Though her heart wasn't quite there, she was convincing her brain that she needed to get out there and meet people, even if just to make a friend to talk to, to help her understand herself and this new world she may be entering.

She had commented on a couple posts on the woman's wall and "liked" a few things when a private message from Kristy came through. Her heart skipped a beat for a moment, feeling almost as though she'd been caught spying or looking through a window.

Kristy asked if she were the same Liberty Faulkner that her mother had told her about. When Libby responded in the affirmative, Kristy let out a trail of smiling emojis, making Libby smile even as she felt a bit strange talking to this stranger.

She was amused at her own feelings. Talking to a "known lesbian" felt weird, as though she were taking to a member of a secret club. She didn't feel quite yet that she belonged to said secret club. She'd had many friends over the years who were members of the rainbow alphabet, but this was different. She was inching closer and closer every day to claiming her spot, her letter, but this woman she was messaging with had already claimed hers, had claimed her truth.

Chewing on her bottom lip, she decided to take this opportunity to ask Kristy about herself. The two went back and forth, easily getting along. Kristy was generous in answering Libby's questions about when she came out and how she knew, and she even challenged Libby with queries of her own. "Have you gone down on a woman yet" turned Libby a deep shade of embarrassed, but it wasn't long before the chat turned to more general topics.

Kristy was two years younger, and though Libby enjoyed her mind and certainly her sense of humor, she felt that there was something missing, perhaps a maturity or wisdom that she craved. Libby had no problem with the occasional fart joke or crude language, but it was a turnoff when it was used as punctuation to every sentence. Kristy wasn't quite that bad, but it was enough that Libby did not entertain thoughts of meeting for a drink.

For the moment, she was enjoying the company. She was surprised that it was nearing midnight, and after a yawn nearly cracked her jaw right open, she said her goodnights then plugged her phone in to charge and shut off the bedside lamp for sleep.

Chapter Twenty-nine

Libby's eyes opened only to squint a bit. The bedroom was so bright. She was used to the miniblinds like she had on her windows at home, but the windows in Wyatt and Faith's guest bedroom were covered by curtains that were delicate and white. Libby had opted to leave them be, pinned to the sides of the window rather than pull them to cover it.

Feeling rested and happy as she could see the sky was heavy and gray, she sat up in bed. She was definitely going to have to ask Wyatt what kind of mattress they had on that bed. Super comfy. Dressed in gray cotton pajama pants and white tank top, she padded over to the window and looked out over the day. She was utterly shocked to see how much snow blanketed the ground. Overnight, the snow must have picked up substantially, as there was at least two feet on the ground.

"Holy crap," she muttered. In a way, it made her feel better that she was missing work. With a storm like this, especially since it was still snowing, there wouldn't be much movement in town and most businesses would stay closed.

She walked from the window to the bedside table where her phone was and unplugged it, checking her messages.

"Shit!"

Libby stormed out of the bedroom, looking left

and right in the hallway as if that would give her some sort of idea where Wyatt was. She decided to head to the bedroom, but it was empty. Turning around, she headed back down the hall, plowing down the stairs. She lost her footing and slid down the final three stairs on her side.

"Do not die, darlin'. I may need you," Wyatt called from the living room.

Relieved to hear her voice, as breathy as it was, Libby gathered herself up at the bottom of the stairs, wincing as her ankle made its displeasure known. "How far apart are they?" she asked, limping over to the couch where her friend lay. "And, oh my god, Wyatt, I am so sorry I didn't get your text. I feel like such an asshole."

"It's okay, darlin'. Oh, lordy, this is not fun."

Libby took a seat on the coffee table in front of the couch. She looked down at her phone to mark the time. "How long has it been? And," she added, looking up at Wyatt. "You're not due for like, thirteen days, right?"

"Well, apparently this little one can't read a calendar." Wyatt chuckled nervously. She glanced over at the grandfather clock. "It's been eleven minutes."

"Okay." Libby did the math to get on Wyatt's schedule. She ran a hand through her hair. *What do I do?* "Did you call Faith or your doctor?"

"Left a message with the doctor and, no, I can't do that to Faith. She has such a big day ahead of her."

Libby stared at her. "Wyatt, you're in labor!"

"I know, but it could be a false alarm. I don't wanna mess up Faith's chance here with this factory," Wyatt stubbornly insisted.

"Oh boy." Libby blew out a breath. "Okay, well,

do you think we should get you to the hospital? I mean, I know it could be a false alarm, I know it also could take hours or even days, but I also know that little Abbigail could decide to join us for lunch."

Wyatt grinned then her face contorted in pain. "Oh god," she growled through gritted teeth.

Fear instantly gripped Libby until she realized what was happening. She noted the time then reached out and grabbed Wyatt's hand. "I'm here, Wyatt. I'm here," she said, feeling utterly helpless. She timed the contraction, trying to gather as much information as she could. It was so difficult to see Wyatt, normally such a strong, commanding woman, look so frail and in so much pain.

Seventy-three seconds later, Wyatt seemed to come out of it and relax a bit. She lay back against the couch's throw pillows with her eyes closed, her breathing long and even as she tried to will her body back to normalcy.

"Are you okay?" Libby asked softly.

Wyatt nodded, eyes still closed. "Darlin', can you get me some ice water, please?"

"Absolutely." Libby was so grateful to be given a task, something she could actually control.

She jumped up from the table and hurried to do Wyatt's bidding, phone in hand. Her mind was reeling as she moved about the kitchen, trying to decide what to do. Immediately, the answer came to her.

"Mind if I make some coffee?" she asked softly as she handed Wyatt a glass of ice water.

"Of course not, darlin'," Wyatt said, taking a long drink. "Whatever you want. In fact, as cold as it is today, why don'tcha make a whole pot?"

"I can do that. What else can I get you? Do you

need to go to the bathroom?" Libby asked, not entirely sure where she'd be the most help.

"I'm okay." Wyatt blew out a long, shaky breath.

"Okay." Libby leaned down and gave her a very light hug.

Wyatt chuckled, hugging her tightly back. "I ain't gonna break, honey." She met Libby's gaze as they separated. "Yet."

Libby smiled and made her way to the kitchen. She readied the twelve-cup maker as she considered what she was going to say. Finally, as she hit the Start button, she engaged her phone and went to her contacts list. Finding the number she wanted, she placed her call. Her heart was pounding in her throat as it rang.

As the coffeemaker gurgled and coughed to life, she leaned back against the counter and waited for a response.

"Well, hello, there." The voice on the other end was warm and smooth, like honey slowly spreading over Libby's soul, the timbre just slightly deeper than her own.

"Hey," she said, her voice giving out on her as it cracked from unshed emotion. Hearing her voice made her realize how much she'd missed her. *Damn it.* "I need your help."

"Anything."

"Wyatt's in labor. She can't get hold of her doctor, and with this snow I don't imagine we'll be getting her to a hospital anytime soon. I don't know what to do," Libby explained. She felt a bit stronger as she got into the situation at hand.

"Are you there with her?"

"Yes. Faith is out of town until tomorrow on

business, so as a precaution she asked me to stay. Damn good thing, too." She could hear Grace moving around, doing something on the other end of the line. "Listen, if you're busy, we can—"

"I'm getting the cats taken care of and packing myself a bag," Grace explained. "We don't know how long this could last. When was her first contraction?"

Libby's eyes fell closed, her hand coming up to cover her mouth as her relief and gratitude nearly broke her into tears. "Um," she said, shaking herself out of it and glancing at the clock. "First one was roughly twenty-two minutes ago. Latest one was four minutes ago."

"How long did it last?"

"Just over a minute," Libby pushed away from the counter and turned around to open a cabinet door above the coffeemaker to grab a mug.

"Okay. Make some coffee 'cuz it could be a minute, and I'll be over before the next one hits."

Libby grinned. "I literally just made some."

"See now?" Grace said cheerfully. "You're already doing it right. See you soon."

"And, Grace?"

"Yeah?"

"Thank you. For coming."

Grace was silent for a moment, then said, "Of course, Libby. There's nowhere I'd rather be."

There was an emotion packed into Grace's tone that Libby couldn't quite discern, but she felt it. "Okay. Be safe. Bye."

Libby set her phone down on the counter and stood there for a moment, looking down into the empty mug she'd pulled down from the cabinet. She contemplated the conversation that lasted such a brief time but had affected her so much. Hell, just the sound of Grace's voice had.

Shaking it off, she reached up and grabbed a second cup. "Wyatt? Are you doing okay? Want anything?"

"I'm fine."

"Grace is coming over," Libby explained, walking toward the couch. "I think she'll be a big help."

Wyatt looked at her, confusion on her lovely face. "Why? Because she's a cop?"

Libby shook her head. "She helped her mother for years."

"Helped her mother do what?"

"Deliver babies."

Wyatt stared at her for a long moment. "Well now, why didn't you say so?"

Libby grinned. "I just did." With Wyatt's laughter following her, she went back into the kitchen to get a cup of coffee ready for herself. She felt better, lighter, knowing she wasn't alone in this situation, and that none of them knew how it would end up—not just her. And, as much as she wanted to hold on to anger that had helped her keep a distance from Grace, she just couldn't anymore. She would be happy to see her.

Sure enough, as she was working on her coffee, she heard the familiar whine of a snowmobile. Most Wynter residents had learned the hard way to get their hands on a snowmobile. Even if it wasn't used for fun, sometimes it was needed simply to go buy food.

She grabbed the second mug and poured a cup for their guest, who was making her way up the long road to the house. Libby could just barely make her out in the sea of blinding white. As she stirred in the creamer to the perfect tone she knew Grace liked,

Grace was swinging the large body of the snowmobile around next to the stairs. Libby noticed her Sentra was half-buried. It was going to be a bear getting it out, she thought randomly.

Grabbing Grace's mug, she walked to the front door, unlocking and opening it. She watched as Grace sat on the bright yellow and dark blue machine, which made her think of a bumble bee. The detective was attired in a dark gray snowmobile suit, which, though bulky as intended, somehow still managed to make that incredible body look sexy. She reached up and removed her black helmet, shaking her hair loose and looking for all the world like she belonged in a shampoo commercial. It reminded Libby of a beautiful astronaut, newly landed.

She cleared her throat to try to clear naughty thoughts as she looked away for a moment, then looked back up as though she'd just spotted her.

"Hey," Grace said, helmet held under one arm and her backpack slung over her shoulder as she climbed off the snowmobile and up onto the third stair to the porch. "How is she?"

"Hi," Libby responded. "When you're ready," she said, holding up the cup of coffee. "She's okay. Really uncomfortable."

"Ohhh, you are a sweetheart." Grace removed her gloves and shoved them into the pockets of the jacket, zipping them inside. She took the mug with her hand, her gaze locking on Libby, who couldn't quite keep her gaze steady. The intensity of Grace's eyes made her feel uncomfortable and giddy all at the same time.

"Come on in," she said softly, stepping back so Grace could enter.

Grace entered, though only stepped out of the way so the door could be closed. "Hey, lady," she called out to Wyatt, who had somehow gotten herself up. She stood next to the couch with a bracing hand on it.

"I'm so grateful y'all are here," Wyatt said.

Grace took a drink of the coffee, eyes closing, and nodded her approval to Libby. She quickly set it aside as she went about removing her suit and boots. She wore jeans and a lightweight sweater underneath. Folding everything neatly by the door, she grabbed the coffee again and, in stocking feet, walked over to Wyatt. She gave her a hug, whispering something into her ear that Libby couldn't make out.

Wyatt nodded. "All right."

Grace took another sip before she set the mug down on the coffee table. She looked at Libby. "I need to check her," she said softly. "See how far along in the process we are. I think she'll be more comfortable in her bed than the couch."

Libby nodded. "Okay. What do you want me to do? Do you need any help?"

Grace shook her head. "No. We'll be back." With that, she and Wyatt made their way up the stairs, Grace helping her friend the entire time.

Libby watched them go, not entirely sure what to do with herself. She felt antsy again, nervous. She really felt they needed to let Faith know, and her gut told her that this baby would be coming sooner rather than later, but there was no way she would go against Wyatt's wishes.

In order to be productive, she decided to do some research on the weather for Denver and whether the airport was still open. The storm that had hit Wynter was unexpected, so had it hit other parts of the state, too? Faith would need to know if she would be able to get home.

Poring through the internet on her phone, she saw that, indeed, Denver had gotten hammered as well. Passes were closed, the airport was closed, flights cancelled. "Shit," she muttered. Yes, she felt the only thing to do was to call Faith.

She looked up when she heard someone coming down the stairs. She wasn't entirely surprised to see Grace alone. Libby pushed up from where she'd sat on the couch. "Is she okay?"

"She's dilated to probably about three," Grace said, walking over to the table and grabbing her coffee. "With this being her first baby, it could take hours and hours. But, with her going into labor two weeks early..." She shrugged as she took a sip. "That baby could be impatient and fly out of there. She went into another contraction while we were upstairs."

"I think I should call Faith. What do you think?" Libby asked, her anxiety again amping.

"Definitely. Hey." Grace set her coffee down again before stepping over to Libby, who must have been showing her concern. She reached up and cupped Libby's face, holding her steady as she looked deep into Libby's eyes. "It's going to be okay," she said softly.

Libby swallowed, her stomach lurching. "Can you do this?"

Grace gave her a warm, reassuring smile. "That's why you called me, isn't it?"

Libby returned the smile as best she could and nodded. "Yeah."

"Okay. I'm going to gather a few things that

we'll need whenever this little one decides to appear for her closeup. Why don't you get hold of Faith and fill her in, then meet me upstairs, okay?"

"Okay." Grace's calm words and energy helped calm *her* down.

Grace leaned forward, Libby's eyes sliding closed as the softest of kisses was left on her forehead. "See you upstairs."

Left alone, it took Libby a moment to catch her breath, her heart racing. She shook herself out of her stupor and got Faith on the phone.

"What's wrong? Everything okay? What's wrong?"

Libby smiled at the greeting. "Wyatt is okay, but she's gone into labor, Faith," she said gently, trying to use Grace's tone to keep Faith calm.

"I'm on the next flight—"

"DIA is closed, Faith. We got nearly three feet of snow here last night. I checked already. Colorado is a mess."

"Fuck. Okay, I'm going to see how close I can get then drive the rest of the way. You keep me posted, okay? Are you guys at the hospital?"

"No." Libby shook her head even though Faith couldn't see it. "We couldn't get out if we tried. Grace is here."

"Wait, look, Libby, I love Grace, too, but—"

"Her mother was a midwife, Faith. She helped her for years before she headed off to the army," Libby explained, feeling a sense of pride in all that Grace was.

"Seriously?" A burst of nervous laughter flew across the line. "What doesn't that woman do? Okay, let me hang up so I can explain what's going on and get going. I'll text you as I move."

"Sounds like a plan. I'll keep you posted on this end, too," Libby promised.

"And, Libby?" Faith said softly.

"Yeah?"

"Don't you dare let anything happen to my wife or my baby. Without them, I have nothing."

Libby smiled at the emotion-laced words. "I know. I promise."

≈≈≈≈

Libby gasped, startled awake. She opened her eyes, surprised to find herself lying on the guest bed, which she hadn't even made that morning. Last she remembered, she was going to sit down and text Faith an update while Wyatt climbed into a tub of warm water to help soothe her contractions.

Now, she found herself lying on her side, Grace sitting next to her, fingers lightly running through messy blond hair. The room was dark except for the light coming in from the hallway.

"Hey," Grace said softly.

"Hey. What time is it?" Libby asked just as softly. "I can't believe I fell asleep."

"It's almost two in the morning. And, don't worry. I drifted off, too. It was Faith calling that woke me up."

"How's Wyatt?" Libby asked, feeling as though she had sand in her eyes.

"She's struggling. The contractions are getting stronger. I think we're getting close. Her water broke about an hour ago."

Libby reached up and took Grace's hand, wrapping her fingers around it as she held their hands together against her heart. She looked up into tired eyes. "I want to help."

"I'm so glad to hear you say that, because I need it." Grace smiled. "I'm going to head back into the bedroom. Can you please run down to my backpack downstairs and get the package of shoelaces?"

Libby sat up, releasing Grace's hand before running her fingers through her hair, attempting to get it out of her face. "Of course. Why shoelaces?"

"I'll have to tie off the cord," Grace explained gently.

"Uh..." Fully awake at that thought, Libby nodded. "Okay."

Grace grinned. "Come on. Showtime soon." She pushed up from the bed, sending a quick glance back to Libby before she stepped out of the room. There was so much in that gaze, so much in her eyes that Libby had never seen there before.

She climbed off the bed and headed down the hall to the stairs. Taking them as quickly as her tired body would allow, she reached Grace's backpack and, sure enough, she easily found a brand-new pack of white shoestrings. She was just about to rezip the bag when she heard Wyatt cry out in pain.

Bag be damned, Libby turned and sprinted up the stairs two at a time. Wyatt, naked, sat on the end of the bed in the bedroom she shared with Faith. The two chairs she and Grace had brought up earlier now made sense. They were placed at the end of the bed, one of Wyatt's feet braced on the seat of each one, her legs spread. Grace knelt on the floor between.

"Libby!" Grace called out, focused on the business at hand.

"I'm here," Libby said, running into the room.

"Fill that with warm water," Grace barked, nodding toward the large bowl that had been placed with four clean towels when they'd brought in the chairs. "Hurry."

Without a word and with her heart about to race out of her chest, Libby followed her instructions in the master bath. Trying not to slosh it everywhere, she brought it back out and placed it on the floor out of Grace's way.

"Don't push yet, sweetheart," Grace said to Wyatt. "I know you want to, but just hold on." Grace looked up at Libby, who stood next to the bed and had no idea where she was needed. "Libby, I need you to help brace Wyatt, baby, okay?"

Libby nodded, only just barely catching the term of endearment that she didn't even think Grace had realized she'd used. Pushing it aside, Libby sat on the bed behind Wyatt, giving her physical strength so Wyatt could focus on pushing that baby out.

"I wanna push," Wyatt whimpered, her hair already sweaty.

"I know you do," Grace said.

Libby could just barely see the top of Grace's head over Wyatt's shoulder and swollen breasts and belly. Libby could feel Wyatt leaning back into her, using her as leverage, so she tried to maneuver her body in whatever way was necessary to help support her.

"Okay, sweetheart," Grace said. "Okay. Push!"

Wyatt ground out a cry that was almost inhuman, her entire body tensing against Libby. She reached under her own thighs as she pushed down. Libby could feel the incredible power in Wyatt's body, the power of a mother giving life to another.

"Good," Grace said. "Good, good."

"Good girl," Libby whispered, reaching around Wyatt with Wyatt's own discarded nightgown to wipe the sweat off her face and get her hair out of the way. "Good girl."

"Again, push!"

Wyatt's head fell back against Libby's shoulder, eyes squeezed shut and teeth bared like a wild animal as another primal cry was ripped from her throat.

"I see the head," Grace exclaimed. "She's crowning! Again, push!"

Libby held on as Wyatt pushed with everything she had.

"She's coming! Come on, Wyatt, she's almost out," Grace cried.

Wyatt panted, her body going limp against Libby. Libby left a kiss on a sweaty temple. "You've got this," she whispered. "Almost there, Wyatt. Almost there."

Wyatt nodded, her face screwing up into complete determination as she bore down again, desperation and exhaustion in her cry.

"It's definitely a girl," Grace exclaimed, wonder and laughter in her voice as she moved back a bit, as though to catch a flying Abbigail. "She's beautiful," she said, tears in her eyes. "Libby, I need you."

Libby left one last kiss to Wyatt's temple. "You did it," she whispered, moving a stack of pillows to where she'd been for Wyatt to lean against.

In absolute awe, Libby looked upon the tiny little slimy creature that had just come from Wyatt's body. She didn't know what to say, utterly speechless.

"Give me one of those towels," Grace said, nodding toward the folded stack.

On her knees, Libby reached over for one, opening it up. She was astonished when Grace placed the baby in her arms atop the towel. She used the dangling material to wipe the baby off, birthing juices and a strange white film covering the tiny body.

"What is that?" Libby asked.

"It's called vernix caseosa," Grace explained, gently running her fingers inside the baby's mouth. All at once, a loud cry burst from the tiniest body Libby had ever seen. "It protects the baby's skin from the amniotic fluid. Once we can give her a proper bath, it'll all go."

Libby watched, astounded as tiny arms and legs began to flail, a very unhappy Abbigail Fitzgerald upon them. The cord was still connecting the baby to her mother's body.

"Okay, Mommy," Grace said, standing up. "Libby, can you wrap that towel up, please?" Grace leaned over the bed and gently placed the baby on Wyatt's chest. "Meet your daughter."

Wyatt was crying as she wrapped her arms around her baby. She looked at every aspect of the baby, counting her fingers and toes, looking into squinty eyes. "Hello, Abbigail," she whispered.

Tears freely streaming down her cheeks, Libby grabbed her phone. She called Faith's number then turned it to a video chat. "Faith," she said, looking at her friend, who was behind the wheel of her rental car, driving the twelve hours from where she'd landed in Phoenix. "I need you to pull over." Faith said nothing, but Libby could see she was doing exactly what she'd been told. When she knew it was safe, Libby said, "I'd like to introduce you to someone."

Chapter Thirty

"So, clearly we're not getting your car out right now," Grace said with a grin as she leaned against the cooking island. "When we head out, I can either take you home on my snowmobile, or," she hedged, looking a little shy. "We can go to my house and I'll make you a proper breakfast. We can talk."

Libby studied her, arms crossed over her chest. She was so tempted, but she was also utterly exhausted. "What's there to talk about?" she asked.

Grace let out a tired sigh, running a hand through her hair. "I have some things I need to say to you. Some things you deserve to hear."

Libby nodded. "Okay," she agreed softly. "We can do that." She figured maybe, if nothing else, Grace could offer her some closure.

The sound of voices and steps on the stairs took Libby's attention. Faith, who had arrived back in town just two hours before, was forced to park the rental on the public road and hike her way through waist-deep snow to the house. Wyatt's doctor had arrived an hour later, and Grace and Libby had left the master bedroom to give the doctor, new moms, and baby privacy.

Faith entered the kitchen, a freshly swaddled bundle in her arms. Libby's heart melted as she and Grace stepped over to her.

"Ladies," Faith said quietly. "Our baby girl is in

perfect health, and so is her mama." She leaned over and gave first Grace then Libby a kiss on the cheek. "Thanks to you both."

"I'd like to shake both your hands," the older woman with Faith said, doing just that. "I've seen many home births over the years, but this tops out as one of the smoothest." She smiled. "If either of you ever decide to change your career path, let me know."

Libby grinned, feeling more proud of this than probably anything else she'd ever accomplished. "It was truly the most incredible thing I've ever witnessed," she managed, emotion rising in her throat.

"Want to hold her?" Faith asked.

Libby couldn't even respond verbally, so simply nodded. She and Faith transferred the precious bundle, Libby feeling absolutely breathless at the gift she was getting. She felt Grace move up behind her, looking down at baby Abbigail over Libby's shoulder. She could feel her front lightly grazing her back and it felt wonderful, comforting. Considering they'd done this together, she welcomed the closeness.

She looked down into the tiny face, wrinkled and pink. She smiled at the sprinkling of dark hair on the baby's head. "You're so beautiful," she whispered, truly moved. Suddenly, all her exhaustion went away, the eighteen hours she and Grace had spent with Wyatt through her contractions, tag-teaming to stay with her so the other could eat, grab a little rest, or go to the bathroom. Every second had been worth it as she looked down at that little bundle, tiny though heavier than she expected.

As though Grace had heard her thoughts, she asked quietly, so as not to wake Abbigail, "What did she weigh in at?"

"Eight pounds, one ounce," the doctor said, a large case slung over her shoulder by a connective strap that Libby assumed held a scale of some sort as well as any other things the doctor would need for a proper inspection of mother and baby.

"And," Libby asked. "Wyatt's okay?"

"She's good," the doctor affirmed. "We got her a little help in feeding the baby, as it's a process. Not all babies come out of the womb knowing how to breastfeed. But she did great and is now sleeping." She turned and gave Faith a tight hug. "Congratulations, sweetheart. I'll see you and your girls in the office Thursday." With a wave to Grace and Libby, the doctor left.

"Well," Libby said, figuring Faith wanted some time alone with her wife and daughter. She left a gentle kiss on the soft skin of Abbigail's forehead. "Gonna give you back to your mommy, little one." She paused as Grace reached around her and lightly brushed some of the silky strands on Abbigail's head.

"See you later, baby girl," she whispered.

Faith took the baby, cradling her to her chest. She smiled at both women. "I love you guys. I'll call you later to give you an update."

"Let us know if you need anything," Grace said, very gingerly giving Faith a hug, as did Libby.

※※※※

Faith had lent Libby Wyatt's snowmobiling suit and helmet to wear, as Wyatt certainly wouldn't be needing it anytime soon, to ensure she and Grace could get to Grace's house safely. They arrived at the two-story house and got themselves and their gear into the warmth inside. It had stopped snowing but was still bitterly cold.

"Hello, babies!" Grace greeted her trio of cats, all but Shadow making their dislike of her absence known.

Libby watched, amused and warmed. "I have to admit, I've been contemplating getting a little furry something."

Grace, who had squatted down to give her babies love, grinned up at her. "My life would be so empty without these guys. I know Faith and Wyatt both have struggled without their boy. While Wyatt's been in her third trimester, Faith had her dad and Vickie take him, worried he'd knock Wyatt down."

"Wise." Libby also squatted and, to her joy, all three abandoned their mom and went to her. "Hey, guys. Miss me?"

"So, what would you like for breakfast?" Grace asked, getting to her feet and stripping out of her gear.

Libby stood and began doing the same, watching Grace's example for where she wanted the wet suit. She realized that exhaustion had creeped up on her again. If it hadn't been so cold, she could have easily fallen asleep leaning against Grace on the way to her house.

"Would you be mad if I took a nap for a bit?" she asked. "I think I've hit my wall. Those couple hours I crashed on the bed last night are long gone."

Grace chuckled and shook her head. "No, not mad at all." Both cleared of their riding gear, she reached out a hand, which Libby took. "Bring your backpack and let's go get some sleep."

Changed into the clothes she'd slept in at Faith and Wyatt's house, Libby padded in bare feet from the guest bathroom to Grace's bedroom, where Grace, dressed similarly, was just pulling down the covers.

"This okay?" Grace asked, indicating the bed. "I can crash on the couch—"

"It's fine," Libby said softly, giving her a small smile. "It's just sleep." Libby walked around to the opposite side of the bed and climbed in. Strangely, it wasn't until Grace moved up behind her and spooned her that she closed her eyes and fell into a deep sleep.

☙☙❧❧

Libby wasn't sure how many hours later she woke, though she noted the sun was beginning to flirt with falling from the sky. She lay on her back, covers pushed down to just above her belly button. Turning her head to her right, she saw Grace was still asleep, lying on her side and facing Libby.

Libby's eyes took in Grace's face like a thirsty man drank a glass of ice-cold water. The relaxed eyebrows, smooth, beautiful skin. Her hair trailed back behind her head across the pillow, dark and stark against the light gray of her pillowcase.

As she watched, Grace's eyes slowly opened as though she'd felt she was being watched. It took a moment, but then her eyes focused on Libby. She gave her the smallest smile, which Libby returned.

Without a word, Grace reached her hand out, lightly caressing the side of Libby's face. Libby's eyes grew heavy at the touch. The soft fingertips trailed down along her jaw then down the side of her neck. Libby's heart jumped as the fingertips didn't stop, their slow tour running along one of her collarbones then down along the neckline of her tank top, teasingly dipping just under the material before moving on.

Libby couldn't move, could barely breathe as those fingers continued, Grace never breaking eye contact with her. Suddenly, those fingers were encircling her left breast, fingernails running along the rounded outer side before trailing over her nipple, making Libby gasp.

Grace's hand covered the breast fully, the warmth sending sensations straight between Libby's legs. There was a part of her that was surprised at the bold behavior, but she couldn't stop it, didn't want to.

Libby's eyes closed and her mouth fell open as Grace lifted herself a bit and moved over to her, leaning over Libby's body until her lips found that hardening nipple through the thin cotton of the tank top.

Her back arched, inviting the warmth of Grace's mouth, her fingers finding their way into sleep-messy dark hair. Her nipple was tugged gently between teeth before that mouth disappeared, but just long enough for her tank top to be pushed aside, the mouth returning to her naked skin.

A sigh of pleasure escaped Libby's lips, her hips moving slightly of their own accord as her panties began to feel far too tight. Grace's tongue worked the rigid flesh, batting at it before sucking it into the volcanic warmth of her mouth. A moment later it was released, the coolness of the evening air breezing over the wet breast as Grace moved up to Libby's mouth.

Libby returned the kiss, which was passionate but controlled, much like the attention Grace had given her breast. She accepted Grace to fully move atop her. She sighed into the kiss as one of Grace's thighs moved between her legs, adding a bit of pressure to where the pressure was building. Libby's hands ran down Grace's T-shirt-clad torso until she came to her behind, encased in the pajama pants she wore, the flesh beneath flexing beneath her hands.

Grace reached down Libby's body and cupped the underside of her thigh, encouraging Libby to raise the leg that was outside of Grace's. She did, and whimpered into the kiss when Grace pressed more firmly against her. Intellectual understanding and primal instinct taking over, Libby brought her own leg up a bit, pressing between Grace's legs. Grace hissed at the move, pushing her hips down into Libby. Through two layers of cotton, Libby could feel the intense heat between Grace's legs.

Together they rocked, the kiss breaking as they were breathing too hard. Grace buried her face in Libby's neck, her heavy, hot breaths warm against her skin. Libby's eyes remained closed as she held Grace to her, concentrating on what her body was feeling and what made it feel even better. It only took a few moments before her orgasm overcame her. She gasped, fingers like talons in Grace's hair and the back of her shirt as she came. A moment later, Grace thrust against her, grinding as she moaned in Libby's ear.

Libby wasn't sure what it meant or what would happen next, but didn't have long to contemplate it as Grace left a soft, lingering kiss on her lips before she moved away, off of Libby. On her knees, she reached down and grabbed Libby's hands and gently urged her to sit up. She leaned in and initiated a slow, sensuous kiss, different than any they'd shared previously, all the while easing Libby's tank top up and over her breasts and then her head, returning to the kiss once the garment had cleared and been tossed to the floor.

Sitting there topless, Libby thought she'd feel shy, but the look on Grace's face as she pulled away and took her breasts in wiped any thought of that away. The detective didn't say a word, nor was there a need for her to. Her expression said it all, as did her touch. Her fingers all but worshipped her breasts, nimble fingers tugging lightly at hard nipples, each tug shooting straight to Libby's clit, which was ready for round two.

Wanting to see more, Libby shyly reached for Grace's T-shirt. She looked into welcoming eyes before pulling the shirt up and over Grace's head. For months, the thought of Grace's breasts had haunted her, tormented her. Now, there they were, bared for her to see, touch, even taste if she wanted. And she wanted.

Feeling bold, Libby urged Grace to lie back, which she did. Libby moved to lie beside her, staring down at those gorgeous breasts. Her fingers explored, loving the softness even as her thumb ran across the rigidity of her nipple. Her mouth watered to take their place, so she made it so.

Grace groaned as her breasts were lovingly explored by Libby's mouth, which made Libby hope that she was doing it right. She could say with all sincerity she could have stayed on Grace's breasts all night. She'd never felt such want, such passion and deep, soul-stirring arousal before. The only other time she'd come even close was while reading the sex scenes she'd been devouring in Wyatt's books. Now, it wasn't a novel, it wasn't someone else's imagination, it was just her and Grace, the woman that she... Dare she think it? Say it?

The thought was startled out of her as she was

pushed to her back, a very passionate Grace taking her mouth in a demanding kiss for a moment before Grace pulled away and silently urged Libby to lift her hips as she tugged down her pajama pants and panties in one go, leaving her completely naked. Now she felt shy. The look in Grace's eyes was downright hunger.

Grace removed the last two articles of her own clothing before she slowed her movements, lovingly running her hands down Libby's thighs before gently pushing them apart. Libby watched down the length of her own body as Grace moved between her legs, still on her knees. She planted her hands on either side of Libby's head as she lowered her upper body and her lips, delivering a slow and loving kiss, easing Libby's uncertainty.

"You okay?" she whispered against Libby's lips.

At Libby's nod, she left a last lingering kiss before she began to kiss her way down Libby's body, flicking each nipple with her tongue before moving on. She eased herself down the bed until her shoulders were tucked between Libby's spread legs.

Libby knew exactly what Grace was about to do, but she'd never allowed it before and didn't know what to expect. Her anxiousness was in a boxing match with her arousal, not entirely sure which would win out. She knew the answer to that instantly at the first long, slow swipe of Grace's tongue through her wetness.

Her body relaxed from the release of her anxiety, but then slowly began to tense up again as Grace slowly and expertly built her pleasure back up. Her breathing increased, back arched as her hands once again found Grace's hair, the head in her hands slowly bobbing and moving with the incredible way her mouth and tongue were making love to her.

Finally, her body couldn't take anymore, A second orgasm ripped through Libby as Grace sucked her clit into her mouth, batting her tongue against it mercilessly. It was so strong that Libby's upper body lifted off the bed before slamming back down, her back arching as her entire body shuddered with the intensity of the spasms rocking her to her very core.

She tried to catch her breath as Grace made her way back up her body, kissing and flicking her tongue until she found Libby's mouth again. Her tongue was warm and slick as it grazed Libby's. She barely registered that she was tasting herself in their kiss before she groaned into Grace's mouth.

Grace moved her body atop Libby's, her hips fitting perfectly between Libby's spread thighs. She adjusted her hips until her clit pressed against Libby's, which still pulsed. Libby spread her legs wider while a whole new sensation rushed through her as Grace moved her hips, rubbing their slick, swollen clits together.

Libby's fingernails trailed down Grace's back as her hips began to move with her, their rhythm slow and deeply sensual. Grace broke their kiss and braced herself on a forearm, allowing her other hand to roam freely as she studied Libby's face. The connection was almost painful as Libby met and held that hooded gaze. She saw in Grace's eyes everything she felt in her own heart as they moved together, once again the pleasure building.

Grace braced herself on her hands once again and used the strength in her body to quicken their rhythm, all the while careful to keep their clits perfectly synced to glide against each other with firm but measured thrusts.

Libby could feel her orgasm starting again, the muscles in her stomach tightening. As much as she wanted Grace to speed up, she refused, instead bringing them both to a slow but intense orgasm. Libby's cries erupted from her throat, joining Grace in a fierce and vocal release.

Finally, Grace's body collapsed against Libby's, who wrapped her up in her arms and legs. Her heart was racing, chest heaving against Grace's as she tried to recover from the experience, her body all but melting into molten pleasure right there on the bed.

After several moments, Grace lifted her head from Libby's neck. She brought up a hand and cupped her cheek as she gazed into Libby's eyes. Grinning, she said, "I swear, my intention was to talk to you before this happened."

Chapter Thirty-one

The flames popped in the fireplace, the fire the only light in the entire house. Grace rested back against the couch in the nest of pillows on the living floor, her legs open and Libby between them, reclining back against her front. They were naked except for the banket haphazardly wrapped around them. As the fire had warmed them up in the cold night, more and more of the blanket had been pushed off.

"Want the last one?" Grace held a grape between her finger, the last morsel from the cheese and fruit plate they'd prepared.

Libby glanced over at where it was held close to her mouth. Like a lioness, she snatched it from Grace's fingers with her teeth, enjoying the sweet juices that exploded into her mouth as she bit into it.

"I know you like my fingers in fun places, baby, but I nearly lost one there," Grace said, then chuckled.

Libby grinned and snuggled in a bit more, Grace wrapping her arms tighter around her. She could honestly say she'd never felt so happy, so accepted, so content. Even though she was tired, she didn't want to go to sleep because she was so afraid that the moment she closed her eyes, the dream would end. There were still things left unsaid.

"So," she began, fingers absently stroking the soft flesh of Grace's right thigh. "Now that we've made love in your bed, in the shower, on the couch—"

"In the kitchen," Grace offered.

"In the kitchen," she agreed. "And, here on the floor."

"I think we got it covered. Oh wait," Grace said, snapping her fingers as though she'd forgotten something. "The studio."

Libby giggled, loving the lightness in Grace's energy. She was happier than she'd ever seen her. "Yes. Of course. So, now that we've covered most of the bases, are we going to talk?" She held her breath, expecting Grace to shut down as she'd done so many times before. She braced herself for it, but instead Grace held her tighter and whispered in her ear.

"Of course, baby."

Libby waited as Grace readjusted her position, getting a bit more comfortable. Finally, she began to speak.

"I never told you this, mainly because I felt like a dirty old thirty-one-year-old woman at the time, but I had a crush on you when you used to make my coffee before you moved away."

A bark of laughter escaped Libby's lips. "You are kidding me."

"Nope. I never would've done anything about it at the time, though."

Libby nodded, able to understand that. "I've grown up a lot since then."

"You have. You were always beautiful, and sexy as hell, I might add, but you've become an incredibly strong, intelligent, amazing woman."

Libby was surprised by the words being murmured against the side of her head. Wanting a serious conversation, she pulled out of the embrace and turned around in the space between Grace's legs. She urged her to put her knees down so she could straddle her hips. Grace placed her hands on Libby's hips while Libby rested hers on the couch behind Grace. She smiled down at the beautiful woman beneath her. "You may continue," she said sweetly.

Grace grinned before dipping her head and taking a swipe at one of Libby's nipples with her tongue, making Libby gasp and playfully swat at her shoulder. "Sorry, it was there, couldn't resist."

"Uh-huh…"

"Anyway," Grace continued, growing serious again. "When we met back up this summer, you were still the goofy, friendly girl I knew before, but something was different. Very different." She brought a hand up and ran her fingers through Libby's hair, tucking it behind an ear.

The look in Grace's eyes in that moment said so much, though Libby did her best to not plug in words unsaid. Instead, she allowed her own fingers to play lightly in long, dark strands.

"You made me embrace life," Grace continued. "You made me laugh, made me think. But," she added softy, "you made me do something that scared the living hell out of me."

Libby's head cocked to the side a bit. "What?"

"You made me feel."

Libby's fingers slid from Grace's hair to caress the side of her face. "Is that why you ran?"

Grace nodded. "I'm ashamed of that. I was a coward. And I'm sorry. Truly and really sorry. When you walked away from me two weeks ago…" She shook her head, as if in awe. "You took part of me with you."

Libby smiled. "Is that why you wanted me over

here?" she asked, teasing in her voice. "To get that part back?"

Grace shook her head, no smile. "No, I don't want it back." She reached up and took hold of Libby's hand, placing her palm against her chest, over her heart. "It's yours," she said softly.

Libby's eyes fell closed. She so badly wanted to believe her, but she'd been so hurt over the past months. She took a deep breath, trying to get a grasp on her emotions. Finally, she asked, "How do I know you won't run away again tomorrow? Or in a week? Six months?"

Grace brought Libby's hand from her heart to her lips, leaving a kiss on the palm before releasing it. "I hate myself for putting such doubt in you."

"I'm sorry, I just—"

"No," Grace said, shaking her head. "No, don't you dare apologize for this. I did this, Libby. And I'm so sorry. I won't run again. I can say that until I'm blue in the face, but the truth is, it's my job to prove it to you. Words, no matter how much they're meant, are ultimately cheap when distrust has been planted. Believe me, I understand that." She smiled. "I'll prove it to you. That is, if you'll let me?"

Libby considered the words for a long moment, looking deeply into Grace's eyes to test their sincerity. She saw nothing but naked emotion there, not the guarded, careful eyes she'd come to know during serious moments like the one they were in. She returned the smile. "So, you're serious, as in show up at my job with flowers and stuff, serious?"

Grace chucked. "Yes. I'm *that* serious."

Libby leaned in, initiating a slow, sensuous kiss. After long moments, she pulled away, leaving them both breathing hard. "I'm that serious, too," she murmured against soft lips.

❦❦❦❦

"Okay, so they want to rent the entire ice cream shop?" Libby asked her employee, who had taken the call from the customer. "Four days before Christmas, and they're just calling about this now?"

"I know, that's what I said. So, what do you want to do? We're supposed to have our Christmas party that night, too," the high school girl explained.

"Crap, you're right." She stood at the counter of the coffee shop with Samantha as the two looked over the printed schedule that Sam had taken from where it was mounted on the wall. A few customers were seated at tables, their orders filled, so they had a few minutes to work on the problem.

"Hey, Libby, I think this one's for you," Sam said.

"Huh?" Libby said, glancing at the girl, distracted.

She followed her employee's gaze to the area right in front of the register on the customer's side. There stood Grace, a bouquet of two dozen red roses in her hands and a smile and a raised eyebrow on her face. A slow smile eased onto Libby's lips.

Epilogue

The sky was blue and shining down on the snowy landscape. The town looked beautiful, white and festive with Christmas just ten days away. The gifts wrapped and housed in the back seat of their new Jeep Grand Cherokee had nothing to do with Christmas, though.

"How is she already a year old?" Grace asked, the fingers of her right hand interlaced with those of Libby's left where they rested on Libby's thigh as Grace expertly guided the SUV through the streets.

"It's just crazy," Libby agreed.

Grace felt happy and content. Actually, she'd been more happy and content over the last year than she had been her entire life. The woman sitting by her side, who had been by her side nearly every single day—and now, every night—was the entire reason for that.

Once she'd let herself go, truly go and let Libby in, they'd grown closer in ways she'd never experienced with another living soul. She absolutely knew that Liberty Faulkner was the love of her life, her soul mate or any other term love songs and romance novels threw out there. She finally realized that just maybe those authors she'd read all those years actually knew what they were talking about. She walked through life with a smile on her face and a bounce in her step.

"Oh excellent," the subject of Grace's thoughts

and undying love exclaimed. "Frankie and Colby are already here. I think they have Noah this weekend, too."

"Colby's pretty proud of the ring," Grace said with a chuckle. "Have you seen it yet?" She pulled the sleek, black SUV into a spot next to Frankie's car.

"No, I'm excited," Libby said, unbuckling her seat belt.

"Hey," Grace murmured, a hand on Libby's arm to stop her from getting out of the Jeep.

Libby turned and looked at her, eyebrows raised in curiosity.

Grace leaned forward until their lips were a hair's width apart. "I love you," she whispered.

Libby's smile was big and bright, as it always was when those words were said. "I love you, too, baby," she responded, accepting the kiss she was given.

They climbed out of the SUV and gathered what they'd brought—gifts for Abbigail and the cake, which the happy moms had ordered from Bessie's and Grace and Libby had offered to pick up and bring to the party.

The house was decorated for Christmas as well as for a most important birthday. It was a holiday/birthday wonderland, Grace thought as they were let in by a very happy Wyatt. She looked tired from chasing a newly mobile toddler but also beautiful, and met them with a mile-wide smile.

"Welcome, y'all!" she crowed, gathering them both in an enthusiastic hug. "Thank you, darlin'," she said, taking the birthday cake from Libby. "Grace, gifts can go over there, hon."

Grace nodded in acquiescence, walking over to the growing pile by the foot of the stairs. She was greeted by a happy—and very pregnant—Frankie, shown the beautiful diamond ring upon her left hand, and accepted a hug from a proud Colby. She'd noted that ever since Frankie had walked into his trailer and then into his heart, he was a different man. Gone was the cocky chip on his shoulder. Gone was a man who was just shy of truly being confident. In his place stood a man who would die for his new and growing family, a man who, after dealing with a mentally ill mother and a father who did the best he could but was gone all the time, had finally found his place.

She also realized that she'd searched, aimlessly for so long, hoping for "it." She'd joined the army, hoping. She'd joined her sisters and brothers in blue, hoping. She was proud of who she was and what she'd accomplished, but still, it had eluded her.

Now, she watched Libby gush over Frankie's engagement ring, watched her place her hands on Frankie's rounded belly, bending down pretending to hold a discussion with the life inside. She knew she wanted to spend the rest of her life with her. And, when Faith carried in a beautiful one-year-old Abbigail in a sailor's dress, her blue eyes bright and head full of dark curls wild, she knew she wanted that for them, too.

As she watched those gathered reunite as though they hadn't seen each other in years, though many had been together mere days before, she knew she'd finally found it. She'd finally found her family.

Check out book 3 - Justice Won next in the Wynter Series

Justice slowly looked back over her shoulder, her body following. The tall, narrow window, like the ones she'd seen from outside, was covered by a blanket, only bits of afternoon sunlight coming in from the top left where the blanket sagged a bit. In the dim light, she was able to make out a chest of drawers, a wooden stand with a water pitcher sitting inside a washbasin atop it.

The bed was narrow, tucked against the wall, covers messy. Her gaze ran across its length and finally to the woman who was sitting up in the bed, the sheet gathered at her waist.

She looked young, not much older than Justice. Her hair was long, draped over her shoulders and down her back. It was such a strange thing to behold as women were never seen with their hair down in public. But then, she realized, this appeared to be her own room, not a public place. She wore a sheer gown, though the room was too dim to see much other than her skin tone through the material.

One thing Justice could see was that she had the face of an angel. Her eyes were light in color, though Justice couldn't tell if they were blue, gray, or green, but they were wide with curiosity.

"I think you've got the wrong room," she said sweetly.

"Um," Justice responded, not sure what to do. She turned back to the door, about to open it when she heard footfalls coming up the stairs, along with the barkeep's booming voice, again trying to stall the police.

"What did you do?" the young woman asked, startling Justice as she suddenly was right behind her.

"Nothing," Justice said in a hiss. "The guy tried to accuse me of stealing, but…" She jangled the coins in her pockets. "Why would I do that?"

The young woman was even more beautiful up close. Justice didn't remember seeing her the previous night. She'd seen a handful of women come and go downstairs, but they'd all been older than this one.

Justice gasped, fear gripping her heart when she heard a loud, firm knock on one of the doors. "Oh god."

The young woman took Justice's hand and yanked her toward the bed, only letting it go when she dropped to her knees, long hair all falling to the side along the floor as she looked under the bed. "Put this on," she said, absently reaching up clutching a white button-down shirt.

Justice took it, noting it was a man's shirt and it was quite large. She quickly put it on over her own shirt, trembling fingers working the buttons as a hat was plopped on her head. She rolled her eyes up, able to see the underside of the dark brim.

"Where did you get this?" Justice asked.

"Never you mind," the young woman said, getting to her feet. She stood in front of Justice, who was taller by a few inches. She glanced up into her eyes before looking down to where her fingers went—which was Justice's fly.

Justice's hips bucked away from her. "Whoa!" she said, trying to bat her hands away.

"Do you want to get caught?" her savior whispered harshly. When there was no further argument from Justice, she continued, undoing her pants and shoving them down along with her undergarments. She gasped, taking a small step back before a small chuckle left her lips. "Well," she said softly. "This just got interesting."

About the Author

Kim has spent her life in Colorado and can't imagine living anywhere else. She's been writing since she was 9 and stumbled into her first book being published in her mid-20s. She's worked in the film industry as a writer, director and producer, but now enjoys the quiet, happy life of a professional author. She can be reached on Facebook and on her website at, www.kimpritekel.com

IF YOU LIKED THIS BOOK...

Share a review with your friends or post a review on your favorite site like Amazon, Goodreads, Barnes and Noble, or anywhere you purchased the book. Or perhaps share a posting on your social media sites and help spread the word.

Join the Sapphire Newsletter and keep up with all your favorite authors.

Did we mention you get a free book for joining our team?

sign-up at - www.sapphirebooks.com

Check out Kim's other books.

Zero Ward - ISBN - 978-1-943353-19-4

Danny Felts grew up in the heart of the Midwest on a dairy farm, expected to follow in her mother's footsteps and marry a farmer and become a mother. Danny had other ideas. As World War II heats up, she makes a decision that will change her life forever as she becomes a lie, serving with the Seabees in the Navy as Daniel Felts.

Kate Adams is about to graduate high school in her prestigious and elite San Diego neighborhood when she's dragged to the USO for a dance with friends and servicemen. There, she meets the person that will catch her eye and her heart, only for jealousy and vengeance to tear her apart.

Are Danny and Kate strong enough to win the battle within and fight for their love?

Connection - ISBN - 978-1-939062-24-6

Julie Wilson lives a charmed life as a beloved teacher and aunt in the small town of Woodland. Close to her brother and guardian of two adorable Yorkies, she loves her life, the only negative being ex-boyfriend, Ray who can't seem to understand the phrase, "We're done." Believing that's her only problem, Julie has no idea what hell awaits her during a normal summer afternoon.

Remmy Foster is the quirky, friendly drifter who has

never found roots after a difficult childhood, as well as the difficulties her very special gift brings into her life. Though she may call it exploring, the truth is she's running from ghosts that haunt her every step.

After a chance meeting with Julie while hitchhiking, Remmy will be thrown head first into darkness she could never have foreseen, regardless of her abilities. As the clock ticks, life and death is on her shoulders to make the right connection.

Warning - Some scenes may be too intense for some readers.

1049 Club - ISBN - 978-1-939062-97-0

Almost two hundred souls, one plane, six survivors, endless heartbreak.

When flight 1049, headed from Buffalo, NY to Italy falls from the sky, a firestorm of drama, pain, angst and sorrow ensues. Can an author, a business owner, a teenager, good ol' boy, veterinarian and ruthless lawyer survive? Better yet, can those left behind?

1049 Club is a story of survival, love, deep regret and miracles. Can the living make peace with the presumed dead? Can the presumed dead make peace with the lives and loves they thought they had before?

Blinded – ISBN – 978-1-943353-53-8

After a horrible explosion sends local television news reporter, Burton Blinde reeling both physically and emotionally, she walks away from her life and the dream job she was about to start at a major news network.

For six long years she hides out in a small mountain town, working at the local library, though is haunted by the life she had, including mysterious messages and gifts she was receiving before her life was turned upside down, a veritable bread crumb trail leading to the unknown.

Unable to resist, Burton begins to follow the clues, which will lead her into the darkest places of human nature that she may not be able to return from.

Damaged - ISBN - 978-1-939062-45-1

Family. A group of people you are related to by blood or love.

Nora Schaeffer has come home to her family after twenty years working around the world as a photographer for National Geographic. She's welcomed into the open arms of her father and siblings.

Family. A group of people who support you, lift you up when you fall.

Shannon, the youngest of the four Schaeffer siblings, has vanished, leaving her five-year-old daughter, Bella, terrified and alone. To help find Shannon, Nora has no choice but to turn to the dark-haired specter who has haunted her for twenty years. Along the way, she finds her own long-dead heart and uncovers chilling family secrets beyond imagination.

Family. A group of people who will stick together to hide the rotten soul at its core at any cost.

Who will live? Who will die? Who will be the most damaged? And who will learn to love again?

The Gift - ISBN - 978-1-948232-47-0

The dead do speak. You just have to listen. Homicide Detective Catania "Nia" d'Giovanni is the only daughter in a large Italian family of six children. The backbone—a position not applied for nor wanted—she continues to create new glue to hold the dysfunctional group together. For Nia, family time feels more like herding cats than spending time with her brothers and feisty, aging parents.

Her heart has always been in her career with the Pueblo Police Department, especially since it will never be okay with her very Catholic mother to openly give her heart to any woman, until she meets a secretive waitress who has her at, Can I take your order?

And then it begins…

Three murders that are so gruesome, so horrible, they rock the small town to its core. Nia and her partner Oscar are left to piece together a deadly puzzle to find the key to unlock the monster they hunt.

Or, are they the hunted?

As they dissect the murder scenes where not one shred of evidence is left behind, more bodies begin to show up, each cleaner than the last, the shadowy specter that is the killer vanishing without a trace, making the woman Nia loves disappear right along with it.

When there is no evidence to follow, Nia must trust her instincts...or, is she being guided?

The Plan – ISBN – 978-1-948232-43-2

As the dark days of the Dust Bowl came to an end, the midsection of the United States tried to rebuild and revitalize. In the small, dusty farming town of, Brooke View, Colorado, teenager, Eleanor Landry and her mother were dealing with her father, a self-appointment fire and brimstone preacher to his congregation of two. A plan to survive.

As the dark era of the robber baron comes to an end, giants of industry and innovation emerged with fabulous fortunes manifested in the mansions that dotted the landscape across the country. Lysette Landon, the teen daughter of the wealthiest family in Brooke View, was everything a good, proper girl of privilege should be. Only problem was, she wasn't dreaming of finding a young man to raise a family with. A plan to be free.

One look, one touch, all plans are off.

Secrets deeper and darker than the grave would bring Eleanor and Lysette together, their families connected by a web of lies and broken promises. A plan to escape.

Be careful because, life has other plans...

The Traveler Book One: The Hunted - ISBN - 978-1-948232-91-3

A story so epic one book can't contain it.BOOK ONE:

1977: In the era between flower power and the yuppie, Sonia Lucas is a young wife and mother, just starting out in life. Without warning, a strange presence and dark force enters her life, clouds building...

1917: ...and a storm brewing as the world reeled from the horrific events of World War I just before it was ravaged by a Spanish flu epidemic that would kill millions. Sephora Lloyd is a 16 year old girl lost in the responsibilities of an adult world helping to support herself and her mother. A beautiful young nun-in-training enters her life, bringing love and hope with her. That is, until a force bigger than either of them threatens everything Sephora holds dear.

Four women - three deaths - two words - one house
THE HUNTED

The Traveler Book Two: The Hunter - ISBN - 978-1-948232-93-7

A story so epic one book can't contain it. BOOK TWO:

1890: In the dying days of the Old West, Sally Little runs her booming brothel with the passion and tenacity the business of sex requires. Savvy and indulgent, there's one itch Sally can't let herself scratch. Afraid of hurting the woman she loves, she instead unleashes...

Present Day: ...her renovation crew and fixer upper TV show on a dilapidated mansion that has known nothing but death since a murder there in 1977. Samantha Leyton sees ratings gold in bringing the sagging old house to life, but instead she discovers only she has the power to unlock the mystery that hunted four women across time, leaving death and destruction in its wake. Can she release her sisters who came before her and finally be granted the gift of love that is stronger than any evil?

Four women - Three deaths - two words - one house
THE HUNTER

Finding Faith - ISBN - 978-1-952270-16-1

Faith Fitzgerald thought that if she got an education and became a high-powered attorney in Manhattan, maybe—just maybe—she'd gain the attention and respect of her absentee father. Considering he was the only parent she had left after her mother's suicide when Faith was just a child, she thought that's what it would take.

She was wrong.

What she dreamed would be glamorous and satisfying turned out to be grueling and thankless. Since she wasn't willing to play the game between the sheets, she was forced to stay in the cubicle jungle doing all the heavy lifting while the men got the credit and the rewards.

Deciding she is done, Faith packs up and, with the flip of the bird to the rearview mirror, leaves New York and heads home to Colorado. She has nothing there: no job, nowhere to live, no relationship with her father. Truth is, she barely has a relationship with herself.

On the drive home, she finds herself in Wynter, a tiny mountain town at the foot of the Rockies. Looking more like it belongs in a made-for-TV Christmas movie than on the map, Faith is utterly enchanted. When she tries her luck and buys a raffle ticket at Pop's, Wynter's charming café, her prize is far more than meets the eye—or the heart.

Enter Wyatt, a feisty, sexy southerner and waitress at Pop's, who just happens to be married to a local sheriff's deputy. All is not as it appears with the All-American boy and his Georgia peach.

A colorful cast of unforgettable and charming characters will teach the jaded attorney that sometimes to find yourself all you have to do is go back to the basics…and have a little Faith.

Other Sapphire books from Sapphire Authors

The Dragonfly House: An Erotic Romance - ISBN- 978-1-952270-14-7

On the outskirts of a small, picturesque Midwestern town, sits a large, lovely old Victorian house with many occupants. This residence, known simply as The Dragonfly House, is home to Ma'am, the proprietor, along with several young women in her employ. One such woman, Jame, is very popular among the female clientele. One such client, Sarah, fresh from a divorce and looking for a little adventure, as well as some gentle handling, becomes one of Jame's repeat clients. Once Sarah enters the picture, Jame and Ma'am, as well as the brothel, will be forever changed.

The Coffield Chronicles – Hearts Under Siege: Book One – ISBN – 978-1-952270-12-3

The year is 1862. The war between the states has been raging intensely for a year now. The country is in complete and utter turmoil, and brother is fighting brother to the death, dying for what each believed. It seems it's all the townsfolk of New Albany, Indiana can speak of, and Melody Coffield is paying attention. Through a series of heartbreaks and sorrow, she settles on the decision to cut her hair and don men's attire.

Going under the alias of Melvin A. Coffield, she leaves her childhood home, the only home she had ever known, and enlists in the United States Army. Chewing tobacco and drinking liquor were ways of men, and she learns quickly how to behave like one. She would soon know the horrors of battle, and what was called the glory of war, through roads that led straight to Vicksburg, Mississippi. However, her biggest concern was making sure she was not detected by the others. Keeping her secret would not only be challenging, but trying as well.

Will she remain in this solitude the rest of her life, never allowing anyone into her heart again? Or will she find love, once more, in a world that was intolerant and unaccepting of who she truly was?

Keeping Secrets – ISBN – 978-1-952270-04-8

What would you do if, after finally finding the woman of your dreams, she suddenly leaves to fight in the Civil War?

It's 1863, and Elizabeth Hepscott has resigned herself to a life of monotonous boredom far from the battlefields as the wife of a Missouri rancher. Her fate changes when she travels with her brother to Kentucky to help him join the Union Army. On a whim, she poses as his little brother and is bullied into enlisting, as well. Reluctantly pulled into a new destiny, a lark decision quickly cascades into mortal danger.

While Elizabeth's life has made a drastic U-turn, Charlie Schweicher, heiress to a glass-making fortune, is still searching for the only thing money can't buy.

A chance encounter drastically changes everything for both of them. Will Charlie find the love she's longed for, or will the war take it all away?

Diva – ISBN – 978-1-952270-10-9

What if…you were offered a part-time job as the personal assistant to someone you have idolized for years? Meg Ellis has just completed the school year as a nurse in the Santa Fe school system. It isn't her first choice of profession, but a medical problem derailed her musical career years ago. The breakup of a bad relationship is still painful. The loving support from her close-knit family and good friends has buoyed her spirits, but longing still lurks below the surface. She can't forget the intoxicating allure of the beautiful diva who haunts her dreams.

Nicole Bernard is a rising star in the world of opera, adored by fans around the globe. When Meg learns that Nicole is headlining a new production at the renowned New Mexico outdoor pavilion—and then is asked to accept a job offer to be her personal assistant—she is beside herself. After a short time learning the routine and reining in her hormones, Meg discovers that Nicole's family will be visiting for the opening. Her responsibility to the charismatic singer immediately becomes more difficult when Nicole's young husband Mario shows up and threatens the comfortable rapport between Meg and the prima donna.

The two women brace for a roller-coaster interlude composed by fate. Will the warm days and cool nights, the breathtaking scenery, and the romance of the music create summer love? A heartbreaking game? Or something very special?

CPSIA information can be obtained
at www.ICGtesting.com
Printed in the USA
LVHW111338261222
735896LV00026BA/538